CW01187902

Producer & International Distributor
eBookPro Publishing
www.ebook-pro.com

The Lost Treasures: The Kingdom of David
Eyal Cohen

Copyright © 2024 Eyal Cohen

All rights reserved; No parts of this book may be reproduced or transmitted in any form or by any means, electronic or mechanical, including photocopying, recording, taping, or by any information retrieval system, without the permission, in writing, of the author.

Translation from Hebrew: Yossie Bloch
Editing: Evan Gordon

Contact: eyalcohen51@gmail.com
ISBN 9798308524830

THE LOST TREASURES

The Kingdom of David

EYAL COHEN

Contents

Prologue 7
Introduction 11
Chapter One: Ammon and Moab 13
Chapter Two: Naamah 20
Chapter Three: I Have Become a Stranger 24
Chapter Four: Shepherd 27
Chapter Five: The Search 37
Chapter Six: The Seer 41
Chapter Seven: Kingship 46
Chapter Eight: Jabesh Gilead 53
Chapter Nine: Jonathan 58
Chapter Ten: Amalek 66
Chapter Eleven: Coronation 71
Chapter Twelve: The Bard 77
Chapter Thirteen: Goliath 81
Chapter Fourteen: Son-in-Law 90
Chapter Fifteen: Escape 94
Chapter Sixteen: Samuel the Prophet 100
Chapter Seventeen: Ahimelech Son of Ahitub 110
Chapter Eighteen: The Madman 113
Chapter Nineteen: Nob, City of Priests 118
Chapter Twenty: Keilah 125
Chapter Twenty-One: David and Jonathan 129
Chapter Twenty-Two: Ziphites 135
Chapter Twenty-Three: The Cave 138
Chapter Twenty-Four: Sunset 143
Chapter Twenty-Five: Nabal the Carmelite 147
Chapter Twenty-Six: The Water Jug 158
Chapter Twenty-Seven: King Achish of Gath 162

Chapter Twenty-Eight: The Necromancer 167
Chapter Twenty-Nine: The Dukes of Philistia 172
Chapter Thirty: Abduction 175
Chapter Thirty-One: The Final Battle 181
Chapter Thirty-Two: The Dirge 184
Chapter Thirty-Three: The Kingdom of Hebron 190
Chapter Thirty-Four: Asahel 195
Chapter Thirty-Five: Palti Son of Laish 202
Chapter Thirty-Six: Abner 207
Chapter Thirty-Seven: Abner and Joab 213
Chapter Thirty-Eight: Baanah and Rechab 220
Chapter Thirty-Nine: City of Jebus 223
Chapter Forty: Uzzah's Breach 230
Chapter Forty-One: The Balsam Trees 234
Chapter Forty-Two: The Dancer 238
Chapter Forty-Three: The Covenant 246
Chapter Forty-Four: Law and Justice 254
Chapter Forty-Five: Hanun son of Nahash 263
Chapter Forty-Six: Bathsheba 267
Chapter Forty-Seven: Clarification 276
Chapter Forty-Eight: The Rebel 281
Chapter Forty-Nine: Nathan's Parable 294
Chapter Fifty: Amnon and Tamar 304
Chapter Fifty-One: Famine 316
Chapter Fifty-Two: Rizpah 325
Chapter Fifty-Three: Vengeance 335
Chapter Fifty-Four: The Lady of Tekoa 340
Chapter Fifty-Five: Absalom 346
Chapter Fifty-Six: The News 368
Chapter Fifty-Seven: The Return 371
Chapter Fifty-Eight: Sheba Son of Bichri 376
Chapter Fifty-Nine: Census and Censure 382
Chapter Sixty: Abishag of Shunem 391
Chapter Sixty-One: Coronation of Solomon 399
Chapter Sixty-Two: Last Will and Testament 407
Chapter Sixty-Three: Afterword 410

In the midst of this came a Great Eagle and knocked on the tower and said to them, "Cease being poor! Return to your treasures and use your treasures."

(Tales of Rabbi Nachman of Bratslav)

PROLOGUE

Wow… This is the first book I have ever written.

As I told you in the prologue to *Genesis Days: The Biblical Story as It Has Never Been Told Before*, I never set out to be an author; the text just burst forth from me, right onto the page.

I remember when I started like it was yesterday, even though it's been about ten years. I was in the southern part of Safed, in a bomb shelter that had been converted into a synagogue. To tell the truth, it was quite bizarre. I had just purchased the parchment to begin writing a Torah scroll. I know I've already told this… By then, I had scribed five such scrolls.

I sat down to follow my regular study schedule, before I began my workday. When I took the parchment in my hands and dipped my quill in ink, I suddenly recalled a conversation with my friends about a month earlier. I was alone in the shelter (as the constant drip of rain drizzling in and creating puddles all winter long had driven everyone else away).

I set aside the ancient scribing tools and instead grabbed pen and paper. I wrote like a man possessed, perhaps out of anger or frustration at the thought that a daily Psalm reader (sometimes even inspired by that same text) might regard the author of those words as depraved and degenerate. To me, it was tantamount to playing Wagner at a Jewish funeral.

To make a long story short, I have already told you about my conversation with my wife that evening and her reaction. (Had she responded differently, I would not have continued writing. It's one of five million things I'm grateful and indebted to her for, throughout the years.)

When I think back, I feel like I've been directed my whole life toward writing these works. (I know it sounds a little bit out there…)

For as long as I can remember, I've read books, a lot of them. True, at first, when I was a little boy, my father — may he be healthy — would harangue me to read, but soon I would do it on my own, becoming a bookworm. I could read the same book dozens of times, sometimes finishing and starting again immediately. Countless times I would lie in bed and read throughout the night, until I fell asleep — and then I had trouble getting up to go to school. (I knew how to provide excuses for both parents and teachers.) I would read books of all kinds: prose and science fiction, fantasy and philosophy, and even the encyclopedias we had at home. Because rereading was a habit of mine, even when I proudly received my Hebrew Bible, I had no problem delving into it over and over again, dozens of times.

As time passed, I began to adopt a traditionally observant lifestyle and got married. A pamphlet came into my possession, explaining a certain form of reviewing the Talmud, and I began to practice the method, adding more books of Jewish law and lore under the same system of study.

In brief, when I started writing the book, things surfaced one after the other, a flood of material surging over the pages in blotchy chicken scratch. (My handwriting is messy and unclear [maybe I should have been a doctor, my late mother would surely have been happy with that], so deciphering it is sometimes harder than writing down the words in the first place.)

After about two years of intense work, this book was published in Hebrew as *The Love of King David*. I distributed most of the first edition to colleagues, family, friends, and acquaintances. The wonderful responses motivated me to keep writing, as I told you in the prologue of *Genesis Days*.

Some people ask me, "Why does it take you so long to write? Some authors have an output of two or even three books a year!" The answer is pretty simple: this is a tale I cannot cut out of whole cloth! Fabricating a story is a matter of inspiration, time, computer access, and a bit of talent. However, when I write these books, I sometimes find myself sitting in front of a mountain of tomes for a week, my computer open, without typing a word. I have to dig through dozens of sources in order to find some missing detail or to clarify a complex point of Jewish law, to turn it all into a comfortable and comprehensible narrative.

To return to our issue, I have often been asked: "Which of your books is your favorite?" My answer is clear: the book you are about to read now! Not because this is my debut, but because of the character of King David, the Sweet Singer of Israel, whom I love so dearly. The versatile and wonderful man who knew how to be hard as a cedar on the one hand, and soft as a worm on the other. A person who reached the heights of physical and spiritual virtue, to stand upright before his Creator, knowing his conscience, and saying unequivocally: "*But I am a worm and not a man, scorned by men and despised by the people.*" The great man who suffered disgrace and persecution all his life (and unfortunately, even today, millennia after his death, there are characters who dare to open their mouths and slander him). The person who, throughout his life, was driven by love — love for his Creator, love for His Torah, love for His people. I am sure that you will also get to know this wondrous figure and share my love for him.

Wishing you a pleasant, enjoyable, and sweet reading — with much love.

INTRODUCTION

The People of Israel stood on the east bank of the Jordan River as their new and inexperienced leader faced the first test of his rule. Joshua proved himself to be a great leader and a gifted general. The people crossed the Jordan River miraculously, conquering kingdom after kingdom with both heavenly and earthly strategies. After his death at the age of one hundred and ten years, there were ups and downs in the people's faith and loyalty to their mission.

Fourteen judges led the people, one after the other: <u>Othniel</u> son of Kenaz, Ehud son of Gera, Shamgar son of Anath, Deborah the Prophetess, Gideon, Abimelech, Tola, Jair, Jephthah, Ibzan (Boaz) of Bethlehem, Elon, Abdon, Samson, and Eli the Priest.

Finally came Samuel the Prophet. We have gone through his story in *Era of Judges*, and he brings that epoch, which lasted more than three hundred and fifty years, to a close. The next period is that of the monarchy, which we will now begin to explore.

King David is the sixth entry in the *Lost Treasures* series. It tells the complete story of David from before his birth until his death. This is the biography of the Sweet Singer of Israel, author of the Book of Psalms, King David of Israel.

I wish you a reading experience that is both enjoyable and exciting, educational and enlightening.

CHAPTER ONE

Ammon and Moab

The week was coming to a close, the afternoon of Sabbath eve. A soft wind was blowing, caressing the leaves, as the sun bent toward the hilltops.

All of Creation seemed to stand still. The flocks of sheep had already been put in their pens. There were only the muted sounds of the household, as its members hurried to finish the preparations for the Sabbath, to be heard among the sounds of the universe.

"Holy Sabbath, oh Sabbath Queen," Jesse, son of Obed, sang.

Chief justice of the Supreme Court, senior sage of Israel, he still sat in his study hall, a Torah scroll unfurled before him. He was preoccupied with the session just concluded, when he had sat with his colleagues, adjudicating the petition of an Ammonite convert to marry an Israelite woman.

"It is forbidden," Jesse ruled, "as it is written in the Torah: 'No Ammonite or Moabite may enter the assembly of the Lord.'"

The convert addressed the court in tears: "But I want to marry her! I love her, and she loves me. I joined the faith wholeheartedly. I believe in God and His Torah; I study the text and keep the laws. I want to be an inseparable part of the People of Israel," he pleaded.

"I'm sorry," Jesse said, "but it is written in our holy Torah that no legitimate daughter of Israel may marry you, even though you have joined the community of Israel. If you really believe in God, and I see that your words are sincere," he added softly, "you should accept it and rejoice in it. As an Ammonite convert, you can earn a share in everlasting paradise by maintaining your distance from an Israelite woman. You need not marry a native-born legitimate daughter of Israel to be an inseparable part of the People of Israel. All you must do is fulfill the Lord's will," Jesse continued. "Find another convert from Ammon, or one from Moab, or even a daughter of Israel born on the wrong side of the blanket. Marry such a woman, and you will be walking in the way of God," he declared softly.

"But I…" the Ammonite convert began to say.

"No buts," Jesse interrupted, in a clear and firm voice. "If you want to fulfill God's command, this is what He truly requires. It is no personal slight to you. Everyone must confront things they don't like — but if it is God's will, there is no other way," Jesse concluded in an authoritative tone.

The man's eyes filled with tears, and he wept softly.

"Listen, my friend," Jesse said in a conciliatory voice. "I will consult some of my acquaintances, and I am certain we'll find an appropriate match for you. This woman is not meant to be with you, but you will find a bride. When you marry, you will rejoice knowing you are fulfilling God's will."

"Father! Father!" came a young voice, choking with tears.

The cries brought Jesse back to the present. He looked up from the scroll to see Ozem, one of his younger sons, who rushed in, in an emotional tumult. Jesse spread out his arms and Ozem threw himself into his father's safe embrace.

"What happened, my dear boy? Why are you crying? Did you hurt yourself? Did someone hit you?" Jesse asked his beloved son, stroking his head.

"Father, is it true?" Ozem asked his venerable father, his tone a plea for a negative response.

"Is what true, son? What are you talking about?" Jesse tried to engage his son. He inspected blue-eyed Ozem, the unruly jet-black hair sticking out from under his skullcap. Jesse noticed that Ozem's freshly laundered Sabbath clothes had already been muddied.

"Father, isn't it true that I'm like a foreigner?" asked Ozem, his soft voice breaking. "The other kids say I am, that I'm a Moabite. They say you're a foreigner, our whole family is foreigners, we cannot marry proper Israelites," he cried. "Father, I don't want to be a Moabite," he stammered, his weeping intensifying. "Father, why do they call me a Moabite? In school too, my classmates call me a Moabite. Father, it's not nice to say that. Why do they keep calling me that?" Ozem burst into heartbreaking tears, the sobs of a child struggling with humiliation and disgrace.

Jesse hugged his son tightly, his mind racing: But in truth, are we really Moabites? My grandmother, Ruth, was a Moabitess who married Boaz. She bore him Obed, my father. It is written in the Torah: *"No Ammonite or Moabite may enter the assembly of the Lord,"* so am I not barred from the assembly of the Lord…?"

"Father, please, answer me, are we Moabites or not?" Ozem was eager to hear his father reject the premise. He was desperate to hear anything, but his father remained deep in thought.

After a few moments, moments that seemed like an eternity to his son, he replied: "No, my boy, no. We are not Moabites. We are not Moabites," he repeated hesitantly, as if he were conscious of lying to himself.

He lapsed into thought again: I knew it would come out at some point. After all, the question arises, why aren't we Moabites? I know the law from Moses at Sinai, that those who are forbidden entry to the assembly of the Lord by marriage are the men of Ammon and Moab, not the women. And my grandmother Ruth properly converted, so she was allowed to enter the assembly of the Lord, as we are…"

"Father, the children told me that Grandma Ruth was a Moabitess, and it is forbidden to marry Moabites, so we are Moabites and forbidden to enter the assembly of the Lord," Ozem whispered in a broken voice, as if divulging a secret. "Is that true, Father?"

"No, my son, no," Jesse said to his son, "We must consider the law. It states that the prohibition applies only to Moabite men, who may not marry the daughters of Israel. Moabitesses are allowed to marry Israelite men, so we are not Moabites." Jesse went on to explain, "The Torah doesn't simply bar Ammonites and Moabites, it also gives the reason: *'For they did not meet you with food and water on your way out of Egypt.'* When the Israelites left Egypt, they passed by the borders of Ammon and Moab. The Israelites asked them for bread and water, but they refused. That is why the Torah says that such cruel and vicious people do not deserve to marry into the assembly of the Lord. But who is expected to go out and offer hospitality? The men, not the women, so it is only men who are forbidden to marry the native-born of Israel." Jesse continued to hug his beloved son, a tear welling up in his eyes. "My righteous little man, you are an Israelite, not a Moabite." Jesse kissed the head of his beloved son and said, "Well, well, we need to go and pray. After all, we are Israelites, and the Sabbath is approaching. Hurry, my righteous little man. Don't tarry, for the Sabbath Queen waits for no one. We must hasten to afternoon prayers."

Ozem lifted his head and looked lovingly at his father's face. "Well, Father, I'll run, but you'll wait for me, right?"

"Of course," Jesse said.

"Holy Sabbath, Sabbath, holy Sabbath, holy Sabbath, Sabbath, holy Sabbath." Jesse's house was filled with the sounds of the sacred melodies.

All the children sat around the table. Jesse, with his snowy beard and bleached clothing, looked like an angel at the head of the table, his sons singing with him. His wife, Nizebeth, served her husband and children the delicacies she'd prepared for the Sabbath. Her face beamed with joy, as she thought: I get to serve my husband and children food made by my hand.

Every Sabbath eve, she toiled in honor of the Sabbath. The serving girls were sent to their homes, and she was left alone. She would not let someone else cook for her loved ones for the Sabbath. Nizebeth would never surrender the privilege to serve her dear family their Sabbath meals.

As she sliced and seasoned and simmered, she constantly murmured: "In honor of the holy Sabbath." Her heart bore a prayer. "Please God, let us merit to truly honor the Sabbath, to welcome the Sabbath with holiness and joy. May we have the privilege of keeping Your commandments sincerely and wholeheartedly. May our children be righteous and pious; may they carry out Your will in truth, joy, and love. May our children study the Torah and observe its commandments. May my dear husband and I be privileged to raise them in the spirit of Your Torah. And may the food I prepared be pleasing and bring honor to the holy Sabbath." Her lips moved in prayer, and her hands did their work as if on their own. Her lips bore a soft melody:

"To observe, to fulfill, to follow Your will…"

Nizebeth looked lovingly at her husband and her precious children: the boys — Eliab and Abinadab, Shammah, and Nethanel; Raddai, Ozem and Elihu; and the girls, Zeruiah and Abigail. A look of satisfaction settled on her face. Her husband, her seven sons, her two daughters — all sitting at the table, singing Sabbath tunes.

"Father, what are you thinking about? Did something happen?" Eliab asked softly.

Every Sabbath, Eliab knew, Father would sit at the head of the table, his face radiant. He'd sing Sabbath tunes with joy and holiness. However, today everything looked different. Father sang in a whisper, as if he weren't there.

"Did something happen in court?" he probed.

"No, nothing special," Father replied. "We discussed the matter of an Ammonite marrying an Israelite woman."

"An Ammonite marrying an Israelite woman?" repeated Eliab. "They cannot marry the daughters of Israel," he said in a firm voice.

"You're right," his father replied, his expression guarded. "Yes, that's what we told him."

Mother served the meat: "Eat, eat, before the meat gets cold," she said, a smile on her face.

"Enough, Father," she said. "You're not at work now. Leave it alone. Eat, in honor of the holy Sabbath."

"Yes, you're right," he replied. "In honor of the holy Sabbath," he said, taking a bite.

The Sabbath meal was over. The children had gone to bed, and the house was shrouded in peace and quiet.

Jesse was studying Torah again, his voice nearly inaudible, but filling the house with holiness. His wife, Nizebeth, sat in the corner of the room looking at her husband, her eyes full of love and admiration.

She thought: How blessed am I, that my soulmate is a Torah scholar, a righteous man loved by all the people. He always speaks calmly and gently. How lucky am I! How did I get such a husband? Still, something is bothering him; he looks different tonight. Something must have happened. Should I ask him? No, I better not. He shouldn't be disturbed now, while he's studying. We can talk later.

Still, her mind was troubled by what she saw. She mused: I've never seen him like that. He looked thoughtful and very sad. Is that a tear in the corner of his eye?

Jesse lifted his head and saw his wife in the corner of the room looking at him. He said to himself: What can I do? How can I do this? She's the best woman in the world. How can I hurt her? It will crush her! But I must.

The thought weighed heavily on his mind: I've no choice. It borders on a Torah prohibition, and I cannot live in sin.

Nizebeth stood up and walked over to Jesse. "What's going on, my husband? Why are you so upset? It's not right for you to bring work home and especially not on the Sabbath," she said, looking at her husband.

Jesse shifted uncomfortably. "We have to talk," he managed to get out, his voice cracking. "There's a big problem. Sit down, dear."

She sat down, her face tense. "What's wrong?" she asked, "Something about the kids?"

"No and yes," Jesse said, a determined expression on his face. He had to get it over with. Jesse stopped himself from bursting into tears: "You know I value your righteousness. There is no better woman in the world than you! I am aware that I have the best wife, that our children have the best mother, that you are the best person in the world. But I don't deserve you," he said, tears welling up in his eyes. "I am not worthy of you, because…" Jesse silently wept, tears running down his cheeks. "I don't know how to tell you this," he continued, gasping. "I don't deserve to enter the assembly of the Lord. I am a Moabite, and I am not allowed to marry an Israelite woman. In fact, I have no right to serve on the court. Oh, how many laws I have violated!" Jesse put his head down on the table and continued to sob softly. "What I have to say is difficult for me and pierces my aching heart. But I've come to the conclusion that we have to separate. This is God's will. Please, my dear, do not be aggrieved. But there is nothing to be done. I don't know if my grandmother Ruth deserved to enter the assembly. It is written: *'No Ammonite or Moabite may enter the assembly of the Lord,'* and I am a Moabite on my grandmother's side. Please, my dear, forgive me," Jesse continued to cry.

Nizebeth looked at her husband with feelings of pain. Yes, she too had heard whispers behind her back. She too, knew what her neighbors and friends were talking about behind her back. To herself, she said: I knew this would come one day. I thought it was inevitable.

Tears washed down her face. She whispered: "Oh my righteous husband, my dear companion, you know that what they say is not true. You know the law," she said, praying that her words would enter her husband's heart. "You know it says Ammonite, not Ammonitess; Moabite, not Moabitess."

"Yes, yes, you're right, dear. But I can no longer live with the doubts and the whispers. I hear what people say, I know how they look at me in court, I feel everything. But enough! It's decided! We have to part; we can no longer live with this doubt," he said in a determined voice as he wiped tears from his face. "I hope you understand me and forgive me someday, but the morning after the Sabbath, we must say farewell."

She burst into tears, knowing there was nothing more to talk about. Her pious husband would not back down. "I understand what you are saying," she told him. "And I forgive you… You are the best husband there is in the world, and I thank God for every day I get to live with you."

"I thank you, my dear, I'm sorry to cause you this grief."

Jesse and Nizebeth sat at the table, tears streaming from their eyes, sorrow covering their faces.

CHAPTER TWO

Naamah

"Naamah!" Jesse called. "Can you come here for a moment?"

"Yes, my lord, how may I serve you?" Naamah, a maidservant in Jesse's house, was tall and attractive. Her cascading red hair was gathered at the nape of her neck. Her outward appearance was quite similar to that of Nizebeth, daughter of Adiel, Jesse's wife, from whom he had separated about two-and-a-half years previously. Remarkably similar, except for her red hair.

"I need to talk to you," he said. "Please sit down." He pointed to the chair in front of him.

Jesse thought: Naamah has the legal status of a bondwoman. If I bring a child into the world with her, the child will be a bondman. Then I will be able to emancipate him, and he will become a free Israelite in every respect, like a newborn baby — but without the stigma of my Moabite heritage. When non-Israelite servants are set free, they join the Israelite nation fully, severing any connection to their biological parents. A clean slate, a tabula rasa, untainted and unsullied.

For a long time, Jesse had been pondering this; the decision had already been made in his heart.

"Naamah," he said. "I want to ask you something. You don't have to agree, but I want you to consider it carefully."

Naamah nodded, "Yes, my lord."

"You know that two-and-a-half years ago, I separated from my wife. You must have heard the reason. I was concerned about the fact that my father's mother was a Moabitess, and that might make me ineligible to enter the assembly of the Lord. This was an extremely difficult decision for me, but I was committed. I am eager and anxious to purify my progeny — at least my future progeny. According to

Torah law, if I father children with a maidservant, the children will be bondmen. Then I may free them, and they'll become fully worthy of joining the assembly of Israel. I know you from your youth — your character, your virtue, your loyalty. So I thought you might agree to be like my wife. Realize that this won't truly be a marriage, as there will be no bridal canopy or consecration ceremony. The children born to us will be bondmen, but once I emancipate them, they'll become free Israelites in every respect."

Naamah looked at Jesse and couldn't believe her ears. "Yes, my lord," she repeated.

"If you agree, I'd like you to prepare yourself. I don't want this to be made public. When you're ready, let me know. Do you agree?" asked Jesse. "You don't have to give me an answer right now, you can think about it," he added.

Naamah looked at Jesse, finding it hard to believe. She thought: He wants to take me for a wife. This revered man, whom all the manservants and maidservants look on as a father — this considerate, kind, merciful, and gentle man wants me. The master who treats his servants as equals, who never raises his voice. Does this honorable man want me to be his wife?

Naamah bowed her head: "Yes, my lord, I agree. It's a great honor for me, my lord."

Still she pondered: But what about Nizebeth? How could I do such a thing to her? She's like my sister and mother. My lady treats all the servants so well!

It had been two-and-a-half years since the awful day that Nizebeth had left Jesse's house. Naamah had cried over her separation from her lady day and night.

Lowering her gaze, Naamah declared: "Yes, my lord, it shall be as my lord says."

There was a knock on Nizebeth's door. Standing in the kitchen, baking challah for the Sabbath, chanting a soft melody, she thought: maybe it's one of the kids. That's interesting, it's still early. They usually come later to have lunch with me and take food and challah for the family.

Jesse had bought her a nice house a few blocks from his, so that the children could visit her at any time. Two-and-a-half years had passed since their separation. Jesse took great care that his children visit their mother every day. The daughters, Abigail and Zeruiah, who lived with their mother, continued to visit their father every day.

Every Friday, she would cook and bake for the Sabbath for her children and Jesse. Every Friday, the boys would come to eat with their mother and take the Sabbath meals home. Some of the children would stay overnight with Nizebeth, some with Jesse.

"Yes, it's open, come in!" she said, as she went to the door and wiped her hands.

The door opened a crack, and her old maidservant stood on the threshold. Nizebeth felt the fear that surrounded Naamah. "What happened Naamah, my love? Is everything okay with the family?"

"Yes, my lady," Naamah replied, "everything is fine with your family, but I need to talk to you about an urgent matter."

"Sit down, my dear," Nizebeth said, bringing Naamah a drink. "Drink, catch your breath, and then tell me what is bothering you."

Nizebeth pondered as Naamah drank the water: She is a good woman, very devoted and humble. She has a good heart and is loyal.

The two women had shared many heart-to-heart conversations. A deep friendship had developed between the maidservant and the lady of the house, and they'd shared each other's secrets. Many joys were celebrated together, many crises, and many recoveries.

"My lady," Naamah's voice was weak and hesitant. "I don't know what to do. Your husband, my lord Jesse, turned to me and told me he wanted to take me as a wife." Naamah continued in confusion: "He spoke so strangely: he wants to purify his seed, so he wants me to be like his wife. What shall I do, my lady? I can't betray you!" she said, bursting into tears.

A few moments passed. Nizebeth, who understood her husband's plan, stood up and gave Naamah a motherly hug. "Calm down, my dear. Don't worry, everything will be fine. I have an idea."

"My lord, I did what you told me," Naamah said to Jesse mildly and diffidently.

"Very good. Tonight, after midnight, I will come to your quarters," Jesse said, returning to his study.

Since he'd separated from his wife and resigned from the court, he had become more immersed in his studies. His doubts gave him no rest. What about him? What was the status of the children he'd already had? Had he done the right thing? All the legal inquiries he'd made with the Torah scholars showed him that there had been no reason to separate from his wife. Had he wronged her for no just cause because of unnecessary strictness? He felt feverish with the endless questions.

Trying to quell the surge of emotions within him, he thought: Enough! Enough! I've already made my decision! I have ruled, and the verdict is final. This way my future progeny will be free of all doubt! Yes, they will have to be emancipated and converted; but after a few generations, that will have no meaning. I must do it!!!

The Sabbath commenced with a wintry wind, and trickles of rain moistened the earth. The chill penetrated deep into the marrow of the bone. Jesse quietly opened the door of his house, fastening his cloak around him. The children were already asleep; they had slipped into slumber immediately after the hearty dinner sent to them by his wife, Nizebeth.

Quickening his pace, he thought: "Oh, Nizebeth, my wife, just don't break down when you find out. At least you're not alone. Abigail, Zeruiah, Ozem, and Abinadab are with you. You are such a good and dedicated woman.

Jesse walked quickly toward the servants' quarters.

A few more steps and he'd be there.

Jesse hesitated, standing by Naamah's door. His hand refused to rise to knock on it. "I have to!" Jesse knocked slowly on the door.

"Yes, come in," came a whisper.

Jesse opened the door and quickly went inside, shutting the door behind him. The room was enveloped in darkness. The candles were out, and the thick clouds covered the moon and stars, as if they were his partners in crime.

"I'm here," came the whisper.

Jesse walked toward the voice.

CHAPTER THREE

I Have Become a Stranger

"Calumny and disgrace…"
"She has no shame…"
"She always pretended she was righteous…"
"No wonder her husband left her…"
"Adulterer…"
"Three years since Jesse left her, and suddenly she's pregnant…"
"Separated from her husband, yet with child…"

Nizebeth walked down the street, hearing the ridicule and the sounds of venom and hatred from the people of Bethlehem. It had been five months since that night when she and Naamah, her bondwoman, had switched places. Naamah, her devoted servant, had told her about her husband Jesse's plans and asked for advice. That Friday night, after the children had fallen asleep, Nizebeth had left her house. The breeze blew gently through the trees as rain drizzled. Nizebeth, wrapped in black, watched to make sure there was no one on the street and slipped into Naamah's room in the servants' quarters at Jesse's house, in the dark of night.

A light knocked, and the door opened. "Come in, my lady," Naamah had whispered as she closed the door behind her. "Come in and I'll go to your house to look after the kids." Naamah left the house, and Nizebeth entered the darkness.

"Lord, only you, Naamah, and I know that I did not violate a prohibition. Only You know the content of my heart and the reason for my actions. Only You know that I act for his own good and for the good of our children. Only You know that I am righteous and not wicked…"

A clout on her back.

Nizebeth fell on her face and stomach, the basket she had in her hand dropped, and the half-rotten fruits and vegetables she had collected from the market scattered everywhere. She could hear their jeering laughter.

"Just leave Bethlehem..."

"How are you not ashamed to stay here?!"

"What a disgrace..."

"With any luck, you will miscarry that bastard in your belly..."

Nizebeth had grown accustomed to the curses and slander, the jeers and mockery, even the shoves and blows. All of Bethlehem spoke ill of Jesse's wife. The children no longer came to visit; Jesse did not send them to take food for the Sabbath. Jesse had divorced her, telling her she had forfeited her settlement by her actions. Nizebeth lived on the verge of starvation; no one was willing to help a woman of ill repute — except Naamah, who saved some of her own food to give to her lady.

"Who's the father??? Do you even know???"

"Must have been a slave or some foreigner..."

"Get out of here..."

"Maybe the father was a bastard, like the child in her belly," one of the women attacked her, spitting in Nizebeth's face, as she tried to look up from the dirt.

Only with great difficulty, Nizebeth scraped herself off the ground, collecting the rotten vegetables and fruits. She stumbled slowly toward the hut where she lived, hugging her stomach painfully.

On the night of the Festival of Shavuot, celebrating the Giving of the Torah at Mount Sinai, Jesse sat with his sons as they read and discussed the holy texts.

The door of the study hall opened, and a young boy came in to whisper something in Jesse's ear and then departed.

Jesse's face fell. His sons looked at their father with questioning eyes. "What happened, Father?" asked Abinadab.

Jesse rubbed his neck. "You have a brother," he told them, "a brother brought into the world by your mother." He spoke as if unable to believe it. "What ignominy! What shall we do?"

There was silence. Everyone knew the child wasn't Jesse's: the family, the neighbors, all of Bethlehem. There was nothing to hide.

This couldn't be concealed.

"Father, you mean he's a bastard?" asked Shammah, tears in his eyes.

"Yes," Jesse replied, "you have a brother from your mother, a bastard."

The silence was overwhelming; the feeling of distress increased. Their gazes were downcast, refusing to believe.

"Truly, Mother gave us a beautiful gift for Shavuot, a bastard brother," Eliab hissed from between his lips. "It's a shame they didn't die in childbirth," he added. "A shame, a disgrace! A bastard in the family. My mother played it so righteous," he went on sarcastically. "Honor the holy Sabbath. You have to learn Torah. Keep the commandments. Love God," he muttered, mimicking his mother's tone. "Villainess! Hypocrite! Too bad they didn't die..."

"Enough! Stop talking about Mother like that!" Little Elihu burst into tears. "That's my mother. I love Mother."

Little Elihu didn't understand; he was only about seven years old. He didn't understand why Mother didn't live with them anymore, why she lived in another house, why Father wouldn't let him go to her. He didn't understand what a bastard was. "Father, tell him to stop talking about Mother like that," Elihu pleaded, as he ran to safety in his father's arms.

Jesse hugged his little son. "Enough, Eliab, you are not allowed to talk about your mother like that," he said firmly. "After all, despite what she did, she is still your mother, and you must respect her."

"Respect her! What is there to respect? The Torah says: *'Both the adulterer and the adulteress must surely be put to death.'* She should be executed! She is lucky that there were no witnesses who saw her and warned her, otherwise she would have already been subjected to the death penalty. Respect her?! Not me!" he shouted. "I wish she and her bastard would die. I'd love that!"

"Enough! Silence!" shouted Jesse as he hugged his little boy. His eyes were filled with tears, just like those of Elihu. "Enough, she's still your mother," he whispered, his eyes gazing at his sons' faces.

Eliab stood up noisily. "No, she's not!" he declared and left, slamming the door behind him. "No, she's not..." the echo sounded.

CHAPTER FOUR
Shepherd

"Someone stole sheep from my herd last night," said one Bethlehemite.

"Someone? You know it's the bastard son of the adulteress, Nizebeth daughter of Adiel."

"That's for sure," another added. "Everyone knows the wretch is a rustler. If I catch him red-handed, I'll break his bones. I'll take apart that misborn body piece by piece, until his own unkempt mother can't identify him."

"Would you believe that the other day he broke into my coop and stole three hens?" the poultryman complained. "That baseborn crook ought to be killed!"

"I've been trying to catch him for years, but the scoundrel is stealthy," the shepherd muttered.

"Yes, yes," said his neighbor, "Today he stole my pie! I put it on the windowsill to cool down, and the delinquent stole it from there."

"You saw him?" her friend asked.

"No, I didn't see him. But who would commit such thievery but a whore's son? Too bad his harlot mother didn't die in childbirth, along with him. Wouldn't that have been better for everyone? Instead, she stays here, unashamed. Pretending she's righteous. Modest. Charitable. What a villainess! He steals, and then she distributes the loot to paupers."

"And Jesse doesn't drive her out of the city. He suffers her to live in his town. Thank God he resigned from the court, that unworthy Moabite," she continued angrily. "Blood will out. He's a Moabite, his children are Moabites, his wife is a harlot, and her son is a bastard. Really, quite the wonderful family," she summarized with a smirk.

In the fields of Bethlehem at dusk, the sun inclined to the west, painting the horizon in hues of crimson. The notes of a shepherd's flute were a counterpoint to the flock's bleatings. The blades of grass sing to their Creator, bending and bowing before their Maker. The trees rustle their leaves, as if applauding the Shaper of the World.

"From where the sun rises to where it sets, the name of the Lord is praised."

The voice of a young man could be heard, singing softly like chimes tinkling in the wind.

"The Lord is exalted over all the nations, His glory above the heavens," the tune continued. The youth played a gentle melody on the shepherd's flute, encouraging the young lambs to gather around him.

David himself was the black sheep of his family, but he herded Jesse's flocks in the hills around Bethlehem. For years, his only friends had been the animals in his care, along with the sky, the trees, the flowers, the sun, the moon, and the stars. The Kingdom of the Creator was the only society David fit into. He found no human companions; he was shunned by everyone. He was alone in God's Realm.

As he counts the flock, he thinks to himself: *There is no other besides Him*. Fifteen years of shepherding. Distinguished from the rest of man. Bastard. Stranger.

For a decade and a half, his mother had been telling him, "Don't worry son, one day you'll know everything." In the meantime, his siblings continued to detest him, despise him, and degrade him. He had no consolation except the tender embrace of his Creator. Whom he clung to. Whom he pined for. The true love of his life.

He did not know his father. Nizebeth's other children he knew were Jesse's, but not David, as everyone constantly reminded him. Jesse was not particularly welcoming to David, but he did not insult the boy.

Once, years ago, David had overheard a conversation between Jesse and Eliab. Eliab denounced David as the disgrace of the family, better off dead. Jesse had replied, "What do you want from the child? He's done nothing wrong." Eliab had been unrelenting, determined that David should be eliminated by any means necessary.

Yes, David knew the word bastard. He heard everyone say that his mother sinned while married to Jesse, who had divorced her upon learning she was pregnant.

Still, his mother was always there for him. Even when they kept him from studying Torah, Nizebeth remained by his side, to teach, help, explain, clarify — and she never stopped praying for him. Her eyes were usually sad, grief clouding her face. "Mother, don't be sad," he would say. "Mother, this is also for the best, and we should be happy about it. The main thing is that I love you, as does our Heavenly Father. God is everyone's father, and He loves us as we are. We should find happiness in Him."

Reflections...

Thoughts...

A maternal grin, a charming, rare smile.

David would spread his arms and hug his mother.

"Thank you, my dear son, you are my comfort. Do not worry; one day you will know the whole truth."

David has been away from home for a week. Tonight the Sabbath would commence. Before midday, he would have to return the flocks to Jesse's pens. His mother's ex-husband let him graze the flock, as he alone would give David a job.

David reflected: He is a righteous man. He treats me like a person and pays me a fair wage. Whenever we meet, he is not hostile, though I am the embodiment of his wife's infidelity. He seems sorry, his eyes full of compassion for my situation. Do we have something in common? I suppose we do. I am a bastard, and he may be a Moabite. That's why he separated from Mother in the first place. We actually have a few other things in common. We have the same nose, the same eyes, the same hands. Not the same build or hair color, but still…

David completed his head count and decided: Enough musing, I have work to do! In dismay, he realized he was one short. How could he tell Jesse that? How could he disappoint him? In the end, he'd think David was a thief too!

David put his flute to his mouth and played the tune he used to call the sheep home. Perhaps he would hear it.

He fell silent...

Listening...

Listening...

A faint bleating could be heard in the distance. Light-footed, David ran toward the sound. In the distance, he saw the lamb desperately slaking its thirst by the stream.

"Oh, poor dear," said David to the lamb, "You were thirsty, and I didn't notice." David waited until the lamb finished drinking, picked it up in his arms, and brought it back to the flock, like a parent carrying a lost child.

"Heavenly Father, thank You for finding the lamb for me. I am so much like it! Yes, Father. I, too, am a lost lamb. Search for Your servant! All you need to hear from me is the sound of my bleating, asking you to find me, as I so desperately desire You and Your commandments. *I have strayed like a lost lamb; seek Your servant, for I have not forgotten Your commandments.*"

Two candles sat on the shelf, a white cloth on the table. Nizebeth and David sat together to eat the Sabbath meal. The wood-burning stove spread pleasant heat and lit up the cabin.

Nizebeth looked at her little son, embracing him with her soft gaze. He was all she had in the world. She thought: My little boy is not so little anymore. My youngest son is already a man. He recently turned twenty-three years old, but he is still a bachelor. When will he marry? Whom will he marry? How will he marry?

Nizebeth surveyed her son's face. She could see, like no one else, how much he resembled his father: the same bright eyes, the same nose, the same cheekbones. Yes, she remembered Jesse in his youth, the eyes shining with vitality and tenderness, with courage and conviction behind them. The eyes she loved so much. Now her son looked at her with the same eyes.

"Mother," David began, breaking her reverie. "I met Jesse this afternoon when I went to get my pay. He's a very nice man." David hesitated. "He asked me if I wanted to get married."

Nizebeth looked at her son: "Yes?"

"I told him I wanted to, but who would become my wife? I told him he knew I'm not to enter the Lord's assembly because I'm baseborn." There was no grievance or disappointment in his voice about his status; he fully and happily accepted his fate.

A shocked Nizebeth looked at her son. She had never heard him express that he was a bastard. "Yes?" she said in a trembling voice.

"Jesse said that in the nearby village, there is a very fine, nice girl, who is also baseborn. We could meet, and if it's a good match, we can marry. If not, I can wed a maidservant, and..."

"Enough!" Nizebeth shouted, "Enough with such talk." David looked at his mother; he had never seen her in such a state. Trembling, agitated, losing control. "David, you won't marry a bastard or a slave!"

"But Mother..."

"David, heed my words," Nizebeth tried to calm the storm of her emotions. "You must hear me out. How many times have I told you that one day you would learn everything? Today is the day." A tremor ran through her hands.

"David, my dear boy... You're not a bastard! You are welcome in the assembly of the Lord. I never committed adultery! I'm not wicked, even though everyone thinks that way about me..."

Nizebeth burst into heartbreaking tears. The dam broke as years of humiliation and disgrace, decades of keeping her son's secret, came to an end.

"David, you spring from Jesse's loins! Do you understand? You are his trueborn son! When your father, Jesse, decided that he was going to separate from me and bed a maidservant instead, I couldn't live with the thought that your siblings would be forbidden to marry native-born Israelites. After all, he married off Eliab even before you were born; he didn't worry at the time that Eliab was unworthy to enter the assembly of the Lord. Even later, when Abinadab and Nethanel got married, he wasn't afraid of it.

"Your father, Jesse, is exceedingly righteous. He has never sinned, but excessive severity and piety sometimes cause a person to do illogical things. Sometimes doubts and fears motivate a person to act foolishly, confusing their mind.

"After your father separated from me, he turned to our maidservant Naamah and asked her to bear his children so he could purify his seed. Naamah told me about what he was planning, and we switched places.

"For more than twenty years, he has been trying to purify his seed through Naamah. Every time he tells her they'll try again, we switch places. You've known Naamah for a long time; she's like a sister to us, she's like your second mother. How many times did she look after you, when you were little, and I "had to go somewhere?" The place was always Naamah's room, so to this day, the poor woman has not had a child. You might ask why you're a redhead, but with the Torah you've studied, you should know better than I. The mind is very powerful. Whenever your father was with me, he was sure he was with ginger-haired Naamah. His intention determined the color of your hair. Do you understand? You are worthy of entering the assembly of the Lord like any other native-born Israelite; in fact, you are prohibited from marrying any bastard or bondwoman. I'm sorry, son, that you suffered such injustice, but I had no choice."

Nizebeth finished her remarks, the years-long burden removed from her heart.

David looked at his mother, like a sleepwalker suddenly awakened: "I'm not a bastard? I'm permitted to enter the Lord's assembly? The righteous Jesse is my father?" Tears flooded his face: "I am Jesse's trueborn son?" he asked in disbelief. "Oh, Mother, thank you. Thank you, Mother." David got up, ran to his mother and hugged her. "Thank you, my dear mother, I always knew you were righteous. My whole life I was convinced that what they said about you couldn't be true. I couldn't bear to hear it. Mother, I love you."

Nizebeth burst into tears, weeping all that she'd held back for more than twenty-three years, the crying discharging the burden on her heart, sobs of letting all the misery go.

"David," came the voice.

"Yes, my lord," David approached Jesse, his heart beating hard, as if it might tear the clothes from his body.

"David, did you think about what I told you?" asked Jesse. "Enough! You're already grown up and need to marry. It is true that there are not many options, but what I offered you is better than remaining unmarried. The girls I suggested to you would make good brides. It's a shame every year that passes. You've long since passed your twentieth year."

David looked at Jesse. With all his soul, he wanted to shout "Father!" and run into Jesse's arms, to embrace the father he'd never had, but his mother had ordered him not to divulge his secret. He thought: Oh dear Father, if only you knew.

"Well, David, enough daydreaming, what do you say?"

"I'm sorry, my lord, I can't... I want to," David stammered.

"Why, my boy, why?" asked Jesse, his eyes full of compassion for the unfortunate lad. "You are not to blame for your situation; you haven't done anything wrong. You must not punish yourself for things others have done! I know you, David, I know that the thievery and robbery they accuse you of is unfounded. I know you study the Torah. Yes, yes, I know you do, when you are in the field shepherding the grazing flock."

Jesse met David's shocked gaze. "I must tell you how many times I followed you when you were in the field tending to the grazing flock. At first, it was to see if you knew how to look after the flock, if you were diligent, and also to see if what they said about you was true. But when I saw how you behaved when you were shepherding, I continued to follow you and learn about your Godliness. I have often heard and seen your crying and singing to the Almighty; and often I wept with you. I heard you sing: *'As the deer pants for streams of water, so my soul longs after You, O God. My soul thirsts for God, the living God. When shall I come and appear in God's presence?'* I heard how you yearn for God's closeness, how you study Torah carefully and honestly, interpreting verses and resolving problems. I know it's wrong that I used to follow you without your knowledge. Still, I couldn't help myself. You may be illegitimate, but our wise men say that a baseborn scholar is superior to an ignorant high priest. I apologize for following you. For our purposes, you know, *'It is not good for man to be alone!'* It is better for you to have children with a maidservant and then emancipate them. Then they'll be allowed to enter the Lord's assembly."

David lowered his gaze. He hadn't known anyone was following him. Everything he did in the service of God was secret and private, in the fields, far from prying eyes or ears. No one but the Creator could have heard him, or so he had thought.

"Sorry, my lord, I can't. One day you'll know why." His gaze still lowered, he mumbled: "Excuse me, my lord. I have to go; they are waiting for me."

Jesse looked at David walking away from him: "Poor fellow, poor fellow, such a decent and loyal young man. A true servant of God, I wish that I were like him! Poor fellow, he suffers such anguish through no fault of his own. A righteous fellow, but an unfortunate bastard.

"I wonder what he meant when he said, 'One day you'll know why?'"

"*The heavens declare the glory of God; the skies proclaim the work of His hands. Day after day, they pour forth speech; night after night, they reveal knowledge. Without speech or language, without a sound to be heard. Their voice has gone out into all the earth, their words to the ends of the world... The law of the Lord is perfect, reviving the soul; the testimony of the Lord is trustworthy, making wise the simple. The precepts of the Lord are right, bringing joy to the heart; the commandments of the Lord are radiant, giving light to the eyes.*"

Night, moonlight and the stars illuminated the darkness as David sat with the flock lazing around him. Moonlight shone on the sheep like the painting of a ripple on the surface of the sea. He had a small campfire going, the flames seeming to play with each other, swaying with the rhythm of the wind. The whispering coals told an ancient story human ears had never heard.

David looked up at the stars of heaven, servants of the Creator of All. "I thank you, dear Heavenly Father. I thank you that I am not a bastard. I thank you that I am of the People of Israel. I thank you for being allowed to enter Your assembly. I thank you for the *neshama*, the soul, and the breath, the *neshima*, that sustains it. *Let every soul that draws breath praise the Lord. Hallelujah!*"

David was immersed in his reflections, in his conversation with his Creator. Joy flooded his heart, gratitude for all the good he was experiencing.

Suddenly, from the side, a thunderous growl burst through the darkness, startling the flock, which scattered far and wide. Bleats of terror foreshadowed disaster. David jumped to his feet and saw a large black bear carrying a sheep from the flock, loping toward the nearby forest from which it had emerged. Moving as lightly as a lioness protecting her cubs, David began chasing the bear.

"Please, God, don't let me disappoint my father. Please save the sheep from the cruel paws of the bear." Light-footed, David chased the bear, the tall and powerful formidable animal that terrorized all the forest animals; it was only yards ahead of him. With courage and confidence, David leaped on the back of the monstrous beast. The bear lost its balance, falling on its face while dropping the injured sheep from its mouth. David hugged the bear's neck and tightened his grip. The surprised bear extended its claws, trying to slash the flesh of its attacker. "Please, God, help me. If I let him go, it will be the end of me — and a bitter one at that."

The bear tried to rise to its feet to shake its assailant off, but David strengthened his chokehold. A fierce struggle, a struggle of power against spirit, the savage strength of the bear versus the will and heroism of David. He felt that he must protect his father's flock; even though no one knew he was Jesse's son, David could not disappoint him.

The ongoing struggle seemed endless, and David sensed his body weakening. "I must not surrender. Please, Heavenly Father, give me the strength to subdue the bear." David knew it was a life-and-death struggle, not only physical but also mental, a struggle between the forces of evil and good, a struggle between the emissary of the Angel of Death and him, a struggle of material versus spiritual: "I must not despair ... I must not break ... *I lift up my eyes to the hills, from where does my help come? My help comes from the Lord, the Maker of heaven and earth.*"

David recalls the story of Jacob's wrestling with the angel representing Esau. Not merely a physical struggle, but mostly a spiritual one. Who has the fortitude not to surrender? Who will never despair? A new spirit came upon David. He felt as if the soul of our forefather Jacob was entering his body and imbuing him with new energy. "I do not surrender, I am from the seed of Jacob," he hissed. "*He will not allow your foot to slip; your Protector will not slumber. Behold, the Protector of Israel will neither slumber nor sleep.*"

David felt his ursine opponent weakening, its muscles slackening, its limbs drooping; but he wouldn't let go until he was absolutely sure the bear was dead.

David stood up straight, over the carcass, his body aching and sore all over.

He looked up at the starry sky, the lone witness to his battle. The moon and the host of heaven that watched seemed clearer and brighter than ever.

"*How can I repay the Lord for all His goodness to me?*" David said. "Thank you, dear Heavenly Father, thank you so much for everything."

The wounded lamb, which until a few moments ago had been in the jaws of the bear, approached David, rubbing against his legs, grateful. It locked eyes with David, appreciating its rescue, as if to say: Thank you for putting your life on the line to save me. Thank you for not giving up on the least of the members of your flock.

David leaned down to it and picked it up, taking it in both arms as if it were his wounded child. "Come, my poor dear, let us go back to the flock. I will tend to you there…"

CHAPTER FIVE
The Search

"Will we ever find them? We've been searching for three days already, and we're no closer to finding them since we started. We're running out of water and provisions, and there's nothing on the horizon."

Two people walked through the wilderness, looking for lost she-donkeys. Saul, son of Kish, head and shoulders above all the rest of the Israelites, was handsome and good-looking; a war hero and courageous, yet modest and unassuming. He possessed the sum total of all virtues, his face as fierce as that of a chiseled eagle, his neck like a lofty tower overlooking all, his body as sturdy as cast steel. Saul was a righteous and upright man, a man following in the ways of his forefathers. He loved everyone and was beloved by everyone. He was no spring chicken, well into middle age, but his spirit was that of a young man. He left his wife and six children for a few days at the command of his father to carry out Kish's order.

"We'd better go home," Saul said to the boy who walked with him. "My father will start worrying about us. We have wandered all the way from Benjamin to the Land of Zoph!"

Three days earlier, Kish discovered that some of his she-donkeys were missing. He'd asked his son Saul to take one of the household servants and look for them. Saul, a devoted and loyal son, hastened to fulfill his father's command and recruited one of the lads he was friendly with to accompany him on the search for the wayward beasts. The boy loved his master's son dearly.

The lad reflected: Working with Saul is a privilege. He's so pleasant and gentle. He never raises his voice or loses his temper; he treats me as an equal. He's like his father in many ways. We mustn't return empty-handed and disappoint Kish.

"My lord," the boy suggested, "I have an idea. We are indeed in the Land of Zoph, and we are not far from its capital, Ramathaim Zophim. That is the town of Samuel the Ramathite! Samuel the Seer will be able to tell us where the she-donkeys are. It's not far off. It would be a shame to leave without seeking his guidance. Everyone knows Samuel possesses the Holy Spirit; the inspiration of God rests in him. He'll certainly be able to help us. You shouldn't let your father down by giving up now."

"You are right," replied Saul, "but what shall we bring to Samuel the Seer as a gift? The way of the world is to present tribute to the righteous for their trouble. True, Samuel neither demands nor accepts such homage, but Father once told me that people do leave donations in the prophet's home surreptitiously." Saul sighed: "Samuel the Seer — it would be a privilege just to set eyes on him. Father says that he looks like an angel, that he is as great as Moses and Aaron combined. How I would love to see his beaming face, to learn from him. But what can we bring him? I have nothing. I'm ashamed to come empty-handed like this," Saul admitted.

The boy went through his pockets, looking for something: "I found it!" He beamed with joy. "Look, a quarter shekel. Here, I've got it. That's something for Samuel the Seer," the boy declared, "We have at least a pittance to offer. This is also a tribute. Let us not return empty-handed."

Saul laughed while patting his servant on the back. "Well, we will go to Samuel the Seer, and with God's help, he will reveal to us where the she-donkeys are."

Samuel the Prophet sat in the study hall, his face deeply creased by advanced age and the burdens of office. His head, sideburns, and beard were now as pure white as snow. Samuel sighed from the bottom of his heart. His shoulders slumped in a physical expression of the onus upon him, his head bent.

His sons, Joel and Abijah, were good people, judges in Beersheba, but they did not completely follow in his footsteps. Samuel had never asked anyone for a favor; everything he did was for heaven's sake. At the age of two, he had been entrusted to Eli the High Priest by his mother Hannah, and since then, he had been dedicated to a life of holy devotion. For nearly half a century, he had served the People of Israel. He had traveled the length and breadth of the land, adjudicating their disputes and guiding their decisions. He never asked for wages, never took anything from the people who came to him. But his sons often asked for recompense and remuneration for their work.

Samuel was aware that people left behind all sorts of little things in his home so he could make a living. He appreciated it very much and was grateful to the people who supported him. All his life, he had kept busy studying Torah, praying, and serving the Holy People. He gladly surrendered every aspect of his life to the Israelite nation.

He commanded his sons: "When anyone comes before you, do not seek or take anything from them. As our Holy Torah states: *'Do not accept a bribe, for a bribe blinds the eyes of the wise and twists the words of the righteous.'* A person who takes a bribe may not seek to pervert the law, but they will be unable to find that party guilty. This is the way of the world, once you have received a benefit from any person, you see them in a positive light; your heart finds all kinds of reasons, arguments, and responses in their favor. Even if your mind says something else, your heart will mislead you."

Unfortunately, his sons ignored this directive; they even went as far as to demand favors from those who appeared before them in court. "Father," they told him, "we have no choice. We have to pay the salaries of the court scribes and the rest of our staff. How else will we support them? How else will we support our families?"

Samuel was about fifty but looked twice that age. "Oh... Oh... My Heavenly Father, what should I do?" he murmured.

About an hour ago, the elders of Israel had left his house. They complained to him about his sons not following in his footsteps.

"You are old," they'd said bluntly. "Unfortunately, you do not have the strength to continue judging Israel as you have. You yourself taught us that there are three commandments to be fulfilled upon entering the Promised Land: to wipe out the memory of Amalek, to crown a king, and to build the Temple. Please, Lord Samuel, give us a king like all the nations to fight Amalek and then build God's House."

Samuel was shocked, as if he'd been stabbed with a sword. The Israelites seek a king like all the nations? The Israelites are tired of me and my sons judging them? In heartfelt prayer, he turned to God: "Father, what can I do? The people are weary of me and my sons, asking for a king like all the nations. Please, Father, answer me."

Samuel felt the Spirit of God rushing over him; his limbs shook, his soul detached. He heard the Word of God in his heart: "No, my dear son! It is not you of whom they are weary, but Me. Since I took them out of Egypt and brought them to the Holy Land, they have had enough of me. They see the commandments, laws, and statutes I've given them as a burden. They love you as a person but reject your teaching. They prefer to worship idols and statues of wood and stone rather than Me; the gods they manufacture are not as demanding as I. They worship their impulses rather than Me, to satiate their lusts with no qualms. That's why they say they want to be like all the nations."

Samuel sighed, "But..."

"No, my son, no. Consider carefully their request. If they really wanted a king like all the nations, they would not ask you to appoint a king for them; they would do it themselves. Now, my son, tell them, what such a monarch would be. A king like all the nations would seize their sons as soldiers and their daughters as serving girls. Their silver and gold would be forfeited to the kingdom's coffers. Unlimited tariffs and taxes would be levied upon them. He would rule over them with an iron fist, until they would cry out to the Lord their God to save them from His hand."

Samuel trembled all over his body, cold sweat dripping from him as if he were in another world. "But they are your children, whom you took out of Egypt! You must not appoint a king like all the nations to rule over them. Please have mercy on Your beloved children! Is not each of them like Your only child?"

Samuel grasped the fading wisps of his vision, his entire being subject to his conversation with his Creator. It has been nearly forty years since his first prophecy, but no one could grow accustomed to the experience. There was always the feeling like it was the first time.

"My dear son, gather the elders of Israel and teach them the law of the king. Explain what a flesh-and-blood monarch is and let them know that I will crown a king after My heart."

CHAPTER SIX

The Seer

Saul and the boy went up the hill toward Samuel's place. As dusk neared, the shadows lengthened. Saul thought: We must hurry, to find the seer before dark.

He picked up the pace, excited about the meeting, his back straight, his posture tense. The fatigue was not noticeable, even though it had been more than a day since their last meal. The boy followed him, trying to catch up with his master, his body bent as if it were about to snap under the burden, looking at Saul, trying to draw strength from his power.

"Come on, brother. Hurry up, soon we'll get to the city and find you something to eat and drink. Be strong, brother." Saul patted the boy affectionately on the shoulder. The boy recovered and hastened his pace.

"Here's a well," the lad shouted happily. The two approached the well: "There are girls there drawing water. We can ask them where Samuel the Seer is," he added, running toward the well.

"May we have some water?" the boy pleaded.

The girls gave the two of them enough water to restore them. Saul and the boy drank until their thirst was quenched.

"Thank you very much," said the boy. "You have revived us. Do you know if the seer is in town? Do you know where Samuel the Seer is?"

"Yes, yes, we know where Samuel the Seer is," they replied, looking at Saul even as he kept his gaze downcast. "He came to town today and said he was going to bring an offering. Samuel the Seer called upon all the elders and Ramathite notables to come to the sacrifice," the girls continued, keeping Saul there so they could enjoy his company; they found him attractive though he was old enough to be their father, perhaps grandfather. "Go into town and look for the high place, where he needs to go. Today he is bringing an offering and making the blessing of the sacrifice. If you go fast, you'll probably make it on time, before he gets there."

The girls were eager to continue explaining, but Saul was in a hurry.

"Thank you," Saul replied without looking up. "Make haste, maybe we'll get to meet the seer." Happiness filled Saul's heart, accompanied by holy reverence. "We are going to meet Samuel the Seer."

Samuel had received a prophecy the day before: "Tomorrow I will send you a Benjamite, by the name of Saul, son of Kish, to crown as King of Israel."

Two months had passed since the Israelite elders had come to Samuel to ask for a king, two months of anticipation. In the meantime, the Philistines were assailing the Israelites; attacking and killing men; accosting women, the elderly, and children, and destroying crops. Every week, a delegation of elders would come to Samuel, begging him to crown a king to lead them into battle, a monarch who would unite Israel against their enemies. Every time, Samuel would put them off: "Another week, soon, we're looking for the right person; we must find someone worthy."

The elders and the people were impatient. "If you cannot find us a king, we will do it ourselves. Stop wasting time!" one of them snapped at him the last time.

Finally, the Word of God had reached him, and Samuel could delay no longer. The animal was slaughtered and prepared; all the dignitaries of Ramathaim Zophim were at the high place, waiting for him; yet Samuel the Prophet dallied. "A few more moments, and we'll begin." Samuel was excited. True, he'd been displeased by Israel's request for a king "like all the nations." Samuel knew that Israel would have a monarch before the day was out — not aping their neighbors, but one fit for the Chosen People.

"This is the man," Samuel heard the Voice speak inside his head. "This is the man I said would be king over My people." Samuel's heart began to beat hard; his eyes took in Saul approaching, and he thought: King of Israel!

Samuel stared at Saul, observing every aspect: his stature, his gait, his noble visage. How exciting! Soon Israel will have its king.

"Excuse me, my lord," Saul hesitated, delicately asking the man with the snow-white hair and beard standing before him: "Do you know where the seer is?"

Samuel reached out and took Saul's hand in his, caressing it. "I am the seer."

Excitement gripped Saul, and he bowed his head and bent down to kiss the prophet's hand. However, Samuel withdrew his hand, eschewing the sign of respect.

"Come to the high place, my lord, everyone is waiting for you," Samuel said as he placed his hand on Saul's shoulder. "Go up there, and all your questions will be answered. Don't worry. Your father's she-donkeys have already been found. Ascend, my son, ascend," Samuel led Saul with his hand toward the high place. "Just go up and I'll explain everything. *And upon whom is all the desire of Israel, if not upon you and all your father's house?* Worry not about the beasts."

Saul was confused, thoughts consuming him: What's going on here? Why won't he let me kiss his hand? Why should I go up before Him? What did that mean, *"And upon whom is all the desire of Israel, if not upon you and all your father's house?"*

Saul was reluctant. What does he want from me? Why is he treating me like this?

"My lord, beg your pardon, perhaps you have confused me for someone else? Who would wait for me? I am from the tribe of Benjamin, the youngest of all the tribes; my clan is not notable, and I am the youngest in my father's house. Why await me?"

"I don't mean anyone else," Samuel gently replied, amazed by the humility in Saul's voice. "Go up and I'll explain everything to you."

A bemused Saul went up to the high place before Samuel the Prophet, finding thirty of Israel's most important elders there. The table was set for them, and all were sitting and waiting for Samuel to ascend and recite the sacrificial blessing.

Samuel approached them, introducing an unfamiliar man who appeared, and in front of him an unfamiliar, youthful-looking man and his servant. Samuel led Saul to the head of the table. "Sit here, my friend. And you, boy, sit next to your master."

Saul hesitated.

"Sit down, my son, sit down," the prophet urged him, beckoning the cook. "Bring me the leg and what's attached to it, and set it before Saul," he whispered. The cook ran off and returned with a tray. Samuel took the tray from the cook's hands, handed it to Saul and the boy, and sat down on Saul's right. "Make the blessing, my son; everyone is waiting for you. After you've eaten, come stay the night with me, and I'll explain everything to you."

Despite Samuel's promises, what Saul learned that night left him confused and shocked. His mind kept racing as he tried to digest it all: What's going on here? Is it a dream? I arrive in the city, Samuel the Seer comes out to meet me, sits me down at the head of the table of dignitaries, offers me to eat first and lead the blessing, then finally takes me to sleep in his house. After that, he talks to me all evening about the reality and uniqueness of God, about serving the Lord. Samuel the Seer speaks to me with deference. What does he want from me? He explains to me what an honor it is to serve the people, that a monarch — and anyone who holds authority over others — must recognize that the reality is that of accepting a yoke of responsibility. A public servant must serve the public, not expect the public to serve them! Still, what does this have to do with me? He tells me that the People of Israel want a king for themselves, and God wants to appoint a ruler over His people. What does this have to do with me? All I did was ask where my father's she-donkeys were, and he casually replied that they'd already been found. Since then, he hasn't stopped talking about all sorts of higher matters. He is a fascinating conversationalist; his words are full of wisdom and morality, and every utterance that comes out of his mouth is imbued with fear of God. But why is he even talking to me? I am the baby of the family; we are a minor family in the tribe, and our tribe is the most junior in the nation. I am heir to no fortune, nor to a great house. Why must he do this to me? Now he's letting me sleep in his bed, and he's napping on a chair in the corner. What's going on here?

In the background, the lad's rhythmic breathing could be heard.

Saul mused: He fell asleep a long time ago. The boy is overjoyed at this turn of events. He went from being hungry and thirsty, to feasting and toasting among the most notable men in Israel. Poor boy, he was really famished.

The sleeping Samuel's labored breathing could be heard in the room.

The torrent of thoughts clouded Saul's mind, confounding him; but eventually, fatigue overwhelmed him, and he fell asleep.

CHAPTER SEVEN

Kingship

The sun was shining, painting the world in shades of a reddish-orange hue along the horizon. The sounds of birds chirping, as if to express gratitude for a new morning, merged with the bleating of the sheep and the crow of the roosters in wonderful harmony. Human voices echoed down the street.

Saul blinked but hadn't opened his eyes yet.

He thought: It must have been a dream.

Then he opened his eyes and saw the figure of Samuel the Seer looking at him with a loving fatherly gaze.

"Wake up, my son. You need to go to your father's house; he's worried about you. Get up, get organized, eat some breakfast, and head back to your father's house," Samuel said, smiling.

Saul got up from Samuel's bed, washed his hands, and woke up his servant.

The two stood in prayer.

After each had eaten his heart's fill, Samuel addressed Saul: "Come my son, you have to go; your father is worried. I will accompany you." Samuel handed the boy a bundle of food and provisions for the road, and the three set out from Samuel's house for the city gates. They were open, and the streets were bustling. However, the passersby froze when they saw the trio. People were amazed: "What is Samuel the Seer doing with these two? Escorting them out of town? He's acting oddly." Word of what happened yesterday had spread like wildfire, the news that Samuel had taken an unknown, young-looking man and his lad and seated them at the head of the high table. "Who is this man?" The crowd looked at Samuel with love and admiration, at Saul and the boy with wonder and envy.

Samuel, Saul, and the lad left the city: "Tell the boy to go ahead of us. I have something to tell you. I must pass on the Word of God," Samuel whispered to Saul, who did as he was told, though he moved as if in a dream.

Samuel and Saul stood facing and looking at each other. Samuel excitedly reached into his cloak, pulling out a small cruse of oil. "The Lord told me to anoint you as king over Israel. You are chosen by God to rule over His nation, to sit on the throne of His Holy People." Samuel spoke excitedly, noting Saul's expression of amazement and thinking: He looks fit to be king.

"Saul, son of Kish, kneel before your God, and I will anoint you as king over the People of Israel," Samuel said, his commanding voice forcing Saul to act.

Saul knelt, and Samuel poured persimmon oil over Saul's head.

"Prostate yourself to the Lord, and give Him your gratitude," Samuel continued.

Saul felt that he was still in a reverie as he received this command. "I thank You very much, God, but I am unworthy to be king over the People of Israel," Saul said, bowing to the ground. "I am unfit. This must be a dream," Saul protested, weeping.

"Please rise, Saul, son of Kish, King of Israel," said Samuel gently, stretching out his hand, helping Saul to his feet. "You have been chosen to be king over the People of Israel." Samuel kissed Saul, but he could sense the other's disbelief.

"Behold, I will give you signs, so that you may know that what I have told you is true, and that it is God's will. When you leave me and reach the Benjamite border, by Rachel's Tomb, you will be met by two people, who will tell you that the she-donkeys you were looking for have been found, and that your father is now worried about your well-being. Then you will reach the Oak of Tabor, where you will find three people ascending to Bethel. They will ask how you are and give you of their provisions. When you reach where the Ark of the Covenant is located in Kiriath Jearim, you will meet a group of prophets, and there the Spirit of God will come upon you. You will prophesy among them, becoming a new man. When you witness these signs, you will know that everything I have told you is true, and God is with you. In a week, I'll meet you in Gilgal and tell you what to do."

Saul's lad, who had waited for him at a distance, was confused. He wondered: "What did the prophet tell you?"

"Nothing special," Saul said, avoiding the boy's gaze. "He said the she-donkeys had been found, and my father was worried about our well-being. Let's go home."

The two went together. When they arrived at Rachel's Tomb, they were met by two people. They told Saul that the beasts had been found and that Kish was worried about him.

"We already knew that," the boy laughed in his heart. He didn't know that this was the first sign given by Samuel the Seer.

At the Oak of Tabor, they met three Bethel-bound pilgrims, who gave them provisions. The boy, unaware of Samuel's signs, thought: What nice people!

At their next stop, they encountered a group of prophets. The boy froze; he was anxious and frightened, as he'd never seen a coterie of prophets before.

Saul approached them, but suddenly felt a tremor run through his whole body, sweat covering him. He fell to the ground, shaking, and prophesying.

The lad was horrified. He saw his master fall to the ground, his body trembling. Very quickly he ran to help Saul, to help him get to his feet. An old man walked toward the boy and took his hand, pulling him away from his prone lord.

"Let me go, let me help him! He's sick, he needs help, something happened to him!" the boy shouted as he tried to free himself from the elder's grasp.

"Calm down, son," said the old man, "he's not sick, he's prophesying. Apparently, your lord is worthy of prophecy, and here, near the Ark of the Covenant, the spirit of prophecy has taken him, and he is prophesying."

"But he collapsed on the ground," the boy continued, not understanding the meaning of the old man's words, "Let me go! Let me help him!"

"No, my son, you don't need to help him; you'll just disturb him. When a person prophesies, the Spirit of the Lord comes upon him, so he cannot stand on his feet. The body is unable to contain the great light that emanates, so it falls down. Moses, lord of all prophets, was an exception; he could speak to God while on his feet. Samuel the Seer is very close to this level too. However, all other prophets are laid low when the Divine Voice speaks to them. The intensity of the revelation of God's reality in the world via prophecy disrupts the body. The light that flows into the soul of the prophet is almost beyond the ability of any flesh to contain; the human soul seeks to abandon the body and cleave to the Creator. Don't worry, son, in a few minutes, your lord will rise and recover. Tell me, my son, who's your master? What's his name?" asked the elder, not letting go of the lad's elbow.

"Saul, son of Kish, of the Tribe of Benjamin," the boy replied, looking at his master in admiration and awe.

"Saul, son of Kish!" The cry arose: "*Is Saul also among the prophets*?"

"Have you heard the strange idea that Samuel the Seer said? He summoned all Israel to Mizpah, where the great altar and house of prayer are, and he will cast lots to see who King of Israel will be."

"A lottery for the throne? That's how you choose who wears the crown? A king should be a warrior and hero, strong and brave, intelligent and clever. He's holding a raffle?"

"Yes, that's what Samuel the Seer said. He will make a lottery among all the tribes of Israel, and whoever wins will be king. Let us hope it isn't some dumb old weakling. Let's hurry up! Who knows, maybe you or I will win the raffle for the crown!"

In Mizpah, the people thronged with sounds of amusement and bemusement arising from the bustling crowd. By midday, the People of Israel had assembled, with participants from all the tribes of Israel. The nation had ascended to Mizpah to answer the call of Samuel the Seer.

"What's the idea?"

"A lottery for the crown?"

"Who will be chosen?"

Samuel stood at the podium, flanked by the twelve tribal princes and the high priest. The eyes of the entire nation were raised to Samuel the Seer as he loomed above the crowd. He raised his hands, and a hush fell over the crowd. The era of the Judges was officially ending, and the era of the Kings was beginning — by Samuel's casting of lots, of all things! His voice could be heard from afar, all of creation awaiting the words of the prophet.

"This is what the Lord, the God of Israel, says: 'I brought Israel up out of Egypt, and I rescued you from the hands of the Egyptians and of all the kingdoms that oppressed you.' But today you have rejected your God, who saves you from all your troubles and afflictions, and you have said to Him, 'No, set a king over us.' Now therefore present yourselves before the Lord by your tribes and clans."

Samuel lowered his hands and picked a scrap of parchment from the bowl. He unrolled it and read the name: "The Tribe of Benjamin! The King of Israel will be from the Tribe of Benjamin."

The Benjamites greeted this result with jubilation, but the other tribes' disappointment was louder.

"Hush..." Samuel said, and the crowd quieted. "Prince of Benjamin, approach!"

The prince approached, with lots containing the names of all the Benjamite families. "Prince of Benjamin, draw your lot," Samuel commanded.

The prince complied and announced: "Clan of Matri!" The Matrites rejoiced.

"Patriarch of Matri, approach!" Samuel exclaimed. The patriarch climbed up to the podium with lots of his own, containing the names of the individuals in the clan. "Patriarch of Matri, draw your lot!" The patriarch complied and announced: "Saul, son of Kish!" This time, there were only a few cheers from the audience.

"Who is Saul, son of Kish? Where is he?" the crowd began to buzz.

"Saul, son of Kish, approach!" Samuel ordered, but there was only utter silence in response. Throughout the crowd, people craned their necks and looked around. Where was the royal raffle winner? No one moved, no one came to the podium.

"My lord, high priest," said Samuel, "please consult the Urim and Thummim to confirm the Lord's choice for King of Israel."

Consulting the Urim and Thummim was one of the high priest's most sacred duties. The Breastplate of Judgment he wore contained twelve precious stones, each engraved with letters spelling out the names of the twelve tribes of Israel, as well as those of the patriarchs

Abraham, Isaac, and Jacob. When he closed his eyes, focused his mind, and sought divine guidance, letters would light up on the Breastplate of Judgment, spelling out the answer. The high priest would put the words together to know what to do. As Samuel requested, the high priest said aloud: "Who is to be King of Israel?" As the crowd eagerly waited, the letters lit up" S-A-U-L S-O-N O-F K-I-S-H. "Saul, son of Kish, is King of Israel," announced the high priest, "so say the Urim and Thummim."

"My lord high priest, where may we find Saul, son of Kish, King of Israel?" asked Samuel the Seer.

The high priest directed his heart toward his Heavenly Father and the letters glowed once again: B-A-G-G-A-G-E. "The baggage, he is hiding among the baggage," the high priest announced.

A few young Matrites ran toward the area where the Israelites had stored their baggage, finding Saul cringing in the corner. "Rise, Saul, son of Kish, King of Israel! Come, Samuel the Seer and the high priest are waiting for you. You are chosen both by lots and by the Urim and Thummim. You are King of Israel."

Saul rose to his feet, embarrassed, and reluctantly went to the podium. When the people saw Saul approaching with the youths, the crowd split in two like the parting of the Red Sea. Between the two rows of people walked Saul, his gaze lowered as if to convey that he thought himself unworthy of the honor.

Neither callow youth nor hoary elder, God's chosen one was head and shoulders above the people, a striking visage, but moved reluctantly toward the podium.

"Ascend, Saul, son of Kish, King of Israel," declared Samuel, "because the Lord has selected you, from all the tribes of Israel, to sit on the throne."

Saul climbed to the podium slowly, hoping to avoid assuming the position.

Samuel approached him. "Israelites, see that this is our monarch. King of Israel, there is no one like him among all the people!" Samuel proclaimed.

"Long live the King! Long live King Saul!" The shouts swelled.

Slowly, one by one, the people began to pass before Saul to meet him, wish him success, and pay tribute to the new king.

The youths thought: For years we have been asking for a monarch, and God has chosen for us a king worthy to wear the crown!

They approached their new sovereign, swore allegiance, and asked to serve in his forces.

However, some of the people turned away from the king, rejecting his authority.

"A royal raffle? Saul, son of Kish the Benjamite, a king? What a joke! Samuel the Prophet has taken leave of his senses. A crown by lots? Not my king!" they said to each other.

Saul heard but remained silent...

CHAPTER EIGHT
Jabesh Gilead

"Saul son of Kish, King of Israel, help us," the delegation begged, kneeling and bemoaning their fate.

Saul had arrived home in the early evening from his work in the field. He had assumed none of the trappings of royalty. He thought: If the people do not want me as king, I cannot force them to.

He had heard the cries of contempt coming from the people when Samuel proclaimed him king. He mused: They're right; I'm unworthy of being King of Israel.

Saul went on with his life as usual, except for a few young men accompanying him, enthused to play the role of king's guard. Saul was shy by nature; he refused to accept the yoke of kingship and exercise his authority over the people.

However, now that had become untenable. The messengers looked at him pleadingly. "Please, Your Majesty, we are emissaries from the city of Jabesh Gilead. We have come to the King of Israel to beg Your Majesty. King Nahash of Ammon attacks us, slaying our townspeople. Anyone who goes out to his fields doesn't return home. Nahash and his soldiers have imposed a curfew on the city, and the town is starving. Our elders sent messengers to Nahash suing for peace; we agreed to pay him tribute. The villain agreed to end the siege, on condition that we become his slaves; that everyone's right eye be put out; and that our Torah scrolls be burnt, since they say: 'No Ammonite or Moabite may enter the assembly of the Lord.'" The tearful delegation begged: "Please, Your Majesty, we've no other hope. He agreed to give us a week to consider his terms, but if Your Majesty does not come to our aid, we will have no choice but to submit!" They broke down sobbing.

"Burn the Torah?! Blind yourselves?! Degrade God and the People of Israel?! I will not allow it!" exclaimed Saul. His body shook with fury, outraged by Nahash's audacity. "Men of Jabesh Gilead, arise! Nahash of Ammon, your end is near! The People of Israel do not abandon their brothers in trouble! Your plight is the plight of us all. Who dares harm the Lord's nation? Jabesh Gilead, cry no more. Your salvation comes. Your countrymen ride to your aid, to save you from your foes!"

Saul gestured to his young men: "Bring me a pair of oxen!" His voice became authoritative and majestic.

The youths, who were eager to serve their king, ran to fulfill his command. "Slaughter them and dissect them into chunks! Go out to all the tribes of Israel and tell them: 'Whoever does not come with me and Samuel the Seer to war, this is what will happen to his cattle.'"

The youths, who had wondered about Saul's fitness not long ago, saw the change that had taken place in him. A heroic spirit filled him, legitimizing his crown and his throne. They were now truly the king's guard, promulgating the royal edict.

Three days later, many Israelites had gathered for war under Saul's command. The Ammonites were a mere thorn in their side compared to the Philistines, who ruled the land with a heavy hand. In every province, there was a Philistine prefect who oppressed the people. The Israelites were not allowed to engage in metalwork. Their mattocks and plowshares were manufactured and repaired only by the Philistines. Any Israelite who engaged in metalworking would be put to death, the Philistines decreed. So great masses gathered for war, but without weapons — no spears, no lances, no swords. A people that for many years had been enslaved to foreigners who continually issued harsh decrees.

At noon, the sun stood high in the sky as if watching what was happening. King Saul and Samuel the Seer stood at the podium, surveying the assembled people. The crowd looked at their new monarch and aged seer, yearning to hear a rousing royal speech. Their roiling emotions were mixed: fear and joy, enthusiasm and anxiety. Decades of oppression had taken their toll on the people. They worried that the assembly itself would encourage the Philistines to enact new edicts and abuses.

The wicked Philistines never shied away from harassing Israel. Debasing women, the elderly, and children was Israel's daily lot. The Israelite women that had been captured to serve the Philistines were severely abused. The young men of Israel were trampled under the feet of the Philistines by hard labor. The Israelites had forgotten the taste of freedom. Their identity as a people hung by a thread. Every city, province, and tribe was controlled by Philistine officials, and there was little connection between the tribes. They were only linked by the Hebrew calendar and its holidays, a fragile, fraying bond. Each focused on their own troubles, trying to survive the day.

Saul commanded his youths to take a census of all those assembled. Each soldier presented a potsherd, which was carefully counted.

When the census was handed to him, Saul mused: Three hundred and thirty thousand soldiers. So many troops, yet we are trampled under the feet of our foes!

"People of Israel," he declared, with a firm, majestic, and loud voice that reverberated throughout the area, silencing the masses. "We are the progeny of Abraham, Isaac, and Jacob. We are one people! We are children of the King of Kings! We are sons and servants of God, and only His! From today, we will begin to behave as befits us. From today, we will cease to be slaves of other nations; we are returning to worship our King." His voice echoed in all directions, stirring their hearts, igniting a new spirit in them, igniting the fading ember deep in the people's hearts. Sounds of joy and encouragement were heard from all sides; the nation was reviving.

"*Hear O Israel, the Lord our God, the Lord is one,*" Saul exclaimed. His voice seemed to go from one end of the world to the other. The call moved their hearts. "*Hear O Israel...*" the people shouted enthusiastically. Their voices rose and burst into the sky, shaking the Heavenly Throne, the cry of a nation already free of the shackles of the mind fastened by oppressors, a people restored into nationhood.

"Today the people of Jabesh Gilead will be saved, and soon the People of Israel will be saved," the monarch decreed.

"Long live the king, long live the king!" the cries rose. "Long live King Saul!"

Before daybreak, the stars glowed like small diamonds in the sky.

The moon sank, making way for the sun yet to rise. Darkness still covered the land. The people marched slowly, approaching the Ammonites besieging Jabesh Gilead. Nahash's camp was full of mirth and merrymaking. The townspeople had sent word that they accepted his terms and would surrender in the morning to their fate.

"Cowards! Weaklings! This is the Chosen People? We'll let them choose which eye we blind and which one we leave!" This mockery was met with guffaws.

The people continue to advance surreptitiously.

"I think I'll take an Israelite woman for myself. They're so comely; they have the most beautiful eyes. Oh, pardon me, I meant 'eye!'" Gales of drunken laughter followed.

Saul, bent low to the ground, led one division, while Jonathan, his eldest son, led another. Samuel led the third division.

The Ammonites' victory party was in full swing; even the sentries had abandoned their posts to join the revelry. Still, the Israelites moved like rebellious slaves, still wary of open combat with their erstwhile masters. They had planks and poles,

The Israelites approached the camp, still feeling like slaves rebelling against their masters, afraid of warfare. They had planks, poles, pickaxes, and plowshares — a pathetic hodgepodge to wield against trained, armed troops.

Mere yards from the encampment, watching tensely, Saul rose to his full height, pulling out a shofar. It was a striking tableau: one man facing the entire Ammonite camp, the town of Jabesh Gilead behind him, the horizon turning golden with the first rays of sunlight. Night began to shatter, as the burgeoning day was about to erupt. Saul's cloak danced around him in the soft wind.

He lifted the shofar to his mouth and blew it, and the mirth and mockery came to an immediate halt. Now there were shouts of shock and surprise, but the three Israelite divisions were already among the amazed Ammonites, whooping for war.

The Ammonites, drunk on the feeling of victory beating in their hearts, were totally unprepared for the sudden attack, striking in all directions with clubs and sickles. The shock of the unexpected assault paralyzed Nahash's men.

The battle lasted about three hours. At its end, the Ammonite fatalities were in the tens of thousands. Few fighters fled for their lives, just individuals fleeing in panic.

King Nahash of Ammon surrendered. He was released only after vowing never to attack Israel again.

"Long live King Saul, long live King Saul," the shouts echoed. The daring Israelite warriors, who the day before had been enslaved and oppressed, now carried Saul, Samuel, and Jonathan on their shoulders. The joy of victory was intoxicating. There was hope. Israel had a king. They could seek freedom from foreign oppression. Feelings of admiration filled the hearts of the fighters: there was a king in Israel!

Samuel the Seer spoke up: "Come, my brothers, People of Israel; we will go to Gilgal and hold the coronation there."

The troops shouted for joy as they made their way to Gilgal.

"Samuel the Seer," came the call from a number of warriors, the young men who had initially supported Saul, "All those who once defied King Saul must be punished! They must be killed!" There were shouts of yea and nay in response; the people were roiled by emotions: fear and hatred, vindictiveness and regret.

"Enough!" shouted Saul, holding up his hands. Silence descended on the masses. "Enough! Enough with this talk. No one will be put to death on this day, because today God has wrought salvation for Israel. This is a day of triumph, a day of Israel overcoming its enemies. Not a day of revenge against our brethren, but a day when the People of Israel are once again one people. Today we will go to Gilgal for the coronation, rejoice greatly, and offer sacrifices of gratitude."

A burst of cheers and relief rose from the crowd. Even the major opponents of Saul's kingdom accepted his kingdom willingly after the great success. The fear that had gripped the hearts of his critics faded, the fear of revenge by the king.

"We are going to Gilgal," cried Samuel the Seer, "for the coronation of King Saul."

The people lifted their feet, singing and praising God with open mouths and full hearts.

CHAPTER NINE

Jonathan

Six months after the ceremony in Gilgal, the Philistines were still tyrannizing Israel.

The People of Israel remained oppressed, enslaved, and tormented under the yoke of the Philistines. After the rout of the Ammonites, the Philistines tightened their grip on the Israelites, suppressing any gatherings for fear of revolution.

King Saul chose three thousand warriors for his army, two thousand with him at Michmash, and one thousand with his son Jonathan at Gibeah of Benjamin. Unarmed soldiers, behaving like ordinary people, hiding their affiliation with Saul...

Jonathan was as tall and handsome as his father, humble and righteous, with a heroic spirit. In his mid-thirties, he was a sharp-eyed archer who never missed. Jonathan gathered his troops silently and engaged the Philistine prefect stationed at Geba. Until this time, Israel had not dared to fight the Philistines.

The Philistines were a numerous people, uncountable as grains of sand on the beach. They were skilled warriors equipped with iron chariots, horses, and cavalry. Well-armed, they had a fierce and brutal army, fighters experienced in countless battles. A nation that controlled all its surroundings with an iron fist. A terrible empire, terrorizing all its neighbors. Warriors in iron helms and armor, eager for battle.

King Saul heard about his son's deed and decided it was time to start confronting the tyrannical enemy. Saul sensed that his subjects expected deliverance from the hands of the Philistines, the real enemy of Israel. The victory over the Ammonites had given the Israelites a taste of freedom, the rush of success that was required to spur them on to continue until they were an independent nation again.

He thought: I need advice. What to do? How do I free Israel from the Philistines?

"My lord Samuel the Seer," he began. "Behold, you have heard what my son Jonathan did, striking down the Philistine prefect at Geba. Now the Philistines are coming to take revenge on us, and you have crowned me king over the People of Israel, and the nation awaits deliverance from the hands of their enemies. What am I to do?" he asked in an excited voice. "Please help me!"

Samuel, as a father who felt sorry for his sons, felt King Saul's distress: "Gather the people to Gilgal, and in seven days I will come to you there. I will offer peace offerings and thanksgiving offerings there, and then I will tell you the path to follow and what you must do."

Saul's soldiers were in a flurry.

"I'm running away from here. Do you think I'm crazy? You think I'm going to stay here to die? Have you seen what kind of army they have? Thirty thousand chariots, six thousand cavalry, and hundreds of thousands of skilled soldiers. They are a skilled army with weapons of war. We have no chance of winning; they will slaughter us all! Our sons, daughters, and wives will be taken away by them. They will not leave any of the men alive; they will abuse women and children. I tell you, if you have some wisdom, take your wife and children and run away before they arrive, before it's too late. Don't be such a martyr. Better to be a living coward than a dead hero. We have no chance. If I thought there was any chance of victory, I would stay. You know me, I'm not fainthearted, but in this case, there's no point fighting. I want my wife and children to survive. There are almost no soldiers left, almost all of them have fled toward the Jordan or to the caves. The few who remain think that if they beg for mercy, the Philistines will not kill them. Stupid! They don't know the Philistines. I repeat to you: take your family and run for your life."

"Listen to me," replied his comrade, "at least come to Gilgal and hear what King Saul says. Samuel the Seer is going there to give the king advice on how to defeat the Philistines. You know Samuel; he will surely give wise counsel."

"Counsel? I already gave you the best advice you'll ever hear to save yourself: take your family and flee while you can. That's all. Brother, if you have sense and love your family, just do as I do," the erstwhile warrior said, turning away, leaving his friend undecided.

"What should I do?" the man thought, torn between his loyalty to the king and his concern for the welfare of his family. "Almost everyone has fled; there are fewer than a thousand people left. Saul is going tomorrow with Samuel to Gilgal. What advice can he give? Fewer than a thousand fighters against a mighty army? Maybe my friend is right. I should run away while we're still alive..."

"King Saul," came the call from the crowd, "where is Samuel the Seer? You said he would come today. Are you trying to delay the issues? Night falls soon. You said he would come to bring the offering, but there's no sacrifice at night! Perhaps he escaped to the caves too? If he ran away, we should run too! He probably won't be coming today! Bring the offering! Maybe God will be pleased, and the Philistines will flee."

With a smirk, one man said: "If you don't bring the offering now, we're all gone."

"Yes, he is right, bring the offering; at least let us fulfill another commandment before we die," said another. "Bring the offering, and perhaps the spirit of prophecy will descend upon you again, and you can give over the Word of God to us. You have prophesied before, so bring the offering and prophesy!"

Saul heard the voices of his soldiers, broken and frightened. They spoke like condemned men, deep in despair. He mused: Samuel the Seer told me that he would come today. The sun is about to set, and we haven't yet brought the offering. There is no time to wait for Samuel. People are already starting to walk away. They're right, what could Samuel the Seer say? There is no chance of salvation and victory; we have fewer than a thousand fighters against this mighty army.

Saul stopped thinking. "Bring me the sacrifice," the king commanded in a firm voice. Saul offered the sacrifice, but was granted no prophecy...

"Here comes Samuel!" a murmur ran through the people.

Samuel the Seer, wrapped in a white robe, approached the high place. The warriors gave ground, retreating in terror from him. His face was wrinkled and sullen, but his eyes shone with righteous fury. Samuel advanced on Saul.

Saul, who only a few minutes ago had offered the sacrifice, took a hesitant step toward Samuel, aware that he had sinned by transgressing the words of the prophet. He reflected: What could I do? I had no choice!

Saul moved slowly as Samuel sped toward him: "Peace be upon you, my lord Samuel the Prophet," he said, regret in his voice. "Welcome!"

"What have you done?" Samuel demanded fiercely.

Saul answered weakly, as if apologizing: "The crowds were dispersing. I waited so long for you, and you didn't come. I brought the offering, fearing you'd never arrive. I thought maybe God would absolve and forgive us. How could I go to battle without bringing an offering? I couldn't help myself, so I went ahead without you."

Samuel looked at Saul, his gaze full of contempt and consternation, mixed with compassion. He thought: I should never have anointed him king. He follows his heart, which is always swayed by those around him.

Samuel stared at Saul, his gaze piercing Saul's heart: "You were frustrated, so you behaved stupidly. What, do you think God wants sacrifices and offerings? Do you think He's hungry? He wants you to obey His word and follow His ways! But you do as you please, following your heart. If you had listened to me and waited, you would have merited an eternal dynasty. But you are impatient, afraid of what may happen, lacking in faith. God wants a king over his people who will obey Him and follow His ways. You have demonstrated that you are not that man!" Samuel turned his glowing gaze on Saul, who looked at his feet.

Samuel turned away, leaving Saul watching with bitter disappointment until he disappeared from sight.

Pain pierced Saul's heart: "I have sinned…"

At midday, the sun beat down, making the heat unbearable.

Jonathan sat on a hillside overlooking the Philistine camp, in a ravine between two high mountains. Saul and his men were hiding in the crevices of the rocks.

He thought: There are only about six hundred fighters left. Naturally, we have no chance of winning.

From his position, he surveyed the Philistine camp that filled the valley, its ends beyond sight. At this height, Jonathan saw the Philistines milling about like an endless swarm of ants.

He reflected: And that's just a third of their forces.

The Philistines were divided into three camps, facing north, east, and west. Three human swarms who want to destroy the People of Israel.

He mused: Three human swarms could wipe out our nation just by walking through the land, let alone using their war engines. And it's all because of me. Maybe I acted hastily!

His comrades seemed disheartened, drooping and dreading the onslaught.

Jonathan considered: I caused this shameful situation. I should not have acted so rashly by killing the prefect; now these family men worry about their loved ones. Their loyalty to their sovereign is undeniable, throwing their lives aside for the sake of their countrymen. Their faces show that they know that our fate is sealed. They're right! The Philistines will not rest until they have executed all the men; the women and children will be taken prisoner. And it's all because of me!

Jonathan's face fell as he was overcome by guilt.

The Philistines usually sent an advance force to survey the area, discovering traps or groups of enemies in hiding. Jonathan looked at the outpost in front of him, thinking: They are excellent fighters, and they have very defined and orderly methods of operation. Twenty troops man this outpost, as they explore the field. It won't take them more than a few days to end the war.

His despair grew, despondency washing over his entire being. His face crumbled and his back bent as he curled inward, as if already in mourning for his nation.

Jonathan murmured: "They are like a swarm of ants, a huge swarm of ants..."

Suddenly, a shock ran through his body. His slumped shoulders straightened, and his slackened face stretched into a grin. "Yes, there's a huge swarm of ants here! Several hundred thousand ants! Is it because they are many that we cannot defeat them? After all, war is in God's hands He can save us, whether we are few or many! *There is no other besides Him.* He can do anything!"

He was imbued with a new spirit, awakening him to action: "There is nothing to fear from them! You can wipe out this swarm of ants in one fell swoop! It is not we who make war, but the Creator of the Universe!" The blood that had flowed slowly through his body began to pump rhythmically, rousing his dormant frame to action. *"For the Lord will not forsake His people; He will never abandon His heritage.* We need to have faith and fortitude, and the Creator will lead our battles. *The Lord will fight for you; you need only to be still."* Jonathan felt the spirit of faith carrying him, filling his heart with hope and confidence.

"Come with me," he said to his arms-bearer.

Jonathan and the boy descended from the hillside toward the Philistine outpost. The sun was about to set, twilight spreading, darkness spreading its wings. The world seemed to begin to prepare for sleep.

Two men approached the Philistine outpost. About twenty troops manned the outpost, fierce fighters. Jonathan and his arms-bearer approached. The boy was an orphan; his parents and siblings had been murdered a few days ago by the Philistines. The boy had managed to escape and joined the ranks of the army; now he sought revenge for his loved ones.

"We'll get to the post soon," Jonathan whispered: "When we arrive, we'll stand up. If the fighters at the outpost tell us, 'Stand in your place,' we will stay and not engage them; but if they say, 'Come up to us,' we will rise up and fight them. This is a sign to us that God has given them into our hands, because God can save us, whether we are few or many."

"Do what you think is right," the boy whispered. "I'm with you, my lord, whatever you do."

A few yards from the Philistine outpost, Jonathan and the boy rose to their feet. The former held a sword, one of only two in the Israelite armory (Saul had the other); the latter held the blade of a plow.

"Who is it there?" came the voice of one of the Philistine warriors. "Here the mice are starting to come out of their holes," his friend replied. "They surely want to surrender, to turn themselves in."

The man shouted: "Come, come up to us."

Jonathan whispered to the boy: "Come, brother, the Lord has given them into our hands." Jonathan began running toward the fighters, followed by his arms-bearer. The Philistines, who were expecting them to surrender, were shocked by the reaction, and fear paralyzed their bodies. The historical memories of Israel's courage in battle and military prowess in ancient times flooded their minds. The people who conquered and destroyed thirty-one kings when they entered the Land of Canaan, after their exodus from Egypt, were not a cowardly or weak people. The fears hidden deep in the Philistines' hearts became real. The popular tales of Israel's heroes of yore — from Joshua to Gideon, Samson and Jephthah — were recalled, leaving them helpless. The Philistine warriors, who had earlier projected fearlessness and confidence, turned out to be cravens, frozen by fears of the past.

Jonathan drew his sword, striking everywhere, and the lad followed him, confirming his kills. The screams and shouts of devastation from the throats of the attacked fighters tore through the silence of the night, reaching the complacent main camp of the Philistines. The yells and cries of terror filled the valley, piercing the hearts of the warriors, evoking ancient fears from deep in their hearts.

Jonathan pulled out his shofar and blew a staccato call to arms. "Salvation is the Lord's!" he shouted loudly. His fierce voice echoed from between the two mountains, striking deep into the souls of the Philistine warriors.

Their shouts were panicked:
"It's an ambush!"
"They're coming at us!"
"They will destroy us like Nahash of Ammon and his army!"

Their deep-set fears bloomed and blossomed, unmanning them. They were blinded by dread, seeing everyone as hostile. The Philistines drew their weapons, hacking indiscriminately in all directions, killing their own comrades. Some of them climbed to their feet to flee for their lives. The commotion broke the silence, shaking the valley. The cavalry trampled infantry, galloping recklessly anywhere. Chariots ran over those fleeing on feet, before crashing and overturning, crushing their occupants to death. Fire spread from tent to tent, igniting the night.

The Hebrew slaves seized by the Philistines to serve them in the camp realized their salvation was at hand. They seized the weapons dropped by their captors and joined the battle. Thousands of them instantly became warriors, attacking their foes.

The warriors of Israel, hiding in caves and rocky places, heard the sounds of combat. They streamed from their hiding places to join their brethren in delivering Israel from the hands of the Philistines.

CHAPTER TEN

Amalek

In the late evening, the Israelite encampment was quiet.

The royal tent was bathed in oil light, as the four members of the war council sat together: Samuel, Saul, Jonathan, and Abner, Saul's uncle and army chief.

Abner, son of Ner, was a veteran, renowned for his valor, bravery, and strategic mind. He was just a few years older than his nephew, and he regarded him with obvious affection. He reflected: We played together as children, and now he is King of Israel, leading the Chosen Nation into battle and emerging victorious. He is maintaining his momentum, capitalizing on the success of Jonathan's assault. All of our hostile neighbors now fear us, from the Ammonites to the Philistines, from Moab to Aram-Zobah. Such a sweeping triumph! You can see he has help from the Heavens!"

Abner realized his comrades were waiting for him to share his opinion. He shook his head and then met their gaze, reporting: "Our army is growing. We have standing forces of over twenty thousand, trained, tested, and fitted out. We now have all the arms and armor we need, and the entire nation stands behind us. We have subdued Ammon, Moab, Edom, Zobah, and Philistia." Abner concluded his analysis: "We have addressed every crisis, save one: the Amalekites in the Negev. They constantly infiltrate at night — killing women, children, and the elderly — then flee. They are a wretched and cowardly people, afraid to fight against men. Just this week, they entered a town in the Negev and murdered a woman and her five children in their sleep. We must deal with them. Our brethren in the south can neither sleep at night nor work their fields during the day. These terrorists paralyze the south and demoralize the whole nation. We have to eliminate their threat."

Jonathan looked at Abner with admiration, thinking: He's a man after my heart. It's true, these accursed evildoers do not hesitate to raid us. They may be far from us, but they carry out these attacks almost daily, seeking to maim and kill Israelites for no reason. Abner is right, they must be destroyed."

King Saul looked at his son and uncle, Israel's heroes, with pride.

Suddenly, a tremor passed through Samuel's body, which immediately became drenched with sweat. The others whipped toward him, and Jonathan began to rise, shaking at the thought that the righteous prophet might be falling seriously ill. Saul raised a hand to halt him. "Stay right there, he's prophesying!" he whispered.

Jonathan's eyes widened as he observed Samuel. He had never witnessed the phenomenon, and he grew emotional. "The Spirit of the Lord is in him now! The Creator of the Universe is talking to him right now, giving him a message!" Excitement and a bit of envy of Samuel's lofty spiritual level flooded his heart.

The only sound was the whisper of flames licking the wicks in their cups of oil.

Aged Samuel abruptly relaxed, opening eyes seemingly fixed on the horizon, his white beard damp with sweat. His wrinkled palms gripped the armrests tightly: "*This is what the Lord of Hosts says: 'I witnessed what the Amalekites did to the Israelites when they ambushed them on their way up from Egypt. Now go and attack the Amalekites and devote to destruction all that belongs to them. Do not spare them, but put them to death…'*"

As the Israelite troops returned to their encampment, they shouted in triumph — mitigated with sorrow and pain. Combat with Amalek was not difficult; despite the vast numbers of the Amalekites, they were a craven and cowardly people, their fighters unaccustomed to facing men in battle. Their favorite tactic was to maim and murder women, the elderly, and children. The war lasted about a week. The Amalekites occupied the Negev, small and large cities, villages and towns. An unorganized army, their fighters had no experience in battle. By contrast, Saul had standing forces of twenty thousand with reserves ten times that. The Israelite army was organized, with a daring commander at its head. There was a general for every thousand and a colonel for every hundred, skilled and disciplined, leading well-equipped soldiers.

Still, despite their sweeping victory, the fierce fighters of Israel were wiping away tears. To utterly destroy Amalek was the commandment — to erase every memory of it. The Israelite soldiers were battle-tested veterans, but they were gentle souls, men of impeccable virtue. To wipe out Amalek was no easy assignment, taking its toll on the soldiers. With tearful eyes and heartbreaking sighs, they did as they were told. The People of Israel must fulfill the Creator's will, despite their qualms.

"We must not let emotion prevail in this matter," Abner had told the fighters at a pre-war briefing. "We cannot allow the slaughter of the People of Israel to continue! Strengthen your hearts, my brothers, and be courageous. Fortify yourselves with bravery and boldness; do not give in to fear or dread. I know that this mission is a harsh one; we are all sons of Abraham, merciful children of merciful parents. Mark my words: whoever makes himself merciful toward the cruel one, ultimately makes himself cruel toward the merciful ones. And the Amalekites are unquestionably cruel, a bitter lesson we learned at the very birth of our nation when we left Egypt. To feel sorry for them would be cruelty to our children and their children. This is a war in which we must take no prisoners and no booty. The name Amalek must be blotted out. No remnant of these sinners may persist; everything must be obliterated." Abner looked at the faces of his warriors, who expressed wonder and astonishment. "God is the Merciful One, and even the Amalekites are His creations. It is He who commands us to wage this war, and it is blasphemy and betrayal to be softhearted in pursuing it."

The victorious army returned from the war, with Saul at their head.

Samuel the Prophet went out to greet the army returning from the battlefield. His eyes were anguished, tired. He hadn't let sleep touch his eyes all night, praying to God to cancel the decree, but to no avail. "*I regret that I have made Saul king, for he has turned away from following Me and has not carried out My instructions"* was the prophecy at nightfall, and it remained at dawn. Saul had failed in his mission.

The people, seeing the magnitude of the victory and the vast booty, had taken from the sheep and cattle that belonged to the slaves of the Amalekites: "This is to make sacrifices thanking God for the victory," they said. All the property of the Amalekites was plundered, rather than being confiscated, as Samuel had commanded Saul. Also, King Agag of Amalek was taken prisoner. Agag, who, according to his orders, would set out to slaughter Israelite children and women. Agag, a cruel king, never spared or pitied any of his captives; with his own hands, he tortured and murdered whomever his men abducted.

Samuel looked up, seeing Saul advancing toward him, his arm outstretched in greeting. In an instant, his tired eyes became disapproving, the muscles of his face tensed, and his slumped shoulders straightened.

Saul's eyes were still aglow, but he had forced himself to smile. "*May the Lord bless you. I have carried out the Lord's instructions.*"

Samuel's eyes shone too, but with blazing fury, not triumph. "Why then do I hear the cows bellow and the lambs bleat?" he replied defiantly.

"Cows and lambs?" Saul repeated in an apologetic tone. "You must mean the cattle and the sheep which the people saved to offer to your God," he murmured, with a half-smile on his face. "They want to express their gratitude to the Lord."

Samuel replied angrily: "Who asked for sacrifices and offerings? God told you to destroy Amalek and its property, and you violated His command. The Creator of the Universe needs neither sacrifice nor offering. Do you think Him hungry? God lacks nothing! But you followed your heart, you pursued greed, you took your booty. And now I must tell you, even though in your eyes you are small, you have been chosen as King of Israel; but you have proven yourself unworthy of the throne. You rejected God's Word, and He has rejected you. You have transgressed the command of the King of the World, and now God has revoked your kingship." Samuel turned to leave, turning his back on Saul.

Saul grabbed the hem of Samuel's robe, trying to delay and appeal to him, to justify and explain his actions. The robe tore. Saul looked with dread at the piece of cloth in his hand.

Samuel turned to Saul, his face expressing rage and contempt, mixed with pity and disappointment: "The Lord has torn the kingdom of Israel from you today and has given it to your fellow who is better than you. Moreover, the Glory of Israel does not lie or change His mind, for He is not a man, that He should change His mind."

Saul's eyes welled with tears, his spirit breaking within him, knowing that he had erred: "Please my lord, I have sinned; but please come with me before my people, and honor me that I may bow down to the Lord."

Samuel agreed and Saul took him to the high place, where the king prostrated himself before God.

"Bring me King Agag of Amalek!" shouted Samuel, and his eyes filled with bottomless hatred for the cruel man, his soft face becoming as hard as a rock.

The guards brought Agag, manacled and chained, to Samuel. Agag was not only a merciless and awful monarch but an evil sorcerer as well. He walked toward the prophet gently and indulgently, murmuring: *"Surely the bitterness of death is past."* He regarded Samuel smugly, knowing that while the prophet had been berating Saul, he had managed to seclude himself with a serving girl who now carried his seed. Agag thought: My dynasty will not end now; the day will come when my progeny will return to fight Israel.

Samuel looked at Agag's smiling face, pulled a dagger from his robe and said to Agag: *"As your sword has made women childless, so your mother will be childless among women."* Samuel grabbed Agag and slit his throat.

Agag fell to the ground wallowing in his blood, but the grin never left his face: "The day will come," he whispered, gasping his last breath.

CHAPTER ELEVEN

Coronation

Samuel sat in his study hall despondent; his strength had abandoned him. The hopes he had pinned on Saul had been dashed, to be replaced by disappointment. The chosen king had sinned.

Almost every day, Saul sent messengers to Samuel asking him to meet, but Samuel refused. His tired eyes closed of their own accord, and his body sank into slumber. Suddenly a prophetic vision filled his mind. An echoing voice rebuked him: "How long will you mourn for Saul? I have rejected him. Get up, take your horn full of anointing oil, and go up to Bethlehem, to Jesse's house. There I see a man after My heart, one worthy of being king over Israel, from the sons of Jesse, son of Obed, and Nizebeth, daughter of Adiel. There I will tell you who deserves the crown."

Samuel, as if refusing to believe it, replied: "Saul is still alive, moody, irritable, and fickle. Saul knows that his kingdom will not last; if he discovers that I have gone to crown a king in his place, he will kill me."

The voice clarified: "Go to Bethlehem, take a bullock with you. You may use it to justify your journey, under the pretext that you are going to bring an offering. There I will reveal to you my choice, and you will crown that man king over My people."

"Peace be upon you, my lord Samuel the Prophet; it is a great honor for our city that you grace us with your presence." All the elders of Bethlehem came out to greet Samuel. The news had spread like wildfire; the most revered figure in the nation was in their town, bringing a bullock with him.

"What brings my lord here?" an elder asked the question in everyone's mind.

Samuel the Prophet had rarely left his home to travel across the Land of Israel in recent years. An old and feeble man, he had shut himself up in his study hall. His face showed his age. "I come to bring an offering," he said. "Tell Jesse, son of Obed, that Samuel wishes him to come with all his sons to bring the sacrifice. I'll go to his house shortly. Tell him to make sure he and his sons are ritually pure so they can partake in the sacrifice. Don't worry," he added with an encouraging smile, when he saw the worried face looking at him. "I just want to bring a thanksgiving offering alongside Jesse; I have good news for the House of Obed."

"My lord, please come in. It is a great honor for me and my family that you have graced us with your presence," Jesse said, leaning and kissing the hands of Samuel the Prophet in complete submission.

A short time ago, a boy had come to tell Jesse that an elder had sent him to ready the household to offer the sacrifice in purity. Samuel the Prophet had come to the city and wanted to bring an offering with him and his sons. Jesse quickly gathered all his sons, sanctified and purified for the altar, excited about meeting the prophet.

"To what do we owe this great honor?" asked Jesse. His obvious enthusiasm masked the fears hidden in his heart.

"You'll soon find out," Samuel said, smiling. "Have you summoned all your sons?"

"Yes, indeed," Jesse replied, "They are waiting outside the room."

"Please call them in, one by one," Samuel asked Jesse.

"Eliab, please come in," Jesse exclaimed.

The door opened, and Eliab, Jesse's eldest son, entered. He was in his fifties, tall, broad-shouldered, handsome, and intense.

Samuel looked at Eliab and thought, "This one looks like a king," but when he closed his eyes, the Divine Voice disagreed: "*Do not consider his appearance or height, for I have rejected him; the Lord does not see as man does. For man sees the outward appearance, but the Lord sees the heart.*"

"Call the next boy," Samuel asked.

Jesse called Abinadab.

"He's not the right man to reign either," said the Voice.

Jesse, at the prophet's command, summoned Shammah, Nethanel,

Raddai, Ozem, and Elihu. "None of them are worthy," said the Voice. Samuel asked: "Call the next child."

"I have no more sons," Jesse replied hesitantly. "These are all my boys."

Samuel stared at Jesse unreservedly: "There are no more that Nizebeth, daughter of Adiel, bore you?"

"Ahhh... Nizebeth daughter of Adiel, who was once my wife, did bear one more child," Jesse replied awkwardly. "I mean, he is my wife's son..."

"What do you mean, your wife's son?" demanded Samuel impatiently.

"Ahhh... My wife, I mean my ex-wife," Jesse stammered in shame, not knowing how to speak to the seer of his family's shame. "She became pregnant from another man while we were married, and I divorced her," Jesse whispered.

"Wait..." Samuel interrupted Jesse, "Call this boy here, immediately."

Jesse sent one of his lads: "Run, my son, run immediately to the flocks, to David, son of Nizebeth, and tell him to come with haste; Samuel the Prophet awaits him."

"My lady, my lady." The door flew open as a panting and breathless Naamah burst into Nizebeth's tiny house: "Come my lady, come quickly, come on, come on, come on," Naamah said as she took Nizebeth's hand and dragged her to the door.

"What happened, Naamah? Did something happen to one of my children? Has anyone been injured?" she asked worriedly.

"No, no," Naamah said, "Samuel the Prophet has come to my lord's house. He told Jesse to gather all his children. Jesse brought seven sons, and Samuel said he wanted to see another son that he and you had. They went to call David from the pasture. Come quickly." The two women ran toward Jesse's house, with the hope in their hearts that soon the truth about David would be revealed.

"Here, let's go up and look through the window," Naamah whispered, pointing.

Nizebeth peeked in to see Jesse, her seven sons, and Samuel the Prophet sitting around the table, waiting for the arrival of her youngest, David.

The door opened softly, and David entered, bashful, hesitant. A redhead of about twenty-eight, his brown eyes full of wisdom and tenderness, he looked around.

"My lord summons me?" he asked submissively. "One of the lads said you called me." David wore his shepherd's garb, with his staff and pack. He peered at his father, his seven brothers, and the old man sitting at the head of the table. He noticed how Eliab still looked at him with loathing and disgust, staring at him as if they wanted to tear into his flesh. David was used to it. He thought: Poor dears, they don't know. They are unaware that we share a father as well.

The old man sitting at the head of the table quickly rose to his feet: "The King of Israel is standing, and you sit?" The Voice echoed in his heart: "Rise up to anoint the king, in front of all his brothers!"

Jesse and his seven sons rose to their feet and saw the prophet jump from his seat, standing in honor of the supposed bastard entering the room.

Samuel looked at David. He mused: A redhead? Like Esau? So a killer too?

"Yes and no," replied the Voice. "Fiery hair, but with a pleasant countenance; he will shed much blood, but only for a good cause. Unlike Esau, he will take life only in the cause of justice, slaying the wicked and cruel to protect the innocent."

"I have come here," Samuel said solemnly to Jesse and his sons, "in order to anoint a new king over Israel." As they stared at him, he declared: "I rise before the King of Israel!"

Jesse was stunned by the turn of events. He wondered: "But he is misbegotten; can a bastard sit on the Throne of the Lord?" he whispered in the prophet's ears.

"He is no bastard! Jesse, he is your son from Nizebeth, daughter of Adiel. She will explain everything later. Hurry up, we must anoint the King of Israel!"

"But, even if he really is my son, he has questionable Moabite status — just as I do. He must not enter the Lord's assembly. Can such a man reign?" he pressed.

"No, my friend, you do not have questionable Moabite status. You are all fit to enter the Lord's assembly. I know the law from Moses at

Sinai, that those who are forbidden entry to the assembly of the Lord by marriage are the men of Ammon and Moab, not the women. It says Ammonite, not Ammonitess; Moabite, not Moabitess," Samuel ruled. "Now, something must be done."

"David, son of Jesse, come to me!" declared Samuel.

David moved toward Samuel shyly, lowering his eyes, trying to avoid the stares.

"Kneel down to honor the Lord," Samuel said to David, pulling out a full horn of anointment oil from the depths of his robe.

David knelt down, acting according to the prophet's instructions, ashamed of his status, feeling unworthy of greatness and power, but fulfilling the will of his Creator. He thought: I have not changed since this morning. Then, my Heavenly Father wanted me to be degraded and humiliated, and now He wants me to be exalted. Like a baby in his mother's arms; wherever she takes him, it makes no difference, because he is always safe there. So am I in the arms of my Heavenly Father; wherever He wills, He will lead me." David felt the oil being applied above his eyes, then poured on his head. It seemed to envelop his entire being.

"David, son of Jesse, son of Obed, is King of Israel," Samuel proclaimed, kissing David's head. "Arise, David, son of Jesse, King of Israel."

Jesse looked at David: "Are you my son, David?" he asked in a whisper.

"Yes, Father! I am you son," David said, running into his father's arms: "Father, o Father, how many times I wanted to call you by that name, but I couldn't." Tears flooded his face, his voice choked.

Jesse was also crying as he hugged his youngest. "My son David, my dear little son David, oh my son, oh my son."

Through the window, Naamah's shout of joy and Nizebeth's heartbreaking cries could be heard. The years of shame and disgrace were at an end.

Her sons looked at her as if dreaming, tears streaming down their cheeks. They seemed to say: Mother, o mother, we're so sorry.

David still hugged Jesse, reveling in the feeling of the father he never had, savoring the paternal embrace.

"I'm so sorry, my son, so sorry," Jesse replied, sobbing and weeping. "I love you, Father," David replied in a strangled whisper.

CHAPTER TWELVE
The Bard

"Get out of here! Get out before I kill you!" shouted Saul, his eyes flaring, picking up a glass from his table to throw it at his servant.

The servant, accustomed to shouting and beating, scurried from the room, bending to escape the glass flying toward his head.

"Get out! Get out of here immediately!" Saul shrieked cacophonously after the slave had already fled the room.

Jonathan stood outside the door, heard his father's voice, agony showing on his face. Sighing, he thought to himself: Since the Amalek War, my father has not been well. His mood shifts unpredictably, acting like a madman. Old age seemed to jump on him in an instant, his coal-black beard whitening all at once. His intense face is suddenly creased with wrinkles. What did Samuel the Seer tell him when they met after the Amalek War? Since then, he has been acting strangely, as if an evil spirit had entered him. Samuel has ostracized Father ever since, ignoring every invitation. He just refuses to meet him!

The sound of footsteps made Jonathan look up. He saw Doeg the Edomite, chief justice of the Supreme Court, coming toward him. Doeg was energetic, still in his early thirties. He had grown up in the Land of Edom, but his background was Amalekite; his family had converted years earlier and joined the People of Israel.

Doeg looked at Jonathan's drooping face: "What happened? Did an evil spirit seize your father again?"

Jonathan nodded. "Yes," he replied weakly. "I don't know what to do. The situation is getting worse. I want so badly to help my father and I don't know how. I feel helpless when I see my father in such a state and can't help him. I need advice; what should I do?" A tear welled up in the corner of his eye.

"I think I have a good idea," Doeg said, placing his hand on Jonathan's shoulder: "We'll bring your father a bard; he can play and sing happy songs for your father, restoring him. Music soothes the saddest heart. Your father knows his situation; he is no fool. He seeks an escape from these foul moods which consume him. I'll talk to him. Don't worry, it'll be fine," he concluded with a smile, entering King Saul's room.

"Your Majesty," Doeg turned to Saul, looking at his hunched figure leaning over the table. There were shards of glass on the floor, testimony to the anger that had overtaken Saul a few minutes ago. "Your Majesty, something must be done. You cannot function like this. You must seek counsel on how to improve your mood; you must find a path out of this despondency which has such a hold on you."

Saul lifted his head from the table, his eyes shut, empty, staring: "What can I do?" he asked softly. "When the evil spirit seizes me, I can't stop myself. The rage suddenly surges inside me, I lose control and act like a maniac. What am I going to do?" begged Saul, his eyes moist with tears. "Doeg, you're a wise man, have you any advice for me?" he asked, hoping and expecting the counsel to save him.

"Yes, Your Majesty, I have an idea," Doeg replied. "The bardic arts have the power to release a person from sadness and gloom. There is a Bethlehemite, a son of Jesse, son of Obed. I heard that he knows how to play and sing exceptionally well. Not only a musician and singer, he is also a wit and a scholar, and quite handsome too! If you agree, I'll have him summoned. He can ply his trade before you; perhaps it will have a positive effect and restore your good cheer."

"Let's try him," said Saul weakly. "It may not help, but at least it won't hurt."

"Yes, Father, you called me?" asked David. Referring to Jesse in that way still gave him a thrill.

"David, my son, King Saul has sent emissaries to ask you to play and sing before him, to lift his spirits," said Jesse, placing a hand on his youngest son's shoulder.

David reflected: Two days after Samuel the Seer left here, Father called me and Mother. She was very nervous, not knowing what to expect. When we arrived, he looked at her for a long time. "Nizebeth,"

Father gently said at the time, "you know that I separated from you out of fear that I might be a Moabite. Then I divorced you, because I thought you'd been with another man, and according to law, a woman who commits adultery must be divorced. But two days ago, when Samuel the Seer was here, he said that there was no doubt about my fitness to enter the Lord's assembly, and that David is our son, mine and yours, not a bastard." There was clear joy in his voice. "And Samuel said that our son would be King of Israel." His voice shook. "I asked Samuel the Seer about our marital status. He replied that the divorce was void, because it was based on an error; so you are still my wife, and we don't need to remarry."

David looked into his mother's eyes and saw the tears leaking out. His mother could not stop herself; she fell to her knees, sobbing.

Jesse looked at his wife with tears of longing, tears bursting from his eyes like a spring. "My dear wife, forgive me," he said to Nizebeth, his voice gentle. "Forgive me, my son," he said to David.

Nizebeth looked up, gazing into the face of the love of her life. "Do you forgive me, that I tricked you?" she asked her husband with a mischievous smile, a smile not seen on her face for many years.

"David, my son," David heard the voice as if from a dream.

"Yes, sorry, Father, I must have been daydreaming. You said that King Saul asked me to come sing and play before him."

"Yes, my son," Jesse said, and there was concern in his voice: "You know, son, everyone says that the king suffers from very strange moods. Sadness haunts him. He is constantly depressed. Doeg the Edomite told him that you could get him out of his situation and lift his spirits. My son, you must go; Saul still functions as King of Israel. But be very careful, my son, lest he learn what happened here with Samuel the Prophet. King Saul must not know about this. Apart from the family, no one knows what really happened here. The whole city believes the story that Samuel gave the elders, that he had come to bring the thanksgiving offering with us, after receiving a prophecy about your being my legitimate son and all of us being eligible to marry freely. Be very careful, my dear son. Saul is a bitter man; if he knows that you are fated to reign in his place, he may hurt you. Go, my son, but take care. Try to come home every few days. Say that your old father needs you by his side, that you need to cheer him up too."

"*Hallelujah! Praise God in His sanctuary. Praise Him in His mighty heavens,*" David's voice came from Saul's chamber — the sweetness of his singing, the poignant melodies and tunes flowing from David's throat. Saul joined in, beaming. His eyes, once burnt out, lit up once again, ever since the arrival of the skilled bard. His pleasant face, his powerful and rapturous singing, his shy smile — David's presence filled everyone around him with joy, illuminating his surroundings.

Doeg the Edomite, Jonathan, and King Saul sat at the table set before them. In front of them stood David, harp in hand. He played and danced, singing and chanting before the king.

A week after David's arrival, Saul's spirits were high. Happiness had returned to his expression, and his eyes shone.

Jonathan looked at David fondly. From their very first meeting, they had felt a deep bond in their souls. David's overflowing joie de vivre overwhelmed everyone around him. Even the stern Doeg the Edomite sat smiling and joined the song. David's melodies and chants enthralled every heart.

"What a brilliant idea," Jonathan whispered to Doeg, "I've never seen Father so happy. This fellow knows how to bring a soul back to life."

"David, my son," Saul said happily, "you have revived me, my son. I want you to always be with me, so you shall be my arms-bearer. I know you need to go back to your father, but you must go and come back. Spend three days here and three with your father. Your father and I will share your time equally — a bit for me, and a bit for him." Saul laughed: "I'm so glad you're with me, my dear friend, so go and come back. If I don't feel well, I'll summon you straightaway. All right, son?" concluded Saul, a note of pleading in his voice: "Truly, you resuscitate me."

CHAPTER THIRTEEN
Goliath

It was dusk; the sun had collided with the horizon and painted the sky crimson as blood. The trees rustled with fear, as if all creation were bowing its head for the evening creed: "*Hear O Israel, the Lord our God, the Lord is one.*"

In the Israelite camp, they steeled themselves for the coming onslaught. At sunrise and sunset every day, the time for their recitation of the creed, testifying to their faith in the Creator and His Oneness, the Philistine giant arose to blaspheme.

Almost ten feet tall, Goliath was as broad as he was tall. His sinister face testified to his craving for slaughter. A bronze helmet sat on his head, and his whole body was swathed in chainmail from his leg to his neck. Goliath the Giant had become notorious throughout the region as a warrior cruel to his enemies, abusing any who fall into his hand until death. He is the son of Orpah, sister to Ruth the Moabitess, daughter-in-law to Naomi of Bethlehem. Orpah turned her back on Naomi on their way back to the fields of Bethlehem, going to join the Philistine camp.

Goliath carried a huge bronze spear and a large sword on his thigh. In front of him marched his shield-bearer, to guard him from sword or spear. The giant emerged from the camp of the Philistines and stood in front of the camp of Israel defiantly, cursing the Creator of the world, His people Israel, and their king.

"Who is craven King Saul of Israel?" he shouted toward the Israelite camp: "Who is Saul and who is his Master to battle me? To fight Goliath of Gath, who killed Hophni and Phineas, the sons of Eli the High Priest, and captured the Ark of the Covenant of this wretched people? A spineless nation! Send a man out to me and fight me; if he is victorious, all the Philistines will be slaves of Israel, and if I defeat him, you will all be slaves of Philistia. Come, cowards, come, and fight Goliath of Gath," he yelled, his laughter echoing far and wide.

Goliath stood in a ravine between two mountains; on one stood the camp of Israel and on the other, the camp of the Philistines.

Saul's warriors hid, frightened.

Silence reigned, even the birds and forest animals were silent. Dread and foreboding enveloped everything.

"Cowardly King Saul, come down to me and fight against me! Lord of cowards, ruler of weaklings, come to me with your Master. Meet me on the battlefield, and we will see who emerges victorious, I or you."

"David, my son," Jesse said to his youngest son. "You know that there is a war going on between Israel and the Philistines. My three eldest sons, Eliab, Abinadab, and Shammah, have joined King Saul's ranks. I want you to go to them; take them provisions so they have something to eat. I also have some documents that need to be signed."

"What are these scrolls?" asked David.

"These are writs of divorce that I want your older brothers to sign. The war is bloody; it is impossible to know who will live and who will die, who will be taken prisoner, and who will go missing. That's why I prepared conditional bills of divorce for your older brothers here. If they return safely from the war, the writs are canceled; but if, God forbid, they go missing or are taken prisoner and we don't know their fate, their poor wives will not be chained to them, unable to remarry. You know how many poor women will never be able to remarry, because we don't know what happened to their husbands. I think that it ought to be enacted that any Israelite who goes to war must write a conditional bill of divorce for his wife, so that the unfortunate women may be spared great sorrow."

David took the scrolls from his father and placed them in his shepherd's pack. His father's worried face made it clear how dire the situation was. "Don't worry, Father, I'm sure that in a few days, the war will be over, and the People of Israel will win; in a few days, God willing, Eliab, Abinadab, and Shammah will return home safe and sound. The soldiers of Israel are righteous and heroic, and with

God's help, they will defeat the accursed Philistines and return home," David declared, his face full of optimism and faith.

"Good to see you, my brothers," David said to Eliab, Abinadab, and Shammah, his face beaming. The sun was about to burst forth, banishing the shadows of the night. David had arrived at the Israelite camp, searching through the tents until he found them. He glowed with joy and pride. David mused: My brothers, heroes of Israel, fearless and dauntless warriors, select troops of the king! How I admire you!

Since Samuel the Prophet had been in their home, David's brothers had restored their mother to her rightful place and had begun treating him as an equal — with the exception of Eliab, who remained sullen and stern, hardly exchanging a word with his redeemed brother.

David looked at Eliab's expression and thought: It's hard for him to get used to the idea that I'm really his brother. It's hard for him to accept the idea that I was chosen to be king and not him, the eldest of the sons of Jesse.

"What are you doing here?" demanded Eliab resentfully. "Are you here to make sport? Go home right away, boy. You have nothing to do here! You're a weak child, go home! This is war, not child's play!"

Suddenly, they heard the echoing voice: "Saul, lord of the lily-livered, I summon you to battle. You're too much of a coward, as is your God, to challenge Goliath of Gath. I will throw your flesh into the sky and drink your blood to the last drop. Come, cravens, fight me. Select your champion and let him face me."

David looked at his brothers' faces in amazement: they looked scared, petrified. Suddenly, they didn't seem to David like war heroes but rather, like frightened little children. He thought: Who is he to mock the God of Israel, the King of Israel, and the People of Israel? Who is this brazen man who dares to do so?

Anger flooded his heart. David felt his legs carry him out of the tent as he ran toward the sound.

A number of frightened Israelite sentries were cowering, looking at the giant standing a few hundred yards away from them, a shiver running through their bodies and their faces drooping.

"Who is this?" demanded David in a firm voice. "Who is this that blasphemes the ranks of the Living God?"

The guards hadn't noticed David before, but now they grabbed him by his shirtfront and pulled him to the ground: "Silence, young man, silence! You must not let him hear you. This is Goliath of Gath, an audacious and fearless warrior. He is a fierce giant, battle-hardened. Oh, what can we do? Who would dare fight Goliath of Gath? King Saul has promised that whoever engages Goliath of Gath in combat and defeats him will marry Saul's daughter, receive great wealth from the king's hand and even exempt his entire family from taxation. But who would dare fight him? Who could defeat Goliath of Gath? All who challenge him prepare themselves for their funeral, not their wedding. Even our greatest heroes tremble with fear at the thought that the king might order them to fight Goliath."

A hand grasped David's shoulder, and he whirled around to confront Eliab's angry face: "I told you to go home, boy, to your mother. This is no place for children."

David shook off his brother's hand and walked away from him.

"Please show me where King Saul's tent is," David asked the guards.

In Saul's tent, silence prevailed, all faces were gloomy and scared. Scant minutes had passed since Goliath issued his proclamation. Saul's face was wrinkled, as if he had aged several years in the previous month. Standing next to him was Jonathan, his face also drooping as he thought: What a shame. We are all afraid. There is no one willing to fight the Philistine, all our war heroes are gripped by fear and terror."

Abner sat alongside, contemplating.

The high priest was also in the tent, his face drawn.

Doeg the Edomite cleared his throat: "Your Majesty, it seems to me that there is no choice but to surrender." His voice faltered: "No one is willing to fight Goliath. Even if you order one of your heroes to accept the challenge, you'll be signing his death warrant, and we will become slaves to the Philistines. It is a shame to send one of our men to certain death, because in any situation, in the end, we will become the personal property of Philistia," he concluded.

The flap of the tent opened, and one of the guards entered. He whispered something in Doeg's ear and left. Doeg chuckled.

"What happened? What did he say?" demanded Saul.

Doeg replies with a smile: "Your Majesty will never guess who has decided to grace us with his presence: your favorite, David the bard. He must have a magnificent sense of humor. He's now wandering around the camp looking for the king's pavilion. He claims he will confront and defeat Goliath of Gath." This brought a smile to everyone's face. "He says he believes God will give the Philistine over to his hand if you consent to send him out to battle with Goliath. The son of Jesse explains that he cannot bear to hear anyone talk about God and the King of Israel in this way." He added with a chuckle, "This young man is the sweetest, I dare say."

A glimmer of hope sparked in Saul's eyes: "Then we have two options: either to surrender and become slaves, or to let David try to fight Goliath," Saul summed up. "Summon David, son of Jesse, to come before me," the king commanded.

The tent flap was lifted to admit David. Saul looked at him, thinking: Just a youth. Almost thirty years old, yes, but still so boyish in his frame and bearing. All he bears is a shepherd's cloak, pack, and stick. That shock of red hair, those eyes shining with a pleasant playfulness that captivates the heart! How I love his fine appearance, his soothing voice, his sweet musicianship! But a warrior? Goliath will trample him in an instant! What a shame, what a waste to lose such an artist!

"Your Majesty has granted me an audience?" came David's voice.

Saul reflected: His tone is different; it is not the sound of bells, but the voice of a firm and courageous man. Aloud, he said: "Yes, my dear son, come in. They tell me you want to fight Goliath of Gath."

David nodded his head decisively, "Yes, Your Majesty."

"Have you seen him?" asked Saul, puzzled.

"Yes, Your Majesty, I have seen this… thing," David declared scornfully.

"And you're still ready to fight him? You are not a military man, while he is a fierce giant, combat-tested and battle-hardened! All the soldiers are afraid to face him, and you want to answer his challenge?" he inquired with growing puzzlement.

"Yes," David replied, "I will fight this wretched Philistine, and I will kill him. True, I am no warrior, just a shepherd. Still, when I was but a child, I defended my father's flock from a lion. Then a bear came to devour my father's flock, so I fought and killed it. I am not afraid of this Philistine; he is no more frightening than a bear. Also, it is natural for a bear or lion to attack sheep; but this uncircumcised Philistine wants to kill the people of God, to spite the Lord and his Messiah. I know clearly that God will give him over to my hand, and I will be able to defeat this Philistine," David asserted, his usually soft eyes full of firebolts. His expression was sober, determined to defeat Israel's enemy.

Jonathan gazed at David with admiration; the bard's powerful faith and devotion filled the prince's heart with love.

Saul was inspired as well, hope filling him at the sight of the boy who had become a man. "Go with God!" he affirmed. But as David turned to leave, the king ordered him to wait. Saul took his tunic, armor, and bronze helmet and put them on David. Miraculously, the military gear tailored to Saul's massive frame fit the short and slender David. Saul unbuckled his sword and strapped it on David. "Remarkable!"

David looked into Saul's eyes and saw the wonder and amazement there, tainted by a hint of hatred and jealousy.

Saul thought: My gear fits him as if it were tailored for that purpose! How?

However, David had never been trained to move armed and armored. "Your Majesty," he demurred, "I cannot walk in this out; I am not accustomed to such gear. Indeed, I don't need this to defeat the king's enemy. I shall defeat the enemies of God in the uniform of a common shepherd." David took off Saul's attire and reclaimed his stick and pack. "With these, I will conquer our foes, for today is a day of salvation for Israel."

David left the tent, but everyone's eyes continued to follow the skinny youth as he set out to confront the cruel enemy.

"Genesis, Exodus, Leviticus, Numbers, Deuteronomy," David murmured to himself as he gathered five stones from the path, walking to the Philistines' camp. David's appearance might be boyish, but his heart was that of a king. He was the ruler of Israel, even if only in secret; still, it was his royal imperative to save his people. In his mind, there was not a trace of fear or dread — either of Goliath or of death.

His lips moved as he prayed: "O Lord, in the five books of the Torah, You gave Your people, You promised us that You would not abandon us, that You would save Your people Israel from the hands of the nations. Please, for the sake of Your great and awesome name, act for Your people Israel and give this wicked Philistine over into my hands. For Your sake, God, not for us, cast down this Philistine before Your people Israel, so that Israel and all the nations may know that You are the King of the World." Finally, David stood in front of the Philistines' camp.

"Goliath of Gath! Where are you, misbegotten mongrel? Come out and fight the puniest Israelite!" yelled David, his voice echoing through the Philistines' camp.

Goliath, readying himself for his twice-daily blasphemy, was surprised by the call. Evening beckoned, cheering Goliath, who was eager to go out and kill the champion of Israel, winning the war. His shield-bearer hurried before him.

Goliath was stunned to find, not an armed and armored warrior, but a slight shepherd with his pouch, a stick in one hand and a strip of leather in the other.

His anger grew. He fumed: They send a little boy to confront me? I am Goliath, the giant, champion of Philistia. They choose a scamp to beat me with a branch? He shouted, red with fury: "Am I a dog that you come to fight me with a stick?"

David looked at Goliath with calm, dismissive eyes: "Don't flatter yourself, you're worse than any mongrel."

Goliath's eyes narrowed, his rage surging: "Soon I will spill your blood on the earth, and your corpse will feed the birds of the sky," Goliath shrieked as he rebuked David and his God.

David stood on a rock and met Goliath's gaze: "*You come against me with sword and spear and javelin, but I come against you in the name of the Lord of Hosts, the God of the armies of Israel, whom you have defied. This day the Lord will deliver you into my hand. This day I will strike you down, cut off your head, and give the carcasses of the Philistines to the birds of the air and the creatures of the earth. Then the whole world will know that there is a God in Israel. And all those assembled here will know that it is not by sword or spear that the Lord saves; for the battle is the Lord's, and He will give all of you into our hands."*

As Goliath's anger reached a fever pitch, he began to run. with his shield-bearer ahead of him, toward David.

Goliath expected David to flee, but the youth ran toward him.

David took one stone out of his shepherd's pack. As he ran, he placed the stone inside the sling, two leather strips attached to a smaller piece of leather. David began to aim the sling, as only a few yards separated them: "In the name of God, the Lord of Hosts," David called out, releasing the stone. The stone flew toward Goliath's forehead, the small gap between his brass helmet and his eyeline. The stone acted as if it had taken an oath at Mount Sinai to fulfill the Will of its Creator, piercing Goliath's brazen forehead, and sinking deep into the giant's skull.

The mighty giant Goliath fell on his face. The mouth which had blasphemed the ranks of the Living God sank into the dust.

David did not hesitate; he immediately ran toward Goliath, took his spear and sunk it into the cruel heart. Then he drew the Philistine's sword to remove his head, only to find that chainmail covered his entire neck. David looked at the shield-bearer. "Who are you? What is your name? Where is the key to the armor?" David asked the servant. "Give it to me immediately," he commanded.

The shield-bearer, also a daring warrior, looked at David: "I was Goliath's slave," he replied calmly. "My name is Uriah the Hittite. But why would I give you the key? You're going to try to kill me anyway."

David looks at the warrior who challenged him: "If you give me the key, I won't try to kill you."

Uriah boldly argued, "And who said you could kill me at all? I'm willing to give you the key, but I want something in return."

David was shocked by his boldness. "What do you ask in return for the key?"

"An Israelite woman as a wife," Uriah replied, his expression stern.

David pondered for a few moments. "You were Goliath's slave, but now you ought to be mine, since I defeated him. Accept that, and I can emancipate you to convert and become an Israelite. Only then will you be worthy to marry a daughter of Israel."

The shield-bearer quickly unlocked the armor around Goliath's neck. David beheaded him with one stroke and raised the severed head aloft.

A Voice from Heaven declared: "By your life, if you are so cavalier with the dignity of a daughter of Israel, your own will be forfeit."

David returned from the battle with Goliath's head in his hand, followed by the shield-bearer, a slave to his new master. David lightly ran up the hill to present his prize to King Saul, Lord Commander Abner, and Chief Justice Doeg.

"Whose son is this young man?" asked Abner, "I know that he is a son of Jesse, from the tribe of Judah. But which clan? If he is a Perezite, he is eligible to sit on the throne; but if he is, say, a Zerahite, then he is fated for greatness, but not fit to wear the crown."

Doeg laughed: "You speak of thrones? Ask first if he is fit to enter the Lord's assembly. His ancestress is Ruth the Moabitess, and *'No Ammonite or Moabite…'*"

"Correct," Abner replied, "this is the law for Moabites, but not Moabitesses — Ammonites but not Ammonitesses."

"So," laughed Doeg, "what about the verse, *'No bastard may enter the assembly of the Lord, even to the tenth generation he may not enter the assembly of the Lord?'* What would you say, a bastard but not a *'bastardess?'*"

Abner frowned: "The Torah doesn't simply exclude Ammonites and Moabites; it also explains: *'For they did not meet you with food and water on your way out of Egypt.'* The Torah says that such cruel and vicious people do not deserve to marry into the assembly of the Lord. But who is expected to go out and offer hospitality? The men, not the women, so it is only men who are forbidden to marry the native-born of Israel. That is utterly irrelevant when it comes to those of illegitimate birth."

Doeg continued to laugh: "The men ought to have welcomed the men, and the women the women. What don't you understand?"

Abner was silent. He knew what Samuel the Ramathite had taught — Moabite but not Moabitess — but what could he say to Chief Justice Doeg?

CHAPTER FOURTEEN
Son-in-Law

"Saul struck with his thousands, and David with his ten thousands," the women chanted when David returned from the war.

After David had placed Goliath of Gath's head in his tent, he set out at the head of the division to fight the Philistines.

"There is no time to waste, Your Majesty," David told Saul. "Now we have the chance to pursue the Philistines and defeat them."

"Just a moment, David," said Jonathan, son of Saul. "I want you to take my gear, my sword, and my bow." Jonathan took off his attire and dressed David; miraculously, it fit him perfectly. "This is how the king's champion should dress."

David did not wait for the order, running to lead the troops into battle. The soldiers, who had been scared and intimidated just a few minutes ago, saw their new hero holding Jonathan's sword and leading the chase against their enemies.

"To battle, follow David!" they shouted excitedly.

"Victory is the Lord's," David cried.

The morale of the Israelite troops rebounded as they followed him to pursue the Philistines. Their legs, heavy and frozen with terror until a moment ago, moved like the wind. Their hearts swelled with new life as they turned to the Philistines.

David, dressed in the princely garments of Jonathan, ran like a gazelle to catch up with the enemy miraculously. The war lasted only a few hours, as the Philistines scattered in every direction. Soon the earth was saturated with their blood.

The thrilled warriors returned from battle carrying their new hero on their shoulders. The ferocious champion who fought like a combat veteran against the enemy, a boyish hero, with the spirit of the fiercest warrior. David heard the cries of the women: "Saul struck with his thousands, and David with his ten thousands."

Saul heard it, too. He thought angrily: Soon they will make him king! I was given thousands and David tens of thousands.

An evil spirit overtook Saul, a spirit of sadness and despondency.

Saul mused: David is trying to win the hearts of the people and depose me.

The love in Saul's heart for David was erased, and jealousy took its place.

At dusk, a pleasant breeze was blowing. The horizon was painted a reddish hue. The room was redolent with delicacies, merging with the cloud of incense that perfumed the atmosphere. King Saul sat at his table and listened to David's melodies, sweet tunes inspiring love and tenderness in his audience. David played and sang to God songs of longing, faith, and gratitude.

Saul had asked David to come and play before him, as the spirit of jealousy that enveloped his entire personality had turned into a spirit of gloom.

David glanced at Saul's face and saw that his songs did not please the king's heart. David began to play happier songs, trying to lift Saul's spirits, but to no avail; the king's face remained frozen.

Suddenly, David saw Saul's face change. He raised his voice in greater joy, thinking: Maybe it's starting to penetrate his soul. "*There is no other besides Him*," he sang in a rhythmic melody.

Saul raised his hand, a spear in it. David pictured the weapon flying toward him. A moment later, the spear would catch him, impaling his body on the wall behind.

Saul thought, a devilish smile on his face: He's already dead. That's it! This is now his end! To him, they credit tens of thousands, and to me, thousands? No more.

A split second separated David from death. David shifted his body. A loud thump echoed in the chamber, as the spear lodged in the wall behind him, making a hole in the stone. David slipped out and left the room.

A stifled cry was heard: "What's going on? What's happening to me? Why am I doing this?" Saul sobbed as David listened through the door.

"My dear brother David!" Jonathan exclaimed with obvious joy. "My father desires that I give you the good news: he wants you to marry my sister Michal. You are to be son-in-law to the king!" he added, when he saw that David did not look happy but dissatisfied. He leaned over, as if sharing a secret: "Do you wonder about my father's ... situation? You know an evil spirit gets the better of him from time to time, and his mood swings this way and that. He seeks your forgiveness for trying to hurt you. You know he loves you. Only you can lift his spirits. Because he realizes what's happening to him, he does not summon you anymore. He also told me to appoint you as a general, to command his regiments." Jonathan saw David still wasn't pleased. "Aren't you interested?" he asked, disappointed.

David looked at Jonathan and thought: He's a true friend.

The love and friendship that developed between the two was beyond compare. They were like twins who had developed in the same womb, brothers in arms and brothers in books. On the battlefield, they would fight side by side, defending each other bodily — often from certain death, each putting their life on the line to save the other. Afterwards, they would sit in the study hall poring over the Holy Torah, the heat of combat replaced by the heat of study. The eyes which shone in battle would shine in academia, analyzing complex issues of law and lore. From the clash of steel in combat to the lunges and parries of scholarly debate, theirs was a comradeship of blood and soul.

David recalled the last issue they'd studied together, the terms for holy matrimony. To consecrate a woman as his wife, a man must present her with something of value; can her pleasure at becoming his bride be considered that item of value? David smiled. "My brother Jonathan," he said as they returned to study, "if we say that I am to marry your sister Michal, I have nothing physical to give her for consecration. You know that I have nothing; I only herd the sheep of others. In addition, I am not important enough that your sister, the princess, could accept the value of becoming my wife as her item of consecration. Furthermore, your father promised that whoever defeated Goliath of Gath would receive your sister Merab as a wife. Nevertheless, though I fulfilled your father's behest and defeated Goliath, he gave Merab to Adriel the Meholathite. How can you tell me he won't maltreat me again? My dear brother, maybe this is just a trap your father is trying to set for me!"

Jonathan looked at David's face, the sincerity and truth evident from his sorrowful words. The prince thought: I have never met such a man. The character, virtue, honesty, truthfulness, and fidelity are inherent in his soul, a truly noble soul.

Aloud he said: "My brother, I have spoken to Father about everything; he is not asking for a bride's price, but a hundred Philistine foreskins to take revenge on the king's enemies. As for Merab, she was wed to Adriel without Father's knowledge. You know she's already past her maidenhood. That's why my father wants to give you my sister, Michal. He has already spoken to her, and she is eager and willing to be bound to you in holy matrimony. Please, David my brother, accept this in the spirit it is offered. There is no scheme behind this. I verified it myself. Trust me and say yes. You don't even have to meet with my father."

"Well then, my brother Jonathan, I'll agree to that."

Jonathan gave David a true brotherly hug: "I'm so happy, brother! It's time for you to get married. Soon, we'll be family in every sense!"

CHAPTER FIFTEEN
Escape

In the morning light, the smell of blossoms filled the expansive fields, as the small hills seemed to hide from the new day. A light breeze blew, whispering schemes in its currents.

Saul and Jonathan stood on a small hill in the fields, looking out at the horizon.

"Father," Jonathan asked hesitantly, "why are you frowning? Yesterday we had the privilege of marrying Michal to David, your faithful warrior. You asked for a hundred Philistine foreskins, and he brought two hundred. There is no one like him! There is no more loyal subject, no more valiant soldier, no more distinguished scholar. He will be a wonderful husband to little Michal."

Saul looked at Jonathan, his eyes shooting fire: "Tell me," he demanded angrily: "Are you a fool? Don't you understand that David is our greatest enemy? Don't you understand that he represents the downfall of our kingdom? The whole nation looks up to him and looks down at me as superfluous, unneeded, and unwanted. Do you think I wanted to give him Michal? When I ordered him to bring me a hundred Philistine foreskins, it was so that he might die in battle! You don't realize that he's no good for us; he's dangerous. Were I not certain it would cause unrest among the people, I would have killed him with my own hands."

Jonathan found this hard to believe, complaining to his father: "What did David do? What fault have you discovered in him? He fought Goliath of Gath, imperiling his life in order to save you and your kingdom from the hands of your enemies. David fights your wars, plays and sings before you as a faithful servant when you are despondent, and you want to kill him? You heard the women's song:

"Saul struck with his thousands, and David with his ten thousands?" Well, David heard that too! He told me that this means that you only need a thousand soldiers to defeat your enemies, whereas he, your inferior, needs tens of thousands of troops when he fights. David adores you as a man and as a king. He would never hurt you. He himself refers to you as the Lord's anointed."

The whispers of Doeg the Edomite, day and night, had poisoned Saul's mind: the so-called danger David posed to the kingdom, his so-called plans to depose Saul. He saw in his son's eyes the truth about David. Saul thought: My son Jonathan is the flesh of my flesh; he would never mislead me. Jonathan is the crown prince who will reign under me. He knows David better than anyone. They share secrets, they fight and study together. Jonathan surely knows the whole truth about David.

"You're right," Saul said aloud. "My son Jonathan, you're right. I don't know why I believed the slander against David. Why do I listen to Doeg's venom? I swear to you, son, that I will not hurt David. I swear I will not trouble him again."

Jonathan looked happily at his father's face, and his face lit up; he saw that his father's words were sincere. The grass in the fields, which had seemed to whisper schemes, changed its murmur to a song of praise.

Early in the evening, Saul's chamber was filled with the sounds of David's harp playing. His pleasant voice lit up the dank room, his elated face singing songs of thanksgiving. David's heart beats to the rhythm of his playing. Joy surrounds him, the joy of a lost son returning to the embrace of his beloved father.

About a month had passed since Jonathan had told him of his father's oath, his promise not to harm him. About a month had passed since his marriage to Michal.

The thought crossed his mind, bringing a smile to his face: The wife of my youth; although I am no longer a youth, she is the wife of my youth. A woman of valor.

His melody of gratitude intensified, as he thought: I am privileged to be the king's son-in-law. A general in the army of King Saul, a good and kind king.

David had already deleted the past from his mind. "The past is gone, the future is yet to be, and the present is the blink of an eye," as he used to say.

David reflected: What a victory we had in the last battle, God's victory over his enemies, with the help of King Saul's warriors. The battle was hard, Jonathan and he fought back-to-back, protecting each other. His rhythm changed to the rhythm of combat: "*I pursued my enemies and destroyed them; I did not turn back until they were consumed.*" David's voice sounded as if he were in the midst of a battle.

Saul listened to the song of thanksgiving. His table was laden with his favorite foods, prepared by his daughter Michal and delivered by David.

Saul mused: What a lovely pair. The finest match! He recalled the happiness he saw in his daughter's eyes when she came to visit him.

Suddenly, Saul awoke to the shift in the melody, to a martial theme. He thought: What's this? "*I pursued my enemies and destroyed them?*" He means me! He wants to kill me! He wants to seize the throne! He's an enemy! He will soon rise to kill me! "*I did not turn back until they were consumed*?" He will kill me and destroy all my seed! He's an enemy! I have to kill him before he kills me! Here he is turning to me to kill me!

The thoughts ran through his mind, threatening to devour him. Saul swung the spear upon his knees and threw it in David's direction.

David, in the heat of his melody, heard a sound behind him. Out of the corner of his eye he saw Saul swinging the spear and throwing it at him. David bent down, and the spear stuck in the wall. The melody abruptly ended, replaced by the voice of Saul, shouting frantically: "Catch him, kill him, he wants to kill me..."

The door slammed violently, shaking the timbers of the building.

Michal had been in the kitchen preparing dinner for her new husband, who had gone to make her father happy. She thought: Soon he'll be back, and we'll sit down to eat together. David, my husband, my soulmate, the champion of my youth. I have the best husband there could be! A modest, humble, gentle soul who is also a fearless hero. What beautiful songs he sings! All the wise men come before him to settle issues of law, dilemmas of faith. Loved by everyone, but Father..."

Michal, startled by the sound of the door slamming, jumped from her chair in the dining area and ran toward the entrance.

"What happened? What happened?" she asked her husband in a panic, as he hurriedly latched and bolted the door behind him. Sweaty and frightened, he leaned against the door, trying to thwart any intrusion by Saul's warriors. His body shook. He stared, and in his eyes were feelings of anger, panic, and disappointment.

"What happened?" she asked again anxiously, her voice breaking.

David looked at his young wife. He thought: How can I tell her? After all, she loves her father and me. She will be torn between the two of us. There's no escape, I have to tell her the whole truth.

David caught his breath and spoke: "My wife, my wife, you know that in the past, your father tried to kill me. Then he regretted it and swore he wouldn't hurt me." Michal nodded. "Today, while I was playing in front of him, he tried to kill me again. He threw his spear at me, and if God hadn't performed a miracle for me, I'd be dead. Your poor father has gone crazy again and tried to murder me. When I fled, he ordered his guards to catch me and kill me. I don't know what's happening to him."

The smart and clever Michal, Saul's little girl and David's beloved wife, looked at her husband with admiration. "My dear husband, I will tell you why Father seeks your death. About a year ago, when Father returned from the Amalek War, I overheard a conversation between him and Mother. He told her that the troops took spoils from the war, and he did not object. When he met Samuel, the prophet told him that he would lose the crown because he disobeyed God, that the kingdom would be torn from him and given to another man. Since then, Father has been down in the dumps; every now and then, an evil spirit takes over and compels him to act out." She knew what was to come and was ready for it. "You've no choice! You must escape as soon as possible, my dear husband. You mustn't sleep here tonight. My father isn't stupid; he knows the people love and admire you. He knows that no one deserves to be king more than you. Therefore, he won't kill you tonight; he will wait until morning, when it is possible to put you on trial. He will assemble the court, and you will be condemned as a rebel against the kingdom. Your sentence will be death.

The people will have nothing to say, and my father will continue to reign," she said sadly. "That's why you have to flee. If we tie our bedsheets together, I can let you out the window." She set to it right away.

Michal looked out to see if any guards were waiting to ambush him. Since the coast was clear, she let down the makeshift rope and turned to her husband.

David was tearing up. "My wife, we will be reunited. I will come for you," he said, trying to smile.

David hurriedly climbed out and down. When he reached the ground, he walked slowly, until he could be sure no one was in the royal gardens. Then he began racing, like an animal fleeing a hunter's trap.

"Open the door! In the name of King Saul, open the door!" There was a loud thump against the door, threatening to pull it from its hinges.

The door opened, and Princess Michal stood in the doorway. With her regal bearing, she regarded the four guards angrily.

"Why do you raise your voice so? How dare you pound on my door in such a manner? Do you think you have the right to disturb King Saul's daughter while she is resting?" She glared at them, a mistress rebuking her servants for their failure. "What do you want at such an hour?" she demanded from the lieutenant defiantly.

"K... Ki... King Saul said to bring David to him, Your Highness," he stammered, wary of making the princess angrier still.

Michal opened the door wide enough for them to see the bed, which was clearly occupied, a human form under the blankets. "As you see, Prince David is sleeping right now. He's not feeling well. Tell His Majesty that Prince David will soon rise. Then he will break his fast, gather his strength, and present himself to the king."

Her reply didn't allow opposition, and she slammed the door without another word.

They returned to the king and told him what his daughter had said. Furious, he shouted: "Bring him here immediately! If you must, carry him here in his bed!"

The guards went back with trepidation, caught between the ire of the king and the irritability of the princess. The lieutenant knocked weakly on her door.

"What now?" asked Michal dismissively as she opened up.

"Your Highness, the king said to bring Prince David in his bed," the lieutenant announced. He steeled himself, leading his men into the princess's bedchamber. However, as they positioned themselves around the bed, they realized with astonishment that the shape under the bedclothes was nothing more than teraphim, a life-size statue. It was now the lieutenant's turn to be irate. "Your Highness must come with us, to explain your actions to His Majesty, how you conspired with an enemy of the kingdom to let him escape!"

The guards brought Michal to her father. "Your Majesty," the lieutenant began, "Princess Michal deceived us. She helped David escape, then placed teraphim under the blankets and pretended he was sleeping. We have brought her before you to explain herself."

Saul looked at Michal with bitter disappointment in his eyes: "Princess Michal, my own daughter? Why would you help my nemesis flee?"

Michal, with the downcast eyes of a little girl caught red-handed, replied contritely: "Father, he said if I didn't help him, he would kill me." Michal burst into tears. "Sorry, Father, I had no choice," she said tearfully, meeting the king's gaze.

Saul regarded his little girl lovingly. "It is not so bad, my daughter, not so bad," he whispered. He went over to hug and comfort his little girl.

CHAPTER SIXTEEN
Samuel the Prophet

As a fugitive, the road seemed long. The open fields and endless expanses once beloved to David had become the enemy. David knew that Saul was resolved to kill him and would give chase. The bitter Saul would not rest until he saw David's body.

"I need to find a hiding place. Saul will send men to my father's house, so I cannot flee there. Where can I run? Where can I hide? Anyone who helps me will pay with his head for it." David ran on, sweaty and tired, his legs heavy, his body weary.

"Just a bit more. Soon I will reach Ramah, where Samuel the Seer lives." The journey seemed endless. Each patch of forest served as cover for the fugitive. When soldiers could be heard coming down the road, David dove into a thicket.

"They've passed. They don't seem to be looking for me. Time is pressing. There's no way of knowing how long Michal will be able to delay them."

Dawn was about to break: "It will be harder by day; I must press on." David ran and hid, concealing himself as he desperately tried to save himself from the clutches of the king.

He mused: Saul is so strange. Some people are distinguished by outward characteristics, such as skin color; Saul is distinguished by his inner characteristics, which motivate him to act so bizarrely.

Trying to force his body to keep going, he realized: It's not far now. After this hill is the study hall of Samuel the Ramathite. In a few more minutes, I will shelter under the wings of the prophet. Saul will certainly not send messengers to Samuel. Everyone knows that since the Amalek War, Samuel has cut all ties with the king. Everyone knows that these two pillars of our society stand on opposite sides.

David stopped at the top of the hill, bending low as he surveyed the area. His combat experience told him to reconnoiter. Were any of Saul's troops around?

He saw only a group of acolytes, apprentice prophets under Samuel's tutelage, standing outside the study hall to play their instruments and sing soulful songs.

"It appears safe." Still, David moved slowly, watching for any sign of a trap or ambush. He looked at the acolytes with longing: "If only I could sit at Samuel's feet, enjoying his presence, drinking of his Torah, learning to be a servant of God worthy of receiving prophecy…"

"David, my son, what's wrong with you?" Samuel asked David as he entered his room. "What happened? You look exhausted and discouraged."

Looking at his face, Samuel mused: King of Israel, but his throne is only theoretical at this point. He looks more like a fugitive than a monarch.

Samuel had kept himself updated with the latest news from the palace. He knew of Saul's attempts on David's life, after he had defeated Goliath and led Israel in other wars. He was aware of Saul's hatred for David and David's love for Saul. He knew everything.

David walked over to Samuel and leaned over to kiss his hand.

Samuel pulled his hand back. "It is inappropriate for the sovereign of Israel to kiss my hand. Please sit, King David of Israel. Sit down and tell me what's going on."

David sat in front of Samuel and told him about everything that had happened to him since Samuel had left Jesse's home. The upheavals and transformations, the joy and sorrow, the sanity and the madness.

Samuel looked at David's face with admiration, "He's still a young man, but he's going through so much. He accepts everything with love and equanimity, be it good or ill, speaking of them in the same tone, accepting the decree of the King of Kings.

David was weary but calm. The long road he had taken was already behind him; he was now in the home of Samuel the Prophet. A smile settled on his face, happiness in his radiant eyes. David talked to Samuel, telling him of the many kindnesses the King of Kings had bestowed upon him. He even spoke of King Saul in a loving and compassionate tone. The wars, battles, trials, failures, and victories were all the same to him. David explained it when he saw the unasked question on Samuel's face. "This is the path God wants me to follow, so I will walk it happily. How would sadness and bitterness help me? What good would sobbing and crying do? They will be not only counterproductive but harmful. The Good Lord wants only what is good for me; He tests me so that I may rise and grow. He loves me and so gives me hard trials to see if I will withstand them or fail. When I think about it, I realize that there is no such thing as failure — except failure of the mind. How will I accept everything I am going through? Will I be happy or sad? If I rejoice in a failure, it becomes a victory. There is nothing to be anxious about. You call me King of Israel, but I am only a slave. People see me as a champion, but I'm weak. There is only one King and Champion, the Lord of the world. But no matter what I am or who I am, the only thing that matters is whether I'm happy. And I'm trying!" David continued with a beaming face. "As long as I have trials, it strengthens my feeling that God has not given up on me, that He still believes in my abilities, that He wants to see me as living, breathing, active. Thank God, there is no shortage of trials," David concluded with obvious joy.

Samuel looked at David, and his admiration grew. "David, my son, what do you want to do now? Do you want to rest? To eat? You look tired. You had better eat and rest," Samuel decided

David gazed into Samuel's eyes — full of love, like those of a father looking at his weary son. "My lord prophet, I am not tired or hungry; thank you very much for your concern. But I have a request, are you ready to teach me Torah? There is something I want more than anything else, I would like you to teach me the plan of the Temple: how it should be built, what tools should be prepared, what are its measurements, what materials must be gathered to build it. After all, if I am King of Israel, one of my duties is to build the Lord's House."

Samuel the Seer and King David sat all night studying the centerpiece of the universe, God's Temple.

"Where is David hiding? In the name of King Saul, tell me where the enemy of the kingdom is hiding," ordered the captain of the guard.

The rumor that David had fled and was hiding with Samuel the Seer had reached Saul. "Bring him dead or alive," Saul had roared at the captain of the guard. "You don't want him to slip out of your hands. That would be the end of you."

The captain of the guard was determined to apprehend David; he valued his men, not to mention his own head. Everyone was aware that David was an enemy of the kingdom who wanted to commit regicide. Doeg the Edomite explained to them David's treasonous plots: "Saul is King of Israel, anointed by Samuel the Seer, by the Lord's command; David tries to subvert God's word and depose King Saul. David is a traitor, rebelling against the king; the sentence for such a crime is death."

"A few more moments, son," Samuel told the captain of the guard. "Please sit here next to the acolytes, and I will enter and bring the king's enemy out to you. I didn't know that David was a traitor to the crown. I was sure that David was the king's son-in-law and one of his generals," Samuel remarked innocently.

The squad sat down, listening to the music of the prophets, a gentle melody inspiring love of God, like the sound of the ministering angels standing on high, praising and glorifying their Creator. The tired guards listened to the tune, the sweet notes plucking their heartstrings. The acolytes sang songs of longing and yearning for a spiritual world stripped of corporeal bodies. The rhythm intensified, the sounds of the flute sailing through the depths of their souls, lifting their spirits to the skies. The guards closed their eyes in delight, their souls bound to the notes of the harp that carried their spirit to the infinite expanses of the Lord of All. Their muscles relaxed, and they sank into tranquility. Some of the acolytes began to prophesy, receiving a vision of God, clinging to the divine glow. The captain of the guard, with his eyes closed, began to experience spiritual feelings that he had never felt before. His urgent mission dissolved and passed from his mind, replaced by a passion for closeness to God. He began to murmur, his words mixing with prophetic scenes, coiling and twisting with his desire to fulfill the will of the King of the world. The other guards also laid down their weapons, most of them lying on the ground, prophesying: "David will be King of Israel; touch not my anointed ones."

The experience lasted for a while, Samuel standing aside, looking at his new acolytes with a loving, fatherly smile.

The captain of the guard rose, walked over to Samuel and threw himself at the prophet's feet: "My lord, we want to stay here with you. Please accept us as your acolytes." His men joined him. Divine intimacy filled their entire being. The brave warriors quickly became men of spirit, seeking closeness to their Rock. The feeling of mutuality, desire, pleasantness, friendship, and closeness to the Supreme Pleasance excluded them from any desire other than closeness to God.

"I've already sent three squads of soldiers to Samuel the Ramathite's school, one every day. They stay there and don't come back. They betray me too!" screamed Saul at Abner. "I told you to send good soldiers there, not weaklings. You seek my death too! You rebel against me too!" shrieked Saul, madness in his eyes. "Get out of here. Get out of here immediately, turncoat!" he continued to yell as he threw the glass in his hand at his army chief.

Abner dodged the glass and left the chamber.

Saul continued to scream madly: "You all hate me! You are all traitors to the kingdom! You want to kill me! Guard! Guard! Come here immediately!"

Two guards entered Saul's chamber in fear: "Get my horse ready and bring a hundred mounted soldiers, I'll go kill David myself."

The guards went outside in a panic to fulfill their king's will.

Samuel and David looked out the window at the morning light. The warm sun caressed the world with light and heat.

"My lord," David turned to Samuel, "what should I do? What does God want from me at this time? I know there is a purpose to everything that happens, and I want to do what is good and proper." David looked at the horizon, preparing for what was to come. Outside, the apprentice prophets sat, some studying, some playing. Among them sat the new acolytes, the soldiers of King Saul.

"Saul will not rest until he catches me," David continued. "It seems to me that his verdict is final: to kill me, and not just because an evil spirit grips him. Apparently, he deems me a traitor to the kingdom, deserving the death penalty. What am I to do?"

Samuel looked at David's face, calm and smiling as he awaited an answer. "My son, the loving bond between you and Prince Jonathan is well-known. It seems to me that you should talk to him and clarify the matter. If Saul is indeed set on killing you, you must flee and hide in the desert until God grants you the throne. If the situation is different, and King Saul does not really want to kill you, stand before him again as in the old days. Only your friend Jonathan can tell you which it is."

The two stood contemplating, while in the background, the prophets played, sang, and uttered words of prophecy when so inspired. Suddenly, galloping horses could be heard, disturbing the pastoral tranquility of the spot. "These are Saul's soldiers," David observed, bending down to hide from them.

"I'll go out toward them, and in the meantime, you can run away. Go talk to Jonathan. Saul will not look for you near his home; you will find out through Jonathan what his state of mind is and decide what to do. I will try to detain them here while you escape," Samuel said as he went to greet the newcomers.

Saul and his soldiers were about to arrive at Samuel's study hall. Since the day Saul had returned from the Amalek War, he had not met with Samuel the Prophet.

Saul, mounted on his horse at the head of his men, advanced rapidly. He thought: I'll catch him. Beyond the hill is Samuel the Ramathite's academy. In a few minutes, he'll be in my hands, and then...

Fuming and furious, he told himself: Just one more moment...

Suddenly, a strange feeling washed over him, as if something was going on within him. The background music of the acolytes reached his ears, and started to penetrate deep into his soul. His breathing became regular, and his obvious anger subsided. Saul felt calm and pleasantness filled his being. The horse continued to gallop. Its hooves, eager for battle, pounded the ground to the beat of the melody and singing.

Beyond the hill... That's where the enemy is... Who is the enemy??? What am I doing here??? David, the fiend??? David, the friend???

His thoughts were disturbing, disturbed, turned upside down.

A feeling of tenderness penetrated him. Saul slowed the pace of his horse and relished the pleasantness. The study hall appeared before him, groups of acolytes playing, singing, prophesying.

Saul dismounted and ran toward the prophets, taking off his royal clothes to experience prophecy, unparalleled pleasantness, the closeness of God filling his being. Feelings of love and connection surrounded him. His physical body vanished along with his clothes. Saul fell to the ground, prophesying... Many long hours passed of incorporation with his Creator.

Samuel looked out the window at Saul metamorphosizing and prophesying...

David fled urgently, with the goal of meeting Jonathan. "Soon we'll find out what I need to do. Soon I'll know the way I need to go. Soon my future will become clear."

It was a long way. The verdant fields that David loved so much seem limitless. The hills, ravines, and forests delayed his return.

Back to where he had fled from.

Back to the lion's den.

Back to where he was a wanted man, a rebel with a death sentence waiting.

Or perhaps Saul the prophet had conquered Saul the paranoid, and David's path was clear to return to his wife and his post?

The place was visible from afar: Jonathan's house. "I must not be seen," David realized, waiting for the cover of night. When it came, David made his way to the house, availing himself of the tracking skills of a lifelong shepherd. He observed that the front door was guarded, but not the back. David went to the rear window, peering into his soulmate's house. Jonathan was poring over a book and studying.

David knocked gently. Jonathan lifted his head and saw his beloved friend in the window. "Shhh... Come in, brother, quietly," Jonathan whispered. David, tired and exhausted from his two days on the run, still brightened when he came in. The two shared a brotherly hug. "What happened, brother? You look exhausted."

Jonathan gave David a drink, while David told his best friend, son of his worst enemy, everything that had happened in recent days.

"It must be the evil spirit that prevails over my father; that will pass soon. I don't think he really wants to kill you! He will surely come to his senses," Jonathan asserted, though his voice sounded disbelieving.

"My dear brother, you must find out for me what your father intends. Samuel the Prophet told me that you're the only one who can probe his true feelings. It's a matter of life and death. Your father will probably come back here in the morning, and you need to find out if I should flee or if I can stay around," David argued.

Jonathan whispered to David: "Tomorrow and the day after is the New Moon celebration, when Father hosts the feast for his closest courtiers. I can use that occasion to bring up your name in conversation, and I'll find out his attitude toward you. You, my brother, must go into hiding. In two days' time, I'll go hunting with my lads. I'll bring my bow, and if I say, 'The arrow is beyond you,' you must run away; but if I say, 'The arrow is before you,' you will know that Father doesn't really mean you harm, and you can go home. Now, brother, go hide in the field."

David left as he had entered, making sure not to be seen.

On the second day of the New Moon celebration, Saul's chamber had a table set for the most powerful men in the kingdom: the king and his three sons, the high priest and his two sons, the army chief and the chief justice — nine notables, with the tenth chair empty. The atmosphere was tense, the conversation forced, as if they were trying to push away the silence, to drive it into the dark corners of the room.

Saul thought: He wasn't here yesterday either! He keeps dodging! He's not coming back here! And what happened to me the other day? Prophecy! It's been a long time since I first prophesied … so many shifts, changes, upheavals…

He sank into the mists of thought, his mind wandering.

"And where is the son of Jesse?" came Doeg's faux innocent voice. "He wasn't here yesterday either. Because of him, we didn't have a quorum at the New Moon celebration yesterday. We're one man short."

Saul roused himself from his musings to echo Doeg: "Indeed, where is the son of Jesse? Yesterday he didn't come, but I thought maybe something came up. Where is he today?" He fixed his gaze on his son, Jonathan.

Jonathan, looking at his father, decided to lie, realizing that his father would know that he was lying. "David asked me a few days ago to go to his father's house in Bethlehem. Jesse was holding a New Moon celebration for his entire family, and he asked my permission to attend his father's feast." Jonathan saw his father's face filling with rage and madness.

Saul began to tremble with anger: "Rebellious and perverse son!" roared Saul, "I know that you choose the son of Jesse over me, and you want him to rule after me. You know he wants me dead, and you're willing to help him."

"What did David do to you that you want to murder him?" replied Jonathan, anger growing: "What did he do wrong?"

Saul hoisted the spear upon his knees and aimed it at his son. It flew at Jonathan, who shifted his body, and the spear stuck in the wall.

Jonathan ran out heartbroken, slamming the door behind him.

"The arrow is beyond you," Jonathan called to his arms-bearer.

The lad, unaware of what was happening, ran toward the arrow, picked it up, and returned to his master. "That's a good fellow. Please, take the bow and arrows and head home now. I'll stay here for a while longer and come back on my own."

The boy ran lightly, fulfilling his master's will.

David, who was hiding nearby, rose and approached his friend.

"You're right, brother," Jonathan began. "He acts like a madman. He tried to kill me too. I don't understand what he's going through. You are in great danger! You must flee while you still have the chance." Jonathan burst into tears.

David approached his faithful friend and hugged him. He thought: None could be more faithful than he! The clash of loyalties tears him apart — loyalty to his royal father versus loyalty to his comrade. David hugged his friend: "Don't worry, brother, everything will work out in the end. This too, is for the best."

"Please, brother," Jonathan begged David: "I know that my father's kingdom will fall. You, my brother, will be the next man to sit on the throne of Israel, not I. I know this is God's will, and I accept your sovereignty gladly. My father, however, will never accept it. I know he'll try to hurt you. Please, my brother, forge a covenant of friendship and loyalty with me, with me and with my seed. Swear not to harm my progeny when you rule Israel, though they be the descendants of your most bitter enemy."

David burst into tears: "Oh, my brother, my friend, my mate. You are my compatriot, my comrade, my companion, my confidant, beloved of my soul. I will never hurt you or your seed — or your father, though he seeks to kill me. I must flee and leave you, but my love for you will remain in my heart forever, oh my brother Jonathan..."

Two brothers, cut off from each other by the king's edict, stood in the field embracing, sobbing over the separation that had been decreed.

CHAPTER SEVENTEEN
Ahimelech Son of Ahitub

A troop of royal cavalry galloped past as David hid himself in a rock crevice.

He thought: Saul is after me; I must find a hiding place until his anger subsides. At the moment, there is nothing to do but hide from him. He has decided I am a traitor to the kingdom, and he has already condemned me to death for rebelling against the king. I have neither food nor water, sword nor spear. I must find shelter. Two days since I parted from Jonathan, I've spent running and hiding. Soon I won't be able to keep walking; fatigue and hunger will overwhelm me — which could kill me as easily as Saul's sword. Perhaps the news has not yet reached every town. I will turn toward the city of priests; perhaps there I will find balm for my soul. It's a long way, but I dare not take the king's road, which royal troops watch constantly.

Springtime was not a pleasant time to travel cross country: the midday sun beat down mercilessly, while the midnight chill cut to the marrow of the bone.

David told himself: "A few more hours of walking and I'll be there; a little more effort, and I'll have a place to hide."

David stumbled on leaden legs, lacking the strength to continue. "Just a few more steps, beyond this hill. Just a few more steps, after this rise."

David pushed himself, trying to keep his spirits up: "Come on, David, another little effort, you can't break down now. You have many tasks in life, you have a role in the world, you must not surrender."

His words breathed a little more life into his body. Every footfall, every step required strength of mind and body. "Here is Nob, city of priests. Come on David. High Priest Ahimelech is there; he will help us," David urged his body.

"You have to be careful lest any of the king's men catch sight of you. You must enter cautiously."

David stopped to observe, looking over the city. "Apparently the coast is clear..."

"David, my friend, what happened to you?" asked Ahimelech, son of Ahitub.

David fainted to the ground. His body had borne him as far as it would. His clothes were torn from his falls, his hands and feet were bruised, his tongue was swollen from thirst, and his eyes were mad from hunger.

"I need to eat and drink," he whispered, pleading: "Please, my lord high priest, let me eat and drink."

Ahimelech commanded one of the young priests to bring water to David, which he eagerly guzzled.

"I must eat." His lips barely moved in a whisper: "Please, let me eat, or I shall surely die," David begged desperately.

"My lord Prince David, I regret to inform you that we have no unhallowed food. Everything we have here is sacred, to be consumed only by the Aaronite priests, and my lord is no descendant of Aaron," Ahimelech replied sorrowfully.

"Give me food from him, it's a matter of life and death; If I don't eat now, I'll starve. Please, my lord high priest, it is permitted to save a life!" David begged.

Ahimelech gave the order, and the Holy Showbread was brought to David.

David ate his fill, finally recovering. "Thank you so much! You have revived my soul! If it weren't for that, I would be dead. Thank you, my lord high priest."

Ahimelech looked at David and wondered: "Prince David, what are you doing here alone? Why aren't you with your soldiers? Why don't you have provisions and water? Why don't you have weapons?"

David realized that the news hadn't reached Nob yet. "Shhh... I was sent on a secret mission by King Saul, an urgent assignment. I sent my men before me, and I came to you alone to consult the Urim and Thummim about our prospects. No one must know that I've been here. This is a top-secret mission," David whispered to Ahimelech, as if speaking to his longtime confidant.

Ahimelech consulted the Urim and Thummim. The Breastplate of Judgment's twelve precious stones gave the answer as individual letters lit up: "R-I-S-E A-N-D S-U-C-C-E-E-D." Ahimelech reported the message to David.

David, his spirits refreshed, decided to address another issue. "Do you have a sword or a spear? I was in such a rush to carry out the royal command, that I left without my gear."

"In the Tent of Meeting, we have the sword of Goliath of Gath, whom you killed. We keep it as a symbol of the Lord's victory over His enemies," the high priest reported.

"Please bring it to me," David requested.

Ahimelech went and brought the sword to David.

"There's nothing better than it, thank you very much. I must continue on my way to carry out the king's word." David strapped on the sword, amicably bidding farewell to High Priest Ahimelech.

Suddenly, David saw Doeg the Edomite's face looking through the window, witnessing the scene with a mind teeming with thoughts of wickedness...

CHAPTER EIGHTEEN
The Madman

"There is no choice. I have to leave the borders of the Land of Israel."

King Saul was relentless, sending battalions of soldiers to search everywhere. He seemed to consider David a venomous snake threatening his household, and he made every effort to root him out. Saul's troops left no stone unturned. They investigated and interrogated, searching every house and every hovel, every hut and every hutch, every hole and every hollow. When they were unsuccessful, the king lashed out at them, verbally and physically, from the lowliest soldier to the highest-ranking officer. He fired officials and appointed others in their place, blaming everyone he could.

"There is nowhere left to hide."

The noose was tightening around David, as he struggled to stay one step ahead of his pursuers.

"I must go beyond the control of King Saul. I must go to the one place where he would never look for me: Goliath's hometown of Gath. There, at least I hope that they will not recognize and identify me. Here, they shall inevitably catch and kill me."

King Achish of Gath sat on his throne, watching with delight as the troupe of performers sang and danced before him. The table before him held all manner of delicacies, and Achish nibbled on them tranquilly, savoring every morsel. As he hummed along, he drummed with pleasure on his stomach. The crown upon his head was magnificent, gold and gleaming with precious stones, testament to his vast fortune.

Suddenly there was noise and commotion, shouting and screaming. Achish shook his head with dread, muttering: "Not again, not now, not again."

The door opened, and two women burst into the room shouting: the queen and the princess. The latter chased the former, screaming inanity and insanity, while her mother yelled too — whether in gladness or madness, no one could tell.

Achish puts his hands to his face. "Not again..." he groaned.

The pair of madwomen stole the stage from the troupers, throwing objects at each other in an obscene juggling routine. Their hair and dress were in disarray as they fought, paying no heed to the onlookers. Their struggle brought them near the throne, and the queen seized a goblet from her husband's table to throw at her daughter. The princess crouched and the goblet sailed over her, to smack into Achish's crown, which fell upside down into his soup with a noisy splash. The women stopped fighting for a moment, as they looked at Achish and his soiled crown. The queen seemed to regain her faculties for a moment, as she approached the king contritely. "Sorry, dear husband, I didn't mean for that to happen."

Achish's expression was furious, anger surging within him like lava in a volcano about to erupt. His hands shook as his eyes sparked. He mused: Would that I could execute the madwomen who tax me so, but they say there is sanctity in the insane, and they must not be harmed.

The guards in the room couldn't help but burst out laughing. The scene was hilarious, horrific, and hysterical.

The queen bent down to pull the crown from the soup bowl and place it back on her husband's head. The soup poured out, running down Achish's apoplectic face.

"Pardon me, my royal husband, but you left some soup in your bowl," she said as she upended the remainder over his head.

The thick-fleshed Achish roared: "Get them out of here! Get them out of the city, out of the country!" He tried to get up, but his wife pushed him back down. Her chuckles merged with the princess's giggles and the guards' snickers. They could not help themselves.

Some hours later, the chief of Achish's army came before him. He whispered urgently: "Your Majesty, we have apprehended Prince David. He is the son-in-law of King Saul of Israel. He tried to cross the border anonymously, but one of the servants recognized him as the slayer of our champion Goliath. We have him safely in custody," he declared with obvious joy, as if he had won the war single-handedly.

"Bring him here now, Lord Commander. I'll show him what the king's justice tastes like," Achish grinned.

The door opened, and two guards led David into the throne room. His plan had backfired, and he had to think of a new one quickly. An unbridled laugh erupted from his throat. He glared wildly, drooling on his beard, rending and ripping his clothes.

Chanting...

Crying...

Chortling...

Screeching…

Cutting into the doors with his fingernails...

Capering and waving his arms bizarrely...

"Here's the scoundrel! You owe me a hundred thousand gold pieces, and your wife fifty thousand!" he shouted as he jumped, jabbing an accusatory finger at Achish.

Achish stared at David, thinking: My nightmare returns, another madman in my castle. This is Saul's son-in-law? This lunatic? This maniac? Well, all Israelites look alike. That slave must've been wrong... Perhaps he was confused; perhaps he wanted to jape at me too. Perhaps he had a death wish, like those guards who sneered at me.

His anger rose until he shouted: "What possessed you to bring him here? You see someone go crazy and present him to me? Do I lack lunatics? Do I need more maniacs? Get him out of here immediately! Send him back to Israel; let them deal with their own madmen. I have plenty already!" shrieked Achish.

The King of Gath's decree was fulfilled, and David soon wandered the wildernesses of Israel again. It was a long way, with neither food nor water nor aid. David understood that anyone who helped him would be in mortal danger at Saul's hands.

He thought: I must flee to one of the caves, where I will hide from Saul until it pleases the Creator to seat me on the throne. The road turns east here, going all the way to Benjamite territory. I must travel off that road, until I reach the Cave of Adullam.

His path took him through fields of thorns and thistles which scoured his flesh.

David was occupied with thoughts of his kin.

He reflected: King Saul has taken leave of his senses, so I must worry that he may hurt them in order to take revenge on me. He may imprison them, even kill them, just to get to me, to wound me. I have to worry about the safety of my parents, of my brothers and their families. My sisters and niece are already married, so I need not worry about them; they are safe in their husbands' homes.

David took an unexpected step, sneaking into his parents' home. Under cover of darkness, he quietly entered their home, stepping noiselessly toward their bedroom. "Shhh, don't say a word," David whispered. "There are soldiers all over the city. I'm fleeing to the Cave of Adullam. Make your way there. Bring my brothers and their families with you, but don't tell them where you're going and where you're headed."

Without waiting for an answer, David went out the window, fleeing to the Cave of Adullam.

The cave of Adullam was a vast network of grottoes and caverns, offering shelter not only for David and his family, but for an assortment of refugees and renegades, debtors and deserters. At first it was a handful of individuals, then dozens, then hundreds.

One day, David approached Jesse. "Father, I fear you'll be in danger if I drag you with me from place to place. I don't know how long we can stay here, as rumors are starting to spread. Each day, more desperate men come, four hundred already. We must head east, to Moab. You, Mother, and all our family should seek asylum there. We have no quarrel with them; indeed, Grandma Ruth was the aunt of the current king. I'll escort you there and request that he shelter you until I know what God will do with me. You're not of an age to be on the run from King Saul, while your sons have wives and children of their own. It's not safe."

Jesse nodded, marveling at his youngest son's optimism and faith amidst such distress and suffering. "You're right, son, we're also putting you at risk by being here. We hinder your movements, the king of Moab is a decent man; we will go to him."

They resolved that David's family would seek refuge with the

Moabite royal family, while he and his men took shelter at the stronghold.

However, there was one voice of dissent: Shammah, thirdborn among Jesse's sons. "After all, I am still unmarried. I have no family of my own. I ought to stay with you, my brother David, to fight by your side."

David appreciated the offer but declined it. Embracing his brother, he persuaded him: "You must not, brother. Stay with Mother and Father and help them. Soon you will all join me."

"Lord David, an old man has come to us and wishes to see you." The sentry, a fresh arrival, regarded his new master with awe. Throughout their time in the stronghold, David had taught his men wisdom and morality, examining and expounding issues of faith and duty for an Israelite in the world.

"Please admit him." David looked at the sentry, who had not long ago been a criminal on the run and was now a new man.

An aged, venerable man entered, and David rose to walk over and greet him. "What brings you here, Lord Gad the Visionary? I hope you bring me good news."

"I have come to you on a mission from God. You must leave this place and return to the land of Judah. Go to the Hereth Forest near Bethlehem. You are beloved among the Judahites there; they will help you with whatever you need. This place is too dangerous for you. If Saul comes looking for you, your tribesmen will let you know. You must hurry." Having spoken his piece, he bade David farewell like an old friend.

CHAPTER NINETEEN

Nob, City of Priests

"This is high treason! You have all conspired against me with Jesse's son. What did he promise you? Fields? Vineyards? Maybe he told you that he would give you respectable positions in his kingdom? The insurrectionist already has an army of his own, twenty platoons of twenty. Four hundred rebels who want me dead."

Saul had finally heard the rumors about men joining David. The revolt he'd feared so much seemed to be taking shape before his very eyes. Saul gathered all his ministers and servants in an emergency meeting. The king sat on his throne, spear across his knees. He seethed at his men, looking for a target upon whom to vent his ire.

"You all hate me! You collaborate with the enemy! You rejoice in the revolt by Jesse's son! You and the entire tribe of Benjamin are waiting for Jesse's son to smash my head and seize the crown. None of you care about me; none of you love and support me. Even my son Jonathan has made an alliance with my enemy."

Saul's men were anxious and apprehensive; on whom would the fury fall? Who would be the victim of the madness gripping the king this time? Everyone's eyes were lowered, afraid of being caught in the king's gaze, lest he pour out his anger on them. The people shifted uncomfortably, praying for the meeting to end. They had heard the rumors, but no one had wanted to inform Saul, lest he turn his wrath on the messenger.

Saul continued: "How is it possible that he manages to escape and evade for so long without assistance? How is it possible that he assembled an army, without your knowledge and help? You are a bunch of rebels! You should all be executed for treason against the kingdom!"

One man pushed forward from among the assembled notables:

Doeg the Edomite. As Saul had lost faith in his courtiers and counselors, even those bound to him by blood, Doeg had maneuvered ever closer to the king's ear. His face was youthful and fierce, his eyes cruel and cunning: "Your Majesty asks who assists the son of Jesse in the rebellion? Who lets him know where you're looking? I'll tell you who!"

Saul looked Doeg in the eye, anticipation in his gaze. He thought: Finally someone who cares about me! Doeg is wise, loyal, and devoted.

"The collaborator is none other than the High Priest, Ahimelech, son of Ahitub. With my own eyes, I saw Jesse's son come to him in Nob, the city of priests. As if that Bethlehemite wore a crown, the priest consulted the Urim and Thummim on his behalf. Then he gave him bread and provisions, not to mention the sword of Goliath of Gath. If Your Majesty seeks insurrectionists, look no further than Nob. All the priests saw how your enemy came there and assisted him; they are the rebels against the kingdom," Doeg concluded.

Silence reigned in the chamber. The priests, led by the high priest, were traitors? Such a thing was unthinkable. The very idea defied belief. No one else could accept it, and it showed on their faces.

Doeg challenged them: "You don't believe me? Question the sanctimonious lot yourselves. They don't lie, so just ask them!" he sneered, grinning maliciously.

Saul rose to his feet and roared: "What are you waiting for? Send a great battalion to Nob and bring those priests here immediately!"

It was an overcast day, but only a few drops of rain fell slowly to moisten the earth. A delegation of Nobite priests, headed by Ahimelech the High Priest, stood anxiously before King Saul. The troops who had brought them had told Ahimelech the charge – high treason! His heart was full of fear and foreboding; it was common knowledge that King Saul was prone to foul moods and lashing out in violent outbursts.

The atmosphere was tense. Saul looked them over as if they were his lifelong enemies, from whom he was about to exact his vengeance.

The Nobite delegation numbered eighty-five, the most venerable of the priestly city.

Saul stared at Ahimelech. With venom in his voice, he demanded: "What do you have to say in your defense?"

"Your Majesty, what crime have we committed?" Ahimelech replied to King Saul.

Saul's eyes narrowed as the muscles of his face tensed, and his gaze bore into Ahimelech: "What crime have you committed? I'll tell you what crime! You have given aid and comfort to a traitor to the kingdom! You knew that Jesse's son was a rebel, yet you gave him food and drink. You armed him with Goliath's sword, so he might commit regicide! Worst of all, you consulted the Urim and Thummim for him, as if he were the king! Then you feign innocence and ask what crimes you've committed?" he shrieked.

"I beg Your Majesty's pardon," Ahimelech replied in horror. "Prince David, a rebel? He is your most faithful servant, obedient and honorable, not to mention your son-in-law! David said that he was on a royal mission and needed arms, so I gave him the only weapon I had, Goliath's sword. Your Majesty knows that ever since David's appointment, he has come to me to consult the Urim and Thummim. My king, there must be some mistake. David is no traitor, and we are certainly not, God forbid!"

Saul's furious expression did not waver, as if he had not heard a word. "Ahimelech, son of Ahitub, I find you guilty of high treason and sentence you to death by the sword — you and all your father's house," he roared, a verdict decided before the accused had arrived. "Guards, execute the priests, who knew about David's rebellion but hid it from me and gave him succor. Kill them all!" shouted Saul.

The guards did not move a muscle. Who would dare kill the priests, the servants of the Lord, including the high priest? The holiest men in Israel? The guards could not fulfill this royal command; their faces showed their terror and horror. They knew what was likely to happen to them for refusing the king's orders, but harming a priest was more unthinkable.

The king looked at his guards in disbelief. A rebellion within his own throne room? The king's guard defying the king's word? Then an idea came to him: there was one man upon whom he could always rely. Faithful Doeg had revealed the truth, faithful Doeg would deliver the consequences. "Doeg, draw your sword and carry out my sentence," the king commanded.

Doeg, happy to do it, unsheathed his blade and slashed through Ahimelech's neck.

The chamber exploded into gory chaos, a bloodbath.

The priests were not men of war; they tried to flee for their lives, but there was no way out. The doors were barred, and Doeg's face radiated cruel joy, murdering and massacring the priests. The slaughter took but a few moments, blood splashing on the walls of the chamber as it became an abattoir of holy corpses. The guards were stunned and sobbing as they witnessed the carnage. Eighty-five priestly bodies, including the high priest, holy of holies, littered their floor. Doeg stood over them, sword dripping and eyes bloodthirsty. "Anything else, my king?" he asked cheerily.

"Yes," Saul shrieked madly. Part of him could not believe what he had done, but part of him — the greater part — still sought vengeance on his enemies. "Go to Nob city of priests. Take soldiers with you, not like these weaklings," he ordered, pointing at the disobedient king's guard. "Form a battalion of the mercenaries in our army, and go to Nob, city of priests. Kill every last living thing, man and woman, child and animal. Leave nothing alive. Rebels, traitors, collaborators with the enemy. Go, go quickly before word gets to them and they run away."

Doeg bowed low before the king, happy to carry out the command. Doeg took with him about a hundred bloodthirsty mercenaries. Every last Nobite was executed, male and female, old and young. A furious massacre, a frenzied bloodbath, led by Doeg. "Let no one escape," he shouted to his men, egging them on. "All the spoils will be yours. Kill, my brothers, kill, have no compassion upon them." Rivers of blood, horror, screams, shouts, cries and groans. "Only the families of the priests," Doeg yelled at his men. "The Gibeonites did nothing; they don't need to be killed."

Then there was silence...

Doeg and his men went through the corpses to take their booty and verify that they were all dead.

The Gibeonites, water carriers for the priestly families, had fled the scene, leaving their water jugs behind. Doeg looked at the sight of thousands of scattered bodies, and his soul was filled with joy.

It was late. David's Hereth Forest camp, not far from Bethlehem, had settled down for the night. While most of the men were asleep, some studied, while others kept watch. The silence was periodically broken by growling foxes and howling jackals.

David's tribesmen were for the most part loyal to him, watching the encampment and protecting it from afar. Rumor had it that Samuel the Seer had declared that David would be king after Saul, even anointing him a year earlier. David's reputation rose in the eyes of Judah. He provided security for all those around, saving them from raiders and bandits. His men were known for their honesty, manners, and Torah observance. They never harassed or hurt anyone. They always spoke calmly and patiently. They were happy and cheerful people, and their ranks swelled thanks to their sterling reputation.

The sentries manned their posts; they did not anticipate any problems, but there was no way to guarantee what the night might bring.

Out of the darkness, a man materialized before the sentries. His torn and bloody garb was that of a Gibeonite servant, a pack on his shoulder. His eyes were haunted by death, overcast in pain and sorrow.

"Halt! Identify yourself!" demanded one of the surprised sentries.

"I am Abiathar, son of the High Priest, Ahimelech. I need to talk to Prince David," the man replied in a tired, feeble voice.

The guard approached the man, looked at his face, and observed his garb. His attire was that of a simple laborer, but his countenance was angelic — the face of a righteous man who had undergone severe suffering. "Come brother, I will show you where Lord David is." The sentry accompanied the man, musing: Yet another refugee from the hands of King Saul.

"My Lord David," the sentry whispered to David, who was in his tent. "A young man has arrived. He says he is Abiathar, son of the High Priest, Ahimelech. He wants to meet with you."

"Please bring him in," David replied.

The flap was opened and Abiathar entered the tent. He stood before David, who rose to greet him. "What happened to you?" asked David. Abiathar's face did not bode well. "Please sit down, rest and drink, and then tell me what happened."

Abiathar sat down, drank and told David the whole story — the murder of his father and the priests by Saul, the terrible massacre in the city of Nob — as tears flooded his eyes.

"My Lord David, I have more bad news for you; a rumor reached my ears from the fields of Edom. A bitter and difficult tale. You and I are partners in distress, we are both mourners and orphans. Your father and your mother, your brothers and their family — they were all slaughtered by the evil king of Moab, who promised you that he would protect them. After you left, the king of Moab rose up and slaughtered your entire family."

David sobbed, tearing his clothes and slipping to the ground in mourning...

Mourning for his father and mother...

Mourning for his brothers and their families...

Mourning for the High Priest and all the priests and their families...

David's weeping could be heard throughout the camp. Those who were asleep awoke, while those who were studying stopped to approach the tent.

The sounds of David's sobs shattered the silence of the forest.

"Oh... Oh... Because of me, this slaughter was committed. Because of me, my father and mother were killed; because of me, my brothers and their families were killed; because of me, all the Nobites were killed; and because of me, the High Priest Ahimelech was killed. Oh my! I should have known that the king of Moab, a foreigner, could not be trusted. I should have understood, when I saw Doeg the Edomite looking at your father who had helped me, that he would go and tell Saul, and that Saul would not accept it quietly... Because of me, your father and your entire family died... Because of me, all my family members died. Oh... How can I make amends for all the blood spilled due to me? How can I make atonement for my sin…?"

David wallowed in the dirt, tears running down his face, weeping over the murdered servants of God.

The sound of crying could be heard throughout the camp, the voices of the fighters mourning for the Lord's holy ones who had been slaughtered, for the murdered family of their master.

"My brother Abiathar, stay here with me. He who seeks your life also seeks mine. Our fates are intertwined. Stay with me, my brother, through thick and thin."

All night long, the sounds of crying could be heard in the camp, fighters weeping for the slain martyrs. The sobbing of men overwhelmed the growling of foxes and the howling of jackals.
    Heavy rain began to fall...
    Heaven wept for the martyrs who had been slaughtered...

CHAPTER TWENTY
Keilah

"Our Lord David," the Keilite envoy began, "the Philistines are besieging our humble town; they kill and thieve, with no one to stay their hand. Each day the body count mounts, as they steal and loot rampantly. The people are afraid to go out to their fields. The Philistines lurk everywhere. I made my way here only by taking my life in my hands and sneaking out under the cover of darkness. You must come and save us. We turned to King Saul and told him about the situation, but he ignored us, as he is preoccupied with pursuing you. Please, Lord David, save us."

David considered the situation: Saul's soldiers scour the country looking for me, as he neglects everything to focus on his sole obsession. He is a king uninterested in how his subjects fare. His belief that I have turned traitor gives him no rest; hunting me down is all he thinks about. This injustice is occurring because of me.

"Summon the High Priest, Abiathar," he ordered.

Abiathar entered David's tent; they were brothers in misfortune, fellow fugitives.

"My lord high priest," David turned to Abiathar, "please ask the Urim and Thummim, shall I go and attack these Philistines at Keilah?"

When the High Priest, Ahimelech, had been seized along with his deputies, the young priest had taken his father's vestments, including the Breastplate of Judgment, and concealed them in a common shepherd's pack. He had dressed as a Gibeonite water carrier, barely escaping from the city as the awful massacre began. Now, Abiathar, in his father's stead, was the senior religious authority in Israel. He wore the holy garments and focused his mind as he had seen his martyred father do so many times. His eyes closed, and his heart sought his

Heavenly Father: "Should David go and attack the Philistines?" A few seconds later, the answer came through the Urim and Thummim, as the letters engraved on the precious stones lit up, one after another: G-O S-T-R-I-K-E S-A-V-E. Abiathar, eyes still shut, said: "Go, strike, save."

The men in the tent were not convinced: "Lord David, our place here is secure. You are beloved in the eyes of your fellow Bethlehemites, who warn us of any threat. This is the safest place in all of Judah for you. If we go down to Keilah, we will be in a hostile region. We will need to guard ourselves from the Philistines to the southwest and Saul's supporters to the northeast. It makes no sense to leave our refuge here."

David, realizing the plight of his people, turned to Abiathar: "My lord high priest, please seek again the word of God."

Abiathar asked: "Should David and his men go to Keilah to fight the Philistines and save the Keilites from the Philistines? Will they achieve victory over the Philistines?"

The Breastplate of Judgment delivered the reply: "*Go at once to Keilah, for I will deliver the Philistines into your hand.*"

David looked at his men: "My brave brothers, we are all Israelites, all descended from the same father. Our Keilite brethren are in trouble, and they have no advocate. We have a holy mission: God has chosen us to be His agents to save them. We have nothing to fear, as we follow the command of the King of the world to deliver His children from their oppressors. We must fear neither the Philistines nor King Saul. We must go into battle with joy; our Heavenly Father marches at our head. My brothers, let us save our people. Do not fear or hesitate, for God will give them over into our hands."

The people who until recently were haunted felt the new spirit pulsing within them, a spirit of faith in the righteousness of the path. David's fortitude instilled faith in their hearts, igniting their souls for their brothers in trouble.

"Keilites, we are coming!" the shout arose. David's militia, which now numbered six hundred, followed their master to save their people.

The battle was bloody, but David's soldiers were brave and ready to lay down their lives for their brethren. His militia, a force of freedom and faith, defeated the army of well-trained Philistines, who retreated, fleeing in every direction. The impassioned militia pursued the fleeing warriors, avenging their helpless brethren who had been slaughtered. They emerged from the battlefield victorious, a force forged anew in combat, bearing their commander on their shoulders and booty in their hands. They marched into Keilah, to be greeted as liberators by the citizens freed from their fear.

Shofars were being sounded throughout Israel, the clarion call of combat. The Israelites gathered and assembled in response to the rumors that Saul was about to free the southern city of Keilah from the raiders of Philistia. "King Saul summons all men of war to save the Keilites from the Philistines," the crier announced.

The soldiers gathered at the staging grounds. Tens of thousands of warriors answered their king's call to save their people. The atmosphere was uplifting. The fighters had been aware of the situation at the border, the neglect of the frontier and the plight of their brethren in settlements close to Philistia; they were happy to save their countrymen.

"Maybe the hunt for David will finally end and we'll deal with the more important things," said one of the fighters. "For more than six months now, our army has been seeking David for no good reason. I hope King Saul is ready to address the truly important issues."

"You're right. But it's not just in Keilah! I have family in the north of the country who suffer trouble all the time. I pray that the time has come to teach our foes a lesson," his friend replied.

"Brave men of war," Saul's voice resounded, "we are going to war today against our enemies. We are going to save our brethren from their oppressors. We set out to liberate the city of Keilah from the hands of its enemies. Heroes, gird yourselves with strength and courage to defeat our enemies forever."

"Keilites, we are coming!" the shout arose.

But while his army set out for war against the Philistines, Saul set out for war against David. About two days earlier, a Keilite had brought a secret message to Saul: David's militia was in their city. The Keilites had no desire to share the fate of the Nobites; they dreaded the violence that Saul would wreak if he caught them sheltering the fugitive. Fearing for their lives and those of their families, they were ready to surrender the man who had saved them from the Philistines to his nemesis.

"Treachery! Duplicity!" David's guard reacted in shock.

A Judahite had arrived with a message. "Saul gathered all the men of war under the pretext that they were going to save the Keilites from the Philistines, but he knows that you already saved Keilah. He is coming to apprehend you. Apparently, a Keilite informed him of our presence. Jonathan witnessed the conversation, and he sent me to inform you of what had happened, so you might escape. King Saul has raised a mighty army, and the Keilites will hand you over without a second thought." The messenger bowed and left.

The guard, embittered and enraged, turned to David: "This wasp's nest must be destroyed. We risked our lives for them, and they want to betray us, handing us over to the enemy? It's a shame we helped them."

David walked over to the guard, placing a fatherly hand on his shoulder: "No, son. That's not the way. These people are small and scared; they've heard what King Saul did to Nob, the city of priests. They worry about what will happen to them and their families. They are not bad people. They are frightened, so they sent a messenger to the king. They are aware of his temperament and fear what he might do. We did the right thing by fulfilling the Word of the King of the world; we must not regret the commandment we carried out. It looks like we're done here; let's move on. Come, my friend, we will go and ask the High Priest, Abiathar, what we should do now." David and the guard left the room to consult him.

The High Priest, Abiathar, focused his mind. David asked, "Will the Keilites hand me and my people over to Saul?"

The answer came through the Urim and Thummim, "They will."

David and his men left the city immediately.

Once Saul heard that David had left Keilah, he sent his troops back home. He claimed that the Keilites had already engaged the Philistines and defeated them.

CHAPTER TWENTY-ONE
David and Jonathan

Days, weeks, and months passed. The chase continued, and David continued to evade pursuit. Saul's entire goal was to capture David and his men, a militia that grew day by day. However, David was no longer merely the head of a fighting force; he provided a place of refuge for all who fled the terror of Saul's rule. David's people multiplied as he became favorably viewed throughout Israel. His militia gained a reputation for guarding the borders and saving their countrymen from raiders. Saul might wear the crown, but the scepter and the sword were firmly in David's grasp.

Saul's army searched relentlessly for the rebel alliance, ready to root it out. Their orders were clear: take no prisoners, show no mercy; the only sentence was death.

David's people moved from place to place, from deserts to caves, from forests to valleys; there was no rest. By cunning trickery, they avoided Saul's army. David's directive was determined: "We must not harm Saul's men; they are our countrymen, soldiers of Israel, doing a job they may detest. They follow the orders of the anointed King of Israel. Do not harm them; just avoid and evade."

Escaping...
Evacuating...
Eluding...
Evading...

In the Wilderness of Ziph, David found a wooded area. It was big enough to accommodate his entire encampment.

The sky was blue, the spring sun filtering through the trees, playing games of light and shade. David sat on a small rock at the edge of his camp, watching his people.

"Sunshine and shadow, light and darkness, all mixed up. How long will my people be able to dodge and flee? How long will they hold their fire and not injure Saul's soldiers?" Birds chirped, singing and praising their Creator. "We've been here too long, more than a week. We must move on. It won't be long before Saul arrives, and I must not endanger my people."

Cheers and shouts came from the sidelines, as a veteran warrior taught swordsmanship to a new recruit. The boy managed to defeat his teacher, and he shouted for joy.

David smiled. "For some, it's just a game. The boys don't understand the horror of battle. They're excited as if they're playing a childhood game. They still haven't experienced the bitter taste of war."

A doe ran out of the bushes, distracting him. "Merciful Father, have I made the correct choice? Do I have the right to endanger these boys? How much longer will they be able to endure persecution, repression, and hardship? I know, Father, that every trial is only a lever of faith. Every difficulty strengthens the human heart, every effort bears fruit at the end.

"But the situation in Israel is not good; we are at the mercy of the surrounding nations, made miserable by the looting and massacring. The people of the land, Your nation Israel, cry out for saving, but there is no savior. The truth is that they are looking for salvation in all the wrong places. A flesh-and-blood king, a human deliverer, a corporeal king — he cannot help, only You can!"

David spoke to his Creator as if He were a friend. His mind was no longer among the trees of Ziph, but grasping at its root, the Sovereign of the universe.

The noises of the encampment faded from his perception. He was in absolute communion with God, finding the answers to his questions deep in his heart. "In order for faith to be taught, it must take root deep within the human heart. True faith is not something to take for granted: it must be learned, and it must be practiced. In every Israeli heart, there is a kernel, a holy seed waiting to bloom and blossom. Every Israelite knows that there is only one Source to seek aid from in times of trouble and distress. The seed must be watered. The kernel must be nurtured. The people must be raised up, the holy seed that believes utterly and completely. They must be trained in the ways of faith and inculcated with truth. Truth is the source of faith, and falsehood is the opposite. We need a core, indeed a corps, of people of truth, in order to spread the true faith among the people of Israel. Samuel the Prophet is a man of truth and faith, but he did not succeed in instilling these virtues among my people. The holy flock requires a faithful shepherd…"

A hand placed on David's shoulder tore him out of his communion with the Creator.

David looked up. "Jonathan?" he said, as if waking from a dream.

The two best friends embraced with great love, overjoyed at their reunion.

Jonathan sat with David in his tent, relishing the closeness and companionship. The two friends sat together, along with Abiathar and the senior officers. Food and drink were presented, the best that the humble camp could offer. The occasion was very unexpected on David's part, only happening thanks to Jonathan's devotion. Their faces shone with joy.

As David looked at Jonathan, feelings of affection filled his heart: the love of fellowship, the love not dependent on anything, the love of brotherhood. Twin souls forced to separate against their will. "My brother Jonathan, what brings you here? How did you find us? You have taken your life in your hand, my brother; if your father learns of this, he may not spare you."

Jonathan looked at David: "If only you knew how much I love you, my brother David! How I longed to see your face again, to talk to you, to study with you. My dear brother, Father already knows you are here. The informers and gossipmongers are not hard to find.

"Recognize this: on the one hand, Father badly wants to catch you; on the other hand, he fears harming you. At the moment, his inclination toward the good is greater, so he is not here with his soldiers. My father is afraid to hurt you, because he heard that Samuel the Seer anointed you as king of Israel, and that you will succeed him."

This revelation stunned David's officers. There had been all manner of rumors, but they'd had no explicit confirmation. David had never told anyone what Samuel had done in Jesse's home. Now they could say it aloud: David, King of Israel!

Jonathan continued: "You know that Father confides in me. He pours out his whole heart before me. So he told me what happened at the end of the Amalek War: that Samuel the Seer came to him and told him that God had decreed that he would lose the throne to another. Since then, his spirit has been disturbed, and he began to look for who that alternative might be, in order to put him to death. When you defeated the Philistine Goliath, and the people began to flock to your side, my father understood that you would be the one to succeed him, so he went after you.

"You must understand that madness seizes him suddenly. After he ordered the massacre of Nob — an order which Doeg was only too glad to fulfill — he began to pursue, of all people, the Gibeonites. They were the woodcutters and water carriers of the priestly city, nothing more, yet he claims that they knew of your high treason — as he alleges — yet failed to inform him. So now the Gibeonites are traitors to the kingdom as well, sentenced to death! He even screamed at Doeg for not slaughtering them alongside the Nobites, if you can believe it. Now their lives are forfeited by royal edict; they are fair game for anyone who wants to kill them and seize their property!

"Oh, David, it is true what they say, that no man who acquires power ever relinquishes it willingly. Father cannot set aside the notion that I will one day succeed him, but I know that won't happen. You, my brother, will be king over Israel, and I will be your deputy. There will be no man as happy as I when you become King of Israel. I know you well, and I recognize that you are the one who deserves to wear the crown."

David looked down, embarrassed; only his family had known about Samuel's anointment. Now his men looked at their master — no, their king! — as their joy outweighed the shock that enveloped them. Until that moment, they had felt some pangs of conscience for being David's soldiers, rebelling against the lawful King of Israel. Now they realized that they were the legitimate military of the sovereign, the ruler chosen by the Creator. They were not insurrectionists, but soldiers in the army of the true king. They had always known that David deserved to rule, but they hadn't known he was the monarch chosen by God and anointed by His prophet.

"My dear brother, I have a great surprise for you," Jonathan smiled and turned to one of David's guards. "Please bring in the man who accompanied me."

The guard came out, and a few moments later he returned accompanied by a man not much older than David, but bearing a striking resemblance to him…

David jumped up as if a snake had bitten him. "Shammah? My brother? Are you truly alive?!" He ran to hug the unexpected guest. "I was sure you were dead, my dear brother," David said, tears of joy welling up in his eyes. "How did you come to be here?"

"Oh, my brother David," Shammah cried. "I will tell you the whole sad story. You know that I wanted to stay with you, but you sent me to escort Father, Mother, our six brothers and their families. The king of Moab presented himself as a great ally, welcoming us warmly, but it was all a ruse.

"One day I went for a little walk to amuse myself. Then I returned to the home we had been granted in the capital, and I saw the horror. They were all murdered: Father and Mother; our brothers, their wives and children."

Shammah sobbed bitterly, reliving the memory of the massacre.

"I wanted to bury them, but I knew that if I tarried even one moment, they would catch me too and kill me, so I fled the place while I still had the chance.

"I was confused and frightened. I don't know why, but I fled over the border to Ammon. The king of Ammon protected me and granted me asylum.

"Then I set out to return to the Land of Israel. King Saul's soldiers caught me and delivered me to Prince Jonathan. He brought me to you."

David looked at his longtime friend, feeling the rush of love for his brother in spirit, who had saved his brother in flesh. "My dear brother," he turned to Jonathan, "how can I ever thank you? I pledge my life to you and your seed."

"David, my brother, my king, all I ask is that you make a covenant with me today before the Lord and before the High Priest, Abiathar. I will be your servant, your viceroy, and you will spare me and my seed when you sit on the throne of your kingdom."

David rose from his chair to hug and kiss his brother Jonathan: "My brother Jonathan, I make the covenant with you and your seed forever. No friend or companion compares to you. You have my pledge and my heart."

The brothers parted in regret and sorrow. Jonathan returned home, while King David remained with his army and his brother Shammah.

CHAPTER TWENTY-TWO
Ziphites

"Your Majesty King Saul, the traitor against the kingdom lurks in the Wilderness of Ziph. Why haven't you come to apprehend him? For quite a while he has been sheltering outside our town, but you have not responded! Delegation after delegation we send to notify you, with no reply. He is a bird in the hand, Your Majesty; all you need to do is close your fist around the rebel! Is he no longer treasonous? Is the reward for assisting in his capture no longer in force?"

The Ziphites were insistent and persistent. There was a price on David's head, and they were determined to collect it. Exemption from the king's taxes was a worthy prize, and the Ziphites wanted to earn it. For about two months, David and his army had been near their town, but the royal soldiers had made no move to catch him.

Saul was weary of the chase; the crown weighed too heavily on him. He was besieged on all sides, but his thoughts were occupied with David. Half of Saul's being longed to catch David, half held him back. He yearned for his dynasty to last but knew with stunning clarity that David would succeed him. He desired to defeat David and preserve his rule, but he was overwhelmed by the feeling of betrayal in his relationship to the Creator of the universe.

"King Saul, if you have changed your mind and do not want to apprehend these traitors to the kingdom, just tell us. We will go back home and send no more delegations. If David knows we have sent messengers to you, he may hurt us. If you have chosen not to catch the rebels, please don't endanger us, your loyal servants. These renegades dwell tranquilly in the Wilderness of Ziph, savoring the quiet as their ranks expand. Every day more people join the insurrection! If you don't destroy this nest of vipers quickly, they will overrun the land, destroying you and your house. We who are loyal to the Crown have only your best interests at heart. The rebels have grown accustomed to the area and are reluctant to leave. If you come with your army, Your Majesty may apprehend these traitors to the kingdom. We only seek your benefit."

The earnest appeal roused the weary Saul. He mused: I was anointed in Zoph; now I'll save my kingdom in Ziph. These folk are loyal and true. I mustn't disappoint them.

Saul came to his senses: "Son, I thank you for your loyalty and for your desire for the good of the king and the kingdom. Go back to your place, locate where the traitors are hiding, and I will follow you with the army to seize the rebels and their leader."

Thousands of soldiers appeared on the horizon, a mighty army making its way to capture the king's enemies. The sun was about to rise, painting the sky in crimson hues, as a fierce wind blew, trying to shatter the trees. Mountains loomed threateningly over the soldiers making their way through the shade. Saul's entire army had been mobilized for the mission, leaving the towns and villages of Israel unguarded. The national mission was to preserve the kingdom, to make the enemies of the king pay. Saul's warriors in the valley, at the foot of the mountain, drew their cloaks around themselves more tightly against the chill as they prepared for battle.

The treasonous force was on the other side of the mountain, and soon the revolution would be no more. The rebels numbered about six hundred. In a few hours, David's army would either surrender or die.

"Where is King Saul?" asked a messenger who appeared out of nowhere before the king's guard. "I must speak with him. It's urgent."

The courier appeared before the king, "Your Majesty, I bring bad news. When the Philistines heard that you went south with your entire army, they began to raid northern and central Israel. The people are in great danger. Each settlement is barely garrisoned, with the few remaining soldiers afraid to fight. Your Majesty must save your people. Time is of the essence; if you delay, you will have no home to return to!" The frightened messenger, broken and tired, described in horrific detail the situation at the border. "The Philistines are pouring through to murder and plunder. It's awful! Women, children, and the elderly are being slaughtered with no one to save them!"

Saul was conflicted. His subjects were in mortal danger, but his quarry was at hand. The king's heart was divided: half to save his people and half to shatter the rebels.

"Your Majesty, there is no time. Every moment is an eternity. Every minute counts. Your people are being murdered throughout Israel; its king must come!" The messenger pressed and urged Saul to act.

The king sighed: "There is no choice."

He thought: I have an obligation to my subjects; I must go back to save my people. The son of Jesse and his rebels will have to wait. Their time will come.

Saul mounted his horse, shouting to his soldiers: "Back north! We must save Israel from the hands of the Philistines. "

The army turned to wage war against the Philistines.

David and his men were forgotten, for the time being.

Until the chase resumed...

CHAPTER TWENTY-THREE
The Cave

Around the oasis at Ein Gedi was a vast expanse of arid desert. Ibexes leaped across the mountains, but the region held few human inhabitants. The flocks of sheep grazing far from human settlement grazed on wild grass. Water was hard to find in the area. There were few springs to quench the thirst of those sheltering in the desolate desert, to breathe life into those hiding from the scorching sun. High up in the hills, massive caves offered the only shelter from the day's heat or the night's chill.

Ein Gedi was a godsend for David and his men; the oasis had enough shade and water to provide a respite, as they knew that Saul would find it difficult to track them through the harsh, arid terrain.

At the oasis, the warriors would sing as they practiced their swordsmanship. Others were engaged in conversation — whether silently with their Creator or boisterously with their fellows.

The sun was hot, but at least a light breeze dissipated their sweat.

David sat at the entrance to a cave, lost in thought: *The last time we were saved by a miracle; I only learned after the fact that Saul's army was so close to us. I can't count on marvels. God works wonders, but they must be minimized as much as possible. Too many miracles can make us excessively complacent, shirking all effort. Every time spared unnaturally and at the last minute — that could be our undoing!*

David noticed a spider climbing atop his leg, slowly advancing toward his arm; the arachnid swung on its web and began to descend. David observed wonderingly: "Lord, what skill and wisdom did You imbue in this small creature to weave these webs? To what end? What does this add to Your world?"

Praying...

Pondering…
Puzzling…
Proposing…
David was frustrated. His thoughts remained unsettled. The endless escapes prevented any deep study. Concern for his men, uncertainty, and restlessness disturbed him.

A guard approached David: "Your Majesty, there seems to be an army advancing in our direction. It looks like you have to go into the cave. "

David came to his senses: "Gather all the fighters into the cave immediately. Quietly, so that they won't notice us. "

The warriors hurried to hide in the cave, which was long and dark, its air still. Deep inside, David and his men held absolute silence. Even their breathing was inaudible.

"Your Majesty, there are people's footprints here, quite fresh. A few hours ago at most, a few hundred people came through here. I think they're the men we're looking for." The tracker had a sharp eye, a lifelong desert-dweller. He could read the signs: a broken branch, a scrap of clothing snagged by a shrub, remains of human waste, tiny tracks in the rocky soil. "Be very careful, Your Majesty, they may be lurking nearby. The hills are filled with caves, and you must make certain they aren't there. Otherwise, they're likely to start a rockslide and bring the whole mountain down on our heads." His eyes darted to and fro, looking for his quarry.

Saul turned to the tracker: "Find me a modest spot, a cave where I can relieve myself. My stomach is bothering me. Quickly, find me a decent, secure place."

The tracker wanted to do his best for his monarch. "Here, Your Majesty. See this cave a bit up the hillside? The entrance is thick with cobwebs. Obviously, nothing has gone in there for ages, man or beast. I'll clear them out with my sword, and then Your Majesty may enter with no worries. It's safe!" he declared. Within a few minutes, he had fulfilled his promise. The cobwebs melted before his blade, and Saul went in.

Silence… Stillness… The tension inside the cave increased. David and his men hiding in the cave overheard Saul and the tracker. The cave, which had been miraculously sealed in a few minutes by thousands of small spiders on a mission to conceal David and his men, had been opened by the tracker's sword to provide Saul a private chamber to relieve himself. They dared not move a muscle.

"Your Majesty," David's warriors whispered, "this is your opportunity to kill Saul. The time has come for you to reign, as God decreed."

"Quiet," hissed David, "God forbid I harm the King of Israel, God's anointed. Quiet!"

Saul went in alone. He was quite fastidious, unwilling to relieve himself around others. The excellent tracker had said the place was safe, and the king trusted him.

David softly approached behind Saul's back, his knife in his mouth, sneaking up like a lion about to pounce on its prey. Inside, the cave was complete quiet; outside, Saul's men desperately looked for the nest of vipers in order to destroy them.

David thought: The Lord has given my foe into my hand. I can end the persecution and pursuit if I want. That's what my men want, to close the book on this so they can go home to their towns, not wander the desert endlessly. One more step and I can go back to Michal. She will be the queen of Israel!

David raised his knife and brought it down soundlessly into the soft material of Saul's cloak. He sliced off the edge, then recoiled in horror. Why had he done that? Why had he cut the king's garment? He slunk back into the dark.

Saul, none the wiser, finished his business and arranged his clothing to leave.

David slowly crept toward the cave entrance to see the retreating backs of Saul's army. Three thousand men, the king at their head, were calling off the chase. The prey could now become the predator, as the pursuers moved on to search elsewhere.

"Your Majesty King Saul!" The call echoed through the desert, and the hills seemed to shake in shock. "Your Majesty King Saul!" It was the cry of a faithful servant to his lord.

Saul and his entire army were stunned into immobility. The unexpected call came from above. Everyone turned toward the sound.

"Your Majesty King Saul!" repeated David, bowing before his master.

Saul was astonished. He could not believe his eyes. At the entrance to the cave he had just left, David stood, his men clustered behind him, bowing.

David spoke in a booming voice, but with the tone of an obedient servant: "*Why do you listen to the words of men who say, 'Look, David intends to harm you?' Behold, this day you have seen with your own eyes that the Lord delivered you into my hand in the cave. I was told to kill you, but I spared you and said, 'I will not lift my hand against my lord, since he is the Lord's anointed.' See, my father, look at the corner of your cloak in my hand. For I cut it off, but I did not kill you. See and know that there is no evil or rebellion in my hands. I have not sinned against you, even though you are hunting me down to take my life. May the Lord judge between you and me, and may the Lord take vengeance on you, but my hand will never be against you. As the old proverb says, 'Wickedness proceeds from the wicked.' But my hand will never be against you. Against whom has the king of Israel come out? Whom are you pursuing? A dead dog? A single flea? May the Lord be our judge and decide between you and me. May He take notice and plead my case and deliver me from your hand.*"

Saul, thunderstruck, disbelieved his ears. He lifted the hem of his cloak to find a strip missing. His eyes filled with tears, saddened by the injustice he had committed, the insane pursuit and the baseless hatred. Saul turned to David in a cracked voice: "*Is that your voice, David, my son?*" Saul burst into tears and declared: "*You are more righteous than I, for you have rewarded me with good, though I have rewarded you with evil. And you have shown this day how well you have dealt with me; for when the Lord delivered me into your hand, you did not kill me. When a man finds his enemy, does he let him go away unharmed? May the Lord reward you with good for what you have done for me this day.*" The sound of Saul's crying was overwhelming. His men were stunned, looking at their king weeping before his alleged foe, deeply regretting his attempts to capture his faithful servant. "*Now I know for sure that you will be king, and that the kingdom of*

Israel will be established in your hands." The king continued in supplication: *"So now, swear to me by the Lord that you will not cut off my descendants or wipe out my name from my father's house."*

Saul growled, sobbing in remorse, recognizing that his life had been in the hands of a man who had every reason to despise him, but gave him his life as a gift. Saul knew he had given in to obsession, a misconception that turned his greatest ally into his worst enemy.

"Father, I never wanted to hurt you or your house. I swear to you, Father, that I will never harm you or your seed. "

David bowed before his king, and Saul returned home.

CHAPTER TWENTY-FOUR

Sunset

It was twilight. The heavens were tinged an ominous blood-red. The sun bowed its head in mourning. Clouds hid it from view, veiled and shrouded like a griever before a loved one's corpse.

The voice of creation was silenced, with the gathering-in of the righteous.

> *A voice is heard in Ramah,*
> *Mourning and great weeping,*

The entire nation of Israel was bereaved, like an orphan howling for his parents.

They were a flock without a shepherd, wandering mutely. Where were they headed? To whom could they turn? Who would lead them?

Screaming…

Sobbing…

Sighing…

Saluting…

In every Israelite town, men, women, and children sat on the ground mourning.

The sun had gone down, its warm glow which had once been cast over the entire land now had vanished, taken to serve its Creator elsewhere.

Void…

Loss…

Samuel the Seer had returned his meritorious soul to its Maker. Samuel the Ramathite, who visited every town in Israel, sharing the people's sorrows, adjudicating their cases, praying on their behalf, was gone.

Great mourning...

Pain...

Regret...

Let the Lord's congregation not be like a flock without a shepherd...

The man who had the ability to pray to God as if he were a wayward son was gone, never to return.

Confusion...

Consternation...

Saul no longer acted as a king; he was not a fit shepherd for Israel.

What would happen?

Who should fill the gap?

Who could step into the shoes of the great man taken far too soon?

Cries of devastation and desolation rose from all sides. Prayer rallies of public supplication were held, as the people tried to compensate for the loss, the void, the lack. Without Samuel the Seer to petition for the people, how would the Israelites survive? He was their precious pearl, sunk forever beneath the waves.

It had not taken long for the news to disperse of Samuel's ascent to heaven. The word spread as quickly as wildfire, scorching the hearts of listeners, leaving them burnt out and ashen.

Gad the Visionary had been the one to come out of Samuel's chamber to somberly break the bitter news, the sorrow and grief flowing from him to all the nation.

But Samuel the Seer had one last gift for his people.

In the morning of that awful day when Gad would break the bitter news, all the elders of Israel had gathered at his house in Ramathaim Zophim.

Samuel had wanted to address the elders before he died; therefore, from all the tribes and towns of Israel, the leaders had gathered there.

"My brethren and comrades, sages of Israel," Samuel had begun feebly, leaning back in his chair, looking older and weaker than all those around him. Samuel the Seer was nearly blinded by his overgrown eyebrows. Still, his fragile body contained a vital soul. "I asked you to come to me, because I no longer have the strength to go out and travel to your towns. I'm sorry that I bothered you all to come to me, instead of making the trip myself."

The elders shifted awkwardly. Was the Master of Israel apologizing for inconveniencing them? Samuel's humility spoke to them, the pleasantness of his demeanor evident on his face.

"Today I am going to return my soul to its Creator. This is my last day to serve you, and I must tell you something before I die."

The people moved restlessly, resisting and rejecting his verdict.

"Hush..." Samuel said, "I did not call you to cry for me and ask for mercy on my behalf. I didn't gather you so you could express gratitude and appreciation." His eyes opened wide, as if he were imbued with a new spirit. Samuel spoke firmly. "I must inform you of the continuation of the people of Israel, the continuation of the Kingdom of Israel." There was silence, tense silence. "After Saul's war with Amalek, God informed me that He was done with Saul as king, that He wanted to replace him. The man chosen by Him is..."

There was a sharp intake of breath by the audience, in anxious anticipation.

"David, son of Jesse."

"David? The rebel? King Saul's son-in-law?" The room was full of disbelief.

"Yes! David, son of Jesse, is the King of Israel. Already anointed with the anointing oil, about a year ago. He is the king, by the Word of God. King David will reign over you after Saul. This is not a subject to question or debate, it's what the Blessed Creator wills. You must accept him as king and treat him with the respect that the King of Israel deserves. King David is a wonderful man, honest and humble, pleasant and God-fearing. He is a war hero with a fierce spirit, a man of truth and peace. I got to know the man, and you are receiving a man fit to wear the crown."

The people looked at each other, and their eyes said it all. Everyone knew that King Saul had already ceased to function as king, and that he should be removed from his position, but David, son of Jesse?!

"Now, my brethren and comrades, I am about to return my soul to its Creator. I hope I did not offend anyone from Israel; if I did, I hereby ask your forgiveness and the forgiveness of all of Israel. I am happy that I was privileged to serve the Chosen Nation and hope that I have done my job faithfully, to be a servant of the Holy People and the Holy King of Kings."

Samuel closed his eyes to proclaim one last time: "*Hear O Israel, the Lord our God, the Lord is one. And you shall love...*" With the word "love," his pure soul returned to his beloved, God.

Heavy mourning reigned throughout the Land of Israel, in every village, town, and city. The people gathered for eulogy and mourning. The faithful shepherd had ascended to Heaven. He left behind an orphaned people, bemoaning its fate. But as was shortly revealed, Samuel the Seer, buried in his hometown of Ramah, had transmitted his last will and testament to the elders of Israel moments before his death — not only his will, but His Will, that of Israel's True King.

David, son of Jesse, would rule over Israel, as God's anointed, after Saul.

CHAPTER TWENTY-FIVE
Nabal the Carmelite

The weather was changing. The nights were now longer than the days. The arid heat of summer was long gone, as the cold began to creep in at the edges, heralding the beginning of the rainy season.

For one group of shepherds, it was time to gather the flock for shearing. As a rule, shearing was an annual springtime event; but this flock faced the clippers twice a year. "When there's less wool on the sheep, the fleece is better," the owner claimed, ignoring the discomfort the lambs would suffer from the chill of the rainy season. The shepherds had become accustomed to the fact that their sheep were shorn even for the winter, and both the shepherds and the owners celebrated the shearing holiday accompanied by dining, drinking, dancing, and debauchery...

In Carmel, the flock was gathered. The shepherds met with their old friends, sharing their experiences across the lonely vistas, rejoicing at their reunion. They numbered in the dozens, their herds about three thousand sheep and about a thousand goats.

Their owner, Nabal the Carmelite, sat at the head of a long, elaborately set table with his shepherds.

The event took place this time just as planned, to the shepherds' surprise. After all, only three days before, the bitter news of Samuel the Seer's passing had arrived. The Nation of Israel was still in a state of mourning and grieving. The shepherds asked their lord if it was not appropriate to postpone the festivities in honor of Samuel's memory.

"Work won't wait! It's been three days since he died. There's nothing we can do; death comes to everyone. Do you want us to abandon our occupation every time the Angel of Death visits? Then we'd never do anything. No, we'll keep to our schedule."

The shepherds knew there was no persuading Nabal. Once he'd decided, he would never back down. Shearing would proceed as planned, lest they be fired or beaten.

Nabal added: "He has sons, and they will observe the week of mourning. He wasn't my father or yours, so we need not continue grieving for him."

The shearing was a two-week affair of feasting and fun. However, despite Nabal's dismissal of the idea, they still could not forget their sorrow. The joy was incomplete.

Meanwhile, Nabal was happy, delighted to watch his flocks come and go. He thought, smirking: David, son of Jesse, will be king, they say. What nonsense! He doesn't deserve the crown. That geezer Samuel must have lost his mind before he lost his life. His regimen of fasting and privation probably drove him mad. King David? Maybe in Moab, but not in Israel.

A week into the shearing festivities, about half of the flock had been stripped of their wool, feeling the relative coolness, after taking away their warm clothing. The rest were waiting to be sheared. The week of mourning for Samuel had ended, leaving the shepherds in a better mood: the festive tone made its mark, imbuing elation and joy.

"My lord," a young shepherd came to Nabal and announced, "a group of warriors from David's army have arrived. They want to meet with you."

"What do they want?" asked Nabal coldly, "Why have they come here?"

"My lord knows that David's soldiers constantly guard us from the thieves and rustlers who abound. They also treat us very well, with great respect. Would my lord please speak to them?" The boy, who admired the warriors and appreciated their decency, looked at his master with pleading eyes.

Nabal reluctantly replied: "Very well, bring the rebels here."

"Peace be upon you, my lord Nabal the Carmelite," the head of David's delegation said. "Our Lord David sends you his best wishes on this festive occasion. May you enjoy long life, and may there be peace for you, your house, and all that is yours."

"Yes, yes, what do you want?" His voice expressed contempt and disgust.

"Our Lord David has sent us to request a small gift from you, for him and for his people. This a season of joy for you, which our lord desires to share for our service."

The young shepherd offered the soldiers drinks as they waited for Nabal's reply, but the wealthy rancher immediately shot to his feet, a frown on his face. "Who does this David think he is? What do I care about the son of Jesse? Many servants defy their masters nowadays! A Moabite? A bastard? An upstart? This rebel has no shame! He revolts against the King of Israel and want me to help him?! A lowborn man who wants to seize the throne from King Saul! I'm not going to give anything to this insurrectionist!" His face reddened: "We work hard all year, and he wants me to give him my sheep and my wine? Get out of here quickly before I show you the back of my hand — or my fist!"

"But my lords..." the young shepherd tried to dissuade his master.

"No ifs, ands or buts! Get these rebels out of here, before I really get angry," Nabal screamed, his body shaking with rage.

David's fierce warriors hadn't expected such a response from Nabal. In disgust, they turned around, returning to David to tell him the words of Nabal the Carmelite.

In the early evening, David listened to his men's report of Nabal's hostility and villainy, which jibed with his reputation for stinginess among his shepherds.

David had already heard about what Samuel the Prophet told the elders of Israel. The whole nation knew that David had been anointed as King of Israel by Samuel. The crown was David's by right, but he would not dishonor Saul by deposing him. David would bide his time, until the day came for him to sit on the throne.

Still, he had begun to think of himself differently. He had found a wife, Ahinoam of Jezreel, while his three nephews Joab, Abishai, and Asahel, the sons of his sister Zeruiah, led his army. Though he had no castle, his royal court was taking shape.

David thought: Nabal the Carmelite knows the truth. He is aware that I am the rightful King of Israel, yet he speaks this way? It's beyond effrontery, beyond ingratitude. My men and I have watched over his flocks and his shepherds all year. In fact, Nabal is a traitor to the kingdom. He commits high treason, and the sentence for that is death. No one may question God's will that I reign. David saw the anger on his men's faces over Nabal's words: "Summon High Priest Abiathar, please."

David, Abiathar, and his senior officers sat down to determine Nabal's fate.

"Your Majesty," said the high priest, "This is high treason. Whoever rebels against the king forfeits his life. Nabal the Carmelite must die. This must not stand!"

The officers nodded. The law was clear. The man had rebelled against the king.

David turned to his men: "Four hundred soldiers will come with me, and two hundred remain to guard the gear. Strap on your swords; we are moving against Nabal."

Four hundred warriors, led by their king, began to march toward Carmel, to defend the new kingship.

"My lady, my lady, please open the door, I have to tell you something."

The door was gently opened by a striking and statuesque woman, famed for her majestic beauty, the desire of every man. Her character was impeccable, diametrically opposed to that of her husband: Abigail, wife of Nabal the Carmelite. Her modesty and tenderness concealed her intelligence, but those who knew her praised her great heart and great mind; she was a true woman of valor.

"What did you want to tell me?" asked Abigail. The boy looked agitated, panting and breathing hard, with sweat drenching his body.

"My lady, Lord David, son of Jesse, sent a delegation to your husband. They requested something from the celebration that your husband was making, so that David's men would have something to eat. Not only did Lord Nabal refuse, but he insulted David most grievously, calling him a rebel, a bastard and a Moabite. He threw out the messengers in disgrace. My lady, you must know: Lord David's men defend us from thieves and rustlers. Whenever they are about, not one lamb or kid goes missing. They guard Nabal's flocks and shepherds, but he denies all they've done for us. Also, we know David was anointed by Samuel the Seer as King of Israel, but Nabal cursed and derided him. This is the end of him and his house!"

Abigail's face was filled with worry. She was well acquainted with her husband's bad temper. She had been crying over her fate ever since she had fallen into the hands of such a vile man, sold off by her father at a young age. Her life had been bitter ever since. Nabal's wickedness, boldness, and stinginess almost overwhelmed her naturally joyful soul. She faced a litany of abuses, finding rest and peace of mind only when her husband wasn't around. Then she spoke to God, her Rock, her Creator, drawing strength from Him to survive. But now Nabal had gone too far, defying the rightful King of Israel!

Abigail's forehead furrowed as her mind worked feverishly: King David will not let this stand; he cannot ignore such an outrage. He will condemn him as a rebel against the king. He may hold us guilty as well, for not resisting Nabal. I must forestall the bloodbath that may result from my husband's reckless actions.

"Quickly run and bring two hundred loaves of bread, two skins of wine, five butchered sheep, five measures of roasted grain, a hundred clusters of raisins, and two hundred cakes of figs. Bring the best of our lads and our donkeys, and we will intercept the King of Israel. Fast! There's no time! Soon it will be dark, and King David won't tarry."

Late at night, a soft wind whistled ominously through the mountains. The chill penetrated deep to the bone, the men shivering as they came down the mountain. Four hundred warriors embarked on their first mission as the army of the King of Israel, declared by Samuel the Seer, to make the rebels against him pay.

Their hearts thundered in their chests. The vile man had degraded their king, disgraced and cursed him. It was time to set things right. Ingratitude toward one fellow is tantamount to ingratitude toward the Creator. Dozens of times, David's men had laid down their lives to save Nabal's flocks and shepherds, but now this humiliation…

"Hurry up, lads! Go ahead of me; it's night already. We have to intercept David and his men," Abigail urged.

Darkness fell over the earth as fear fell over their hearts. "If we don't find them before they get there, it will be a disaster." The sliver of the new moon was concealed, the first night of Rosh Hashanah, a day of judgment. The chill of the night grew, heralding the approaching rains, as their palms froze around the reins. Abigail gripped them tightly, trying to keep her mount. Going down the mountain atop a donkey was frightening and dangerous. The ride, the terrain, and the time were unfamiliar to her.

"Here, there is a large group of people before us. It may be the king and his men," Abigail whispered to the boys in front of her.

"Halt immediately!" came an authoritative voice. "Who goes there, and what is your destination!?" It emerged from the void, surprising Abigail and her lads. David's trackers popped out from the rocks, swords drawn. The panicked boys retreated.

"I am Abigail, wife of Nabal the Carmelite. I bring a gift to the King of Israel, David, son of Jesse." The chill and fear shook her clear voice. "Please don't hurt us. We have no ill intent. We wish to meet the king and seek his pardon and forgiveness for the misunderstanding. We have food and provisions for the king and his army."

The trackers, prepared to fight, were surprised by the answer. The frightened woman's voice touched their hearts, as she spoke truthfully. "Please, my lady, we'll show you the way to the king." One of the trackers walked over to Abigail and grabbed the donkey's reins, leading her safely to a meeting with the king.

David's forces advanced, while the trackers arrived with donkeys and several people. The night was dark, and David could not see the faces of the newcomers. A tracker approached David and whispered something in his ear. David came over.

"Well, what brings you here!?" David demanded in a firm voice.

The woman hurried to dismount. Her nobility and gentleness were evident from her actions. Her enthrallingly beautiful face was visible in the hood covering her head, and her tall body was swathed in modest clothing. Abigail prostrated herself before the King of Israel. By accident, her thigh was exposed, seeming to glow in the dark, like a bonfire in the heart of the valley.

David frowned. He'd heard about Nabal's wife, her reputation flying far and wide like a shooting star in the darkness. A woman of valor held captive by her villainous spouse. Still, he was wary. After all, he had a sister Abigail, and her son Amasa chose to stay with Saul when David had fled — unlike his cousins, the sons of Zeruiah.

Abigail covered herself, embarrassed about exposing a handbreadth of her flesh. "Your Majesty, David, son of Jesse, King of Israel. I am Abigail, wife of Nabal the Carmelite, whose flocks and shepherds my king has guarded. The disrespect shown to the king and the king's men shames me. Your Majesty, please listen to your handmaid and hear me out." She cried in supplication. "Please, Your Majesty, do not pay attention to my husband Nabal. His name means Wretch, and his deeds are wretched. He is worthless and heedless, evil in thought and deed. Please, I was unaware of Your Majesty's delegation. The household of Nabal has done nothing wrong; they couldn't stop him from talking about the king the way he did. Fear and terror grip them even at the sight of his face. They are not to blame, and Your Majesty ought not to harm them. My husband Nabal is not even worth your time to punish him."

David looked at the woman kneeling in front of him. Her eyes begged for mercy, as she risked her life to save her husband and his men. "You have given me good reason to spare you and the household, but what of Nabal himself? He deserves death as a traitor to the kingdom. Whoever rebels against the king forfeits his life." David, amazed by the woman's boldness, continued: "That is the verdict, and that means he is as good as dead. Your reputation has spread far and wide, and you have suffered for many years. An evil and cruel man like Nabal is not worthy of a woman like you. You deserve all the good that an Israelite woman can receive; you deserve a decent man. Since your husband is as good as dead, will you marry me?"

In a moment of embarrassment, Abigail changes the subject of the conversation. Ignoring the unexpected question, she pulled out a small piece of cloth. "Your Majesty is known as a Torah scholar. I have here a spot of blood. Can you tell me if it is the sort which renders one impure or not?"

David was confused by the shift: "That is not for me to say, wife of Nabal the Carmelite. By the Torah, you know you cannot inspect a blood spot at night."

"Your Majesty, even though you have been anointed king over Israel, King Saul is still on the throne. Can two monarchs share a crown? Your title of King of Israel has not yet been realized, so Nabal does not deserve death. Also, just as one does not inspect a blood spot at night, one does not judge a capital case at night."

Abigail's words made an impression. David looked at the woman and was filled with admiration for her. He grinned at her intelligence and learnedness.

"Now, Your Majesty ought to thank God for preventing bloodshed today. Think what would happen if you slew Nabal. People would say that if a vagrant asks a head of a household for charity and the head of a household refuses, the vagrant is entitled to murder him. By the same token, thank God for keeping you from a married woman, as my husband still lives. Now, please take the gift I have brought, from my husband's wealth, and give it to your men. Forgive me, Your Majesty, for my boldness, but I only wish to keep the king from making a mistake. Your Majesty is known to be a righteous man who fights the Lord's battles." Abigail lowered her eyes before David.

David declared gratefully: *"Blessed be the Lord, the God of Israel, who sent you to meet me this day! Blessed is your discernment, and blessed are you, because today you kept me from bloodshed and from avenging myself by my own hand. Otherwise, as surely as the Lord, the God of Israel, lives, who has restrained me from harming you, if you had not come quickly to meet me, then surely no male belonging to Nabal would have been left alive by morning light."*

Abigail, heart full of joy at saving her husband's household, was eager to bless the King of Israel: "May you soon sit on the throne and may all the king's enemies fall before him. May the Lord bond Your Majesty's soul in the bond of life. May the souls of all your enemies be cast away as if by a slingshot. May the house of the King of Israel exist forever and may there be none who challenge your kingship or cloud your rule." For so many years, she had kept her gaze downcast, but now she could look up with confidence, to meet the eyes of the King of Israel. David looked at her and saw a woman with a mighty spirit but humble bearing, mixed with a streak of cunning.

"When the Lord is good to Your Majesty, and the king's foe is no more," Abigail continued, her slightly sly look fixed on his face, "do not forget your handmaid."

Nabal's estate was a site of unchecked debauchery and drunkenness. He and his mates reeked. The air was redolent with wine, beer, and vomit. The men were overfed and satiated by the concluding feast of the shearing holiday, their humanity stripped from them by excess and inebriation. The floors were littered with glass shards and potsherds, and the furniture was upended and splattered with food and drink, some fresh and some regurgitated. Broken glasses and plates in all corners of the house. Nabal, wallowing in his retching wretchedness, leaned against the table, blood-red eyes nearly closed. Snorting, he blurted out: "Did you see what I did to King David of Israel's royal delegation?" Laughter arose from the drunks who were still conscious.

One of the few who could still walk, came with a trayful of food and drink, but he stumbled and dropped the platter, sending more detritus flying everywhere.

Nabal laughed: "Never mind, brother, Abigail the animal will come soon and clean it all up. That will do her good, give her something to do. Otherwise, she just prays and dawdles. Make her..." Nabal passed out abruptly in the bowl of food before him.

By afternoon, the house had been cleared of the drunken guests; order was slowly restored. Abigail feverishly scrubbed at the dirt and filth left behind by Nabal and his friends. She was already used to it; twice a year, the nightmare repeated itself. She knew that if the house was not cleaned and spotless, she would feel the back of her husband's hand or his fist. The sound of his snoring came from the bedroom. The lads had helped her remove the guests and put her drunk husband in bed. Nabal was unaware of what had happened the previous night, and the upheaval was worse than normal. Nabal's feast for the end of the shearing had been enhanced by his glee at humiliating David's men. Abigail kept cleaning, praying he'd stay asleep.

Abruptly she heard a noise from the bed chamber. Stumbling, fumbling, mumbling, until swearing rang out. "Abigail," he shouted, "Come here now, you wretched slattern. What's with all the mess? It's a disaster. Come here right now!"

Abigail went, knowing what awaited her. With hesitant steps, she approached her husband, praying that the nightmare would end. "Yes, my lord," she whispered tentatively. A slap in the face greeted her, slamming her to the floor of the room.

"'Yes, my lord!'" he repeated contemptuously. "What is this chaos? Why isn't the house tidy?"

Abigail looked at Nabal, scared to death and in tears. "I beg your pardon, my lord, I didn't have time..." she whispered as the pain burned in her cheek.

"Didn't have time?!" screamed Nabal, as he followed the slap with a kick. "What were you doing that you didn't have the time to do your wifely duty?"

Abigail looked up at her husband's face, so hateful, so cruel. "I went to save your life!" She pursed her lips. "I don't know why I did it; you don't deserve it! I heard what you had done to King David's men, and I knew he'd never let it stand. So I loaded up donkeys with food and wine and intercepted him. He was on his way here with four hundred men to slaughter you and everyone else." Her loathing and pain pushed her. "What a shame I did that! Had I died, I'd be better off than living with a wretch like you." Nabal's face fell. David's pursuit filled him with fear; Abigail's gift saddened him. "His soldiers would have slain you and all the men of the house. The dogs would have devoured your corpse, and the birds would have scavenged it — assuming some mongrel or bitch would be able to tolerate your flesh!" The abhorrence stored in her heart erupted, the years of anguish and agony loosening her tongue. "What a shame I did that! I never would have, but I felt sorry for the innocents who work here. If I hadn't, I would already be free from the hell of living with a wretch like you."

Nabal, who had been flushed from the aftereffects of his drinking, suddenly looked as pale as lime. He leaned against the wall, his legs no longer bearing the burden of his body. He placed his hand on his heart. Then his cumbersome body collapsed with a thump.

Over the next ten days, Abigail never stopped praying; but her supplication was an unusual one for a wife. All she wanted was for Nabal to never wake up again.

Her wish was granted. Nabal died without regaining consciousness on Yom Kippur. The fear and sorrow were too much for his heart to bear.

The widow rejoiced, relieved.

The mourning period for Nabal was shortened. The Harvest Festival of Sukkot, five days after Yom Kippur, arrived with the full moon, and to Abigail's delight, she was freed of all obligations toward Nabal.

A loud rap on the door drew Abigail's eyes to the window. She recognized some of David's men standing outside. Her heart beating fast and hard, she answered the knock.

Abigail stood in the doorway, before David's men. "How can I help you?" she asked with a calm face that hid her agitation.

Embarrassed, the leader replied: "Lady Abigail, our Lord David shares your sorrow over the death of your husband. He sent us to seek your hand in marriage. King David invites you to take your time to answer, as long as you may need."

Abigail felt all her life's aspirations coming true, her prayers becoming a reality. "He hasn't forgotten me... He wants me as a wife..." The thought of a good husband was, until recently, a dream beyond her reach. Now it was within her grasp.

"I would gladly be his handmaid, to wash his feet and serve him," she replied as she fell to her knees, thanking God, weeping for her good fortune.

"Just a few minutes," she told David's men. "Everything is ready. I'll be back in a moment."

A few minutes later, Abigail and her five maidservants stood in the doorway, all of their clothing and small personal belongings stowed in their luggage.

Two days after her husband's death, she had packed up and prepared her girls for the long-awaited journey to King David of Israel.

CHAPTER TWENTY-SIX
The Water Jug

Night fell in the desert. The winter chill froze the marrow of the bone, as a cruel wind cut across the wilderness, carrying grains of sand. The fierce sandstorms blinded the men, as both moonlight and starlight vanished. The darkness that ensued was absolutely terrifying for all those encompassed by it.

Three thousand young men accompanied King Saul. The standing army was reluctant to chase David and his men any further. It was now common knowledge that David had been anointed king, yet Saul was pursuing him to kill him.

Saul issued a call for men to join the chase, with promises of rich rewards for participation. Three thousand youths and boys set out together with Saul and his army chief Abner, son of Ner, to capture David. All the new recruits were untested in battle, propelled by youthful exuberance. It was literally child's play.

The chill cut right through the young recruits, who tried to burrow into their clothing to sleep through the frosty and fearful night.

Saul and Abner sat in the camp's center. The makeshift brigade encircled them.

"Abner, what do the trackers say? Are there any traces of the son of Jesse and his warriors?" Saul asked his army chief in anger and frustration. "According to the Ziphites, they ought to be nearby. I'm tired of chasing him! He needs to be found; He's starting to annoy me beyond what's tolerable. Look at the confidence he projects. He has two wives now, Abigail of Carmel and Ahinoam of Jezreel. He feels comfortable with his wives and men. He must be caught quickly, before the people rebel against me on his behalf. It is already difficult to gather trained fighters to come and capture him.

If we don't do that, there will be a military coup here, the people will move on to him."

Abner pondered the matter, well aware of what was going on, how the whole army and nation were turning against Saul: If you knew how much the people are against you, you would not have pursued this. The Philistines on all sides murder and massacre, while we chase David and his men in the desert. Looking for him here is like looking for a needle in a haystack."

Abner scratched his beard and picked the grains of sand from his mouth. Aloud he said: "In this wind and dark, the trackers cannot do anything. Wait until morning, then they may find something. I've dismissed them for now, and we should catch up on some sleep too, so we have strength tomorrow."

His thoughts made him restless: The king is a righteous man, but he does strange things that seem to go against Torah law. The pursuit of David is understandable; he rebels against the king. However, Saul gave his daughter Michal, David's wife, to Palti, son of Laish. Palti refused, but Saul forced the marriage on him. So were they truly married? Saul maintained that her wedding to David had been under false pretenses. Is that true? King Saul also threatened Michal's life, forcing David to send her a divorce. Could a man be forced to divorce his wife? Poor Palti is a righteous man. They say he won't consummate the marriage. He lives in a house with her but doesn't touch her.

Abner fell asleep, still absorbed in his thoughts. Throughout the camp, the men curled up in slumber. A profound silence surrounded them, aside from the whistling wind.

Peering through rocky crevices, David observed Saul's camp. His men had seen Saul's forces going through the wilderness for three days, searching for David and his men.

One of David's loyal warriors, a Hittite, observed: "They don't look like military men. It looks like everyone is sleeping there. No one's standing watch."

"The professional soldiers don't want to go chasing anymore. The people are tired of searching for us," answered Abishai.

The sons of Zeruiah, bound to David by blood, were the first in his ranks. Joab was army chief, Abishai his deputy, and fleet-footed

Asahel was captain of the guard. Abishai was a youth full of energy and joie de vivre, a brave and fearless warrior.

David smiled: "I want to go down there with one more fighter. Who'll go down with me to Saul's camp?"

"I shall," Abishai answered quickly, lest the Hittite precede him.

The two descended quietly from the hillside toward the enemy camp. David and Abishai passed like shadows over Saul's sleeping men, approaching the heart of the camp, where Saul and Abner slept.

"Let me go, and I will kill Saul," Abishai whispered. "One blow, and that will put an end to the persecution. The Lord has once again given the enemy into our hands."

"Hush... God forbid we reach out to strike down the King of Israel," David silenced him. "If God wants to put him to death, he is in His hands. We will not harm him. Take his water jug and spear, and we will return to our encampment."

Abishai leaned over to take the spear and the jug of water. All he wanted was to end the persecution at this moment, to strike Saul down; but David had refused him.

The two shadows emerged from the camp and climbed the mountain, away from Saul.

"Abner, son of Ner..." The call shook the valley, overcoming the whistling wind, taunting the sleeping brigade. The boys jumped up in fear; the unexpected voice made their young hearts shiver. The echo floated across the desert and shattered the silence of the night.

Abner roused himself, jumping to his feet with his sword in his hand as if to face his invisible enemy. In the darkness, he saw nothing; the echo seemed to come from all sides.

"Who is it that calls in the middle of the night?! Who would dare to wake the king from his sleep?!" shouted Abner into the darkness, searching for the source of the voice.

"Abner, son of Ner, aren't you ashamed to abandon the King of Israel in this way?! Why don't you protect your master, the king?! What kind of warrior are you?! How dare you sleep and leave the king unguarded?! If one of the people came to kill the king, who would save him?! You are all dead men for sacrificing King Saul's life." David's voice echoed through the desert, enveloping the entire camp. "See, Abner, where is the king's jug of water? Where is his spear, which was placed at his head?"

King Saul shook, though it was unclear if fear or cold made his body tremble. The voice was familiar: the voice of his mortal enemy, the voice of his greatest ally. "Is that your voice, my son David?" Saul demanded of the darkness, which seemed like the mists of a dream.

"Yes, Your Majesty, it is I! Why does the King of Israel pursue his servant? What did I do wrong? What is my offense? And now may Your Majesty King Saul hear the words of his servant. If God incited you against me, I pray that He will accept my prayer and quell your ire. And if it was humans who incited you against me, damned are they before God, for making me flee the borders of Israel to become like an idolator, distant from God's inheritance. Why is the King of Israel chasing a single flea in the mountains to catch it?!"

A torrent of tears shook Saul's voice, streams flowing down his face. He knew his life was forfeited to David. "I have sinned again, David," said Saul, "I will no longer pursue you. I know that you are innocent, and I am the guilty party. Please my son, forgive me for making a great mistake."

"Please, Your Majesty, please send one of the king's boys to take the royal spear from my hand and let the king return to his place. May the Lord, who gave you over into my hand, repay me for declining to harm His anointed. Just as I have valued your life, may the Lord value my life, delivering me from all trouble."

Saul wiped the tears from his face, regretting his choice, regretting his chase. In a matter of minutes, the boy handed him the royal spear. A step from death he had clearly been, had David wanted to strike him down. "My son, may you be blessed for your kindness. I know that whatever you do, you will succeed; you will prevail over all your enemies. Know that I will never be counted among them again."

Saul called out to his army chief: "Come, Abner, gather the army. We are returning home. We will pursue David no longer."

CHAPTER TWENTY-SEVEN

King Achish of Gath

"Your Majesty, David the Israelite seeks an audience with you."

King Achish of Gath sprang up from the sofa on which he'd been lying.

"You're bringing me lunatics again? Are you trying to enrage me?" Achish vividly remembered the previous meeting with the crazy Israelite David they had introduced him to not many months ago — the son-in-law of King Saul of Israel, so he had been told. However, David jumped all over the room and carved on the walls that the king and queen of Gath owed him money. The sight of the shaggy redhead and his spittle-filled beard still haunted him; David's disturbed demeanor reminded Achish of his insane wife and daughter.

The messenger trembled with fear; he knew full well what had happened to those who had brought David in the last time. "Your Majesty, David the Israelite comes this time with his six hundred warriors and two wives. We asked him what he wanted from the king, and he replied that King Saul of Israel is pursuing and harassing him. That is why he left the borders of Israel. David is looking for a place of refuge; he is ready to swear allegiance to you and go fight your wars against Israel. Our spies inside Israel say that Saul is constantly trying to kill David. David is King Saul's greatest enemy."

"Go and bring him here. Woe betide you if you have made a mistake; you will face the appropriate consequences if you are lying." The messenger came out frightened, hoping that what had happened to his comrades would not befall him.

"Peace be upon Your Majesty, Achish son of Maoch, King of Gath." David entered the throne room, which he recalled well. A thin smile alluded to his memories of the last time. David, Joab, and Abishai bowed slightly to the king, who was sitting vigilantly on his throne.

"Peace be upon you, David the Israelite. What brings you here today?" Achish looked at David with great suspicion, steeling himself for the unpredictable. "What do you want now?"

"Your Majesty, first of all, I must ask the king's forgiveness for my behavior during our previous meeting," David said with a smile. "I hope I did not cause the king too much distress." Achish snorted in anger but nodded his head. "This time, Your Majesty, I promise you that everything will be different. My Lord knows that King Saul of Israel has been chasing me for many months, trying to kill me and my men. I have realized that our only chance is to join Your Majesty's forces and wage war against Saul and his people. After all, we both have a common enemy; if we join forces, we will be able to defeat Saul."

Achish thought: Judging from his expression, he seems to be telling the truth. He knows the Israelites better than I; he can easily defeat them.

"Your Majesty is aware," David continued, reading the Philistine's thoughts, "that I know the Israelite people and the terrain very well. I know how they think and plan. Beating them will be child's play for me. It would be my privilege to fight Your Majesty's wars."

Achish straightened up on his throne. A general of Israel fighting the Israelites on his behalf? His most elaborate dream was coming true before his eyes! "Suppose I agree, what would you demand? You won't risk yourself and your men for nothing."

"I request only the most equitable reward: half of our booty. Your Majesty would take half, and my men and I would split the rest. In addition, we need a town to serve as our base of operations. There my men may live with their families. Our customs, Your Majesty, are different from those of Philistia, so we prefer not to reside in Gath or its sister cities. I promise the king that he will not regret this course. My men are very skilled warriors. We despise Saul and seek vengeance against him and all our foes. We, Your Majesty, take no prisoners — just booty for the glory of King Achish!"

The king smiles: "I think we can make a deal. I will give you the city of Ziklag, where you and your people may settle. We'll see how it goes."

"My dear boy David!" Achish rose from his throne, moving his awkward body toward the Israelite, embracing him with the affection of an old friend.

He reflected: I never imagined making such a deal. He's loyal to the last, and cruel in war. Why, he never takes slaves, just plunders beyond measure!

"Peace be upon Your Majesty, I am glad to see the king's face." David returned the hug, but inside his heart was nothing but loathing, hatred mixed with derision.

"What did you bring me today? Where did you fight, comrade?" Greed and hatred for Israel suffused his heart.

"Your Majesty, this week we fought in the northern Negev. There was a very large Israelite settlement there, and we took a lot of booty. The casualties numbered in the thousands. We came to them in the dark of night while everyone was asleep. My soldiers went from house to house, executing and slaughtering everyone, men, women, and children. After making sure that no one was left alive, we collected everything that was in the city in honor of the king. This time we bring you about ten thousand head of sheep and cattle, two thousand donkeys and camels, and a variety of clothing, jewelry, and various vessels. We have brought it all to the palace. I would be honored for Your Majesty to see the bounty that his loyal servant has brought."

Achish and David went out into the courtyard, which was crowded and cacophonous with the vast assemblage of animals and other loot. The king's men walked about, admiring the great spoils.

"David," asked the king, "why don't you also take slaves and slave girls? At least the smallest of them, children aged two or three. There must have been many children there who could have been slaves and slave girls for us."

"Your Majesty!" David replied firmly, "I told the king, when we agreed on the terms of our alliance, that I take no prisoners! If the king regrets it, we can end our relationship. I'll take my people and my property, and I'll go somewhere else."

Afraid of losing David and his men, Achish quickly replied: "No, God forbid. If it's so important to you, then fine. I just thought it was a pity to lose all those slaves."

"A pity, Your Majesty? Not in my eyes! They want to kill me and my people, even our children. Therefore, they and their children ought not to live either!" exclaimed David, anger evident on his face. "They wouldn't show mercy to me and my children. Why should I have compassion upon them?!"

"Well, well, my friend. Do as you please, David," Achish mollified him. "My friend, tell one of your men to slaughter some of the sheep you brought me, cook them, and we will have a great feast in honor of you and your fellow warriors."

In his room, David sat with Joab, Abiathar, and several of the high-ranking warriors. Candlelight shone on their beaming faces with a robust glow.

David was reciting the rollicking rhymes of his latest poem in his pleasant voice:

Achish the lush had a brain of mush
He saw a turncoat at first blush
An Israelite ready to slay his brothers
David he loved above all others.
But Maoch's son for a fool was played
For Philistines fell to David's blade.
Achish's brethren died by the sword.
No prisoner was taken from their horde.
The King of Gath reveled in Philistine loot
While David sang songs and played his flute.

The comrades laughed contentedly. It was a rare pleasure to sit on chairs, around a table, with soft beds waiting, after many months of fleeing from forest to desert.

David and Joab were the masterminds behind their stratagem. The men raided the borders of the Philistines, beating Israel's enemies mercilessly. They never took prisoners, because any survivor would reveal the ruse.

David's army was the only effective resistance against Philistia, though Saul had been true to his word and abandoned his pursuit after David had moved to Gath. Saul's army was disorganized, its morale sapped by the realization that Saul's time was done.

David told his nephew: "Achish requests our presence tomorrow;

he has something to tell us. I think it's about the upcoming Philistine offensive. With the blows we've dealt them, the dukes of Philistia are enraged. They think Saul has been attacking them. Now they are gathering all their forces to invade Israel."

Joab looked straight at David: "It's a general mobilization. They're getting ready for all-out war, on every front, holding nothing back."

"We must not endanger Israel by our actions," Abiathar added.

The faces fell with concern over the fate of the People of Israel. There was silence in the room. Fear of what was coming filled their hearts.

CHAPTER TWENTY-EIGHT
The Necromancer

In the midst of night and darkness, Saul and Abner stood on top of the mountain, overlooking the valley. It had been a quiet place, where almost no human had ever set foot, but now being trampled by the boots of the enemy. The ravine between the Gilboa Mountains looked like the sky scattered with stars due to thousands of fires lit by Philistine soldiers, attesting to the army's size. Hundreds of thousands of soldiers eager to fight Israel filled the valley. Countless horses and chariots were readied for war. The air was heavy. The burning night wind blew, carrying the sweat of the observers.

"We are lost! So many soldiers, we have no chance," Abner whispered. "Our army will be wiped out within a day! We had better surrender before they face us. If we do it now, maybe there's a chance they won't destroy Israel."

Saul looked at the Philistine army in horror, fear flooding his heart, fear for the fate of Israel. "They will not agree to surrender. They want to conquer all of Israel and end our kingdom once and for all."

"Let us ask the prophets! The Urim and Thummim! The dreamers. You need advice on how to act!" said Abner, helplessness sounding in his voice.

Saul shook his head: "I have tried everything. The prophets cannot answer me, the dreamers suddenly do not dream. The Urim and Thummim..." His heart flinched. He thought: After I killed Nob, the city of priests, how can I consult them?

"Maybe we should look for a necromancer, a soothsayer who speaks to the dead?"

"A necromancer?!" cried Saul. "Necromancy is forbidden by the

Torah and carries the death penalty. That's why I ordered you to rid the country of their kind."

"Yes, Your Majesty, I killed them all… almost. There is one left, in Endor. I spared her. She's retired — reformed, you might say; but I think I can convince her. Look, we have no choice. I know it's taboo, but the fate of Israel hangs in the balance. We are the People of the Book, but if we must violate one line of it so that the whole of it not be burned to ashes, is that not worthwhile? We must commit this sin for the greater good: the survival of Israel. We have no alternative. It must be done."

"But why didn't you do as I ordered? Why did you spare her?" Saul asked angrily.

Abner scratched his neck: "Because she is my mother. Your Great Aunt Zephaniah. I could not kill her. After all, she only learned the art to teach the sages about it," he said ashamedly, as if revealing a secret.

Saul rubbed his face, nodding reluctantly, "You never told me… But you are right, there's no choice. We must go at once. How I wish David were still here! At least his nephew Amasa still serves with us. Have him saddle three of the fastest horses, and we will ride to Endor. Let us be off as quickly and quietly as we can…"

A knock on the door roused the old woman, unaccustomed to guests in recent years. She opened the door and welcomed three travelers into her house.

The cottage consisted of a single room, with individual candles illuminating the darkness, as the shadows gathered in the corners of the room. A hot wind blew through the cracks, whistling softly. A weathered wooden table rested on a faded rug which smelled of dust. The old woman sat on the rug. The wrinkles etched on her face like furrows plowed in a field over the course of a long and difficult life. Her guests sat across from her, their faces swathed, and their features concealed.

But Zephaniah would know her son anywhere. "Abner, what brings you here?"

"Mother, we need you to bring up someone for us," Abner whispered. "We'll give you anything you ask for."

"Abner, my son, don't you know that King Saul forbade it, and that he killed all those who defied his words? Do you want them to kill me too? Are you trying to test me? To see if I have repented of my actions. Please son, go somewhere else; I no longer practice such divination, not even to teach. If King Saul hears about it, he will kill me." The woman spoke pleadingly, begging for her life.

"I swear to you by the Lord, God of Israel, that nothing will happen to you because of this. You have nothing to fear from King Saul," the second guest replied.

His confident and honest answer was persuasive. "And whom shall I raise for you?"

"Samuel son of Elkanah," whispered the traveler, a tremor running through him. He hadn't seen Samuel in about two years, when the prophet had rebuked him harshly.

That was all she needed. Zephaniah closed her eyes tightly, her worn hands resting against the table. The wrinkles adorning her face deepened her concentration, her lips murmuring unknown words along with Samuel's name. She began to shake, sweat dripping from her face as it made its way through the grooves of her face, like streaming water flowing through ancient channels. Her closed eyes flew open in horror, bulging from their sockets. The slight tremor became an intense vibration, shaking her entire fragile body. Her murmuring lips opened in astonishment, and a cry sprang from her mouth: "Why did you lie to me? You are my great nephew Saul!"

The men flinched uncontrollably. "Don't worry! What did you see?" asked Saul. His face had been revealed when he recoiled.

"Two great men I see ascending from the ground, standing as all people do. One of them is wearing a robe, but they both look like angels." The necromancer had never seen the dead rise headfirst. She was used to seeing them upside down. She had never heard their voices; that right was reserved for the questioners only, who could listen but not look. From her extensive experience in necromancy, she knew that the dead rising headfirst meant that the petitioner was a king, not a commoner.

Saul realized the first had to be Samuel the Prophet, but who was the second? He bowed to the ground and prostrated himself. Then he heard Samuel's voice, as he recalled it from their last exchange, just as disapproving: "Why do you disturb me?"

Samuel the Seer, Father of Israel, had been summoned from heaven: "Samuel, son of Elkanah, you have been summoned on earth." Samuel had been horrified: "What is my sin? Did I transgress the holy Torah? All my life on earth, I had strictly observed God's commandments precisely, and now I am being summoned? Am I to be retried after my death? Then I need a character witness. Our master Moses, son of Amram, will testify there is nothing he wrote in the holy Torah that I had not fulfilled."

The irate voice pierced Saul's heart. The sweat that washed over his body mingled with the tears streaming from his eyes. He spoke as a shattered man: "I am very sorry, my Lord Samuel, but the Philistines have come to war. The prophets cannot answer my questions, nor do dreamers dream for me anymore. I am afraid and helpless. I didn't know whom to turn to or what to do. God has shunned me, and the fate of the Kingdom of Israel is in danger. That's why I called upon my Lord, Samuel the Seer of Ramah, who crowned me King of Israel, to tell me what I should do."

The irate voice responded: *"Why do you consult me since the Lord has turned away from you and become your enemy? He has done exactly what He spoke through me: The Lord has torn the kingship out of your hand and given it to your neighbor David. Because you did not obey the Lord or carry out His burning anger against Amalek, the Lord has done this to you today. Moreover, the Lord will deliver Israel with you into the hand of the Philistines, and tomorrow you and your sons will be with me. And the Lord will deliver the army of Israel into the hand of the Philistines."*

With his final prophecy thus delivered, Samuel returned to his eternal reward. The sudden absence of his voice knocked Saul over. The chilling and intense message overwhelmed him, his body already having been weakened by more than a day of abstaining from food and drink. The mental and physical exhaustion left him as still as a corpse.

Zephaniah was horrified. "Please, Your Majesty! Look, I followed your command; I fulfilled your wish to speak to Samuel through necromancy. Now, I beg, Your Majesty, please sit on the bed. Eat and drink until your strength is restored, so you may be on your way."

Saul, the only one to have heard the prophecy, wallowed in the earth of the cottage's floor; he mourned for his nation, his sons, and himself. Samuel's words were undeniable. He would not see another night. He had no desire to eat, but the others would not relent, encouraging him to prepare for the coming dawn. Saul finally agreed, and poor Zephaniah insisted on slaughtering her only fattened calf, baked some flatbread, and served her honored guests a feast.

"What did the prophet say?" Abner asked his nephew, whom he'd known since childhood. The expression on Saul's face did not bode well for the next day's battle.

"Nothing special. We must go to war," answered Saul, refusing to sap his fighter's morale. "Let's go, we have a busy day tomorrow."

Amasa went outside to ready their horses. The son of Jether and David's sister Abigail, he had remained loyal to Saul all this time — even when his three cousins, the sons of Zeruiah, had left to join David — but now he wondered what his fate might be.

The men mounted and galloped off, back to the army encampment. The moon shone brightly on the horizon, about to sink below it, making way for the blinding sun.

CHAPTER TWENTY-NINE
The Dukes of Philistia

"You're as crazy as your wife and daughter! You have planted a viper's nest in our midst. When the opportunity presents itself, he will betray us without a second thought. He is an Israelite. He will not fight his own people on our behalf!"

The Philistine war council was stormy, as one of the Dukes of Philistia berated the king of Gath, shouting and waving his hands.

Achish had brought David and his men to the staging grounds, but the other Philistines had blanched at the sight of Israelites in their midst, alerting the dukes.

"You don't know him!" Achish countered. "He is my very devoted servant! He has been with me for four months, fighting my wars against Israel, killing and slaughtering them mercilessly. He wallows in their blood. He hates them so much that he won't even take prisoners. King Saul chased him for years because he rebelled against him. I have no braver and more loyal fighters than David and his men."

The duke was unmoved. Red-faced, his blood boiled. "Achish, you're a madman! David was the one who killed your Goliath two years ago. He is the man who, to marry Saul's daughter, killed two hundred of our warriors. In Israel, they sing, 'Saul struck with his thousands, and David with his ten thousands.' The thousands are your Philistine brothers. It is lunacy to put him in our ranks!" Those present nodded.

"I'm telling you, you're wrong! You don't know the man. You haven't seen the joy of victory over Israel every time he returns from battle; the rapture on his face when he tells how many Israelites he and his men killed in a raid; the delight with which he distributes the spoils he took. If he doesn't go to war with us, that's our loss. You have never seen such warriors in your life," Achish insisted. The thought that David and his men would not be his bodyguards in combat worried him.

However, the five dukes were unanimous: David and his men were unwelcome.

"Why do we need them in this war? We will wipe out the Israelites, no problem. Our army, even without this Israelite and his men, is large and strong enough to defeat Israel within a few days. These faint-hearted Israelites only know how to attack, conquer, and plunder a single city. Against our full army, they have no chance, and they know it. Go to your David and tell him to go home. He must not march with us."

The five dukes had come together like a fist. There was no arguing with them.

"My old friend and companion, please come in," Achish exclaimed as David entered the room. The king hugged his supposed servant fiercely.

"Your Majesty called, so I answered," David assured Achish.

They sat at the table. Achish's face was sorrowful, as he was ashamed to disappoint his devoted warrior. David's face lit up as always, a smile on his graceful face.

"Why is my king distressed? Has something happened?" David asked his master.

Achish sighed. "My dear David, you know that in my eyes, there is none better or truer than you. Since you came to me, I have found no fault in you; you are dearer to me than all my ministers and family. All I want is for you to be by my side in the war, to fight alongside you against our common enemy. Unfortunately, the Dukes of Philistia do not share my view." A tear ran down Achish's cheek.

"But my king..." David tried to say.

"My dear David, there is no choice. The decision was unanimous. You are not welcome in the Philistine ranks. As much as I tried to persuade them, to explain to them how much you hate Israel, and what a loyal person you are, they are unwilling to listen to me. Please, my friend, do not cause me more grief than they caused me. They refuse to allow you and your men to come with us," he murmured apologetically.

David saw his plan going awry, a plan he had hatched with Joab, son of Zeruiah, to betray the Philistine camp from within, to attack the nape of their neck like a lion. He was disappointed.

David tried to persuade Achish: "Your Majesty, how have I failed you, I or my men? Since our arrival, I have fought the king's battles. Now that we have the opportunity to strike the king's enemies with a decisive blow, am I to be sent home like a child?"

"Please, my brother, I really tried to convince them, but under no circumstances will they fight alongside you. They fear that you will strike at our heel like a viper. They don't know you! But there's nothing we can do, my dear brother. In the morning, you and your men must depart for Ziklag. When I return from the war, I will see you again, my dear friend," Achish concluded. He saw the sorrow in his friend's eyes, a twinge in his heart over disappointing his most trusted comrade.

At daybreak, an early breeze was blowing ominously.

David and his men were banished by the Philistine army to return to their city.

The Philistine army began to move toward Shunem, facing Gilboa. Flowing streams of myriads of soldiers going into combat, chanting battle songs.

CHAPTER THIRTY

Abduction

Smoke billowed, visible over the hill, black fumes filling the entire land with soot. The hill's slope hid the horror, but the men began to run with all their might toward their loved ones and homes. Horror gripped the hearts of men who imagined the worst. The thick ash adhered to the fathers and husbands through their tears and sweat. They ran though they wanted to stand still, afraid of the horrific sight that would appear suddenly before their stinging eyes.

The town of Ziklag had been burnt...

The city of David and his men had gone up in flames...

Plumes of smoke rose from all corners of the city, casting a pall over the future. David's warriors who settled in the town with their king had smuggled their wives and children out of Israel, happy to be able to reside with their families in their new home. Now the men were returning, from a war they hadn't even fought. In the distance, a vision of terror appeared. Ziklag was in ruins. Primordial fear flared in the hearts of the soldiers, taking shape, manifesting itself before their tearful eyes.

The fighters reluctantly entered the city of embers. The smoke blinded their eyes, blackening their aching hearts. Damage and demolition prevailed everywhere. Fathers and husbands searched for their loved ones, dreading to find the bodies of their loved ones shredded and scorched, hoping not to find them at all. There was destruction, desolation, and devastation at every turn, but there were no bodies.

The fierce warriors were tender fathers and husbands again, as they slipped down to the scorched ground, sobbing and screaming. They feared the worst, distraught over the fates of their wives, their sons, and their daughters. The weeping and wailing filled the streets.

They prayed and pleaded on behalf of their dearest, rending the heavens with their cries.

One of David's warriors spoke to his comrades: "We must find them quickly. Achish must have sent his men to kidnap our loved ones. The scoundrel must have heard of our plan, so he did not take us to war with him, and as punishment, he sent soldiers to abduct our families. I told you not to trust that foreigner. We told David too."

Resentful voices rose from all sides, as furious faces turned to David, blaming him for the situation. "You are to blame for everything! You volunteered us to aid Achish, and that's why he's seized our families." Voices of rage and disappointment, accusing fingers rising from all sides, condemned David.

David turned to Joab: "Run and get Abiathar." He turned to the rowdy crowd: "My friends and comrades, do not let your spirits fall. Our wives, our sons, and our daughters are still alive, and this is merely a trial from the Hand of God. We mustn't despair or become disheartened. With the Lord's help, we will find all our families whole and healthy. Be strong, my friends, and rely on the aid that God will provide."

Joab arrived with Abiathar. "Please, Lord High Priest, consult the Urim and Thummim. Shall we chase these raiders? Will we defeat them?"

Abiathar focused his mind and the letters of the breastplate lit up. He decoded the message: *"Pursue them, for you will surely overtake them and rescue the captives."*

David and his six hundred warriors took up the chase, heading southwest, where the trackers said the raiders were headed. The sun was merciless, beating down on their heads, while they still had a long way to go, as they knew. After a while, the grumbles returned, a rising tide of bitterness from the soldiers losing heart in the heat. Suddenly, a ribbon of water gleamed: The Besor Stream lay before them. The footprints of the raiders and hoofprints of their animals were unmistakable now.

Joab urged them: "Look alive, men! Cross the stream and keep pace!"

Many of the fighters were flagging. The thought of what they might find bedeviled them. "It's no good. They must have already died. Who knows what they've done to them?" Their voices were aggrieved and despairing.

"Buck up, my brothers," Joab said. "The Urim and Thummim promised us victory!"

"Enough! I won't take another step!" declared a soldier, sitting down in the dirt. A chain reaction resulted, by the end of which two hundred men squatted alongside.

David thought quickly: "We need men to stay here and guard our gear. We cannot drag it through the stream anyway. Anyone who wants may stay; everyone else, go!"

Four hundred continued with David and Joab, to save the families of Ziklag.

The afternoon waned, the day fading fast. The sun was low in the sky, painting all of creation in over-the-top purple, aptly reflecting the warriors' mood, who were beside themselves with worry. Whispering branches dancing in the wind made them more uneasy.

A groan came from somewhere in the bushes, and the trackers ran over. They returned with a prize, a young lad, wounded and ill, who'd been hiding in the brush.

"Please don't hurt me," the boy whispered, fear evident in his voice. "I'm so hungry! For three days, I haven't eaten. Please feed me."

The lad was not an Israelite, but the men pitied him. They gave him food and water and bound his wounds, healing his starving soul — a show of compassion totally unfamiliar to him. The boy stumbled after the men as they led him to David.

David looked at the boy, whose body was bruised and broken. "Who are you? And what are you doing here?" he asked gently.

The boy was confused. The tone of the fighters' voices was in stark contrast to their fierce appearance. "I am from Egypt, but I was captured by the Amalekites, who raided the Negev of the Cherethites, the territory of Judah, and the Negev of Caleb, burning down Ziklag. When my master saw that I had fallen ill and could not walk quickly, he beat me vigorously, leaving me there to die without food or drink."

"So it was not Philistines, it was Amalekites. Can you tell us about them? Their guard posts and shifts?" asked David.

"Yes, my lord, I know the camp and the ways of the Amalekites," the boy replied.

"Will you take us down there and show us the way?"

The lad's eyes sparkled. The prospect of revenge on his Amalekite master buoyed his spirits: "Yes, if my lord will swear not to kill me, nor hand me back to my master."

"Of course," David replied, swearing to the lad.

The silence in the valley was shattered by the sounds of singing and dancing in the Amalekite camp, feasting, and revelry. Drunkenness and debauchery enveloped them, due to the great spoils taken during the war. The night covered the valley, hiding David and his slowly approaching warriors seeking the return of their loved ones.

Crawling quietly...

Stopping...

Observing...

It was essential that the Amalekites didn't notice them. The raiders would slaughter all the captives if they perceived that the enemy was coming to attack.

"Joab, take half the men to rescue the captives, while I take the other half to engage the Amalekites." Joab nodded, leading his company toward the prisoners.

The reveling was reaching a climax while the Israelite warriors were sneaking in.

David approached, straightening up only as he was a few yards away from the Amalekites. Then he drew his sword and ran toward the enemy. On the other side of the camp, Joab and his fighters sprang into action to rescue the captives.

The drunken partying was replaced by sounds of war; swords clanged amidst war cries. Screams of fear and terror could be heard from the Amalekites in the camp amidst the onslaught in the dark. It was the latest round in an age-old struggle between Israel and Amalek, and the latter were overwhelmed. The battle raged all night and day, until the next evening. The Amalekite army was defeated and destroyed except for four hundred mounted men who'd managed to flee from David's sword.

Joy surged throughout the camp; this victory was unlike all others. The fighters ran to the freed captives. Each man embraced his son, his daughter, and his wife. David reunited with his wives, Ahinoam of Jezreel and Abigail of Carmel.

Happiness filled the hearts of the Israelites upon realizing that they had been spared casualties: neither combatants nor captives had been lost. The families that thought they'd never see their loved ones again were made whole again.

In addition, the spoils were vast. Thousands of animals, laden with vessels, clothing, silver, and gold, were led by David's people back to their base in Ziklag.

The fighters reached the Besor Stream, where they found the two hundred who had remained with the gear. As the herds and flocks were being driven through the water, the noncombatant company approached David and his fighting men.

"Peace be upon you, my brothers and my comrades," David greeted them cordially. The joy on his face testified to their victory and the rescue of their prisoners.

"Peace be upon you, Your Majesty King David," the rearguard replied, apprehension evident in their faces. How would their comrades, who were fresh from the battlefield, react?

"Peace be upon us? You have no shame," came a mocking voice from one of the fighters. "You betray your comrades, then speak of peace? Easy for you to say, camped out on a stream that's miles from the fighting!"

"Just take your wives and children and get out of here," another fighter snarled.

"Even that is more than they deserve!" a third objected. "We rescued your wives and children, so show your gratitude by taking them and nothing else! You have no share in the property we recovered or the loot we pillaged!"

David listened to the argument; he had anticipated the tension between those who went into battle and those who'd remained behind. "Don't fight, don't fight, there's enough for everyone. Those who went into battle and those who remained to guard the gear will share equally. The rearguard has a role too. We will divide the spoils equally."

This was met with astonishment: "We risked our lives to save their wives and children, and these cowards get a piece too?!"

"Yes, my friend!" David declared. "Had we won the war ourselves, you might have a point that they deserve no share of the spoils, but we have all seen the manifest miracles that took place in battle. We suffered not one casualty. It is God who fights for us, so victory does not belong to us, but to Him. Therefore, all the men will split the booty equally, combatants and noncombatants alike."

David shut his eyes to muse: "All wars are God's. Man does nothing in the world. The Lord does it all, so from this day forward, any spoils taken will be divided equally between those who sally forth and those who guard the base." David opened his eyes and saw the looks of approval from all his men.

David and his men returned to the smoldering Ziklag and rebuilt it. David took a large part of the spoils and sent gifts throughout the Land of Israel to all those who had helped him escape from Saul time after time.

CHAPTER THIRTY-ONE
The Final Battle

In the evening, the crimson sun was setting, painting the sky like a blood-soaked cloak. On a small hill amid the mountains of Gilboa, three men stood, fighting fiercely against the flowing streams of humanity. The three sons of King Saul fired arrow after arrow at the ascending hordes, climbing over corpses whose blood had already saturated the earth. The three brothers were unwilling to surrender, defending their homeland with their bodies, sacrificing their lives for the people of Israel. Jonathan, Abinadab, and Malchishua were the last men standing in a battle lost from the start. Most of their soldiers lay dead around them, heroes struck down in battle. A tiny fraction had managed to escape death, their retreat led by Abner and Amasa.

"Strength and courage, my brothers!" Jonathan shouted. "For the People of Israel!" he screamed, stretching his bowstring taut yet again, to fell as many of the advancing enemy as he could. A faint moan behind Jonathan let him know Abinadab had been felled by a Philistine archer. Tears flooded Jonathan's eyes: "For you, my dear brother," he called out in a broken voice, his bow twanging as he released shot after shot. He hoped for help, but he knew it would not be coming.

An instant later, Malchishua fell at his feet, a spear piercing his body as he murmured: "For your sake, living God." Jonathan stood alone, his end near. The stream of warriors was approaching, and his quiver was empty. Jonathan drew his sword, charging his enemies. Swords clanged, as Jonathan slew one opponent after another, but his body was weary and failing: "*Hear, O Israel, the Lord our God, the Lord is one*," he yelled defiantly as he faced his foes. Then a blade ran through him. Jonathan swooned, falling on his back, a smile of acceptance and contentment on his face. "Heavenly Father, I'm coming to you..." he murmured, as his soul took flight.

"Draw your sword and kill me!" came the king's command. Saul and his arms-bearer stood at the entrance to a cave, watching his sons' final battle. He wept and sobbed and wailed, but his arms-bearer refused to touch the King of Israel.

"Don't you see? They're coming! Within minutes, they'll come here and abuse me. They won't let me die quickly. Their hatred of me is too great for them to kill me right away. They'll torture me little by little, until I die, and they'll make sport of me." Saul begged the lad: "Please help me die with dignity."

"My lord, it is better that we fight than take our own lives. If we commit suicide, we have no part in the afterlife. At least let us have that." His voice broke in fear.

Saul replied: "No, my son, this situation is not considered suicide, for we are dead already. In a few minutes, we will be apprehended and tortured; we are allowed to commit suicide in such a situation. Please draw your sword and strike me."

"I cannot, my Lord, I cannot reach out my hand to strike down the King of Israel, the Lord's anointed." The boy cried. He knew that his master's words were right, but his heart would not let him kill his master.

Philistine soldiers were approaching. There was nowhere to run, nothing to try to fight. Saul remembered what he had been told the previous night. "Samuel the Prophet, I and my sons are coming to you," whispered Saul, as he drew his sword and fell on it. The boy looked at his master and found it hard to believe his eyes; he followed his master's example and set his soul free.

The bitter news of the death of Saul and his sons spread rapidly, like wildfire consuming everything in its path, singeing every heart. People from all over Israel fled to caves and caverns, looking for refuge for themselves and their families. The spirit of the warriors was broken when they heard of the death of their king and his sons.

Warriors abandon the battlefield, hoping to save themselves. The Philistines found the empty cities quite welcoming, rejoicing at the great spoils that had fallen to them. The People of Israel scattered everywhere, like a flock that had lost its shepherd.

"We must not stand idly by," cried one of Jabesh Gilead's elders, beating his fist on the table in front of him. "King Saul saved us from the hands of Nahash of Ammon when he wanted to pluck out our eyes and turn us into slaves. But two-and-a-half years have passed since then, and we have already forgotten the favor he did us. Don't we know what gratitude is?!" The rage appeared in his eyes: "King Saul of Israel and his sons are lying in disgrace, their heads severed and their bodies hanging on the walls of Bethshan, and we stand idly by?!"

The people nodded their bowed heads. It touched their hearts that the king who ended their own humiliation was being disgraced in such a manner. "What does my lord suggest we do?" asked a person in the crowd.

"We will gather all the men of war, and we will bring the bodies of the King of Israel and his sons back for burial, even if it costs our lives," the elder concluded firmly.

The call went out, and Jabesh Gilead's bravest warriors set out to end the outrageous violation of their deliverer. All night they marched silently, until they reached the walls of Bethshan. The Philistine warriors, drunk with victory, did not notice as the corpses were taken down.

Once the warriors of Jabesh Gilead had retrieved the monarch and his heirs, the putrefying flesh was burnt.

Finally, the bones of Saul and his sons were buried in Jabesh Gilead. The place where his sun had first risen was where it last set.

Jabesh Gilead held a week of fasting, mourning, and eulogies for the martyred King of Israel and his three sons.

CHAPTER THIRTY-TWO

The Dirge

At sunrise, a cool breeze was blowing, raising dust and soot. In Ziklag, the people were sifting through the ruins to clear the rubble and begin rebuilding. Only three days had passed since the fighters returned with their families liberated from the hands of the Amalekites. While they were relieved, they also grieved with the report from the Gilboa battlefield, the utter decimation of Saul's forces. The messenger from Achish to David who told of the magnitude of the Philistine victory was quite unwelcome.

David sat in his ash-filled room and prayed for Israel's peace and salvation. Tears rolled down his cheeks, a feeling of bitterness suffusing him with trepidation of what the next message might contain. People moved about slowly. The atmosphere weighed on their aching hearts as they worried about their brethren in distress.

"David, a refugee from Gilboa has arrived — his garments torn, and dirt on his head. He claims to have a message for you. He looks to me like the son of Doeg the Edomite." Joab looked at his uncle's face, sorrow and pain etched on his own.

David rose from the earth, tired from weeping and fasting, soul broken and tormented by the gloom prevailing within him. He struggled to put on an expression of calm and optimism. "I hope he brings good news," he said with a forced smile.

David approached the lad, whose face was tense, trying to gauge the reaction...

"Who are you, and where do you come from?" David asked the boy, his gaze hard.

The lad fell on his face and bowed to David. "I am the son of a convert, and I come from the battlefield of Gilboa. When the combat intensified, I fled, like the others, in an attempt to save my life. The fighting was awful; people were running in every direction, and the dead were innumerable." The boy looked directly at David as if he had good news: "I saw King Saul and Prince Jonathan fall," he said with a half-smile.

David felt his heart being torn apart. The King of Israel?! The Lord's anointed had been killed?! The crown prince had fallen in battle? David held back his tears and turned to the boy: "How do you know that King Saul and his son Jonathan died?"

The lad hesitated, his fears growing. On the one hand, Jonathan was known to be David's best friend; on the other hand, Saul was David's bitterest enemy. "I was on Mount Gilboa and saw King Saul fall on his sword. The king, wounded, asked who I was. I told him I was an Amalekite convert. Saul asked me to kill him, because the Philistine enemy was approaching, and he did not want to fall into their hands alive. I knew he wouldn't live long, so I took my sword and killed him. I also took his crown, jewels, and phylacteries and have brought them to my lord."

Hearing the bitter news, David tore his garment as if he were in mourning for his own father and brothers. His heart broken, David fell to the ground, weeping and lamenting King Saul, Prince Jonathan and the Israelites killed in action. David's people also mourned, eulogized, and fasted until evening. All the fighters wept over the devastation God had wrought. David bemoaned the beloved king and his best friend.

Then David took up this lament for Saul and his son Jonathan, and he ordered that the sons of Judah be taught the Song of the Bow. It is written in the Book of the Upright.

"Your glory, O Israel, lies slain on your heights.
How the mighty have fallen!
Tell it not in Gath;
Proclaim it not in the streets of Ashkelon,
Lest the daughters of the Philistines rejoice,
And the daughters of the uncircumcised exult.
O mountains of Gilboa,

May you have no dew or rain,
No fields yielding offerings of grain.
For there the shield of the mighty was defiled,
The shield of Saul, no longer anointed with oil.
From the blood of the slain,
From the fat of the mighty,
The bow of Jonathan did not retreat,
And the sword of Saul did not return empty.
Saul and Jonathan, beloved and delightful in life,
Were not divided in death.
They were swifter than eagles,
They were stronger than lions.
O daughters of Israel,
Weep for Saul,
Who clothed you in scarlet and luxury,
Who decked your garments with ornaments of gold.
How the mighty have fallen in the thick of battle!
Jonathan lies slain on your heights.
I grieve for you, Jonathan, my brother.
You were delightful to me;
Your love to me was extraordinary,
Surpassing the love of women.
How the mighty have fallen
And the weapons of war have perished!"

When evening fell, the sky took on a black hu d got up from the ground: "Bring the messenger boy to me," he commanded.

The lad approached David, confused. He thought: Why isn't he happy? Why does he mourn for his enemy?

David looked at the boy, thinking: This boy is evil as his father. His heart is cruel and dark, telling of the death of the King of Israel, as a man who rejoices in idleness. He takes pride in killing the Lord's anointed. We must not let such a thing pass in silence. He has sealed his fate by claiming credit for killing the King of Israel.

The boy looked at David. No satisfaction, no joy over the death of his nemesis.

"Whose son are you? What nation are you from?" asked David stiffly.

"I am the son of Doeg the Edomite. Our family is of Amalekite origin but came to join the People of Israel. My grandfather and father converted, and I was born after my father had already completed the process," the boy replied.

"If so, you should have known that it is forbidden to shed blood. Even the simplest Israelite knows that murder is prohibited, but you committed regicide! Even were you not an Israelite, you would still be forbidden to kill! Nevertheless, you did not hesitate to reach out and put the King of Israel to death. For this, you are condemned to die," David ruled. "Joab, draw your sword and execute he who dared kill the King of Israel."

Joab drew his sword and carried out the king's orders, killing the boy.

The week of mourning had passed, but David still wallowed in the dirt. Abigail was sitting next to her husband and trying to improve his mood. David sighed, his face drooping. Despair clouded his mind, and tears still welled up in his eyes.

"My Lord David," Abigail turns to her husband, "please, tell me why you are so sad? For a close relative, one cries for three days and mourns for seven, but you still weep after ten days for Jonathan. Why do you decline solace? Even for a parent, it would be excessive."

David looked at his wife, thinking: She is a wise woman, but she could never understand. "I don't know if I can explain it to you, my dear wife, but I will try. You know that a person has many spiritual powers, and the main one is the power of love. The power of love is also made up of several different forces. There is a power of love that a person bears for his fellow man because it benefits him. There is a power of love that a person bears for his fellow man because he has given his friend all the best. Even a son's love for his father is such a kind of love. There is love between husband and wife, a bond of love created by mutual giving. All these forces of love depend on something; that is, love is fostered because of certain situations between people, and in some cases, this love ends. However, there is love that does not depend on anything, that of a man for his son. This love is a love that will not change under any circumstances; a father loves his son regardless of their relationship. Even if the son condemns the father, it does not stop the father's love for his son. But this love is a one-way street; the son does not usually love his father that way. There is also a kind of love similar to the love of father and son: the love of a master for a student. Here, too, this love is almost always a one-way street. So far, do you understand?"

He looked at her to see if she was following, and Abigail nodded encouragingly.

David continues: "But there is a reciprocal love, similar to the love of father and son, and it is true camaraderie. A comrade who has one of three elements of love: friend, master, or student. These three elements are usually filled by three different people. The first is the friend with whom you can talk about anything a person is going through. The second is the teacher, with whom you can consult and learn everything you need. And the third is the student, who is advised, instructed, and taught. Sometimes you're lucky, and these three elements are concentrated in one person: who is the friend, the teacher and the student. Such a person was Jonathan, son of Saul. A man who was for me a friend, a master, and a student; what's more, he saved me from certain death dozens of times, and I him. It's not an ordinary love. I don't know if you can understand it, but that's the best I can explain it."

David looked at Abigail's face and knew she would never understand. A slight smile rose to his lips from an old memory. "Once, I told Jonathan that it was clear to me why he loved me more than I loved him. I said it was because of the love of our matriarchs, Rachel and Leah. He didn't understand at first, so I explained to him that he was from the tribe of Benjamin, and the mother of the tribe of Benjamin was Rachel; whereas I am from the tribe of Judah, and Leah was the mother of my tribe. And it is known that Rachel's love for Leah was greater than Leah's love for Rachel, for Rachel was willing to give up the right to be Jacob's wife, if only so that her sister Leah would not be ashamed. So he, Jonathan, was willing to give up the throne for me. It is the way of the world that one who reaches greatness wants beloved ones to be prestigious as well; but for a person to give up power so that his cherished ones may rise rather than he — that is a most uncommon phenomenon."

Abigail looked at her husband, understanding and not understanding. "Please, my husband David, I may not fully comprehend this, but you must recover and resume your role. You can't mourn for your friend Jonathan any longer. Unfortunately, King Saul has been killed, and the People of Israel have no leader. You were anointed to succeed Saul. You could put off ascending to the throne for so long, but now the eyes of Israel are upon you. You must unite and gather the scattered people; you must mobilize the forces; you must return to your people and seize the reins to guide them. Only you are capable of doing this job, and the mission doesn't belong to anyone else. As you know, my dear husband, you cannot lead the nation in despair."

David looked into her bright eyes: "As usual, my wise wife is right," he said, bringing a smile to his face.

"Guard!" David exclaimed. The door opened: "Please summon Lord Commander, Joab and the High Priest, Abiathar."

CHAPTER THIRTY-THREE
The Kingdom of Hebron

Amid the shadows of the afternoon, David huddled in his room with Abiathar and Joab. He sat at the head of the table, his army chief and high priest before him. The two of them looked at him, grinning with relief. After ten days of solitude, David summoned them — ten days of pondering and thinking, ten days of isolation, ten days of eating only bread and drinking only water. David's face, clouded by the great mourning which he had wallowed in, now brightened at real food and drink.

"Joab, what can you tell me?" asked David.

"Your Majesty King David," Joab said, a smile forming on his face at finally using the title. "First of all, I am happy to see the king's face again and pray for his well-being; unfortunately, I cannot bring good news today. The situation on Israel's borders is terrible. The Philistines captured almost all the cities and dominate Israel. The people scattered everywhere, hiding in the mountains and beyond the Jordan. The battle was awful, perhaps the worst we've ever seen. Saul and his three sons fell, along with tens of thousands of soldiers, and many women and children."

David wiped away a tear: "What is the mood in our camp and among Israel?"

"In our camp, people say it's time for us to go home again, to go north. Saul is dead, and you have to seize the throne. In Israel, the situation is quite similar: the people have no leader now. They're confused, divided, and frightened. You know that you remain greatly admired among a very large part of the people since the battle with Goliath. A lot of people expect you to take the kingdom in your hands, especially since Samuel the Prophet announced that he anointed you king," Joab replied.

David pondered for a moment: "Is there anyone left in King Saul's family who wishes to assume the crown?" he asked.

Joab cleared his throat: "There remains Ishbosheth, last son of King Saul, whom Abner, son of Ner, wishes to compel to rule. You know Ishbosheth; he does not seek the crown. He wouldn't even go out to war with his father, as he is but a scholar. Abner wants him anyway, so a Benjamite will sit on the throne. It is Abner who seeks to keep the Clan of Matri as the royal family, despite Ishbosheth's wishes."

"Then perhaps going north to assume the throne is a mistake? If I return, it could cause a civil war, which none of us wants," he mused aloud.

Joab replied firmly: "Your Majesty, forgive me, but this is no time for humility! Ishbosheth is not capable of being king, even with Abner by his side. Abner himself does not deserve to be king. Your Majesty has accepted the role of being King of Israel and cannot renounce it. We must head north no matter what. Our people are not willing to continue living like this far from their homes. The people are devoted to you; they gave their lives for your kingship! Now they expect to return to their land with you at their head. You can't betray them just out of fear that something may happen. We must return to our homeland. Let my king consult the Urim and Thummim and see what the Lord's word may be," Joab concluded emphatically.

Abiathar's expression showed his agreement. "My lord high priest, please consult the Urim and Thummim. Shall I go up to one of the cities of Judah?"

Abiathar focused his mind to ask the question, and the letters of the breastplate began to glow. "G-O U-P."

"Where shall I go?" asked David.

"T-O H-E-B-R-O-N."

David did not delay; the fact that Ziklag was still in ruins meant that his people were eager to decamp as well.

They arrived at the outskirts of Hebron, the final resting place of the patriarchs Abraham, Isaac, and Jacob, in the evening. Hebron was the capital of the tribe of Judah, a dozen miles down the road from Bethlehem, David's birthplace.

A delegation of city dignitaries set out to welcome the visitors, followed by the common citizens. The Philistines, who ruled the land with an iron fist, were relentless. Taxes, tributes, and tithes weighed heavily on the survivors of the last war. Philistine troops suppressed any possibility of rebellion or disturbance.

"Your Majesty David, King of Israel," said the head of the delegation, "Welcome to our city of Hebron. Unfortunately, we cannot receive Your Majesty with the honor that the King of Israel deserves. The dukes of Philistia control the city and slaughter anyone they see as disturbing the peace. That is why we greet you here, outside the city, to speak freely of what goes on within its walls. Hundreds of Philistine fighters roam the city, oppressing the residents. There is nothing in the city but a few hundred residents, most of us old and exhausted, with the young people still hiding in the mountains and beyond the Jordan. The Philistines keep us around to serve their needs. We have come to you to tell you that it is not advisable to enter the city. The situation is far too dangerous," the man concluded in a crippled voice.

David could see that the years and the tears had left their mark on the elder's careworn face, though the fierceness of his glorious past was still recognizable. "Don't worry, my dear man, go back to your homes and tell the residents not to leave until morning. My men and I will come to the city and save you."

"But Your Majesty, it's very dangerous. Philistine warriors are everywhere; you must not risk yourselves for us," said the old man.

"My friend, the Lord does not bless us for the sake of me or my men, but for the sake of the People of Israel. I cannot sit by and watch the Chosen Nation trampled by those who rise up against them. A king must unite them and restore to them the glory they deserve. Return to your homes! Tomorrow toward evening, we will speak again, God willing," David concluded.

The delegation returned to its place, and David and his men camped where they stood and began to plan the operation.

Just before dawn, the fighters began to infiltrate the city. Small groups of skilled and daring warriors began to climb the walls. They sprung up from every corner of the city, surprising the complacent sentries. For only a few hours, the combat went on; it was almost one-sided as David's warriors captured the sleeping Philistines. By midday, David's soldiers gathered in the market square, all smiles as the easy victory had been completed without a single casualty. The warriors passed before the king, congratulating him on the conquest of the City of the Patriarchs. All the citizens took the opportunity to greet their savior, who'd rescued them from the Philistines' hands.

"Your Majesty," the elder said, "we residents of Hebron, City of Abraham, Isaac, and Jacob, welcome the King of Israel and his army, with gratitude for liberating us from the Philistine yoke. We residents of the Resting Place of the Patriarchs ask Your Majesty to accept the Crown of Israel in our holy city. We residents of the Town of Four swear fidelity to David, son of Jesse, King of Israel, and accept his sovereignty."

The Hebronites applauded wildly and shouted: "Long live King David."

Three days later, the elders of Judah gathered in Hebron. The atmosphere of joy concealed the fear of a Philistine counterattack. The townspeople and David's warriors gathered again in the market square to receive the Judahite emissaries who had arrived in Hebron, people who'd put their lives on the line to attend the event.

"Your Majesty, we the elders and judges of the Tribe of Judah have come here to swear allegiance to the King of Israel and crown you as our monarch. We know that you have already been anointed by the prophet Samuel, but we want to crown you and accept your rule over the entire tribe of Judah." The Prince of Judah looked at the boldness and tenderness in David's face. He took out a horn. "This is persimmon oil. Samuel the Prophet used the olive anointing oil, but at that time it was all in secret. We will anoint Your Majesty as king once again, this time in public."

David bowed his head, and the prince poured oil on David's head. Applause and cheers of joy rose from the audience. "Your Majesty David, son of Jesse, King of Judah! For now, we, the Tribe of Judah, have accepted your kingship over us. Very soon, the rest of Israel will enjoy that privilege."

The applause grew louder. David raised his hands and a hush fell over the crowd. "My friends, my brethren, my comrades, my tribesmen. I thank you for your loyalty, and I hope that I will be worthy to rule over you. Now there are two kings in Israel, Ishbosheth and myself, and I ask you not to start a quarrel with his people. God forbid that there should be a war between us and the other tribes of Israel. The Lord will crown me over the other tribes as well when He wills it, but civil war is inconceivable. We all have a common enemy, the Philistines, who control most of the country. Them we must fight and attack, not our own people." David sensed the mood in the tribe, and the desire for his kingdom to spread over all Israel was palpable.

"I have heard about what the people of Jabesh Gilead did, laying their lives on the line to retrieve the bones of King Saul and his sons for burial in Israel. I congratulate them for this and express undying gratitude for the kindness they have done regarding our King Saul and his sons. I have sent a delegation to speak to them and ask that they accept me as their king, as you have. For now, they still remain loyal to the Clan of Matri; Ishbosheth is their king."

Some in the crowd resented this, but David stared them down. "Regardless, I praise them. Loyalty is one of the best human virtues. King Saul, son of Kish, saved them at the beginning of his reign over Israel, and these faithful people are not ingrates; they demonstrate their loyalty to Saul and his kingdom. We should not be angry and grumble about it; on the contrary, we must rejoice that the People of Israel are a faithful and grateful nation."

The resentful voices faded, to be replaced by nods of agreement.

"And now, my people, we have work to do. We must rescue our nation from the hands of the Philistines. It is not an easy task, but with God's help, we will succeed."

CHAPTER THIRTY-FOUR
Asahel

For two years after David's sun had begun to rise in Hebron, boys and men flocked to Hebron to recognize his kingship, as the struggle with the House of Saul continued.

Abner, Saul's uncle and army chief, held the dynasty together through sheer determination, aided by Amasa and a few others. Fierce and valiant, Abner was also a Torah scholar. Promoting Ishbosheth tirelessly, he established the new king's capital in Mahanaim, on the east bank of the Jordan, not far from Jabesh Gilead.

Ishbosheth still had his doubts. "Abner, don't you think it would be better if I abdicated in favor of David? I have neither the aptitude nor the desire to wear the crown. I don't know anything about military or political matters. Why assume the burden? The people don't want me as king, and I cannot be the king they deserve."

Abner grumbled: "This again? I told you repeatedly: the throne is your birthright. It's not about personal choice; God Himself made you king when He let your father and brothers die. You are Saul's heir, whether you like it or not." Abner looked at Ishbosheth with irritation and contempt: "True, you do not want to be king; and as a king, you are wanting. So put your faith in me. I will manage your kingdom, and I know my role. You are not a man of war, but I am. Keep doing what you've been doing, and leave the reins of power in my hands."

"But Abner, I hear all the time that more and more people are turning their backs on us and accepting David as their king. He has liberated the cities around Hebron from the Philistines, while we continue to be under their thumb," Ishbosheth objected. "What kind of sovereign am I if my people are under the rule of a foreign power?"

"Stop believing everything you hear! A few cowardly people fled to Hebron to hide under the Bethlehemite's skirts, so what? He freed some hamlets around Hebron from the dukes of Philistia, but that's nothing serious. As for our Philistine overlords, you are right that they still control the territory, but I am biding my time," Abner declared. "You really are no man of war! If you were, you would know that timing is everything: you don't go into battle without properly timed strategies and tactics," Abner chuckled. "Do you doubt me? Let's summon the troops today, and you can lead them into battle tomorrow. Does that idea please you?"

Ishbosheth panicked at the thought. "No, do what you think is right. I'll stay here and study my scrolls. You run the kingdom, and you tell me what to do."

Abner got up and walked out of Ishbosheth's room, contempt evident on his face.

"Lord Commander Abner," said one of Ishbosheth's men, "The Gibeon Pool lies before us. Let us give our men a chance to relax and rejuvenate themselves. They are hot and tired. A rest by the pool, just to wade in with our feet, will restore our strength."

Several hundred fighters were moving from Mahanaim to Gibeon, in an attempt to encourage the people and show them that the House of Saul had endured with its army. However, they were a force afraid to fight, dodging the enemy and avoiding confrontation, lest a battle erupt which would raise the ire of the dukes of Philistia.

"Well, show us the way. Some rest and relaxation wouldn't hurt."

The fighters reached the edge of the pool. Some of them stripped off their clothes, frolicking in the water and enjoying the coolness that stimulated their tired bodies. Others rested by the pool, splashing their feet in the water, savoring the respite.

The pool was very big, the reservoir extending for hundreds of yards. The fighters were all on one side of the pool. Suddenly, they heard a group of men arriving on the other side. Abner jumped to his feet, expecting the worst.

"Lord Joab, we are not far from the Gibeon Pool. Do you think we could let our men rest there for a while? The cool water will wake us up a bit and let our men recover their strength. We can eat our provisions too. The men are weary and hungry."

Joab looked at the officer as he considered the idea. "Send a tracker there to see if the area is clear. I don't want to run into a company of Philistine troops by mistake."

The tracker was dispatched, and he returned soon: "Lord Joab, there are several hundred of Ishbosheth's fighters there, with Abner commanding. They're frolicking by the pool and resting. There are no Philistine fighters in the area, just Abner's men."

"Very well, we can go to the pool, but the men must not engage Abner's people. We are not in a state of war with them, and I have no desire to be."

David's men eagerly went to the pool, reveling in the coolness of the reviving water.

When Abner caught sight of them, he was quickly reassured. He thought: These are no Philistines. These are David's men. Warriors they call themselves, but they're nothing but a group of little boys, playing war games. Joab and his brothers are also here. Joab is a real fighter, but the rest are just small children.

Abner approached Joab: "Peace be upon you, Joab, son of Zeruiah. It's been a long time since we last met. When was that?" he asked, trying to remember. "Shortly after David fled from King Saul. You also deserted and joined the rebel camp, right?"

Joab looked at Abner, sensing the venom in his words. "Yes, after Saul defied the word of God and transgressed His commandments, the Lord made David, son of Jesse, King of Israel. Saul was unwilling to accept this and tried to murder the new monarch. My brothers and I formed the army of the true king of Israel, who received his crown from God. There are those who are not yet ready to accept God's words and are trying to crown an unworthy monarch, just for the sake of power."

Abner looked up at Joab's warriors, ignoring the deliberate sting. "And who are the children you frolic with? A group of boys you took to play?" he asked sarcastically.

"These children, as you call them, are King David's warriors."

"Warriors?" laughed Abner. "Do you call these boys warriors? They are babes in arms, and you've armed them, ha!" he sneered. "For your sake, I hope that the son of Jesse has some full-grown men in his militia too. But you say they're warriors? Then let's have some war games. Put a dozen of your boys against a dozen of my men, and we shall see who emerges victorious!"

Joab nodded, though he didn't like it. David had forbidden fighting with Ishbosheth's men, but Abner's ridicule and contempt angered him. In any case, these were war games, not warfare — mere training maneuvers, a contest of youthful exuberance.

The scene seemed absurd: a dozen hard-bitten veterans from Abner's ranks facing off against twelve of David's youthful fighters.

Abner turned to his men: "Behold, Joab, son of Zeruiah, says that these children are men of war." A smile appeared on his face. "I want you to show them what men of war are. This is no battlefield, and I don't want casualties. I just want Joab to learn his lesson. Don't harm the kids, just subdue them and we'll be on our way."

Joab instructed his boys: "Abner thinks you are children and belittles your heroism; I know what kind of warriors you are. But I implore you: these are our countrymen, not our foes. We must not injure one another. This is a kind of training exercise that we are conducting. Just make Abner's men yield, and he will be forced to acknowledge that King David's fighters are top-notch. Then we'll return to Hebron."

Abner thought: It's a shame Ishbosheth isn't here to see this game. It might change his thinking about our army compared to David's band of boys. It would do him good to see a bit of how our military measures up to David's — whom he wants to hand over the kingdom to! That weakling, that coward really doesn't deserve to be a king.

Abner's warriors, smiles on their faces, began to advance toward Joab's youths. "It's been a long time since we've had a fight," one said to his comrade.

"If not with the Philistines, at least we'll have fun with these boys. I hope they don't run away, poor youngsters," the other replied with a smirk.

"Be careful not to break that one's bones. He's more petite than my daughter!"

The boys approached the men. The youths showed neither terror nor fear; their grins demonstrated that they knew their worth. Young they might be, but they'd fought many battles, defeating their foes.

They were determined to teach a lesson to those who defied their king, to prove David's warriors were made of sterner stuff.

The contest began with wrestling. David's agile warriors showed that they knew martial arts, tossing Abner's veterans to the ground. Their great lightness and dexterity contrasted with Abner's blunt fighting style. His men used more force, to their detriment. David's boys employed technique and skill to subdue without injury.

One of Abner's fighters, humiliated after being thrown to the ground one time too many, drew his sword in frustration and struck the boy in front of him. The boy's eyes widened in disbelief. Screams and yells erupted as the fighters went for their blades.

The war game turned into a bloodbath. Within the space of a few minutes, there were two dozen corpses on the ground. Their surviving companions stopped holding back. David's boys saw Abner's men as legitimate targets, and they were soon slicing through Ishbosheth's forces. Abner and his men began to flee for their lives, frightened by the bloodshed that had erupted, trying desperately to survive.

The once clear pool of water was now stained with the blood of Israelite fighters.

Abner, fleeing the terror of the bloodbath, looked behind him and saw Asahel, son of Zeruiah. Light-footed as a deer in the field, he pursued Ishbosheth's army chief.

"Are you Asahel?" Abner recognized him,

"Yes," Asahel replied with a smile, "that's my name."

Abner, desperate to escape, beseeched him: "Asahel, I beg you, pick another quarry. I don't want to hurt you."

Asahel laughed, quickening his pace, knowing Abner could not get away.

"Turn away from me! Why should I strike you to the ground? How would I ever face your brother Joab afterwards?" cried Abner.

Asahel closed the gap, sword in hand. He sought revenge; wasn't Abner the only one standing between David and the Crown of Israel?

Abner thought: The lad is relentless. He is too swift; in a moment, he'll be upon me, and there's bloodshed in his eyes. Since he is pursuing me with the intent to kill, I am within my rights to use lethal force to stop him!

Asahel thought: One or two steps more and he's in my hands. In a few seconds, my king's adversary will die, and the rightful owner will take the Crown of Israel. Soon—

Asahel fell to the ground, stopped dead by a spear wielded by Abner. The army chief had sharpened both ends, allowing him to impale Asahel with the butt of the weapon.

The chase was over. The point had gone between Asahel's ribs, skewering his heart, and out his back. He collapsed and died without taking another step.

"Asahel..." Joab cried when he found his brother's corpse. Abishai was right behind him. They ran toward the lifeless, crumpled form. His nimble feet would never run another race, his mouth would never again form that mischievous grin. His joy of life had been cut short. His two brothers wept, tears streaming down their cheeks.

"Crying won't help now. We must redeem the blood of our brother. Abner must die. Nothing else will make this right," Abishai told Joab.

The two began chasing Abner, most of their fighters running with them to avenge the blood of their comrade Asahel. The wounded were left behind, guarding the bodies of their fallen brothers in arms, weeping over the loss of their fellow soldiers.

The chase continued for many hours, as Abner and his fighters fled toward the Benjamite border. The sun began to set, painting the sky red. Their legs grew heavy after hours on the run. Here, at the edge of the Gibeon wilderness, Giah Hill was safe Benjamite territory, a vantage point overlooking a nearby stream. Abner stopped and blew his shofar, summoning his tribesmen to his aid.

Joab, Abishai and the handful of fighters still following Abner halted at the bottom of the hill. Atop it gathered thousands of fighters, ready to battle for their army chief.

Abner called aloud from the top of the hill, "*Must the sword devour forever? Do you not realize that this will only end in bitterness? How long before you tell the troops to stop pursuing their brothers?*"

Joab answered the call. He knew that civil war had to be avoided, but he yearned to avenge his brother. "*As surely as God lives, if you had not spoken up, the troops would have continued pursuing their brothers until morning,*" Joab replied. "Why did you even suggest this ludicrous contest? Why did your foolhardy fighter unsheathe his sword and kill one of my boys? This carnage could have been avoided." Joab blew his own shofar: "My brothers, we are returning to our homes. We must not pursue this fight any longer. Enough fratricide!" The people who, together with Joab, had halted, began to turn back to collect those who had fallen in battle.

Nineteen of Joab's fighters had been killed, as well as his brother Asahel.

Three hundred and sixty of Abner's fighters had been slaughtered.

Joab and Abishai carried their brother's body to their father's tomb in Bethlehem.

"Don't worry, brother," Joab whispered to Asahel's body, "the day shall come when I avenge your blood."

CHAPTER THIRTY-FIVE
Palti Son of Laish

"Summon Abner, son of Ner," Ishbosheth commanded. His eyes displayed both anger and fear; he was intimidated by the chief of his army.

A few minutes later, the door was thrown open. Abner, son of Ner, stood in the doorway looking at the King of Israel: "Did you call me?" he asked contemptuously. The most powerful man in the kingdom stared down his monarch.

Ishbosheth looked in awe at Abner, "Yes," he said hesitantly, "I called you." His voice sounded fragmented and weak: "I don't understand how you have taken my father's concubine, Rizpah, daughter of Aiah, as a wife."

Abner looked at Ishbosheth with rising contempt: "What didn't you understand?"

"I mean to say," stammered Ishbosheth nervously, "the law is that no commoner may wed the widow of a king, nor his concubine. So how can you marry Rizpah?"

Abner's disdain and disgust for Ishbosheth were obvious to all. Abner, the fierce warrior who controlled everything that happened in the Kingdom of Israel, scorned the weak and frightened man who sat on the throne. "What are you trying to say?" His venomous voice shocked Ishbosheth. "Why did I take Rizpah? Do you think you're a king and I'm a commoner? What kind of king are you? You sit around the palace all day, oblivious to what your subjects experience. You do not fulfill your role, but you clutch onto your title." Abner was indignant that the weakling had angered him, this pitiful excuse for a king — for a man — whom he was supposed to obey.

Ishbosheth cringed, sinking into his throne as if he could hide from Abner's rage.

"Do you think you're a king? I'll show you! Aren't you ashamed to even ask me such a thing?! It is I who function as king, not you! Do you think I'm some lowly dog you'd throw a bone to? For the past seven years, I have ruled and led men into battle. I manage the kingdom and do all the dirty work. Spoiled brat, you ask me about that!?"

Ishbosheth looked more and more frightened, a tiny fawn facing a lion, trying to shut his eyes in terror of the person standing in front of him. "But Abner..." he pled.

"But nothing! For seven years, I served you as king because of my love for your father, but not anymore. You have proven yourself unworthy! The seven years that you reigned, by my grace, are over. Now I will do what God swore to David. I will make sure to transfer the kingdom, from the House of Saul to the House of David, to establish the Kingdom of Israel as one kingdom, from Dan to Beersheba!" Abner concluded with wrath, walking out on Ishbosheth for good.

That evening, special couriers from Benjamin brought a letter from Abner to David, which he read in his room. It addressed him as "David, son of Jesse, King of Israel," inquiring after his welfare and praising him for his initiative against the Philistines in the greater Hebron area. It went on: "I hereby seek to make a covenant with Israel's rightful sovereign. Your Majesty knows that until now, I have been the de facto ruler of the House of Saul, out of my loyalty to the late king. However, I now see that it is the will of God that Your Majesty succeed him. Therefore, if Your Majesty approves, I would like to make a covenant, pledging my loyalty and committing to use my influence to unite all the tribes of Israel under Your Majesty's rule. I will serve the House of David as loyally as I served King Saul. If Your Majesty approves, send me word with these couriers. Signed, Lord Commander Abner, Chief of the Army of Israel."

David looked at the parchment in amazement. He mused, a thoughtful expression on his face: If Abner comes to our side, the crown of Israel will be mine. I will be able to unite the People of Israel to fight our foes. Abner is an excellent army chief. If I could only reconcile him with Joab, the task of freeing Israel would be simple; but Joab cannot be so easily mollified over Asahel's death. When we spoke of Abner's sentence, he was adamant that Abner deserves the death penalty. I told him that Asahel was a pursuer, which meant Abner was entitled to employ lethal force, but Joab replied that Abner was obligated to injure his pursuer rather than kill him. I suggested that Abner might not have meant to kill, but Joab just laughed. There is no better fighter in Israel than Abner, he told me, and the spear went straight through Asahel's heart. Abner never misses, he insisted; he is a man of war beyond compare, and he knows his craft. For the sake of the kingdom, I must talk to Joab for the sake of the kingdom and the nation, I must convince him to relent, though he feels justified.

David summoned the couriers. "Tell Lord Commander Abner that I am happy to accept him and make an alliance with him, on one condition. My wife Michal, daughter of Saul, is currently living with Palti, son of Laish, though he has not touched her or brought her into his bed. Regardless, Michal is still my wife. King Saul told Palti that our union was invalid, because I never gave her something of value to consecrate her as my wife. Saul said I had wed her in exchange for the wealth I would receive from him. Were that the case, the marriage would be invalid, since I would have given her nothing of value. However, I did present something of value: a hundred Philistine foreskins, which I put my life on the line to get and bring to King Saul. Those have value — one might feed them to a dog. One penny is all it takes to sanctify a woman. So even if Palti had brought Michal into his bed, they would have sinned unwittingly, not intentionally, which means she is still permitted to me. Inform Abner that if he brings my wife to me, I will make a covenant with him," David concluded.

"Your Majesty," a palace guard addressed Ishbosheth, startling him. He had shut himself in his chamber, his face in his hands, his eyes tired, uneasy and anxious. Ever since Abner's departure, there had been an endless parade of petitioners.

"What do you want now?" he asked the man standing in the doorway of his room desperately. "More questions and requests? I told you I don't know what to do. Leave me alone! Do what you think!" Helpless frustration emanated from him.

"Pardon me, Your Majesty, but emissaries from David, son of Jesse, have arrived. They seek an audience."

Ishbosheth stroked his face. He thought: The last thing I need! What does David want from me? He surely wants me to surrender and hand the crown to him. I wish he'd take it away. Then they'd leave me alone. "Tell them to come in," he said.

The delegation entered the dark room where Ishbosheth sat. "Your Majesty," one of the messengers addressed Ishbosheth. "We have been sent to you by our king to deliver this letter to you," said the courier, handing a scroll to Ishbosheth.

It read: "To Ishbosheth, King of Israel, from his servant, David, son of Jesse. I hope this finds you well. I hereby ask that you send my wife, your sister, Michal, daughter of Saul, to me. My wife was mistakenly given by your father, King Saul of Israel, of blessed memory, to Palti bin Laish. Now I am asking you to send me my wife, whom I consecrated with a hundred Philistine foreskins. Best regards, David, son of Jesse."

Ishbosheth looked at the letter in disbelief: "Is that all he asks?! He's not asking me to submit to him? He just wants his wife? He calls me King of Israel and says he's my servant?!" he murmured in a low voice.

His frustration mounted: "Summon my sister, Michal, and Palti, son of Laish. Let them come to me immediately!" he commanded his servants.

"Oh, oh, my dear wife, my beautiful wife, who was never mine!" Palti, son of Laish, cried, voice breaking. "Oh, most beautiful of women, if the world knew the power of my desire to wed you, my longing for you to be mine. If people knew the magnitude of the trial which we have both bravely endured for nine whole years! It was a constant internal struggle I battled for almost a decade. The test of living with you but not being with you is at an end, Michal. Your true husband, David, son of Jesse, King of Israel, wants you back. The fact is that you were always his wife, though we lived together, because we were compelled by your royal father's decree."

Palti and Michal sat in their home, the house where they had lived together for so many years knowing that they were forbidden to each other. The tears flowed freely between them. Knowing that the trial was about to end was gratifying on the one hand, and sad on the other.

"Dearest Palti," Michal replied, "I don't know if there is another person in the world who could withstand the trial as you have. Legally speaking, you were my husband. My father's court declared it so. Nevertheless, you, righteous Palti, refused to accept it. Thanks to you, we avoided a horrific sin — thanks to you, I will be able to return to my husband, David. Don't shed a tear, Palti, we achieved something few people could."

Palti continued to cry: "For this I weep, righteous Michal. This divine command that we fulfilled is about to end. Standing up to any trial in life is hard, but the magnitude of the command is enormous. Until now, we eschewed sin and fulfilled the Word of the Lord at a great cost, but the opportunity is going away. After all, one fulfills a divine command by refusing to violate a prohibition, all the more so when one has the legal justification to rely on."

All night, they sat across from each other and cried — gladness and sadness, grief and joy, pain and relief mixed together.

Early in the morning, David's emissaries arrived to bring his wife home, accompanied by Abner, son of Ner — and Palti, son of Laish, who followed her, weeping over the precious commandment which he would no longer be able to fulfill.

CHAPTER THIRTY-SIX
Abner

All the elders of the tribe of Benjamin were summoned for the general assembly. The streets were usually quiet at this hour, the vendors having gone home, leaving behind the aromas of spices and fruit; but now they were teeming with curious onlookers. It was late afternoon, with the sun leaning to the west, giving way to the stars which would magnificently dot the sky.

"I wonder what Abner wants to tell us," one elder remarked to his fellow.

"It must be a declaration of war against Judah. You know his relationship with David isn't very good; he wants Ishbosheth to rule over all of Israel," his friend replied.

The first elder smirked, "Then you know nothing. Haven't you heard of the row he had with Ishbosheth? Ever since Abner took Rizpah, Saul's concubine, his relationship with Ishbosheth has deteriorated; Abner was furious, yelling at his king."

His fellow was astonished: "What are you saying! Abner shouted at the king?! That cannot be! It is inconceivable for a subject to scream at his sovereign."

"Sovereign? Do you think Ishbosheth is really a ruler? He just keeps the throne warm! He doesn't do anything! Abner leads the kingdom." The elder laughed: "Ishbosheth is as much a king as I am a king."

"Shhh, Abner's coming."

"Dear friends," Abner said, his loud, authoritative voice audible even from a distance, "I have gathered you here to tell you something important."

There was silence, and people waited in anticipation to hear the army chief's words.

"It's no secret that the state of the kingdom is poor," he continued. "The Philistines subdue us with an iron fist. Our countrymen are crushed under the boot of the Philistines, and there is no savior. Ishbosheth has not risen to the occasion, and our situation deteriorates daily: our sons are kidnapped to slave away on Philistine estates, our daughters are seized by thugs to become their property, and innocents are slaughtered wantonly. The young men who can escape live in caves and across the Jordan. To my dismay, we are helpless. We, dear brothers, need a real leader to rectify the situation."

The bowed heads nodded, remembering the family members and friends who had been murdered and kidnapped. Their broken hearts bled anew with the memory

"My dear brothers, this is indeed the situation here, but not throughout the land. In one area, the mood is different," Abner thundered. "Hebron is ruled by David, son of Jesse; the Philistines fear him, and his soldiers stand proudly against our oppressors. David, son of Jesse, was anointed by Samuel the Prophet, by God's command, as King of Israel. Ishbosheth was not." Abner paused to let the crowd express its surprise. "You may ask: Why have I supported Ishbosheth for so long? I admit my error; I had hoped that he would rise to the occasion, but he has failed to earn the crown after seven years. So I have come to the conclusion that the best thing for the Nation of Israel is to unify and recognize David, son of Jesse, as its monarch — king of Israel, anointed by a prophet, at the command of God. He knows how to lead and has proven his fitness; he can lead the army and fight our wars, delivering us from our enemies."

Various chants were heard from the audience, voices for and against, questions and fears. The desire for the tribe of Benjamin to retain the monarchy warred with the realization that Saul's last son was not up to the task.

"Who says the other tribes will agree?"

"Maybe David will take revenge on us for not accepting him as king until now?"

"What will happen to King Ishbosheth?"

"What if David doesn't agree?"

The crowd challenged the idea; the hard-working people wanted change but could not dare to believe it possible. Abner raised his arms, and the masses fell silent.

"My dear brothers, I have already spoken to the other tribes, and they are all eager to crown David over them. I also sent emissaries to David; he assures me that he won't take revenge on or harm anyone for opposing him in the past. If he is willing to welcome me very warmly and cordially, despite my actions against him, he'll surely accept you. King David knows that the Nation of Israel must have one king, and that task was entrusted to him by the prophet. David would never harm Ishbosheth, trust me. You do not know King David; he doesn't have a vengeful bone in his body, and he cares deeply about the welfare of Saul's family. His best friend was Jonathan, and his first love was Michal. He'd never harm their brother, who himself prefers to abdicate. Ishbosheth acknowledges and recognizes that he is unworthy of kingship; he's repulsed by it. If you agree, David will become king over all Israel and save our people. You're the last to give your consent." Abner fell silent, waiting for a response.

Hope glimmered in the people's eyes, the promise of freeing them from the hands of their oppressors and rescuing their loved ones and family members from captivity.

A call came from the crowd: "Come on, Abner, what are you waiting for? Surely we agree; there is no question here at all! Go and tell David that we want him to rule over us. Tell him that he is the sovereign of all Israel. Long live King David!"

Cheers of agreement and applause rose from the entire audience, their broken hearts mended. The desire for freedom and the belief in its potential revived them.

Abner climbed off the platform, joy filling his soul. The process, which began with anger at Ishbosheth, had now become the assumption of responsibility for all Israel — with the realization that David's coronation would pave the path to redemption.

"Your Majesty," the guard turned to David, "Army Chief Abner, son of Ner, has arrived with a delegation of twenty men, and he seeks an audience."

"Please bring them in," he told the guard.

David was beaming. He was familiar with Abner; he knew the

man's virtues and the strength of his heart. They had fought many battles together while David was still serving Saul, and Abner had been his mentor in warcraft, strategy, and tactics.

He had also reunited David with Michal, his first love. David reminisced about the long-awaited meeting, the ecstasy of anticipation. When the messenger had come to tell him that a woman, accompanied by four of Abner's men, had arrived at the city gates, requesting an audience, his heart had skipped a beat. David had run toward the gate, the surprised sentry trailing behind. He had wept for joy when he arrived and saw her for the first time in a decade. His voice was husky as he whispered: "Michal!"

Michal had looked up, meeting the gaze of her youthful champion, the husband she loved so much, the gentle and joyful face that often stared at her, after almost a decade of forced separation. Michal had fallen to her knees, crying. "Your Majesty the King!"

David had leaned down: "Rise, my wife. Come home with me, Queen Michal."

Michal rose to her feet, wiping away the tears from the corners of her eyes.

David mused: Her angelic beauty has not changed over the years, Michal *malachi*, my angel. Her regal countenance has remained the same as the day I had to flee.

David whispered to his wife, "Come, my dear soulmate. Let me take you home."

At home, David and Michal sat together. Michal told David all she'd undergone over the past near decade: her forced marriage to Palti, son of Laish, and the nobility of his soul, the weeping, the pain, the sorrow, the loss, and the mourning. "I knew that in the end, you would return," she told David, "as you promised me the day you fled."

"I'm sorry I couldn't do that before, Eglah." *Eglah* (calf) was David's pet name for her. "From now on, we will never part again," David whispered to Michal.

"Your Majesty, Abner and his men are waiting outside the door. Shall I admit them?" asked the guard, stirring David out of his reverie.

"What? Yes, of course, bring them in," David stood up to greet

Abner, who strode in with his delegation. Abner and his men bowed to the King of Israel.

"Rise, my old friend," David told Abner. "I'm so glad to see your face. Many years have passed since we last met, though no one would know it to look at you. You are still as vigorous as ever." David beamed; the smile on his face revealed the purity of his heart as he talked to Abner.

Abner stood up, observing David's smile. He thought: He hasn't changed. He has the same captivating smile, the same radiant face as when he first played before Saul. As if nothing has happened, as if I haven't tried to kill him as Saul's army chief. "Your Majesty," Abner said ruefully, "First, I must ask the king's forgiveness..."

"You need not do so," David interrupted. "You did what you had to do."

"But Your Majesty—" Abner tried again to apologize, but David held up his hand.

"Enough, Abner, my friend. It is past and passed. What matters is what we decide in the present to do in the future. I'm so glad you came to me, and I want to thank you for sending my wife, Michal, to me." David looked at Abner with gratitude. "Now, my friend, let's sit down and eat something. You must be hungry after not eating all day, I presume. Our meal is ready for us. Come, my friends, we will sit, eat, and talk."

They sat down to a feast, with Abner and David speaking to each other like old friends.

"Your Majesty," Abner said, "in the past month, since I sent the messengers to you, I have traveled through all the borders of Israel and have spoken to the elders and leaders. I have been fortunate enough to persuade all the tribes to accept you as King of Israel. Thank God, there is a consensus. You know the situation at the borders; despair and sorrow envelop the people; however, after speaking with me, they unanimously acknowledge the potential for success under the leadership of the true King of Israel. Once Your Majesty gives the order to summon them, they will eagerly arrive to proclaim your kingship and to swear allegiance to you."

"Well done!" said David. "The people must truly unite; the tribes of Israel must come together. Once we do so, by God's grace, we will be victorious against our enemies. The peace that you and I have achieved is the beginning of Israelite unity; the Kingdom of Israel depends on brotherhood between all the tribes and the desire to unify. You, my friend, have taken a great step toward bringing all our brethren together. Now is the time to gather everyone for my coronation. You, Abner, will be my right-hand man."

"Your Majesty," said Abner happily, "I rise to gather all of Israel to serve the true King of Israel. They shall make a covenant with you, and you shall rule over all that you desire."

Abner stood up to plan his next moves, and David wished him farewell.

CHAPTER THIRTY-SEVEN
Abner and Joab

"Your Majesty!" Joab's eyes flashed with anger, his face furious. "What have you done? Abner came here, and you feasted with him, then sent him on his way? Don't you know what a villain he is? Do you think his agenda is peaceful? Abner is evil! His whole ambition is to reign! He came here to spy on us, to assess our defenses! He is a soldier, not a diplomat! He blinded you with flattery to plan your execution!"

Joab had just returned from a raid on the Philistines — a brilliant victory, with great spoils and no Israelite casualties; but upon his return to Hebron, one of the sentries told him of Abner's visit. Joab's triumph turned into outrage over his brother's killer.

"Calm down, my friend," David said calmly. "I know the man well, even better than you. I also know what brought him here. Many things may be said about Abner, but he is not a traitor. Abner knows that one does not become King of Israel by violence; it is a gift from Heaven. He does not want the throne for himself, and he didn't come here to spy. Abner came to tell me that he has persuaded all the tribes to accept my rule. I know the man's soul; if there is one thing that really matters to him, it is peace in Israel. The man has laid his life on the line countless times for Israel. He knows that Ishbosheth cannot be king, so he convinced the other tribes to accept my rule."

"Are you kidding me?" Joab fumed. "Abner doesn't want to reign? If so, why did he only show up today? If he deems Ishbosheth unfit and the crown as a divine gift, why did he wait seven years to act?" Joab shouted. "Abner is a scoundrel! A vile killer!"

"Joab, you speak out of anger and personal resentment. I understand the personal animosity after Asahel's death," he tried to calm Joab, "but you have to trust your mind over your heart. Don't let fury and petty feelings lead you astray. You know I'm right, that Abner is actually an honest man. Think of the good of all Israelites, not your vengeful instincts. I, too, am saddened by Asahel's death, but think about what we have talked about many times. There is a possibility that Abner did not want to kill Asahel. Think, my dear brother, of the good of Israel and nothing else."

"I know very well what the good of Israel is," Joab said angrily. Joab turned his back on David and stormed out.

David thought: They say it is best to let your fellow's wrath subside before you try to mollify him. I'll talk to Joab later when he cools down.

Abner and his men had said their goodbyes and were on the outskirts of the city. They were eager to spread the word and gather all Israel for David's coronation. The afternoon was growing short, with only a few hours of daylight left. Abner did not want to wait until morning. "Every moment wasted is a shame," he told his men. "We have a very important mission which cannot wait." The delegation turned north.

Suddenly, a sweaty young man ran up to them. "Lord Abner!" he panted.

Abner and his men halted, waiting to hear what he had to say.

The messenger caught his breath, then said: "Lord Commander Abner, the king sent me to ask you to come back to him. He forgot to tell you something very important. It will not take long. Your men can wait here; I'll escort you back afterwards."

Abner told his men: "Wait here for a few minutes. There's no point in your coming with me. Stay here and rest, I'll be back soon." He hurried back with the messenger.

"Peace be upon you, Abner, son of Ner!" At the gate of the city stood Joab, meeting Abner's gaze with his hand outstretched in peace. "You can go," he told the messenger. "I'll show Abner the way to King David." The boy went on his way.

Abner looked at Joab, apprehension in his eyes. He knew Joab's reputation as a fighter. Joab and his vendetta had always constituted the greatest potential obstacle.

Joab saw the fear in his eyes: "How are you, Abner?" he asked with a friendly smile. "It's been a long time since we last saw each other."

"Yes, right," Abner replied, confused by the unexpected meeting. "I owe you an apology," he declared.

Joab nodded slightly, "Yes, that bitter and hasty day! But what can you do? We must go on living. My brother Asahel was young and hot-tempered. He kept chasing you, leaving you no choice. He had the status of a pursuer, and one may use lethal force to stop a pursuer. I should have spoken to him and cooled his hot temper."

"Yes, it's a shame that young people sometimes do stupid things," Abner said amicably to Joab, feeling that the stumbling block had been removed from his way.

"What did King David want?" he asked Joab: "Maybe we should hurry to him; my people are waiting outside the city. Soon night will fall, and we have an important national mission to do … to crown King David over all Israel."

"You're right, you must hurry. However, the truth is that he wanted to ask you about a completely different matter. You studied with Doeg the Edomite for a long time, so he thought you would know the law. I'll ask you and tell him. That way, you'll save precious time," Joab replied.

Abner nodded. "Indeed, Doeg really was a great Torah scholar. He would solve complicated and strange questions very easily and quickly. What's the issue?"

"A childless widow came to our court. Her late husband's brother does not want to perform a levirate marriage, so he needs to release her. However, the ceremony requires her to remove his shoe, and she has no arms. What are we to do for her?"

"His Majesty knows whom to consult," Abner said with a smile. "Indeed, we had just such a situation when Doeg was presiding, and I was on the panel. Doeg thought a little and ruled that she could use her teeth to remove the shoe, and so it was."

"With her teeth?! How would you do that?" asked Joab in wonder.

"What's the problem?" replied Abner, whose love for Torah scholarship was immense. He bent to demonstrate to Joab the maneuver. As Abner leaned down, Joab unsheathed his sword and brought the blade up into Abner's heart.

Abner gasped and died before he knew what was happening.

"This is for you, Asahel, my dear brother," Joab whispered, meeting the gaze of his brother Abishai, the lone witness to the scene.

"Your Majesty," the horrified boy burst into David's room: "Have you heard?"

David, surprised by the outburst, saw the shock on the boy's face: "Heard what?"

"Joab killed Abner, son of Ner," he said in horror.

David jumped up, as if bitten by a snake: "How could that be? Abner left before he returned."

The boy told David the whole tale, who was gripped by shock and surprise. He had been sure he'd be able to quell Joab's rage, and now it was too late. David's grief was unbearable. His appreciation for Abner as a warrior and as a man overshadowed the hostility that prevailed between the two leading lights. David teared up as he whispered: "*I and my kingdom are forever guiltless before the Lord concerning the blood of Abner, son of Ner.* God knows that I had no role in this injustice. I did not want Abner to be hurt. Had I known that Joab would harm Abner, I would have stopped him. And now..." Rage could be heard in David's voice. "*May it whirl over the heads of Joab and the entire house of his father and may the house of Joab never be without one having a discharge or skin disease, or one who leans on a staff or falls by the sword or lacks food.*"

The frightened lad looked at David, whose anger and sadness testified to his good faith and blamelessness. "Now, my boy, it is our duty to give Abner a state funeral with full honors. Get the word out: the funeral will take place in two hours. We must not delay! By royal decree, all shops and businesses must be shuttered immediately. A great man in Israel fell today, and we shall all pay him our final respects."

As the funeral procession set out, all of Hebron was present. King David walked before the body, eulogizing Abner, tears streaming down his face and sorrow choking his throat: "Oh, oh, hearken, my brothers and sisters! The Holy Ark has been seized. A great officer has fallen today in Israel, and all Israel must bemoan the fire the Lord has ignited. Lord Commander Abner, son of Ner, Chief of the Army of Israel, right-hand man of King Saul, Torah scholar, paragon of impeccable virtue, fierce in battle against Israel's foes, has been struck down today. The man who feared no man but only his God has been taken from us; how can you not cry?" He raised his voice: "Tear your garments with me, Israel, and wear sackcloth to eulogize him. The Torah of truth was on his lips, which never uttered falsehood. Now the voice of the Torah has been silenced. Oh, Abner, brave warrior!

Should Abner die
The death of a wretch?
Your hands were not bound,
Your feet were not fettered.
As a man falls before the wicked,
So also you fell."

David's cries were louder than anyone else's as Abner was buried. The grief in his swollen, tear-filled eyes was undeniable. Even after the funeral, David stayed at the gravesite, sitting on the ground as if he had just lost a loved one.

His subjects longed to comfort their bereaved. "Your Majesty," said one, trying to give him a drink, "Please have some water, so you may recover your strength."

David refused: "I swear by the name of the Almighty, may He do the same and worse to me if I drink a drop or eat a morsel! Don't you know that a great officer in Israel was struck down today? By the Lord, I shall not eat or drink until daylight."

Two days later, David still sat in his room, physically and mentally still engulfed in a state of mourning. High Priest Abiathar sat alongside the king, who was lost in thought. "Your Majesty, the people know that it was Joab who killed Abner on his own initiative. However, they still wonder: Why doesn't the king punish him? How has Joab escaped culpability?"

King David was silent, as he pondered the issue deeply. "My dear friend, I have thought about this a lot, and indeed Joab deserves severe punishment. A murderer must be put to death — but the court may do it only if he was warned beforehand and the act was witnessed by two bystanders. Joab wasn't warned; and Abishai, the only witness, cannot testify against his brother. True, I am king, and the crown does not have the limits of a court. Still, after much thought and study of the subject, I have come to the conclusion that it is not the right thing to do." David explained: "You know what the sons of Zeruiah are like; they are very difficult people. If I punish Joab, my army chief, what might Abishai, his deputy, do? The kingdom is still too unstable for me to do such an act and not throw the whole country into crisis. Joab has always resented authority; he leads his fighters as he sees fit. His people are very devoted and loyal to him. If I move against him, he could cause a civil war to break out. The resulting losses would be very heavy, undermining the foundations of the kingdom. Wars with external enemies are difficult enough; we cannot afford internal conflict. It is wrong to take action against him now. God will repay the evildoer for his evil act."

As Joab stood in front of David, feeling his sovereign's animosity, he thought: "My uncle doesn't understand that I did the best thing. David thinks Abner would cast his lot in with us, but he would have been a viper in our midst. He is loyal only to his tribe! Had I not done something, the day would have come when Abner would have turned his sword against David. Now, after the fact, we are seeing positive results.

"Your Majesty," said Joab, "I know you hold the matter of Abner against me, but the king must know that my act bore fruit. From all the tribes of Israel come messengers who announce that the people are with you. I have a census of the fresh recruits.

David looked at Joab with dissatisfaction.

Joab continued, ignoring the king's gaze: "Ishbosheth is left with almost no one, helpless." Joab began to list those who joined David's army.

"From the tribe of Judah, six thousand eight hundred brave warriors, bearing shield and lance.

"From Simeon, seven thousand one hundred brave warriors.

"From Levi, four thousand six hundred. Also, three thousand seven hundred priests arrived with Jehoiada, who was Saul's high priest after Ahimelech had been massacred along with all the Nobites.

His deputy is the young and valiant Zadok, who brought twenty-two officers from his father's house, with their families.

"From Benjamin, Saul's brethren, three thousand who had kept faith with Ishbosheth to this point.

"From Ephraim, twenty thousand eight hundred brave warriors.

"From Manasseh — the western half — eighteen thousand.

"From Issachar, there are two hundred Torah sages known for their scholarship and counsel. They said that the whole tribe is loyal to you, but the sons of Issachar are not warriors. Almost all of them are people who toil in Torah study. The merchants of Zebulun subsidize their livelihood.

"From Zebulun, fifty thousand men, armed and equipped men of war.

"From Naphtali, a thousand officers, along with thirty-seven thousand, bearing sword and lance.

"From Dan, twenty-eight thousand six hundred prepared for battle.

"From Asher, forty thousand fit for service, prepared for battle.

"Also from the other side of the Jordan, from Reuben and Gad and eastern Manasseh, one hundred and twenty thousand men of war."

Joab took in David's astonished look with a smile: "All in all, we already have more than three hundred and thirty thousand soldiers ready to stand at your right hand when you give the order. Israel stands with us, waiting for the day when you dare to take what belongs to you," Joab concluded.

David felt that Joab's desire for war against King Ishbosheth was intense. "Ishbosheth is still before you," David told Joab. "I am not prepared for a civil war to break out. I shall not spill Israelite blood to take the throne. I guess what you say belongs to me doesn't belong to me yet."

CHAPTER THIRTY-EIGHT
Baanah and Rechab

Ishbosheth was enjoying his afternoon nap, overwhelmed by the burdens of the day. The onus of running royal affairs weighed down on the man who had been handed the crown.

The door opened noisily, and Ishbosheth jumped out of bed, frightened: "What happened?" he shouted. "Why are you disturbing my sleep?"

"Excuse me, I am very sorry to disturb Your Majesty," said the terrified messenger, "but I have bitter and difficult news to convey to the king."

"What happened? Tell me!" The stress was audible in his voice.

"Your Majesty, Abner son of Ner is dead. Joab son of Zeruiah, David's army chief, Joab, killed Abner when he went to meet David," he said in horror. "If David ordered that Abner be killed, who went to make a covenant with him, what will he do to us?"

Ishbosheth covered his face with his hands in despair. "This is the end of us!" he whispered, trembling. He hid his face in a pillow, trying to hide for his life.

"Brother, now is our chance to go back to live in Israel. I'm tired of living in Gittaim. We've been living here for years, and what life is that? Our families are in Benjamin while we're here," Baanah, son of Rimmon the Beerothite complained to his brother.

Rechab nodded, "I'm fed up too, but what are we going to do? In Benjamin, we have a death sentence for killing that wheat-seller. That stupid merchant, if he had let us take what we wanted, he would still be alive. But the fool had no honor. Didn't he know that we were officers of King Ishbosheth? He knew very well! But he resisted, so he deserved death and that's what he got. He tried to prevent us from taking what we wanted! He's lucky we didn't kill his whole family! An impudent rebel!"

"He wanted us to pay him for his goods," Baanah added mockingly. "He got paid well enough, with a blade in his heart."

"Yes, Ishbosheth the 'Soft' ordered his servants to bring us to trial," Rechab fumed. "That weakling, how disgraceful to prosecute us for killing some brazen merchant!"

"Now's our chance! David killed Abner, and Ishbosheth is completely helpless. His protector is gone. The officers and men have abandoned him too. He has no defense and is utterly desperate. We must not miss this opportunity," Baanah declared.

The afternoon was quiet in Ishbosheth's palace in Mahanaim. The household staff did their work silently, afraid of waking the king. Despair and sadness were evident in every corner; the sentries were not at their posts. The fear of what was coming cast a dark shadow over the palace. The depressive, oppressive atmosphere encouraged escape into slumber. The world of dreams offered a respite from the ominous reality.

The two men entering the palace went unchallenged by guards or soldiers. The staff asked no questions of the midday callers, as their clothing was that of officers.

At the door to Ishbosheth's bedchamber, loud snoring broke the silence. The two brothers entered the room softly and slowly, barring the door behind them.

"Come, brother, let's deliver this fool from his misery," Baanah whispered.

The blade flashed once, followed by a faint moan of surprise. Rechab and Baanah slipped out of the room, closed the door behind them and left the house with a bundle.

"Your Majesty King David," Rechab said in a solemn voice. He and Baanah had arrived in Hebron and requested an audience. They introduced themselves as officers of King Ishbosheth, wishing to bring gifts to King David. "We have brought Your Majesty a handsome and important gift. We know that the king will value this present more than any treasure. We, Rechab and Baanah, sons of Rimmon the Beerothite, seek to pay him tribute and swear allegiance to him."

David considered the brothers, who seemed suspiciously cheerful. He thought: What do they want to bring me? Usually when Ishbosheth's men defect, they seem apprehensive, unsure if I'll go for revenge or reconciliation. These seem overconfident.

"What did you bring me as a gift, Rechab and Baanah?" he asked.

The men undid the bundle and displayed Ishbosheth's head proudly: "Behold, King David, the head of your nemesis, Ishbosheth. We killed him in his bed! Know that Rechab and Baanah, sons of Rimmon, have secured the throne for you!"

David paled in shock, a reaction the brothers had not expected.

Puzzled, they repeated: "Your Majesty, this is the head of the usurper Ishbosheth! We have come to show you that your enemy is dead. We have taken vengeance on the House of Saul, he who pursued you for years and tried to take your life!"

David's expression became furious; he was enraged at their audacity and outraged at their wickedness, swearing: "*As surely as the Lord lives, Who has redeemed my life from all distress, when someone told me, 'Look, Saul is dead,' and thought he was a bearer of good news, I seized him and put him to death at Ziklag. That was his reward for his news! How much more, when wicked men kill a righteous man in his own house and on his own bed, shall I not now require his blood from your hands and remove you from the earth!*" David's fury was unquenchable.

"Guards," David addressed his men, "kill these evil men who dared to lay their hands on the King of Israel. Cut off the hands that shed innocent blood and the feet which ran to do evil. Hang them by the Hebron Pool. Let all the people know and see what has been done to these wicked people, who have dared to dishonor the Throne of Israel. Take the head of the late King Ishbosheth of Israel and bury it with full honors, alongside the grave of Lord Commander Abner, the chief of his army."

CHAPTER THIRTY-NINE
City of Jebus

Hebron was humming, not with sorrow but with celebration. Trumpets were blown, the sound growing louder and louder. Emissaries from every tribe had arrived in David's capital for his coronation. Thousands of Israel's elders, sages, and judges had arrived to crown David, son of Jesse, as king over all Israel. A festive atmosphere prevailed in the City of the Patriarchs. The streets were crowded with people from all the tribes of Israel wearing their festival finery to honor their new king.

"Your Majesty, the time has come to welcome your subjects," Abiathar said. "The heads of all the tribes are waiting for you."

The king emerged, with Abiathar on his right and Joab on his left. Shouts of joy and jubilation greeted the king and his men, together with cries of delight and excitement. The King of Israel came to the platform, on which stood the twelve tribal princes and the seventy justices of the Supreme Court, waiting to crown him. David and his men ascended.

"Your Majesty," the prince of the tribe of Benjamin began, as a hush fell over the crowd. "*Here we are, your own flesh and blood. Even in times past, while Saul was king over us, you were the one who led Israel out and brought them back. And to you the Lord said, 'You will shepherd My people Israel, and you will be ruler over them.'*"

David looked at the tribal prince with some suspicion: "*If you have come to me in peace to help me, my heart will be united with you; but if you have come to betray me to my enemies when my hands are free of violence, may the God of our fathers see it and judge you.*"

"Your Majesty," the prince replied, "so that you know that in peace and good faith we have come to you, we have brought to you Amasa, son of your sister Abigail, and the rest of your tribe who have found refuge in the battle of our tribe."

Amasa, son of Jether, had been Abner's deputy during the end of Saul's reign and throughout Ishbosheth's. He had been torn between his loyalty to King Saul and his bond to his uncle David. Now he was the last man standing from the fallen kingdom.

Amasa approached his uncle, bowing deeply, declaring:

"We are yours, O David!
We are with you, O son of Jesse!
Peace, peace to you,
And peace to your helpers,
For your God helps you."

David advanced toward his nephew to hug and kiss him. There had been a great deal of love between the two in their youth, a love that was now renewed.

The crowd burst into applause, the sound of divided hearts coming together. "David, son of Jesse, King of Israel, all of Israel's tribes have come to recognize you as our king and to forge a covenant before God. Your Majesty, we have no divisions or disputes anymore. Every Israelite must have the same sovereign. You are the monarch chosen by God, anointed by Samuel His prophet. Let us now crown you over the Kingdom of Israel, all twelve tribes united," Amasa said.

The applause grew louder and louder. The people felt the power of unity.

The High Priest, Abiathar, took out the horn of anointing oil. "Your Majesty, you were anointed by Samuel the Prophet first, then by the prince of the tribe of Judah. Now you are anointed over all Israel, as the Lord has commanded that you lead His people."

David knelt down and Abiathar poured anointing oil on his head.

"Long live King David," Abiathar exclaimed. The voice of the crowd grew louder: "Long live King David! Long live David, King of Israel!"

The divided people united in Hebron, the city of Abraham, Isaac, and Jacob. Their hearts as one, David bowed before God, accepting the crown from the King of Kings.

David, Abiathar, Joab, and the elders of the tribes sat together. The new king announced: "The time has come to conquer the city of Jebus. Even though Hebron is a holy city, I know that the people are unhappy with its being my capital. Hebron is a Judahite city, and I conquered it to become King of Judah alone. The other tribes feel like second-class citizens here. God wills that the capital be elsewhere."

The candlelit conference had a historic feeling. David went on: "While fleeing King Saul, I met with Samuel the Prophet, peace be upon him. He told me that Israel's capital, the site of our temple, must be in Jerusalem. It is the City of Perfect Faith, *yira shelema*: the spot from which the world began to form; where Adam was created from the earth; where our patriarch Abraham bound his son, our patriarch Isaac, to the altar; and where his son, our patriarch Jacob, dreamed of a ladder to heaven. It sits on the border between Benjamin and Judah; neither tribe has yet conquered it from the Jebusites. If all Israel unifies to conquer Jebus, as it is now known, we can make it our unanimous capital."

"Your Majesty," said Abiathar, "What of the oath Abraham swore to King Abimelech that he would not conquer the city? That is why Jebus is not in Israelite hands now!"

"True, but it expired," David replied. "The oath reads: *'Now, therefore, swear to me here by God that you will not deal falsely with me, nor with my son, nor with my son's son.* The last of Abimelech's grandchildren are long gone, so the oath is null and void."

"The city of Jebus is a highly fortified city. I don't know how we can conquer it," Joab mused aloud. "Speaking of Isaac and Jacob, the Jebusites made statues of them: The Blind, because Isaac lost his sight; and The Lame, because Jacob had a limp. They worship them as idols, and on them is written the oath that Abraham swore to Abimelech. They also erected figures of our ancestors at the entrance to the city, holding swords that move tightly in all directions; the swords move wondrously, thanks to the stream running beneath them."

"I know all this," David said firmly, "but Samuel the Prophet ordered it. It is the will of the King of the World that Jerusalem be our capital. We are commanded by the King of the World, and with His help, we will prevail."

"Jebusites," the crier called, "in the name of King David of Israel, we call on you to surrender. Open the gates and let our army in, or we will enter by force."

David's army surrounded the fortified city, with about thirty thousand soldiers. The city of Jebus, atop a mountain in the Judean range, was thoroughly besieged.

Early in the morning, whitish clouds swept hurriedly across the blue skies. A soft wind caressed the faces of the warriors, ready for battle.

The response was a loud laugh: "In whose name? King David? Who is King David? Do you want us to surrender?" Chuckles and chortles echoed through the valley. "You will enter by force?" King Araunah of Jebus stood atop the high wall, mocking the threat: "Tell your David that even if all my defenders were as blind and lame as your ancestors, you would fail to conquer it." The voice became firm: "Go back, you and your David, to the holes from which you crawled, before you anger me. You want to see force, I'll give you more than enough," said the king of Jebus, heading home.

"Your Majesty," said the tracker. "I don't see a way to enter the city. There is only one gate, and in front of it are the statues with the swords. Even if we were to bypass them, the gate is massive and fortified." There was despair on the tracker's face: "We won't be able to open the gate from the outside."

Anger filled David. "These vile Jebusites use the images of our ancestors as idols, confident that we will not succeed in conquering the city. They place statues of our patriarchs atop the tower, then mock us, their descendants. The first man to strike the Jebusites and knock down their statues I so despise will become a lord and chief. Don't worry, son," David told the tracker, "We'll figure out how to get into the city."

Joab pondered aloud: "The statues make it impossible to open the doors from the outside, but if we managed to enter and open the gates from the inside..."

David looked at Joab with admiration; his fortitude and heroism knew no end. "Do you have an idea?"

"I think so. Look, there is a cypress tree that can be used as a catapult," he said, pointing. "You can bend it back and use it as a launcher. Pull the tree back, and I'll climb to its top. Then you release it, and I will be thrown over the wall. Then I can open the gates for you." Joab smiled at David, who looked astonished. "Don't worry, we'll wait until dark, and then we'll do it. In the meantime, pull the army back; the Jebusites will think that we have capitulated. I will enter the city and open its gates."

David was shocked. "Joab, it's suicide. If you make it over the wall, you'll break every bone in your body."

"Your Majesty need not worry. I'll cushion myself well. Nothing will happen to me. Unless my king has another idea?"

David shook his head.

"Look, the cowards are fleeing." Araunah, king of Jebus, shouted at David's retreating army: "You finally wised up! Get out of here before I come after you!"

Night came. Joab, David and a handful of warriors stood by the tree, ready to carry out Joab's plan. They bent the sapling back, launching Joab into the city. Quickly he stripped the cushions from his body, then snuck toward the city gate. The citizens, including the guards, were asleep. David's retreat had given them a sense of peace and security. Their drunkenness and debauchery had given way to drowsiness.

Joab made quick work of the sleeping sentries, who died without waking up. He opened the gates and shattered the statues from behind. David's soldiers slipped in quietly, taking it over before the residents knew what was happening. Joab climbed to the top of the tower to topple the statues there.

In short order, Jebus became Jerusalem. Araunah surrendered at the first chance, begging for mercy in the name of the oath between Abraham and Abimelech.

David stood atop the hill, overlooking Rephaim Valley, which was full of Philistine soldiers ready to fight him. The dukes of Philistia and their soldiers flooded the valley at the foot of the City of David. They could not bear that David had become King of Israel and made the erstwhile Jebus his capital. While Araunah had ruled there, they had been willing to turn a blind eye to the upstart Bethlehemite. Now that David was a true challenge, they had to nip the Israelite rebellion against Philistia in the bud.

David was lost in thought in his room, pouring out his heart before his Creator: What am I to do, Lord? The Philistine army surrounds the city on all sides, waiting for the right moment to attack. We are still in good shape, but how long can we hold out against a superior enemy? Time is on their side; within a few weeks, the city's supplies will run out and hunger will begin to prevail. I need advice! You crowned me over Your flock, but now I am a shepherd lost in the wilderness. Now we are on the defensive, and morale is beginning to weaken. They know that it won't be long before we have to surrender. Please, Father, I need advice. Was I too hasty in seizing the city of Jebus? Did I force the issue? Our besiegers are convinced the city will fall to them without a fight, while despair penetrates the hearts of my men. What should I do?"

At a knock on the door, David raised his head. Joab stood there.

"Your Majesty," Joab reported, sweat dripping down his face, "The walls are superbly fortified. We managed to smuggle a lot of food and water into the city through the tunnels, so we can last a long time." Joab smiled: "They don't know about the tunnels leading to the city! The Philistines think the siege won't last long. They think we won't be able to hold out much longer."

David pondered this, feeling despair penetrate his heart: How long will they go on not knowing? In the end, they'll find the tunnels. How long can we hide in the city?

Aloud he said: "Joab, what is the situation with the Philistines? I know what our people think, but what is happening there?" David looked into Joab's eyes, sensing that the smile was no more than a brave face to hide a feeling of helplessness.

Joab pursed his lips: "They almost feel the war is over. They're confident that we're about to surrender." Joab whispered as if he were sharing a secret: "Unfortunately, I feel the same way."

David rubbed his forehead and ran his hands over his eyes. He felt despair flooding his entire body, commanding him to surrender to the feeling of doom. A scream rose from his heart, echoing through his mind, shaking his body. "You must not lose hope," he shouted through webs of sadness, "Even if a sharp blade is at your throat, never give up on God's mercy. You are not alone in this war. The people are my people, and the city is my city." David felt the blood flowing lazily through his body begin to pulse rapidly.

His grin puzzled Joab: "Is everything all right, Your Majesty?"

The smile turned into a smirk: "That's not what they expect!" said David as laughter bubbled up. "Joab, how many tunnels do we have?" he asked, as if trying to stifle it.

Joab looked at David, afraid that his king was succumbing to madness. "Six," he answered, puzzled by the question.

"Don't worry Joab, I haven't lost my mind," said David, "You said they were waiting for us to fall into their hands."

Joab nodded.

"We," David continued, "will not fall into their hands! They will fall into ours! Gather all the fighters; divide them into six battalions. Each battalion will come out of one tunnel, and in the early morning, we will attack them and defeat them. The best defense is a good offense. They don't expect to be attacked. Once we attack, they'll lose their minds." David laughed out loud: "They won't know where it's coming from."

Early morning lit up the large camp. David consulted with Abiathar the high priest: "Shall I go up to the Philistines? Will you give them over to me?" asked David of the Urim and Thummim.

"Go up, for I will surely give the Philistines into your hand," was the reply.

David and his men emerged from the tunnels, raiding the complacent Philistine camp. Like a torrent of water surrounding the enemy camp on all sides, they fell on the Philistine camp and won the war. The Philistine enemy fled from the valley, leaving their statues and idols behind, which David and his men burned.

CHAPTER FORTY
Uzzah's Breach

The year was 2893 of the Hebrew calendar. After seven-and-a-half years in Hebron, David had a new capital. The town of Jebus, conquered by David a few months earlier, had been renamed Jerusalem. It was the City of Perfect Faith, the spot from which the world was formed. David sat in his modest home in the City of David. With him were Abiathar, Joab, Amasa, the tribal princes, and the justices of the Supreme Court.

"My friends and comrades," David began, "While I was with Samuel the Prophet, a righteous memory, he gave me the blueprints for the Temple and its sacred vessels. This city is where the Temple must be built, but only once God gives the word, which He hasn't yet," he said thoughtfully. "However, although the command has not been given, it seems to me appropriate and proper that the Ark of the Covenant, in which Moses put the Two Tablets of Testimony, should be here at the future site of the Temple. It sits now in Kiriath Jearim, in Abinadab's house, and I have a strong desire to bring it to us." David looked at the assembled dignitaries, who nodded.

"Your Majesty," Joab exclaimed, "if we do this, the Philistines won't take it well. They will gather their entire army to fight us."

"True, but I think it's time to do so. And even if the Philistines come upon us later, we will defeat them!" replied David firmly.

The heads of the nation agreed. It was a popular idea: the Ark of the Lord's Covenant, symbol of the Nation of Israel, its most sacred vessel, to be kept in its capital.

"The sooner, the better," said Abiathar. "Abinadab has watched over the Holy Ark ever since its return from Philistia. Thirty years had passed, and the time had come for the Ark of God to be in its rightful place, even if it means war with the Philistines."

"My brothers and comrades, we must rally the masses to accompany the Ark of our God on its journey. Every tribe must be represented. Bringing the Holy Ark home must be a national endeavor of all Israel." David beamed in anticipation.

It was a sunny day in Kiriath Jearim, an azure sky welcomed the day above the crowds which had gathered for the important event: shining faces, glowing hearts; the tribes having been assembled. The musical accompaniment was melodious, cheerful, and soulful. The priests were resplendent in white — with Abiathar, in blue and gold, at their head, wearing the Breastplate of Judgement, whose multicolored stones sparkled in the sunlight. David's dress was lavishly regal, the gold and jewels gleaming. He stood alongside Abinadab, who had housed the Holy Ark for three decades, thinking: Saul's second son was Abinadab, my second brother was Abinadab, and here is another Abinadab. I hope that the third time is a charm; let this be a good omen.

Uzzah and Ahio, the sons of Abinadab, went to open the doors of the building.

The joy of the crowd surged. After being distanced from God, they were reunited.

The large doors were opened, and the crowd saw the Ark of the Covenant, mounted on a new wagon. Its pure gold reflected the sun's rays, almost blinding the masses. The cherubim atop it were looking at each other, a boy and a girl, shining with love.

The people immediately prostrated themselves, eyes tearing with joy at the sight.

The king rose to his feet, followed by the entire nation: "My brethren and my nation, Children of Israel. This is a great day for our people, a day when the Ark of the Covenant will be brought to its rightful place, our metropolis, our capital of all Israel."

Cries of excitement and exultation echoed over the hill.

"My holy people! This joyous occasion obliges us all to acknowledge how awesome the privilege is that we embrace today!" continued

David. "We welcome the Divine Presence to reside among us. This is no small matter! We must be worthy of such exaltation; we must be pure in thought and holy in action!" David raised his hands: "Please, Lord God of Israel, rest Your Divine Presence in our midst. Let us merit the privilege of being called by Your Name, in sacredness and blessedness!" The Holy Ark glowed so fiercely that they could see nothing through their tears. "My brethren and comrades, we will accept the yoke of His kingdom upon us, may He be blessed." He shouted: *"Hear O Israel, the Lord our God, the Lord is one."*

The people echoed the creed loudly, accepting the yoke of the kingdom of Heaven.

Uzzah and Ahio came to harness cattle to the wagon, which Ahio would steer.

"Your Majesty, shouldn't the Levites carry the Holy Ark?" Amasa asked the king.

"No, my brother, just as the Ark of the Covenant came here from the Philistines, so we take it to its permanent home. It will be as if the Ark of Testimony had never been here and had only just been returned from the hands of the Philistines. That command was for the time of Moses, when there was a Tabernacle. The other parts of the Tabernacle were transported on wagons, while the holiest vessels had to be transported on the shoulders of the Levites. Today we may use a wagon."

There was dancing and joy, singing and music, as the procession made its way from Kiriath Jearim to Jerusalem. The Levites played their instruments — harps, lyres, tambourines, cymbals, and trumpets — while they sang inspiring songs which rose to the skies. The melody joined the hearts of the people to their Creator in perfect union, souls rising up to the Crucible of their Creation. All of Israel danced and sang happily before the Ark of the Covenant, pulled by the oxen on the wagon.

Uzzah walked beside the wagon, chanting and singing. Suddenly, near the threshing floor of Chidon, the wagon went over a large stone, causing the Holy Ark to shift. With bated breath, the procession halted. Uzzah, walking by the side of the wagon, jumped up to grab the Ark of the Covenant, fearing it would fall to the ground.

Two bolts of lightning flashed from the Holy Ark, striking Uzzah in the eyes and killing him on the spot.

The crowd was shocked and surprised. No more dancing, no more singing, nothing but thunderous silence.

David fell on his face, bursting into tears. "I am not worthy to bring up the Ark of the Lord. Because of me, the Lord has made a breach. I am at fault. I deserve to die here, at Uzzah's breach. I should have had the Levites take the Holy Ark on their shoulders, not placed it in a wagon. I relied on my own reason, and I transgressed the Word of God." David cried aloud: "How can the Ark of the Lord come to me? I am unworthy! Here is the house of Obededom the Gittite, a Levite, nearby. Take the Ark of God there, until the Lord wills that I bring it home."

CHAPTER FORTY-ONE
The Balsam Trees

The Philistines, who had retreated, were regrouping and bringing reinforcements for the war. They had heard rumors about all the Israelites gathering for some religious ceremony and their attempt to bring the Holy Ark to the city of Jebus, which raised the ire of the dukes of Philistia. They recalled what had happened to their god Dagon and their cities when they had captured the Holy Ark, and the memory was difficult, bitter, and shameful. They wanted revenge on Israel.

"Shall I attack the Philistines again?" David consulted the Urim and Thummim.

"Do not march straight up, but circle around behind them and attack them in front of the balsam trees. As soon as you hear the sound of marching in the tops of the balsam trees, move quickly, because this will mean that the Lord has marched out before you to strike the camp of the Philistines."

David and his warriors emerged from the tunnel openings, concealing themselves among the trees, the thicket of brush enhancing their hiding place.

A mighty army was assembled by the Philistines to fight David and his men, a host which swept through the valley. The sound of war trumpets increased in volume and pitch, as if provoking their enemies to come attack.

David's army remained lying in wait.

"Your Majesty," Joab whispered, "we must attack now! They are approaching. Soon they will notice us, and then we will lose the element of surprise. We must not wait."

"Shhh..." David whispered. "The Urim and Thummim said we had to wait until we heard the sound of footsteps right above our heads. We must not rush."

"But Your Majesty, we are endangering ourselves and our fighters! We are risking their lives for no reason."

"No reason? Thus commanded the Lord! It is better for us to die following the Word of God, than to live in violation of His imperative. Saul lost his kingdom, because he was not patient enough to wait for Samuel the Prophet's arrival. Reuben, son of Jacob, lost the birthright because he was in a hurry. We must learn from the mistakes of those who preceded us. We are doomed to failure if we defy a divine directive. The power of patience is one of the highest and most difficult virtues. Forcing the issue never works. Nothing in the world acts independently or by the efforts of others; everything is decided in the upper spheres. If we internalize that everything is miraculous and nothing is natural, then we can succeed in everything we do. But if we think that it is ourselves who accomplish anything in the world, or that our tricks can do us even a little good, we will fail not only at one thing but at everything. If you contravene the will of God, you may delude yourself into believing you experience success, but rest assured that it will backfire. You, my friend Joab, must learn to be patient. Nothing bad will happen if we only fully fulfill God's commands."

It was quiet in the camp, with the lurking fighters hiding in the dense vegetation, which covered them like a blanket. The tension was palpable, with the pressure in their chests growing, as they heard the enemy advancing closer and closer.

Anticipation...

Standing by...

Resisting the impulse to attack the enemy seemed unbearable. All their senses screamed in their minds: "This is suicide."

The enemy was approaching...

Their hands gripped the hilts of their swords more tightly. Cold sweat washed over the warriors' backs.

The thought pounded in the soldiers' heads: "We must rise up and attack now," but their hearts invoked faith: "This is what God commanded."

The sound of enemy trumpets was very close. Their hearts were thumping in their chests, seemingly louder than the swords which the Philistines were beating against their shields to intimidate the Israelites.

Every natural impulse screamed to save their bodies from certain death, to burst forth in front of the enemy. The hearts of the fighters were torn. "Now is the time, before it is too late." Still, they were blocked by the wall of faith, which King David had fortified in their hearts.

Soft breathing.

"*From where does my help come?*" shouted the senses, which refuse to wait.

"*My help comes from the Lord, the Maker of heaven and earth,*" answered faith.

"A little more... A few more moments... We must not fail... Do not violate the commandment... By His will, we will succeed, or we will fail..."

David waited, acutely aware of his warriors' distress. He admired their enormous mental powers, forcing their bodies to wait.

A few yards separated the armies...

It was as if the balsam trees were screaming: "Now..."

"A few more seconds of waiting," David thought. He gripped the hilt of his sword more tightly, sweat moistening his palms.

He could hear the enemy trampling the grass, the boot a finger-breadth from his face...

"Now..." David exclaimed, jumping to his feet, toppling the astonished Philistine who had almost stepped on him.

Screaming...

Shouting...

Confusion...

David's warriors appeared out of nowhere in the heart of the Philistine camp, striking the shocked army from every direction. A few thousand Israelite fighters, bursting from the heart of the vast enemy camp, left the Philistines shell-shocked.

The Philistines' fear of David and his men paralyzed them. Soldiers imbued with faith in the righteousness of their path, fighting for a noble cause, terrified the Philistines, who had gone into battle only for the spoils they might win.

The battle lasted only a few hours, a battle that quickly turned into a pursuit of the Philistine invaders who dispersed in all four directions.

"I pursue my enemies and destroy them; I do not turn back until they are consumed," shouted the warriors fighting with the power of faith.

The Israelite army was getting stronger and stronger, a small and high-quality fighting force, engaging the enemies of Israel without fear — led by the valiant chief Joab son of Zeruiah, the faithful king David, son of Jesse, and above all, the Lord God of Israel.

Thirty thousand warriors were reconquering the land of their forefathers, liberating it from the invaders who oppressed the people and the land, terrorizing all who faced them.

CHAPTER FORTY-TWO

The Dancer

David sat in his new home in Jerusalem, a house built by men sent by King Hiram of Tyre. Hiram had sent David artisans and cedar trees to build the palace, as a symbol of the conclusion of a covenant of peace and the surrender of Tyre to Israel.

David's harp was in his hand. As midnight arrived, David chanted before God:
As the deer pants for streams of water,
so my soul longs after You, O God.
Oh, Heavenly Father, I yearn so for Your closeness.
My soul thirsts for God, the living God.
When shall I come and appear in God's presence?

When will my Father grant me the privilege of experiencing the glow of His splendor?
My tears have been my food
Both day and night,
While men ask me all day long,
"Where is your God?"

Those who hate me have said that I am unfit to rule Your people or to raise the Ark of Your Covenant to the Chosen City.
These things come to mind as I pour out my soul:
How I walked with the multitude,
Leading the procession to the house of God
With shouts of joy and praise.

When will I have the privilege of bringing the Ark of the Covenant to Jerusalem and building the Temple?
> *Why are you downcast, O my soul?*
> *Why the unease within me?*
> *Put your hope in God, for I will yet praise Him*
> *For the salvation of His presence.*

We must not despair, we will yet merit such grace.
> *O my God, my soul despairs within me.*
> *Therefore I remember You*
> *From the land of Jordan and the peaks of Hermon—*
> *Even from Mount Mizar.*

You have forgiven sins of greater enormity.
> You have wrought miracles for us.
> *Deep calls to deep*
> *In the roar of Your waterfalls;*
> *All Your breakers and waves*
> *Have rolled over me.*

Each day brings a new crisis, by Your Will, and I have faced many.
> *The Lord decrees His loving devotion by day,*
> *And at night His song is with me*
> *As a prayer to the God of my life.*

When I consider the truth of the matter, Your kindness is evident. However in the dead of night, only faith and prayer keep me alive.
> *I say to God my Rock,*
> *"Why have You forgotten me?*
> *Why must I walk in sorrow*
> *Because of the enemy's oppression?"*
> I feel like a son forgotten by his father, beset by foes on every side.
> *Like the crushing of my bones,*
> *My enemies taunt me,*
> *While they say to me all day long,*
> *"Where is your God?"*

When they say that You have abandoned me, their words are like cutting blades.
Why are you downcast, O my soul?
Why the unease within me?
Put your hope in God, for I will yet praise Him,
My Savior and my God.

David, why do you fall into despair? Pray to your God, and He will save you.

Song merged with supplication, and man integrated into his Creator. Prayer became a conversation as if between a man and his beloved: "Father, I know that I have erred, sinned, and transgressed Your word. Please Father, please forgive my wrongdoing. All I want is to do Your will, to keep Your laws and commandments. I want to be worthy of the role You have assigned me. Your people Israel need a place where they can come and see Your Presence. The place You chose is Jerusalem. Please Father, I am privileged to build Your Temple, to raise the Ark of the Covenant to Your holy city, and to welcome Your dwelling within us. I know of myself that I am not perfect; I have done many wicked things and corrupted myself. Please grant me the privilege to fully repent before you, to see the glow of Your Presence, and to truly do Your will." The tears ran down his cheeks, moistening his beard. Three months had passed since the attempt to bring the Ark of the Covenant to Jerusalem. Three long months of crying, fasting, praying, and heartfelt repentance.

There was a soft knock on the door. David wiped the tears from his face: "Yes, come in," he said in a low voice.

The door opened and there stood Ira the Jairite, the priest, David's Torah teacher. His coal-black beard was streaked with snow-white strands.

David rose from his seat in honor of his mentor and went to greet him: "Peace be upon you, my master and my teacher."

"Peace be upon you, King David."

David pointed to a chair, inviting his master to sit down. Ira sat, followed by David.

"What brings my master here at this hour?" asked David, surprised by the visit.

"I saw fit to come at this hour to talk to Your Majesty about bringing the Ark of the Covenant to our city of Jerusalem." Ira cleared his throat, "I think the king should try again to bring the Holy Ark to us. It needs to come home. I know what happened last time, but now we can do it right, according to the law. The Holy Ark must be carried on the shoulders of Levites, not on a wagon, and it must be covered. Sacrifices must accompany it, and the most important thing is to show true reverence."

"But my master, how can I know what God wants? Perhaps God does not want us to bring the Ark of the Covenant to Jerusalem at all? The people fear the Holy Ark; they say it brings death to all who approach it. Uzzah fell dead after taking six steps."

Ira replied: "Uzzah died because he lacked faith. We all know that the Holy Ark carries its bearers; it doesn't need anyone to lift it. Even in the days of Joshua, son of Nun, when Israel was at the Jordan, God stopped the flow of the river, and the people passed; only the Ark of the Covenant and its bearers remained on the other bank. The water resumed flowing, and the Holy Ark carried itself along with its bearers over the Jordan. Indeed, any ordinary person would jump up to grab the Holy Ark, if he saw that the Holy Ark was about to fall. That was not Uzzah's sin. It is human nature to give in to the inner impulse that compels one at such moments. His error was fearing that the Holy Ark might slip. When the whole nation walked before the Holy Ark, he walked alongside, and for that he was punished. Do people fear the Holy Ark? Look at Obededom the Gittite, blessed from the moment of its arrival in his home — not only has he experienced good fortune, but his entire household has."

"But my master, perhaps I am unfit to bring it up. Behold, I have sinned!" David whispered, and his voice was broken with pain.

"My dear king, you regret what you did! You repented before God! The past has been erased and wiped out … you don't need to ponder over it anymore! You are the king chosen by God, and only you may and must do so." Ira looked at the face of his king, who looked like a child ashamed of his mistake. "Your Majesty, you must take action."

Early in the morning, the tribes of Israel gathered at the house of Obededom the Gittite. Mixed feelings accompanied the assembly.

Fear...

Trepidation...

Joy...

Trembling...

Hope...

"I hope this time it works. I wouldn't want what happened last time to happen again," one attendee remarked.

A tremor ran through his friend's body: "Yes, it was terrible. Poor Uzzah, he was a great righteous man, but he died like that."

"It seems to me that this time it will be different; King David will not make the same mistake twice. I heard that this time the Levites carry the Holy Ark," he whispered.

"The Holy Ark should reside in a respectable place, not in the home of an individual. Although Obededom is a great and important person, the Ark of the Covenant should be in Jerusalem, the city of all Israel."

His friend nodded: "I heard that the king prepared a special house for the Holy Ark, a house built of stone but roofed with leather. I wonder why the roof isn't stone too?"

"Of course, this house is temporary, until the Temple is built. The roof demonstrates that it's just for the time being. If the house were all stone, it would seem permanent."

"Shhh... Here comes the king."

A small platform had been built outside Obededom's door. David climbed onto it, wearing the plain white cloth clothes of a holy servant, with a simple, thin, blue tunic on top. There was silence as the people looked up, to see the king in common garb.

"People of God," David began, "we are assembled to bring the Holy Ark to the City of God. Hold reverence in your hearts! Purify your souls for exaltation! Tremble before the Creator of the Worlds." The silence was total, their eyes full of devotion. "Priests Zadok and Abiathar, enter to cover the ark of God." From the assemblage of priests, the two emerged bearing a sky-blue cloth to cover the Ark of the Covenant.

The tension rose as they went into the building…

A few minutes passed, and the priests came out.

"Levite gatekeepers, open the doors of the house." Four men rushed forward. "Levite gatekeepers," said David, "please go and lift the Holy Ark. Levite musicians, play in honor of the King of Glory." Eight Levites went in the doorway, as devotional music played to inspire the audience, whose hearts pounded with fear and awe. They anxiously wondered: Will the tragedy of Uzzah recur? Will this succeed?

The few minutes seemed like an eternity for the people waiting on the doorstep.

Inside the building, the eight chosen Levites prostrated themselves before the Ark of the Covenant, holy terror enveloping the people who came to carry it. The Holy Ark was two-and-a-half cubits in length, one-and-a-half cubits in width, and one-and-a-half cubits in height, plated with gold. On top of it were the two golden cherubim, and inside were the intact Second Tablets and the shattered First Tablets, both sets made of stone. Each tablet was square, six handbreadths by six handbreadths, with a thickness of three handbreadths. The Holy Ark was swathed in the sky-blue cloth.

The Levites approached the gold-plated wooden staves used to carry the Holy Ark. Four of the Levites in front of the Holy Ark and four behind it bent down in awe to raise the vessel. The eight Levites straightened up as one, not feeling the great weight of the Holy Ark, walking in fear, leaving the house of Obededom.

Uzzah had taken six steps holding God's Ark.

The crowd counted silently. One… Two… Three… Four… Five…

All the Levites were already outside. The audience watched with bated breath.

Six… Seven…

David fell on his face, prostrating himself, arms and legs spread in front of the covered Ark of God.

The Levites, the priests, and the entire nation bowed before the Ark of God.

"*Blessed be the glory of His kingdom forever and ever,*" David declared and the crowd repeated it.

David, the priests, the Levites and the entire nation stood up.

The priests sacrificed seven bulls and seven rams in honor of God. David sacrificed a fattened calf and a bull.

The Levites continued to make sweet music, while the sound of singing started to swell.

The people, including David, began to dance and frolic with the joy of fulfilling God's commandment, accompanying the Holy Ark resting on the shoulders of the Levites.

The procession continued toward Jerusalem, stopping every few steps and offering sacrifices in honor of God.

Intoxication, spiritual exaltation, and the feeling of God's closeness and love beat in the hearts of the people, who danced and gyrated in holy reverence before God's Ark.

The crowd entered Jerusalem, the Holy City, and faced the structure that David had erected for it. David danced passionately in the midst of the crowd.

The Levites carrying the Holy Ark entered, placed it in its spot and left.

Dancing, singing, rejoicing and playing music continued until the end of the day, as elevation offerings and thanksgiving offerings were sacrificed. A royal feast was served to all the attendees, with gifts for everyone to take home.

David, soaked with sweat and joy beaming from his face, ascended a small platform: "My brethren, my friends, my loved ones, People of God. Blessed are you to the Lord God of Israel, Whose Presence is among us. We are privileged to bring the Ark of the Covenant to our capital and to witness God's love for us. My dear loved ones, return to your homes happy and grateful for all the good that God has granted us." David came down to hug and kiss his subjects, wishing them farewell before they headed home.

At the window, Michal, daughter of Saul, a bitter, barren woman who raised her sister Merab's sons, stood, watching her husband abase himself amid the people...

David returned home. His smile of happiness had not left his face, his heart swelling with gratitude to God. In the doorway stood Michal, who looked at her husband's sweaty face and body, and she said with contempt: *"How the king of Israel has distinguished himself today! He has uncovered himself today in the sight of the maidservants of his subjects, like a vulgar person would do,"* she said venomously. "Do you think this is how a king should behave before his people, like a commoner, like a simpleton, dancing and gyrating? Heedless of his dignity, exposing his thighs as he cavorts, carouses, and frolics? My father, King Saul, was a paragon of modesty. He never even uncovered a handbreadth of his flesh in public. He knew how to preserve his honor and the honor of the crown, which you do not!" she snarled, with disgust and disdain in her voice.

David, surprised by the contempt and venom in his wife's voice, replied: *"I was dancing before the Lord, who chose me over your father and all his house when He appointed me ruler over the Lord's people Israel. I will celebrate before the Lord, and I will humiliate and humble myself even more than this. Yet I will be honored by the maidservants of whom you have spoken."* He went on: "I danced not before flesh and blood, but before God Who chose me as king. Before the Lord, personal dignity is of no concern, even that of the monarch, because the king is a servant of God too. I am no better than the rest of Israel; indeed, I am of less concern. If you fear that the people will despise me for this, you are mistaken; they know how to appreciate it. They will also respect that I do not wall myself off from the people as other kings do, that I wear a crown but know Who is above me. He who knows his place and his status fears not the ridicule of others, especially when he fulfills God's command."

"But," objected Michal, "you must preserve the dignity of the kingdom; a king may not act like one of the people to abase himself. If a king forgoes the honor due to him, his honor is not forgone. That is the law!"

"The king is not entitled to forgo the honor due to him before flesh and blood," David explained. "But before God, I am not a king, but a servant, and a servant has no honor," he concluded, turning to leave the room.

CHAPTER FORTY-THREE
The Covenant

The markets were crowded with people, children running through the city streets, playing their games. The city was adorned in a variety of hues, the overloaded vegetable and fruit stalls displaying their bounty of beauty to their buyers. Vendors selling their wares stood at every corner, the faces of the residents beaming, happy to be in the royal capital. Music and melodies echoed in the background, merging with the shouts of the merchants. On this spring morning, the caressing rays of the sun warmed the atmosphere, giving the city a festive air. A revitalizing aura prevailed.

David looked out his window at the people of his city, and beyond the bustling streets, he could see the pavilion of the Holy Ark.

David thought, feeling a twinge in his heart: Almost a decade has passed since I brought the Holy Ark to Jerusalem, but there is still no temple for my people. I destroyed most of the enemies around me, and still the Ark of God is placed in the pavilion. The city is well-built, with homes, bathhouses, and government buildings. Even my palace rises on a plateau, but there is still no temple.

Sorrow filled his being: "God, I swear an oath!

I will not enter my house
Or get into my bed,
I will not give sleep to my eyes
Or slumber to my eyelids,
Until I find a place for the Lord,
A dwelling for the Mighty One of Jacob.

"You commanded us to crown a king, to erase the memory of Amalek, and to build Your Chosen House. Now I am king. Amalek is almost gone, with Joab at war with the remnant. However, the construction of the Temple has not yet begun. All I want is to do Your will, to crown You over Your people Israel, to see You dwell among us."

David moved away from the window and walked over to the door. The feeling of exhilaration that had pulsed within him as he looked out over the city passed and was replaced by a sense of helplessness. Sadness and depression overshadowed the light flooding into the room. "Call Nathan the Prophet," David told the sentry.

"Your Majesty, you summoned me?" asked Nathan the Prophet, bowing to David. They were of approximately the same age, about fifty, but Nathan had a snowy white beard which reached his chest. His bright eyes were full of wisdom, while his face shone with vitality and a perpetual smile, as if savoring the secrets known only to him. His deep, soft voice emanated a sense of fatherliness and closeness in those who spoke to him. His calm and meticulous gait hardly moved the hem of his simple white cloak, which covered his entire body. Its hood covered his head, leaving only his pale face exposed. His snow-white fingers poked out from his sleeves. Purity and holiness radiated to all who surrounded him, his whole life devoted to serving God. Torah study and prayer filled all his days and nights. The people had a name for him: Nathan the White Prophet.

David looked at Nathan, bowing to God's emissary. He thought: Nathan the Prophet is holy and pure. His patience, his exalted virtues, and his joie de vivre are known to all. His greatness in Torah scholarship and his humility earned him the spirit of prophecy. How I wish I were like him!

David looked admiringly at the pure man, aware of the prophet's closeness to God.

"Yes, my lord prophet," David replied. "I beg your pardon. I hope that my sentry did not disturb you by arriving at an inconvenient time, Your Eminence."

Nathan looked at King David, his thin, emaciated face testifying to the fasting and privation that was the king's lot. His slender, slight body was wrapped in a long, simple, blue robe. His red beard tended toward white now, indicating the king's age, but his face was still as soft and pure as that of a child. His eyes, meanwhile, held the wisdom of a venerable elder in the twilight of his years.

He thought: The king's modesty is extraordinary. His purity, his sense of humility, and his desire to serve God and His people know no bounds. His joie de vivre illuminates the hearts of everyone around him; his greatness in Torah scholarship and fear of God allow him to always direct himself toward God's will. His red hair testifies to the bloodlust that lurks within him. Were he a creature of his desires, he would be incorrigible; but he worked on his inner world so devotedly that he changed his whole state of mind. He denies himself carnal pleasures, subduing his basic instincts, turning himself into a different man. He does not let the beastliness of his nature get the better of him. He subjugates his body to his soul. Such a man deserves the crown, because he reigns over himself first and foremost.

Observing David with love and admiration, Nathan assured him: "No, Your Majesty did not disturb me. I am always glad to see the king's face."

"Please, my lord," David gestured, "come and look out the window." They looked down on Jerusalem. "My lord, behold the capital of the Kingdom of Israel! A peaceful city, its streets full of people safe in their kingdom. Almost all our enemies around us have been defeated. No nation dares to attack us; our city and kingdom are secure. The houses of the citizens are beautiful and luxurious, as no one lacks money or resources in our kingdom. The great spoils we took from the nations we conquered have brought us vast wealth and economic security. The government buildings are beautifully constructed, and even the king's palace is large and magnificent."

Nathan listened to the king's words, hearing the tone of his voice, trying to understand his sadness as he elaborated on the success of the kingdom and its people. The prophet allowed his eyes to sweep over the magnificent metropolis.

"Look a bit to the west," David said, pointing toward the pavilion of the Holy Ark. "*Here I am, living in a house of cedar, while the Ark of God remains in a pavilion.*"

Nathan felt the intensity of the pain in the king's words. The prophet peered at David's face and saw the tears welling up from the corners of his eyes.

"I am a lowly human ensconced in a glorious palace, while the King of the World has no place for His Presence to dwell. It is true that the whole earth is full of His glory, but it is our duty to build a special place for the revelation of His Presence, a site that will unite all humanity to serve Him, housing the Holy Ark and Candelabrum and Table, the Golden Altar and the Bronze Altar. Samuel the Seer gave me all the plans, but he did not specify the location of the latter. I know clearly that as soon as we begin building the Temple, God will inform us of its exact location." David looked into Nathan's eyes in supplication: "My lord prophet, may I begin the work of constructing the Temple? Am I worthy to build the House of the Lord God of Israel?"

Nathan met his gaze, thinking: If there is a man alive who deserves it, then King David is the man. His longing for God's closeness is admirable, and his sorrow at not being inspired by the Divine presence is extraordinary. Nathan cleared his throat to declare: *"Go and do all that is in your heart, for the Lord is with you."*

Happiness flooded David's face, tears of sorrow replaced by tears of joy.

But that night the word of the Lord came to Nathan, saying, "Go and tell My servant David that this is what the Lord says: Are you the one to build for Me a house to dwell in? For I have not dwelt in a house from the day I brought the Israelites up out of Egypt until this day, but I have moved about with a tent as My dwelling. In all My journeys with all the Israelites, have I ever asked any of the leaders I appointed to shepherd My people Israel, 'Why haven't you built Me a house of cedar?' Now then, you are to tell My servant David that this is what the Lord of Hosts says: I took you from the pasture, from following the flock, to be the ruler over My people Israel. I have been with you wherever you have gone, and I have cut off all your enemies from before you. Now I will make for you a name like the greatest in the land. And I will provide a place for My people Israel and will plant them so that they may dwell in a place of their own and be disturbed no more. No longer will the sons of wickedness oppress them as they did at the beginning and have done since the day I appointed judges over My people Israel. I will give you rest from all your enemies. The Lord declares to you that He Himself will establish a house for you. And when your days are fulfilled and you rest with your fathers, I will raise up your descendant after you, who will come from your own body, and I will establish his kingdom. He will build a house for My Name, and I will establish the throne of his kingdom forever. I will be his Father, and he will be My son. When he does wrong, I will discipline him with the rod of men and with the blows of the sons of men. But My loving devotion will never be removed from him as I removed it from Saul, whom I moved out of your way. Your house and kingdom will endure forever before Me, and your throne will be established forever."

Nathan jumped out of bed, knowing he had to fulfill God's word quickly. He thought: King David will not wait to begin the work; he is prompt in keeping the commandments and eager to follow them. Early in the morning, he will begin building the house, hiring artisans and laborers, and it will cost him dearly. He might even make a vow about the work, perhaps not to sleep in his bed until the Temple is built, perhaps not to eat or drink until construction begins, and will be hurt due to me.

Nathan hurried to the palace, thinking: He'll be up already. He has vowed to study each night. At midnight he rises like a lion to worship and praise God until dawn. Sometimes he naps for a bit, but he always wakes himself up like a tireless stallion.

He arrived at the palace, and a soft knock brought David to the doorway. Behind him, his desk was full of drawings and diagrams. The king was beaming, overjoyed to be planning the layout of the Temple. David welcomed the unexpected guest, inviting him to join in.

"Your Majesty," Nathan demurred, "I have something I must tell you. Tonight I received a prophecy from the Almighty, and I must convey it to you."

David was silent. The face of the prophet did not bode well.

Nathan closed his eyes and delivered the divine dispatch: "So says the Lord: David, you are as faithful a servant to me as Moses. Ever since I took My People from the land of Egypt, I resided among them in a tent or a tabernacle; no dwelling or domicile of perpetuity. You, like Me, know what it is to wander from place to place; you have been constantly on the move, avoiding your enemies. My permanent home must be built by a man whose throne is permanent, not one engaged in constant battle. The Forever House is a symbol of peace, and a man of peace must build it, not a man of war like you. Your kingship is still temporary; though you control the entire land, your rule is incomplete. It is not a dynasty until you pass the crown to your son. In the era of the Judges, there were periods of peace, but I never asked one of them to build My Temple. I have slain all your enemies, and you have a reputation befitting of the greatest kings, like the Patriarchs. Because I see your strong desire to build My House, I am building your house. You will have a son who will be your heir; he will be the builder of My Temple. Your son will be like my son, not my servant. In his time, there will be peace in the land, so that he may be a man of peace, not war. Your dynasty will be eternal. Your son, who will succeed you, will have a scion for generations to come. Saul sinned before Me, and I took the throne away from him forever, but your line will never suffer the same fate. If they sin, I will punish them, until they return to me. Your house and your kingdom will last for eternity, as they are today."

The prophet opened his eyes and looked at David. There were mixed feelings on his face: sorrow and disappointment at not being allowed to build the Temple, joy and gratitude for securing his dynasty in perpetuity.

"Thank you, my lord prophet, and now there is much work to be done," he said as he approached his table. "Everything must be prepared for the prince who was promised, so he may build the Temple quickly and efficiently." The king sat down with the prophet next to him, planning the layout of the house and calculating everything necessary so that the Temple could be constructed by his heir.

David walked through the streets of the city, heading toward the Holy Ark's pavilion. Dressed in plain clothes, his legs carried him with his characteristic lightness. He brightly greeted anyone who happened across his way, but the passersby were taken aback to find their sovereign walking alone through the city streets in the afternoon.

They were so surprised that they forgot to bow. David radiated joy to his surroundings, invigorating the hearts of all who met him.

David arrived at the pavilion, greeting the Levites serving there, entering with reverence. Fear and awe of God's kingship filled his pounding heart strongly, making him mute. The desire to pour out his heart before his Creator was met with a deafening wall of silence. David settled his mind, calming his heart, and his lips began to sing as if of their own accord:

"A psalm of thanksgiving.
Make a joyful noise to the Lord,
All the earth.
Serve the Lord with gladness;
Come into His presence with joyful songs.
Know that the Lord is God.
It is He who made us, and we are His;
We are His people, and the sheep of His pasture.
Enter His gates with thanksgiving
And His courts with praise;
Give thanks to Him and bless His name.
For the Lord is good,
And His loving devotion endures forever;
His faithfulness continues to all generations.

"God of Israel, I thank You for making me an Israelite and for choosing me to rule over Your people. Who am I to attain this greatness? But that was Your will, straightforward and simple. So You picked a straightforward and simple shepherd, the lowest of men. You have graced me with an amazing gift, the crown of Your people Israel. You have enhanced this gift by promising me that my dynasty will last forever. I am insignificant and puny, yet You granted me fame before the lords and the common people. Even the most minor of men may become magnificent and mighty, for that is Your Will — just as You created the universe by Your Will and chose the seed of Israel to be Your children, without our knowing why. Thus You have chosen me and my seed to rule over Your people, and therefore I will thank You forever. Please, God, let me and my descendants merit to be righteous and pious in Your eyes, that we may be worthy of the greatness You have granted us, that we may truly walk before You. May it be Your Will to bless Your servant's house forever."

David stroked his face with his hands. His sobs of appreciation and gratitude echoed throughout the pavilion.

CHAPTER FORTY-FOUR
Law and Justice

Joab and Abishai sat planning the next attack. The sons of Zeruiah were very similar in appearance, their black beards turning white, their fierce faces lined. The command tent was large and spacious, candlelight flooding the tent, banishing the shadows to the corners. The table held food and drink for the generals recovering from the last battle. A sense of victory filled the brothers, a feeling of exaltation and exultation, knowing the courage of their army and the heroism of their fighters. They reveled in the revenge exacted from a cruel enemy on behalf of their loved ones.

"Cheers, my dear brother," Joab said, holding a cup of wine in his hand.

Abishai grinned: "Cheers to our fearless forces, jeers to our feckless foes." He laughed.

"King David will hail this triumph. Those awful Moabites murdered our grandparents, our uncles, our cousins. For years we've waited for our chance, and now vengeance is ours."

"That's not all that's ours, praise God! So much loot ... gold, silver, and bronze; garments and jewels; chariots and horses; swords and spears; sheep and cattle; manservants and maidservants!" Abishai raised his cup again: "Cheers, brother, it is indeed a great day for us."

Joab sipped as he said: "Send the precious items directly to David. He is very eager to collect them so that there will be more than enough for the building of the Temple. He thinks of nothing else. Take care of it first thing in the morning, brother."

Jehoshaphat, son of Ahilud, court secretary to King David, was honest and loyal, committed to truth and incorruptible. He told the king: "Your Majesty, two litigants have a case before you. The claimant is very rich, and he says he lent a great deal of money to the respondent for his daughters' dowries. The respondent denies it."

"Summon them both," David ordered. "However, make sure they dress the same — either in rich or poor garments, but not one as a pauper and one as a wealthy man."

Jehoshaphat brought the two litigants in shortly after. Their dress was identical, but the expression on their faces made clear who was rich and who was poor.

"Well, what do you have to say?" David asked the claimant.

"Your Majesty, about a year ago, my neighbor came to me and asked me to give him a thousand gold pieces as a loan to start a business and marry off his three daughters. He promised me that he would repay the loan within six months, and right up to this day, I haven't seen a single penny from him. I even gave him an extension. I didn't want to pressure him, because I know his financial situation and how his business has failed. About two weeks ago, I ran into him and asked about the debt. He seemed dumbfounded and said he didn't know what I was talking about. That's why I decided to sue him, Your Majesty," the claimant said.

David turned to the respondent: "What do you have to say in your defense?"

The poor man shifted uncomfortably. Lying in court discomfited him, making it hard to breathe. In a whisper, he stammered: "I don't know what he's talking about."

"Don't know what I'm talking about?" roared the claimant. "I have it here, in black and white! Documented and signed by two witnesses, whose signatures have been verified in court. And you say you don't know what I'm talking about?!"

David looked at the respondent, whose face gave him away: miserable and sweaty, haunted by the massive debt he could not repay. "Please show me the loan."

The claimant approached the king and handed him the scroll. David read it carefully, glancing at the respondent. "Is your name Moses, son of Gedaliah?"

"Yes," he answered in a whisper.

"And are you Simeon, son of Reuben?" he turned to the claimant.

"Yes, indeed!" he answered boldly.

"Thus, Moses, son of Gedaliah, all the evidence indicates that the document is reliable. You borrowed a thousand gold pieces from Simeon, son of Reuben. A lower court has verified the signatures, and this court will not question that ruling. Moses!" he said firmly, "Tell me the truth, and do not perjure yourself. Know you stand before God in judgment, Who does not suffer liars, Who knows the mysteries of the heart, Who cannot be misled. Did you borrow a thousand gold pieces from Simeon?"

The man burst into tears: "Yes, Your Majesty, I borrowed the money from him! I'm sorry I lied. Simeon is a righteous man who was willing to lend me a large sum of money even without guarantors. But my business failed, and I have no means of repaying him. I apologize, Simeon, for wronging you; I apologize, Your Majesty, for lying in court." The sound of the man's crying grew louder, knowing he had no leg to stand on.

David looked with compassion at poor Moses, his sobs piercing the king's heart. David felt a tear in the corner of his eye. Simeon shared a look of sorrow and pain.

David turned to Shavsha the Scribe. "Record the verdict of this court, Shavsha."

"Moses son of Gedaliah," David said authoritatively, calming his voice: "You must pay Simeon, son of Reuben, a thousand gold pieces. You have a week to transfer the entire amount to him. Simeon, if within a week you do not receive repayment in full from Moses, come here again and notify the court. The case is hereby closed."

The shocked Moses wept, his mind unable to process the verdict. "A week to get a thousand gold pieces?! It's impossible. It would take me years to collect such a sum of money. I will never be able to obey this ruling."

The king motioned for Jehoshaphat to approach him, whispered something in his ear, and got up to leave the courtroom.

Jehoshaphat approached the bitterly crying Moses: "Please come with me," he said softly.

Moses, walking alongside the secretary of the court, felt that his world lay destroyed. How would he be punished for attempted perjury and contempt of court?

Jehoshaphat opened the door to the king's chambers and led Moses in. The poor man found himself standing alone, facing King David of Israel.

Moses' eyes teared up. "Please forgive me, Your Majesty," he cried, heartbroken.

David approached Moses and placed an encouraging hand on his shoulder: "Please, sit down. Tell me the whole story, please. Start from the beginning."

Moses sat down heavily, as if his legs could no longer bear his weight. Stunned, he poured out his life story. It was full of poverty and suffering, distress and anguish: pain and humiliation were his lot. An honest man, torn between his desire to provide for his family with dignity and the inescapable hardship that had always been his lot.

"…Then my daughters grew up, and it was time to find them good husbands. I thought if I could just start a business of my own, I might be successful enough to pay back the loan and cover all their wedding expenses. Simeon, my neighbor, was willing to lend me the money, but I pushed my luck with the business. It all went down the drain, along with my hopes of providing for my girls. Now I have to scrape together a thousand gold pieces in seven days…" Moses burst into bitter tears: "What kind of life is this? What does God want of me? How much torment can a man bear?!"

"My son…" David looked at Moses, agonized over his subject's pain. He empathized with the years of suffering, feeling sorry for the miserable soul that lay shattered before him, as if the waves of a stormy sea had slammed it on the rocky shore.

David leaned over and opened a drawer, taking out three heavy bundles and placing them on the table. "My dear Moses, each of these sacks contains one thousand gold pieces. Use the first to repay the loan to Simeon, the second to marry off your daughters, and the third to relaunch your business. Do not act recklessly this time, lest you lose this as well."

Moses looked at the king in amazement: despair being turned into hope, grief being replaced by joy, and pain being soothed by healing. "Thank you very much, Your Majesty; thank you from the bottom of my heart! I thank God for making you King of Israel." He wept with joy of deliverance, filled with anticipation of a new day for him and his family.

"Jehoshaphat," David mused to his secretary, "here I am judging others for not paying their debts, while I have a debt I have not paid. I swore an oath to Jonathan, son of Saul, that I would keep my covenant with him and his seed after him." His heart twinged as he remembered his fallen friend. "Is there anyone left from his house, whom I may show kindness to, for the sake of my beloved Jonathan?"

"Your Majesty, I don't know. However, I know that there is a servant of King Saul who remains, by the name of Ziba. He will be able to answer your question."

"Please bring him to me," the king replied.

The old, bold servant strode into the throne room, slyly looking around as he bowed.

"Are you Ziba, King Saul's servant?" David asked the man standing in front of him.

"Yes, indeed, Your Majesty. I was a servant to King Saul, now I am yours."

"Tell me, Ziba, is there any man living from the House of Saul, your late master? I would show him kindness and appoint him as a minister and judge over my people."

"As Your Majesty surely knows, Rizpah daughter of Aiah, concubine of King Saul, bore him two sons. The late Merab, daughter of Saul, had five sons, whom Queen Michal raises as her own. Aside from them, Jonathan left behind a son, the poor and unfortunate Mephibosheth. He was five years old when his father Jonathan fell in battle. His governess fled with him, but she dropped him in her haste. Since then, he has been unable to walk. Machir, son of Ammiel, hosts him in Lodebar."

"Go and bring him to me, please," the king said to the servant.

"Mephibosheth?" David asked the man who'd flung himself down before his throne.

In a trembling, broken voice, he replied: "Yes, my lord, I am he, your servant." A shiver ran through his broken body as he thought of the death coming to him. He reflected grimly: The House of Saul, which Ishbosheth headed, are considered traitors to the crown, since we did not accept the kingship of David, God's anointed.

David sensed his fear and commanded: "Help him up and seat him in his chair. Do not fear, my son," he reassured him, "for I will show you grace for your father Jonathan's sake. I am restoring the estate of Saul to you, and you are always welcome at my table."

Mephibosheth looked at King David, wondering: What does he want from me? What is he planning? The way of kings is to eradicate the previous dynasty, yet he is drawing me close to him?!" Shocked, he flung himself to the ground again. "What is your servant but a dead dog? Why show me such regard?" he asked with growing astonishment.

"O, Mephibosheth, son of Jonathan, you were tender in years when your father fell in battle. You didn't really know your father," David said, longing for Jonathan. "There was a wonderful love between me and your righteous father, a love that my heart cannot forget. This love persists, in full force. I made a covenant with your father, of blessed memory, that I would show him favor, and his seed after him. Now I have learned that his child still lives, and I desire to uphold my covenant. By the law of the kingdom, all the property of King Saul belongs to the crown. Now I give you all your father's houses, fields, and all his possessions."

David pointed his finger at Ziba: "All that pertains to his estate and to all his house, I have given to your master's son. And you shall work the land for him, you and your sons and your slaves. And the son of your master shall have bread and eat, but Mephibosheth, your master's son, shall always eat bread on my table."

Ziba bowed to the king: "Whatever Your Majesty commands, his servant will do."

"Mephibosheth," said David, "You and your son Mica are always welcome at my table."

True to his word, David sat Mephibosheth at the head of his table, opposite his own firstborn, Amnon. He was the son of Ahinoam of Jezreel, whom David married while he was fleeing from Saul. He thought: Now he sits across from Saul's grandson! Ah, he is so young, handsome, and brave; tall and broad-shouldered. His chiseled face has a beauty that's both bold and benign. His black beard gives him the gravity of an older man. His green eyes are clever and cunning. My prince has a fierce soul! Though sometimes he may be too bold, too self-assured as the eldest son. Such pride must be corrected. His ambition is boundless, and I fear he may outsmart himself!

One day, Amnon announced: "I have some unfortunate news from Ammon."

"What's the news, son?" David asked gently.

"King Nahash has died," Amnon said, knowing his father's gratitude to the late king.

The sadness was evident on David's face: "That is bitter news, my son. My brother Shammah escaped Moab, whose king executed my parents and all my family. The Moabites had promised to protect them but betrayed me. Nahash then granted Shammah asylum, and he is the only one of my brothers to survive. Think about it: his son Jonadab, your best friend, would never have been born had Nahash refused him refuge! I am forever in his debt. Please, my son, select a dozen dignitaries, one from each tribe, to bear our condolences to Hanun, son of Nahash, the new king."

"Your Majesty, King Hanun of Ammon," the Judahite noble began, "King David of Israel sent us to you, twelve representatives of the tribes of Israel, to console you on the death of your royal father Nahash, who was a true friend to King David. On His Majesty's behalf, all of Israel expresses our sympathies for your loss. May his memory be a blessing, and may the Lord bless you to know no more sorrow or pain."

Hanun looked at the well-dressed and well-groomed delegation that had brought this message of consolation. "Thank you very much for your words. I greatly value your king's gesture and offer of solace," Hanun said, his voice expressing sincere appreciation.

One of Hanun's ministers, face twisted in disgust and revulsion, whispered in his ear. "My lords, please excuse me for a few minutes," Hanun told the Israelite nobles.

The king of Ammon got up heavily and went out with his ministers to another room.

The displeased minister was venomous. "Don't you know who

King David of Israel is? Do you think he sent you a delegation to comfort you? He sent them to observe the state of the country! He knows that your father was a very strong man of war. Now that your father is dead, David wants to see if he can conquer the land. David is two-faced! He plays it up like he's sorry for your father's death, but he plans to invade us. I tell you, you must expel this expedition from here before they can reconnoiter the land. If I were you, I would kill them all and send their bodies to David. But I know you won't, so at least send them out of here in disgrace so they won't come back."

Hanun looked at his minister, "Do you really think so?"

"I tell you, you're still young; you've no experience ruling. Listen to me! At least send them back in disgrace so that David knows we don't fear him," the noble demanded.

"Well, if that's what you think is right, do as you will," Hanun replied uncomfortably.

The minister left the room and called his guards to enter the room where David's delegation was waiting. The fighters received a briefing from the minister on how to handle the Israelite spies. The warriors rushed into the room. Each Israelite was seized by four Ammonites, while a fifth shaved half their beards off and tore their clothes to the groin.

The shocked members of the delegation, who could not resist the humiliating attack, were taken away, to be thrown out at the gates of Jericho.

At midnight, David sat in his room, eyes closed, playing and singing his songs to the Creator, holding on to his love for the Almighty, thankful for the favors he had received. The sounds of the harp were muted, blending with the tone of his voice: songs of love and yearning for the Creator of the Worlds.

"God, I want to worship You with all my heart, to follow Your path and be like the Patriarchs Abraham, Isaac, and Jacob, with whom You have deigned to associate Yourself. You are named the God of Abraham, the God of Isaac, and the God of Jacob. I want you to also be called the God of David. My only desire is to cling to You and to be included in Your being. My whole life is full of trials, but I rely on you, and I will not stumble. I know that Your grace directs me and drives me on the path of my life. Each Patriarch faced a trial challenging his nature. Abraham, the paragon of kindness, was told to slaughter his only son. Isaac, embodying might, faced the closeness of his son Esau, who was known to be wicked. Jacob, a man of truth, was forced to lie to his father, Esau, and Laban. And I, my Father, what will my trial be? *Test me, O Lord, and try me; examine my heart and mind.* I want to face a trial, so You know that I am Your servant and that You should be called by my name."

The door opened quickly, pulling him out of his connection to his Beloved in Heaven. David opened his eyes to see a furious Abishai standing in the doorway.

"What a shame! What a disgrace! This man has no respect! We have to go out and destroy them!" Abishai fumed and hungered for vengeance.

David shook off his thoughts: "What happened, Abishai? Why are you so angry?"

"Hanun, son of Nahash of Ammon, humiliated the delegation you sent to him!" Abishai exclaimed angrily. "He shaved half their beards, tore their clothes, and cast them down at the gates of Jericho. Our messengers are deeply humiliated, embarrassed to show their faces in public. They want to bury themselves in shame."

David got to his feet, rage coming over his features: "Tell the people to stay in Jericho until their beards grow back and then come home. Gather the army to fight the Ammonites. We will go and cut off the head of Hanun the Ammonite. He dared to degrade a delegation that came in peace, so we will send a delegation that seeks war. I had gratitude toward Hanun's father. It has been nearly three decades since King Nahash of Ammon granted asylum to my brother, and from then until now, I have refrained from fighting Ammon as an expression of that gratitude. However, his son has demonstrated himself unworthy of such regard. Tell our men we will avenge their shame. Be strong and courageous, Abishai; we will repay Hanun and his people."

CHAPTER FORTY-FIVE
Hanun son of Nahash

Ashen clouds curled in the fiery horizon. The sun's rays burst through the mist, illuminating the valley with crimson beams of light. The golden wheat fields spread wide at the foot of the mountains were carpeted with warriors, who trampled the amber sheaves with their feet and chariot wheels. The thousands of horses chewed the grain with pleasure, anticipating the battle.

King Hanun of Ammon stood on top of a small hill with kings whom he'd hired to join his war against Israel. The faces of the monarchs shone with joy, and the countless warriors, horses, and chariots created an air of security.

The kings of Ammon, Aram Zobah, Rehob, Maacah and Aram Naharaim observed their armies proudly.

"My dear brothers," Hanun began, "I know that even though I hired you with a lot of money to go to war with me against the Israelites, you have not come here solely for financial reasons. David and his Israelites have already crossed every boundary; his desire is to rule over the entire region. His army has already destroyed many peoples and countries in the region, and we must stop him. If we don't stop it now, it won't be long before he takes over all our lands. We are strong when we stand united. I know that I raised David's wrath when I disrespected his people, with the pretext of consoling me over my father's death. That was the claim, but he wanted to spy on the access roads to the city in order to conquer it. His men are on their way here to fight me, they will try to conquer my capital, but it won't be easy for them. The city is well fortified and protected. As soon as they attack, we will strike from the rear, so they will be between the hammer and the anvil, and we will consume them."

The other kings expressed agreement; the possibility of defeating Israel made their hearts sing. The fear of David's army taking over the area kept them up at night.

"My capital is beyond the hills, and David's army is rapidly approaching the city gates. They don't seem to be aware that you're here. My men will be able to withstand the attack until you come to their aid. I will take some of my soldiers out of the gates of the city, and when David's army comes to fight them, they will flee back inside. The Israelite army will try to break in, and then you must attack from behind them."

"It will not be difficult," said the king of Maacah, "I alone command thirty-two thousand iron chariots, hundreds of thousands of cavalry, and countless infantry."

Hanun smiled, "It's time to wipe them off the map."

"Joab, my brother, look back; they're attacking us from the rear," Abishai shouted.

David's army began an attack on the fortified walls of Rabbah. The warriors, standing at the entrance to the city, fled into it, closing its doors behind them.

Joab and Abishai, the military leaders eager to avenge the humiliation of the peace delegation, urged their army toward Hanun's capital. Their eagerness hurt them; their many victories over their enemies led them to shed some of the necessary caution. The army, which was rushing toward its enemies, did not send scouts ahead of them.

Joab looked up and saw the mighty army approaching them quickly. "My brother, we will divide the army in two. I will take half of the fighters, and we will face the army of Aram advancing toward us. You, with your fighters, will continue to besiege the city; they must not come out of the city toward us. If they come out, we will be squeezed in a pincer move. *If the Arameans are too strong for me, then you will come to my rescue. And if the Ammonites are too strong for you, then I will come to your rescue. Be strong and let us fight bravely for our people and for the cities of our God. May the Lord do what is good in His sight.*"

The army was quickly divided, the skilled fighters turned toward the army at their rear. Joab led his half of the Israelites against the

Arameans, who grew alarmed as their flanking tactic was stymied. The attacker became the attacked; the mindset changed from offensive to defensive. Joab and the Israelites let out war whoops that cut deep into the Arameans' souls, terrifying them. Joab's reputation preceded him, and the esprit de corps and joy of victory vanished from Aram, and was replaced by the fear of death. The knowledge that Lord Commander Joab was leading his troops against them brought terror into their hearts. Their ranks dissolved as they tried to reassemble in a defensive posture.

From the other direction, Ammonite soldiers burst out of Rabbah to attack Abishai's army. The Israelites faced an influx of people leaving the city toward them.

"My brothers, block their advance from the city!" shouted Abishai. "We mustn't let them get far; keep them inside Rabbah." Abishai's men met the Ammonite charge head-on, trying to drive them back into the capital.

Joab led the attack on the Arameans, the wind catching his snow-white beard. He kept the pace of a young man despite his considerable age. As he ran, he surveyed the army of Aram, looking for its chief, whom he eventually found trying to withdraw to the rear of his forces. Joab rushed toward him with his sword drawn, his blade slicing through hapless defenders. Finally, he cut down the leader of the Aramean army, leaving the flock with no shepherd. Panic gripped the Aramean camp, as soldiers attempted to carve out an escape route for themselves.

The pursuer became the pursued.

Seeing the Arameans collapse under Joab's attack, the Ammonites retreated back into Rabbah, slamming the gates closed and crying for help against the besiegers.

The Aramean force was wiped out by Joab and his men, and Joab returned to David in Jerusalem to mobilize for the counterattack.

The Israelites and Arameans met again, this time in full force.

The war was bloody, but it ended in victory for David and his men. Aram surrendered to Israel and was required to pay tribute from then on.

Ammon, in the meantime, continued to resist. Entrenched in

Rabbah, the Ammonites refused to surrender, repelling the repeated attacks on the capital.

CHAPTER FORTY-SIX
Bathsheba

In was evening and David had just concluded a briefing with Joab's messengers, who had reported the progress of the siege on Rabbah — or lack thereof.

It was late summer, and the heat of the season still prevailed, with stifling humidity remaining even though the sun had set. David went out to the roof of the palace to enjoy the light breeze. As he beheld the panorama of his capital, he felt a little sadness creeping into his heart, thinking: Still, the Divine Presence has no permanent residence among the People of Israel! Is the Lord to be homeless forever? When will the Israelites be merged with the Creator of the Universe? When will the people have a place where they can come to witness the honor of the King of Kings? When will all humanity perceive that there is a Creator of the Universe, a primordial Mover by Whose unique, unified and undividable Will and Power everything exists and occurs? How long must the earth be riddled by conflict and combat?

A dove landing on the roof drew his gaze. He pondered: Like a dove, the Assembly of Israel has no home and no rest, relentlessly driven from place to place.

David sighed, saddened that his soldiers were still far from home. He reflected: Nearly three decades have passed since I was crowned in Hebron at age thirty; nearly two decades in Jerusalem. Still, I am constantly at war! I may live in a palace, but it is my prison; I am nothing but a servant of the people. Trapped here, I cannot go out into the flowering fields to enjoy the beauty of the blossoms, to smell the plants of the field, to be alone with my Creator in nature.

The doves strutted on the roof, collecting birdseed and cooing.

"I said, Oh, that I had wings like a dove!
I would fly away and find rest.
How far away I would flee!
In the wilderness I would remain."

David sighed again as he remembered his pastoral youth. He longed for the days of shepherding his father's flock alone in the wilderness. His fragile body grew weary with the burden of leadership on his shoulders. Years of serving the public had drained him. Fasting and hardships filled his days. Each troubled individual in the Nation of Israel had someone to turn to for relief and aid. Like a compassionate father, David tended to his subjects, listening to their bitterly recounted sorrows and setbacks. The paternal monarch felt the pain of all those who came to his gate. When his guards wanted to turn petitioners away, he told them: "A king is not one who is served by his subjects; a king is one who serves his subjects. The throne is not a personal possession; everything belongs to the nation. The monarch is a conduit to direct all the resources he receives and controls, so that it can benefit those who need it."

However, the constant torrent of the people's sorrow and pain did have an effect. A tearful mother would ask for the king's blessing to help her sick child, and David would, while silently vowing to fast for the little one's recovery, spend hours in prayer and supplications before God to show mercy, as if the child were his own.

"O Heavenly Father, the People of Israel seek my face in pain and anguish. I cannot save your children; what powers do I have? All I can do is pour out my supplication before You. I am more worm than man, disgraced and despised. Who am I to speak before You, to ask You for anything? But just as a worm's only power is in its mouth, so is mine. As the lightest and lowest of Your nation, I beg You, O Heavenly Father, to give Your people Israel relief from their pain, to let Your children see the glory of Your strength, to behold the pleasure of Your dwelling. You told me, my son, who comes out of my loins, will build Your house, but which one? I do not want to build Your house for My honor, but for Yours. One day I will perish and leave this world; only You know when. Who will reign after me?"

David looked skyward to beg for an answer. The doves frolicked above his head, circling in the air, hovering on the wings of the wind, as if dancing to an unknown tune, floating in the sky. David felt his soul soar among the doves, ascending to heaven in a captivating dance.

Liberty...

Freedom...

Peace...

His soul was enveloped in noble rapture, rising together with the doves over the houses of the city, like a wick catching a flame, so was his soul with the winged creatures hovering above him. A feeling of liberty and freedom filled his being with his dovish dance. Peace of mind suffused him, breathing life into him, cheered by the release from the gravity of murky matter. The levitation continued. David's soul had a dove as a dance partner, touching but not touching, in an aerial ballet. In witness of the couple's aerial choreography, the entire universe fell silent.

The dove rose on its wings, soaring to shine like the North Star in the twilight.

David soared, ascending, rising to catch up to his mate, illuminating the sky with his glow, to fill the universe, with the light then vanishing at sunset.

David advanced...

Approached...

Absorbed...

Suddenly, the dove gathered its wings — like a star falling from heaven; like a stone thrown upwards as it stops climbing and begins falling to earth.

His breath stopped...

The magnificent spectacle turned into a nightmare that was expected to end with a crash to the ground. David dove behind his dove, seeking to catch her, to save her from certain death...

Rooftops of the capital rushing toward them...

The crash was imminent...

Please dear, spread your wings...

Save yourself...

A few yards from the rooftop...
David's soul screamed: Spread your wings...
There is a reason to live...
A few feet from the rooftop...
The dove spreads its wings, landing nobly on the roof of the house.
A sigh burst from David's throat...
David stood on the edge of his roof, returning to himself, catching his breath. He could see his dance partner on the rooftop below, strutting and collecting birdseed. Suddenly a door opened there, and a beautiful young woman emerged from the ritual bath on the roof. Her hair was covered, in the style of a married woman.

David watched, unable to look away from the noble figure; his eyes would not shut, and his head would not turn.

His mind screamed the Torah's commandment: "*And you shall not seek after your own heart and your own eyes, after which you go astray.*" However, his soul was not ready to disconnect. David felt his soul go out toward the woman walking on her roof: his heart clenched with longing for the figure standing in the distance.

"No!" he tried to order his body. "It is forbidden! Turn around and go back inside!"

His body would not obey; it stayed where it was, watching.

David felt his soul striving to connect, to unite, to merge with the woman across the way. His soul had found its mate, its lost partner, the missing piece that would make it whole in a perfect union. It wasn't clear how he knew, but he was rock-solid in the belief that their merging would produce the future king of the People of Israel — a child who had not yet been born; a child who would be worthy to build the Temple, the residence of the Divine Presence among the people of Israel.

On the one hand, his soul screamed: "Forbidden!"
On the other hand, the knowledge arose: "I must!"
"You are the king! You can't do that!"
"You are the king! You have to do it!"

An internal battle, which seemed to last forever. The permitted and the forbidden fought, between the duty of a king to his people and a man's duty to his soul.

Logic shouted: "It won't look good in the eyes of the people! Her hair is covered, so she's probably a married woman."

The intellect replied: "Everything can be cleared up."

David stared, knowing that Israel's fate and his own depended on this decision.

The woman raised her head, as if captive to David's eye, meeting the king's look.

Their gazes met, connected, and merged.

David pulled back and entered his house.

"Please call Secretary Jehoshaphat," David commanded the guard at his door.

The sentry ran to carry out the order, and a few minutes later Jehoshaphat came.

"Yes, has Your Majesty summoned me?"

"Come with me." The king led his secretary to the palace roof. He gestured to the rooftop where the woman had appeared. "Who lives in that house?"

"Uriah the Hittite, whom Your Majesty met when he was Goliath's shield-bearer. The king took him as a bondman and then released him after the battle."

"What is Uriah doing these days?" asked David.

"As far as I know, he is at war with Joab. They are still besieging the city of Rabbah, and Uriah is one of Joab's senior commanders," Jehoshaphat replied.

"Is Uriah married?"

"Yes, of course, he has four wives."

David feigned innocence: "Oh? Which one lives in this house?"

"His youngest and most recent wife, Bathsheba daughter of Eliam, who is one of his comrades — and the son of Your Majesty's counselor, Ahithophel the Gilonite. The wedding was not long ago, and Ahithophel told Uriah that he ought to stay home for a year to rejoice with his wife, as the Torah commands. He refused and said that he could not sit in his house while his master Joab was on the battlefield," the secretary said, and his voice expressed disgust at Uriah's actions.

"Do you know if Uriah gave his wives a bill of divorce before he went to war?" asked David, ignoring Jehoshaphat's tone.

"Of course, Your Majesty promulgated the decree at the beginning of your reign: every soldier must give his wife a bill of divorce before going out to battle — at least a conditional divorce, if not a complete one. Bathsheba's grandfather, Ahithophel, certainly wouldn't have let Uriah go into battle if he hadn't written her a complete divorce," he replied, adding: "This was a wonderful idea. The wives of those missing in action or of prisoners of war would otherwise be trapped! Even those who are killed must sometimes be buried in the field, as unknown soldiers. You have provided for their widows. My own grandmother spent most of her adult life chained in such a manner, as her husband went missing in battle. My youngest daughter was saved from a similar fate, thanks to Your Majesty." Jehoshaphat regarded his sovereign with affection, thinking of his daughter, the young divorcee.

"Thank you very much, Jehoshaphat. You helped me a lot," said David gratefully.

Jehoshaphat left, and David sent messengers to ask Bathsheba to come to him.

David sat in his room, his thoughts disturbed and confused. He was bedeviled by a jumble of conflicting opinions, each one jostling the other.

"It's the evil inclination that tells you to do this."

"You have no choice, you must! You know this is how your heir will be born!"

"You want to violate a prohibition just to satisfy your lust?"

"It's not lust, it's your desire to perfect the nation."

"What hypocrisy! All you want is to serve your vice."

"If it were just the vice of lust, you'd be satisfied with the wives you already have."

"Stolen water is sweet, and bread eaten in secret is tasty!"

"It's not stolen! There is an allowance for you."

"Well done! Become the sort of man who uses allowances to violate prohibitions."

"There's no prohibition! She is not a married woman, she is a divorcee."

"Yes, from now on, every combat soldier must worry that another will take his wife."

"It's not a blanket permit, it's totally different."

"Different because you're a king?"

"No, because you know she completes your soul. Israel awaits such a perfect union, which will produce the king God promised would build the Temple."

"How do you know that?"

"You feel it in every bone of your body."

"That is the bone of contention! Maybe it's just lust after all?"

"There's no doubt about it! All your days, you fast and suffer to subdue your lust, in order to rise above the material, the base, the animal."

"Maybe all this is just a trial to see if you have really conquered your desire!"

"Your heart burns within you, your knees tremble, your body grows lean and gaunt. You already know you're beyond lust, you've conquered your passions."

"What will the people say? How will your subjects look at you?"

"As always, whoever wants to, will think good of you, and whoever wants, will think bad. You must not refrain from the right act because it may be misinterpreted."

"You'll be laughed at, booed."

"What of it? You must do it, despite it all."

The chamber door opened softly as Bathsheba entered. David rose to dismiss the sentries who had brought her. Bathsheba knelt down and bowed to the king.

"Arise, Bathsheba, daughter of Eliam. I have a very important thing to tell you."

"Yes, Your Majesty," Bathsheba said, rising from her knees.

"Listen, my dear, today as I was strolling on the roof of my home, I was deep in thoughts of the restoration of Israel and the building of the Temple," David said, trying to sort things out. "I asked myself who would be my heir, who could succeed me and construct the Chosen House? Who should his mother be, to bear the future builder of the Creator's Dwelling?" David realized he was confusing her.

Bathsheba kept looking down, bewildered and worried, trying to figure out what exactly David was getting at.

"Lost in thought, searching for my path, I saw you on the roof of your house. As soon as I laid eyes on you, I felt that you were my true match, that our union would produce the Prince of Israel, the future builder of the Temple. Every bone in my body told me I had to marry you." He knew his words were surprising and seemingly detached from reality.

Bathsheba looked at the king uncomfortably, her youth quite evident. "But Your Majesty, I am the wife of Uriah the Hittite."

David assumed an expression of wonder: "Really?! You're a married woman?!"

"Yes, Your Majesty," Bathsheba said sorrowfully. "My father married me to Uriah the Hittite, his comrade. The betrothal was just over four months ago. A few days later, immediately after the Festival of Shavuot, Uriah went to war, and he has not returned home since," she said, her gaze fixed on the ground.

David waited a bit, as if thinking about the new information he had received from the young woman. "Did Uriah give you a bill of divorce before he left for the battlefield?" he asked, knowing the answer.

"Yes, Your Majesty, Grandfather Ahithophel forced him to grant me a bill of divorce. Uriah initially did not want to; he said he'd soon be back and didn't need to. But my grandfather insisted on it; he told Uriah that if he came back, he could betroth me again. Otherwise, Grandfather said, Uriah might go missing from the battlefield, and I would remain chained forever. He'd never allow that. I would remain a virgin wrapped in sackcloth for the husband of my youth for life!"

David cleared his throat as if considering the legal issue: "If your husband gave you a bill of divorce before he left, it means you're not a married woman but a divorcee."

The young woman looked up, sinking into the king's eyes. Joy glimmered in her gaze, acknowledging the justice of the royal verdict: "That's true, Your Majesty!"

David's eyes penetrated to the depths of the young woman's soul, piercing her inner self, merging with her. "Look, my dear, you are now a free woman, a divorcee. As I told you, I want to marry you. Our son will succeed me and build the Temple. Your father was entitled to marry you off by the law of the Torah. The circumstances allowed him to accept Uriah's betrothal on your behalf. However, as a divorcee, your father has no further claim on you. The choice is yours. Do you wish to marry me? I cannot force you to do so, nor would I want to. If you want to return to the embrace of your ex-husband, Uriah the Hittite, I will not prevent you from doing so."

Bathsheba, gripped by the king's eyes, burst into tears: "Return to Uriah?! I cannot stand the man! He's rude, insensitive, and inconsiderate. He was never my husband, he was my slaveholder! I'm nothing but a maidservant in his house. On day one, he was already shouting and cursing at me, in front of everyone! He's a beast in human form. The few days I had with him were like hell on earth. I thought about running away, but I had nowhere to go. I wanted to die, but I didn't know what to do. Now that Your Majesty has ruled that I don't have to go back to him, there's no way I'll agree to remarry him." She wept like a prisoner condemned to a life of captivity suddenly rescued, with a sense of relief and deliverance.

Bathsheba cried for a few minutes, then wiped away her tears, coming to her senses: "Yes, Your Majesty, I would be very happy to marry the king."

David looked at Bathsheba, feeling his soul bond with hers in love.

Bathsheba sat with David in his chamber. "Listen to me, my love. Even though everything I have told you is true and valid by the letter of the law, I know that people will grumble that I took you, while your first husband still lives. Return to your home for a few days until I send to call you to come to me. In the meantime, I must develop a strategy to stop people from speaking slander."

Bathsheba looked at him in shock: "But my king..."

"Don't worry, my love," David whispered, reassuring her with his gaze. "Go back to Uriah's house. He's not home; he's still on the battlefield. Don't worry, within a few days, I will bring you to my home to dwell with me forever." David looked at Bathsheba, who seemed terrified at the very idea. "My soulmate, my life partner, I know that parting is difficult. Every day will seem like an eternity to me. But for the sake of both of us, do what I ask. Wait a few days, and you will return to me forever..."

CHAPTER FORTY-SEVEN
Clarification

The shofar of Rosh Hashanah had fallen silent; the day of judgment — when every human is evaluated by the Heavenly Court, when everyone accepts the yoke of the Kingdom of Heaven, when there is a reckoning for every person's actions — had passed. The trepidation and shudder in people's hearts still remained, however. The divine decree had been written, but not signed.

There was still anticipation for Yom Kippur, the day of forgiveness, pardon and atonement, hovering in the air, filling people with a desire to improve their actions and forsake their sins. They hoped the Lord would erase every error committed by His people. There was anxiety accompanied by a feeling of elation ahead of the big day, creating an atmosphere of joy and trembling for the Israelites. Yom Kippur is the day when the verdict written on Rosh Hashanah is sealed.

The crowds of people filling the streets rushed to right their wrongs: paying off debts, asking for forgiveness from friends, returning objects they'd forgotten they'd borrowed. Yom Kippur is a day of forgiveness for the sins committed before God alone, when one repents and resolves never to sin again; but for interpersonal sins, Yom Kippur does not suffice. The sinner must first apologize to and be pardoned by the victim; only then does God forgive too.

Thus, from Rosh Hashanah to Yom Kippur, the Ten Days of Repentance are a period of righting wrongs...

"Have I sinned, Father? Have I transgressed your precepts? Are my acts condemnable? Please, Father, please tell me." David sat on the floor of his room, tears streaming down his face and regretful anguish filling his heart. "My heart tells me I have not sinned, but my mind calls me a transgressor! What is the truth, my Father? Let me know! I beg you to help me find the truth."

David spent many hours crying before God, wearing sackcloth and putting ashes on his head, trying to know and understand the practicalities of the law: a mental struggle penetrating the inner soul, trying to clarify his motivation.

There was a knock on the door. David looked up to see Jehoshaphat the secretary in the doorway: "Yes, Jehoshaphat, my friend, what do you want?" David did not bother to get up and wipe away his tears. Those close to him knew him; there was nothing out of the ordinary in this behavior.

"Your Majesty, a letter has arrived. I would not have bothered the king, but I've been told it's very urgent." Jehoshaphat approached David and handed him the letter. A slight tremor ran through the secretary's body upon seeing his royal master sitting on the ground, his sackcloth soaked with tears. He thought to himself: What a righteous man! He is so God-fearing, fearful of divine justice. Although everyone knows that he is a paragon of virtue, he cries like a child who has sinned against his father. I wish I had a little of the fear of Heaven that He has, a smidge of his devotion and closeness to his Creator.

"Thank you very much, Jehoshaphat," David said to his secretary.

Jehoshaphat looked at the table, the king's breakfast was still there. It seemed as if no one had touched it. "Your Majesty, haven't you had breakfast yet?" he wondered.

"Ahh... Breakfast? No, not now. Thank you, my friend." David lowered his eyes to unroll the scroll. Jehoshaphat walked around him and left the room.

For the glory of His Majesty King David, may the Lord preserve and keep him!

I write this letter to my king in tears, begging and requesting that the king not ignore me. I, Bathsheba daughter of Eliam, servant of my king, would like to inform him that I am with child. About three weeks have passed since the king sent me from him to the house of my ex-husband Uriah the Hittite, promising that he would return to take me to him. So far, I have heard nothing from His Majesty. Nearly five months have passed since my ex-husband left, so there is no doubt from whom I am pregnant. It won't be long before my pregnancy is noticeable. What will people say about me? What will they think of my baby? I make my plea to His Majesty to fulfill his word and not let me be ashamed among my people.

Signed,
Your handmaid, your servant,
Bathsheba daughter of Eliam

David read the letter, joy and apprehension filling his thoughts. "What do you want, my Father, to tell me in this letter? Does the fact that Bathsheba is pregnant mean that my actions are desirable before you? How do I bring her to my home? What will happen with Uriah? What will people say? Does she bear the child the whole world awaits? The one who will build the Chosen House? There's no time. I must develop a strategy to bring Bathsheba to me as respectably as possible."

David rose to his feet, washed his face, and exchanged his sackcloth for royal garb: "Guard, please call Jehoshaphat the secretary."

Jehoshaphat was surprised to be summoned back so quickly, and even more surprised to see that David was now in his regal attire: "Yes, Your Majesty?"

"My friend, tell me: do you know Uriah the Hittite well?"

"Yes, Your Majesty, unfortunately. He is my next-door neighbor, and every time he returns from war, he brings the battlefield back with him. I and my household have no choice but to endure it," he muttered with disgust.

"Please, please tell me everything you know about him. Don't omit a single detail. This is a very important matter," David requested.

"What shall I tell you, Your Majesty? Uriah the Hittite, as you know, is not a righteous convert. When you emancipated him, he automatically became a full Israelite. Now I know why the Torah discourages freeing bondmen. Since you emancipated him, he has become like any other Israelite; he can marry anyone he pleases and act like an Israelite for all intents and purposes. While a righteous convert comes to join the nation because he feels drawn to the Torah and its precepts, the freedman is different. Uriah the Hittite is a prime example of this, as he fulfills no precepts. He enjoys the privileges of an Israelite, while accepting none of the obligations." His tone of disgust turned to rage: "He behaves cruelly toward everyone around him, disrespecting all that is sacred to us. He disobeys the sages of Israel and does as he pleases. He is a brave warrior, very fierce and brutal to his enemies. His eyes are bloodthirsty when he goes to war, anticipating bloodshed like some great booty. He is often seen among the manservants and maidservants, cavorting and carousing. What can I say, Your Majesty? It is a disgrace that he bears the name of Israel." His face fell. "Uriah married four Israelite women, and they are like prisoners of war. Yes, he supports them amply, but he shows them no pity. He wasn't even willing to give them a bill of divorce when he left for the battlefield, until he married his last wife, Bathsheba, daughter of Eliam, granddaughter of Ahithophel the Gilonite, your counselor, who forced him to do it. He wanted to give a conditional divorce, but Ahithophel knew him too well; he insisted that Bathsheba receive a full bill of divorce. So she received that, but the other three have only conditional bills of divorce. I don't know how Eliam, honest and loyal as he is, married his daughter off to this man. Yes, he is a comrade of Uriah's, but it still perplexes me that he would allow this. Uriah is an excellent fighter, and war is his only occupation. He is slavishly devoted to Joab, who made him a senior commander. The soldiers under him despise him. He is tyrannical and arrogant, ruthless and crude." Jehoshaphat looked at the king's face: "Excuse me, Your Majesty, if I have gone on too much, but I cannot bear the man."

David smiled. "Think nothing of it. In what manner is he loyal to Joab?"

"Before Joab, he behaves like a lowly servant, like a dog serving his master. All his pride lies in serving as a general in Joab's army, not the king's. When he drinks, he sings and praises Joab and himself, for Joab's victory over his enemies. Your Majesty is never mentioned in these odes, much less the King of Kings. In short, Your Majesty, Joab is his king, his God, and his beloved," the secretary concluded.

"And what is Joab's attitude toward Uriah?" asked the king.

"As far as I know," Jehoshaphat smiled, "Joab despises him with all his soul. You know Joab, he doesn't like the bootlickers. He uses Uriah, because he really is a great soldier, but Joab despises the man who grovels before him."

"Thank you so much, my dear friend," David said, a smile of contentment on his face. "That will be all. Please, when you go out, ask the guard outside to come in to see me."

David sat down at his table and began writing a letter.

The guard standing at the king's door entered: "Did Your Majesty summon me?"

"Yes, my friend, wait a few minutes until I finish writing the letter. I have a task for you, but don't go alone. Please take two more cavalrymen with you and go urgently to the battlefield. Hand over the letter to Lord Commander Joab, son of Zeruiah."

David finished the letter and handed it to the guard, who hastily set out to carry out the king's order.

CHAPTER FORTY-EIGHT
The Rebel

"Did you call me?" demanded the warrior at the door to David's chamber.

The door, which he had opened rudely and noisily without knocking or asking permission, surprised King David, who was immersed in his study.

"My Lord Commander Joab, son of Zeruiah, Chief of the Army of Israel, told me that you have summoned me," the soldier continued to say in a hurried tone, as if he had been interrupted in an important task by some annoying commoner.

The king looked at Uriah, thinking: A very rude man, indeed! About thirty years have passed since I took him as a servant and freed him. I thought something would change in him during that time, but I guess I was wrong.

"Peace be upon you, Uriah the Hittite," said the king, "we haven't seen each other for a very long time."

"Yes, it's been a long time. What do you want?" asked Uriah.

"I wanted to inquire about the welfare of Joab. How are the fighters? What is the state of the war?" replied David, ignoring the tone of his former servant's voice.

Uriah replied exasperatedly: "That's what you called me for?! Everything is fine! Joab is fine! The fighters are fine! And the war is fine! Is that all? May I go back to my lord Joab, who is on the battlefield?"

"I'm glad to hear that everything is fine. Please go home, wash your feet, rest a little. I will send you a generous repast for you and your house from my table. Relax and rest at home. Then come tomorrow to me, and I will give you a letter to deliver to your lord," said the king.

Uriah turned on his heel, showing his back to the king, and left the room frowning at the annoyance.

"Why are you lying here in the guard's quarters?" one of the sentries asked Uriah. "The king told you to go home and gave you a royal feast. Why are you still here?"

"Why should I go home? Lord Commander Joab, son of Zeruiah, Chief of the Army of Israel, is in the field? Shall I go to my house, sleep in my bed, eat a royal feast on my table? I am a loyal warrior to my lord! If my lord cannot sleep in his own bed under his own roof, neither will I!" answered Uriah firmly.

"But the king ordered you to go home," another guard told Uriah, puzzled.

"So what? My loyalties lie with Lord Commander Joab! Stop confusing my brain! I'm going to sleep, and when he calls me to take the letter, tell me!" Uriah put his pack under his head and promptly went to sleep in the guard's quarters.

"Guard," David called the next day. The door opened, and a sentry stood there.

"Did you call me, Your Majesty?"

"Yes, please go Uriah the Hittite's house and bring him here."

The guard shifted uncomfortably: "Your Majesty, Uriah never went home. He spent the night in our quarters, here on the palace grounds."

"Why? I told him to go home!"

"I beg Your Majesty's pardon, but we also told him to go home, but he insisted he sleep with the guards. He said he would not go home as long as his master, Lord Joab, was in the field. We tried to convince him, but he refused," he apologized.

"Well, then go to the guards' quarters, and summon him," the king requested.

"Did you call me? Is the letter ready?" Uriah asked David impatiently.

"No, Uriah, the letter is not ready yet. Tell me, why didn't you go to your house yesterday when I told you? You haven't been home for several months. Don't you miss your wife? Don't you want to rest and relax a little?" he asked calmly.

Uriah reddened with anger: "Are you kidding me? Miss my wife? Rest and relax? My lord Joab is in the field! He needs me there! Shall I eat and drink and frolic with my wife?! By your life and by your soul, I swear I would never do such a thing!"

The guards were agitated, thinking: How dare he? Off with his head! He speaks insolently to the King of Israel, swearing by the king's life to defy his command!

One placed his hand on his hilt, eager to strike down the rebel for just cause. David stared at him, silently ordering him to stand down.

The king turned calmly to Uriah: "Well, stay today. Tomorrow I will dispatch you."

Uriah turned on his heel, furious at the unexpected delay, bodily pushing the guards around him out of the way in disgust.

The next day, he was again called to the king to dine with him. Uriah sat in front of David and ate. He brazenly drank excessively, as if he were sitting with his comrades. He then got up and went to sleep in the guards' quarters again.

"Your Majesty! In my opinion, this insolent man should be executed as a rebel against the crown," said Jehoshaphat after witnessing this. "He struts around among the king's guard, mocking Your Majesty's orders to go home. He speaks with such disdain and disrespect, saying things like — and I beg Your Majesty's pardon — 'This David is a fool to keep me from serving my master out of pettiness.' I knew he was uncouth and crass, but I underestimated his insolence," he said angrily.

"Calm down, my friend," said the king calmly. "You are biased against him. You said you despised Uriah beforehand."

"Your Majesty, pardon my prejudice, but all the king's guards who spoke to Uriah can confirm what I've said. Everyone agrees that he is a rebel against the king; had Your Majesty permitted it, the scoundrel would have lost his head long ago." Jehoshaphat looked at the guards standing behind him: "Ask them, Your Majesty."

The guards nodded in agreement, their faces sharing fury at Uriah's conduct.

"Well, my friend, I hear you," David said to his secretary. "Have the king's guard bring Uriah to me in an hour's time."

David sat at his desk, quill in hand, writing a letter to Joab. His mind was filled with a torrent of thoughts and deliberations.

"Uriah rebels against the crown. He disobeys you, the king of Israel."

"You knew beforehand that he would defy your order. That's what you wanted."

"So what if you wanted him to be insubordinate? He's a rebel regardless! The law says that a traitor to the kingdom may be executed even without trial."

"If you forgo your honor, then he need not die."

"If a king forgoes the honor due to him, his honor is not forgone. That is the law! It is not yours to dismiss, because this is a role the Lord has given you. Forgoing the king's honor is akin to forgoing the honor of God, and no man is allowed to do that!"

"Oh right, kill him without trial, then take his wife. The people will love that! Uriah is a brave fighter, who laid his life on the line to defend the people of Israel for many years. To execute him as a rebel is a great disgrace to such a person."

"He did it for his own benefit, a mercenary fighting for treasure."

"Even if that's the case, you still owe him for it. Your thoughts have been corrupted; you seek to remove the obstacle that prevents you from taking Bathsheba as a wife."

"What obstacle? She's a free woman."

"Then why did you call Uriah to come to you?"

"To evaluate the man, to understand the competition."

"How is he competition? She's a divorcee."

"True, she is a free woman, but fairness says that a man who divorces his wife so he can fight for his country ought not fear that she may marry someone else while he is at war — all the more so if that someone else is the king for whom he fights!"

"So leave the woman, and when she gives birth, take the child on some pretext."

"You cannot leave her; she completes your soul! To leave her in the hands of Uriah the Hittite is unthinkable."

The flow of thoughts was halted. A flash of a smile appeared on the king's face, as if he had found a perfect solution to a complex and complicated riddle. David began writing quickly. A few minutes later, Uriah arrived to take the letter to Joab.

"Peace be upon you, Lord Commander Joab, son of Zeruiah, Chief of the Army of Israel," Uriah said, bowing deeply to his master. He was sweaty from the long ride.

"What did the king want from you?" Joab asked his devoted warrior curiously.

"Believe me, I have no idea! He drove me crazy! He asked after you, the men, and the war. I don't know why he had to summon me. Any man from the ranks could have told him, no need to trouble me!" He frowned, eyes on the ground in awe of his master. "David sits at home, and instead of letting the fighters do their job, he annoys and upsets them with nonsensical questions. And then he tells me to go home to rest and relax? What's wrong with him? Is he putting me out to stud? Fine for him, he can enjoy his harem, while we do the work!" he said dismissively.

"Hold your tongue! You must not speak about the king that way!" Joab's face reddened with rage. He knew Uriah and his blunt style, but this crossed the line. Raising his voice, he ordered: "Watch your step, and don't push your luck. You're talking about the king of Israel!"

Uriah turned pale, unaccustomed to such a reprimand from his master. "But Lord Commander Joab, why did he call me? David didn't have to keep me away from the battlefield. I should have been here, with you."

"The king is neither 'he' nor 'David!' His Majesty is not your comrade," Joab's said, growing angrier, "but our lord and master, King of Israel, the bravest warrior I have ever had the privilege of fighting alongside. You forget that all your respect and prestige is due to the king! Apparently, you forget you were once his slave! Start speaking respectfully of His Majesty, before I demote you to camp aide or cook or dishwasher — or remove your head!" Joab looked at Uriah with disgust. Uriah stood before him, suddenly lowly and ashamed. His once proudly erect back was bent. His stern eyes and face were lowered, fearing the wrath of Joab, like a disobedient dog cringing from his master's rod.

Joab noticed the letter in Uriah's hand, which bore David's seal. "What do you have in your hand?" he asked firmly.

"Excuse me, Lord Commander Joab, I have here a letter for my master, from His Majesty King David." Uriah had difficulty referring to the king respectfully.

He handed over the scroll, which Joab unrolled and devoured with his eyes.

"Go eat something and then come back. I forgive you now, but next time hold your tongue." With a wave of his hand, Joab dismissed Uriah, who went to his tent.

In the command tent, Joab and Abishai sat alone. All other soldiers and officers had been sent away so the two commanders could discuss the war's progress. The tent was lit by two small candles which barely kept away the darkness of the night.

The toll of the long-running operation was visible on Abishai's face. The six-month siege of Rabbah was draining all of them, from the chief to the lowest foot soldier.

"My brother," Abishai lamented, "Yom Kippur is less than a week away, but instead of repentance, Torah study, and prayer, we are preoccupied with Ammon."

"Yes, I know, but there's nothing we can do. We have to be here, dealing with this. Fighting Israel's battle is a divine commandment too. Don't be disheartened, brother; remember, Israel is one people. That means that each of us has a certain role to perform. Each Israelite is part of one big body; just as the body has different limbs and organs that perform different actions, so too in our nation, each person has a different role. The body has a heart, brain, lungs, hands, legs, nose, mouth, eyes, nails, and many other parts. Each part is a component of the whole. Remove a fingernail, and the body is deficient, and so on with every limb and organ. The same is true for Israel; its integrity depends on all members of the nation. No one is more important than another; every person has a mission in life as a piece of the divine perfection chosen by God. The scholar, chosen for that purpose by the Creator, is not superior to the storekeeper. Each of them has a different role to fulfill with wholeness and faith. The storekeeper who works faithfully, enjoys the lot granted by

Providence, and carefully observes all the precepts, perfectly filling that role in the completion of the world. Meanwhile, a Torah scholar who shirks that duty is a failure and a disappointment when it comes to the world's completion. No role is inherently greater or lesser; all parts are essential for the integrity of the body, and all parts are essential for the integrity of the people. We are privileged to be warriors defending Israel. We are no greater than those whose calling is to draw water, nor are we lesser than those who never leave the study hall. Rejoice in realizing that we are fulfilling our purpose in life, to the best of our ability. Be strong, brother, and have courage. We are fulfilling the Will of the Creator."

Abishai felt his spirits revived by his brother's discourse, a smile crossing his face. "Brother, we should talk like this more often. You have cheered me up. Sometimes, the conditions of war distract us from the truth. I knew all this, but such ideas must be firmly rooted in the heart, enshrined within the soul. Sometimes I fall into a state of sorrow and sadness when I cannot recall a law, chastising myself for not studying all day. Thank you, Joab, for the moral reinforcement — I needed it very much."

Joab laughed, looking at his brother with open love: "The truth, brother? I needed it very much, too. Although I know this truth, sometimes I also fall into a gloomy and miserable mood. When a person speaks the truth in his heart to his friend, he accepts the truth within himself, and he becomes stronger." Joab handed Abishai a cup of wine: "Cheers, brother! When you can find joy in anything, life is always good."

Abishai took a sip, then changed the subject and moved on to practical matters. "I saw that Uriah brought you a letter today from our lord. What did the king write?"

Joab's face grew serious. He handed the letter over: "Here, see for yourself."

Abishai unfolded the scroll and began to read aloud:

To Lord Commander Joab, son of Zeruiah, Chief of the Army of Israel, and my dear friend, peace be upon you!

I hope this letter finds you, your brother Abishai, and our army well. Please let me know how the war is going. How many men do we have, and what is their status? If you need reinforcements, please let me know and I will send more fighters to you.

May God make this new year one of success and happiness. May our enemies soon fall before you, so you may return to our holy capital.

May you be inscribed and sealed in the Book of Life, with all the just and all of Israel, who pray and study for your health and victory.

I close with a request, my brother. Uriah the Hittite, who brings you this missive, is a rebel against the crown. He defied royal orders, mocking and denigrating his sovereign before the king's ministers and servants. Because he is one of your warriors, I refrained from killing him contemptuously as a traitor against the kingdom. I ask you to send him to the front lines, where he will die in combat. There is no possibility of forgiveness and pardon for all the deeds he did while in the palace, but I do not want him to die in dishonor.

Please let me know after you have honored my request.

With much gratitude and love,

Praying for you before our Heavenly King,

David

Abishai finished. He looked up at his brother in astonishment: "Uriah, a rebel?!"

"Yes, so it turns out. This insolent man spoke dismissively of our king when he returned from the capital. I'm telling you, I almost decapitated him on the spot for his disrespect. He talks about the king of Israel like a good-for-nothing — in my presence, as if he expects me to agree! Until I read this, I didn't realize how far he went to disparage the king of Israel personally and publicly. I don't know if he deserves to die as a war hero, but that's the king's will." Joab went out and asked one of the sentries to summon Uriah the Hittite to the command tent.

"Yes, Lord Commander, you called me?" asked Uriah, peeking into the tent.

"Yes, come!" said Joab, irritated. Uriah seemed chastened and downcast. "Uriah, listen to me carefully! Today you truly enraged me! One more word, and I would have spilled your blood. After consulting with Abishai, we decided to give you one last chance to make it right. Tomorrow morning, we are going to attack Rabbah again;

we have spent too long besieging it. I want you to lead the charge; we will be with you, but you will lead. I know what you said was because you were tired and exhausted from riding back and forth to Jerusalem over the past few days." Uriah nodded, his gaze still lowered. "I know that you are an extremely loyal soldier and the bravest fighter in our army." Uriah's shoulders began to straighten; his slumped head rose, looking at his master admiringly. "I entrust you with this important task: to conquer the city. I know you won't disappoint me, and you'll rise to the occasion honorably."

Uriah's face shone: "Yes, Lord Commander, I will carry out the mission to the fullest. Consider Rabbah conquered. Tomorrow, we will toast our glorious victory," he said proudly, standing tall and looking straight at Joab. "Thank you my lord, I will not disappoint you."

"I very much hope so," Joab said. "That's all, you are dismissed."

Uriah bowed and backed out of the tent.

At sunrise, the white rays burst through the thick gray clouds, flaring on the city walls. Dark and light fought for dominion. A cool autumn wind heralded the approach of the rainy season, as if preparing the army for the impending difficulty of besieging the city. The battalions were ready for the impending attack, the fighters looking skyward, praying to capture the city and end the siege, for the long-awaited reunion with their families, children, and wives, whom they had not seen for many months.

Uriah led the soldiers, giving orders to the battalion commanders. With the skill of a veteran, he planned the fateful battle. As he barked orders, he thought: I must succeed, I must not disappoint my lord.

"I and my battalion will break through first toward the eastern gate. Two others will remain behind as my reinforcements for the second offensive. They are headed by Lord Commander Joab and his brother Abishai. Archers! I want a screen of arrows; don't let the defenders stick their noses out of the slits. Two more battalions will attack from the north and the south; you will also have reinforcement battalions for the second and third waves. Ladder-carriers! You will come with the attacking battalions after the second wave, when the soldiers standing on the city walls get tired. While the third wave is attacking, the western side will probably not be protected. Climbers!

You will come quietly from the west, and using your grappling hooks, you will climb the western wall and make your way through the city toward the eastern gate. When you open it, the city will be in our hands." Uriah smiled: "Tonight, we will celebrate our victory."

The attack began with staccato shofar blasts from the north, south, and east. Uriah led the first wave attempting to breach the city, galloping wildly on his horse. His troops struggled to match his pace, as Uriah waved his sword and let loose war whoops, encouraging his soldiers. As he neared the gate, Uriah's grim grin faded; companies of soldiers were emerging from Rabbah, prepared for battle.

"They're counterattacking! They're meeting our offensive," cried the soldiers, who had expected the townspeople to remain entrenched in their city. Swords clanged, but Uriah sped right into the midst of his master's enemies, slashing right and left. The slain fell all around him, as he struggled to make it to the gate. His noble black steed trampled the approaching Ammonites, rearing to kick with its forelegs. The Ammonite army began to retreat, which made Uriah smile in triumph as he pursued them. He thought: A few more yards, I'm almost there. I'll take Rabbah and make Lord Commander Joab happy, appeasing him with my glorious victory.

An endless barrage of arrows shot through the slits in the city walls wiped the smile off his face. One pierced Uriah's neck, another hit his horse's head as it reared, trying to crush his enemies. Uriah held the reins of the mount with the last of his strength, trying to pull it back; but instead it collapsed backwards, pinning his body under it. Rider and steed lay helpless on the ground.

Staccato shofar blasts echoed through the Israelite camp. "Retreat! Retreat!" Joab cried, as Uriah's body lay like an unturned stone, corpses from both sides surrounding him.

David frowned: "What sort of fool tries to conquer a fortified city this way? Who tries to invade in broad daylight?" A messenger sent by Joab from the battlefield had told the king about the course of the battle and the retreat. "Obviously, the archers would fire through their slits," David continued, angered by the illogic of the tactic, which had led to heavy Israelite casualties.

The messenger apologized: "Your Majesty, it was Uriah the Hittite who planned the attack. He thought covering fire would stop the archers, but he too died."

David's angry face softened. He thought: I wanted him to die, but I didn't want other soldiers to die with him. The battle planning may have made some sense.

David turned to the messenger: "Tell Joab not to trouble himself over the attempt. There is a better way to conquer such a city. An underground stream must be supplying water to the townspeople. Tell him that he must find this stream and redirect it, so Rabbah will be gripped by thirst. They'll surrender within days."

The messenger left David, while another was sent to inform Uriah's wives of his passing, as a hero of Israel. The king would come to comfort the grieving family.

Uriah's home, near the king's palace, was crowded. Dusk had arrived, and the autumnal sun moved to the west as the clouds of the distant horizon greeted it. Men and women streamed through the house, where Uriah's wives and children had gathered. The atmosphere of the impending Yom Kippur was felt in the air, with light bursts of crying in the background. The children bounced around, breaking the silence in the mourning house. Uriah's wives sat on chairs scattered throughout the large home, tending to their grieving children. The children sat on mats spread out on the ground, paying their last respects to their father, whom they'd barely known. The wives — ex-wives, really, since Uriah's death meant they had retroactively been divorced before he left — greeted the crowds of visitors.

A hush fell over the crowd when a boy ran into the house, announcing that King David of Israel had arrived to comfort the grieving family. The crowd squeezed aside, making way for the king to approach Uriah's orphans.

"I share in your sorrow," said David. "Your father was a heroic, brave, and daring man who sacrificed his life for the People of Israel. He was privileged to do something that many do not: to die sanctifying God's name, fighting the enemies of Israel. I know that there really is nothing that comforts a person whose relatives have passed away. But know that those who sacrifice their lives for the Holy Nation are guaranteed to dwell in the shadow of the Divine Presence; perhaps this will give you some comfort. May the Lord bless you to know no more sorrow and to heal your pain quickly. From Heaven, may you be comforted."

"Thank you very much, Your Majesty, for taking the trouble to come to comfort us," said Uriah's eldest son. "We appreciate it very much, that the King of Israel has come to our father's house to honor his memory."

David turned to leave. Out of the corner of his eye, he saw Bathsheba sitting in the corner of the room, tears streaming down her face. He thought: Everyone must think they're tears of sadness, but I know they're tears of gladness.

All eyes were fixed on the king of Israel who'd paid tribute to his fallen warrior.

One of the king's guards surreptitiously approached Bathsheba in the corner, slipping her a note from the king. She quickly buried the letter deep in her bosom.

The king and his delegation left the house. Bathsheba waited anxiously for the peace of night, the silence that came upon the house of mourning at day's end. The voices of the children were silent, except for the monotonous rhythm of their breathing in sleep. Bathsheba slid into an empty corner containing the memorial candles lit in honor of the deceased. Quietly she opened the secret letter, crying with joy and relief as she read the text.

To my soulmate, the other half of my heart, my wife, and the mother of my future son!

Being apart from you and far from you is unbearable. Each day is like an eternity to me, as we are prevented from being together. But we must act prudently. Stay in Uriah's house until the month of mourning ends, though you are no mourner. Otherwise, tongues will wag. After that, I will summon you to the palace, so we may wed before all, according to the faith of Moses and Israel. Your pregnancy is still in its earliest stage, so it will still be unnoticed at the end of the month.

Looking forward to the merging of our souls,
Your husband, David

Bathsheba read the letter over and over, memorizing it. She then folded the letter and buried it firmly in her bosom again.

A messenger came from Joab to David with a letter:

To my lord, King David of Israel, blessings be upon you!

As usual, the king has been proven right. The stream was found, as the king knew through the Holy Spirit. The siege of the city is about to end, as the townspeople flee, gripped by thirst.

Your Majesty, Rabbah is in your hands. Please gather the rest of the people to encamp on the city and capture it, lest this victory be attributed to me, when the king's guidance brought it about.

Looking forward to seeing the king's face soon.

Your servant Joab, son of Zeruiah

David gathered the whole nation to war, which proved quite easy. The warriors of Ammon, desperate due to thirst, broke out of the city, trying to break the siege. The dehydrated warriors fell easily before David's forces and the city was captured.

As sweet revenge, David and Joab wreaked their vengeance on the villains who had disgraced the Israelite delegation, whose only crime had been coming to console King Hanun over the death of his father.

Hanun, son of Nahash, King of Ammon, was captured and tortured to death by Joab's warriors. His crown, made of a golden talent and with a precious stone in its center, was taken from him and given to King David, who hung it over his throne.

CHAPTER FORTY-NINE
Nathan's Parable

The sun's last rays burst through the window as the great day reached its zenith — Yom Kippur, the anniversary of pardon, forgiveness, and atonement, bestowed by the Creator for the repentant among His people Israel.

The streets were empty, and the citizens huddled together in their assembly places, becoming stronger in repentance, returning to their Creator. The atmosphere of trepidation was dissipating; thoughts turning to the coming Festival of Joy, Sukkot.

With one exception: a man who hurried through Jerusalem on his way to the palace, stepping ahead of the burgeoning twilight.

The king's gate opened, and Nathan the Prophet stood at the entrance, his garb white as frost, his body wrapped in a snowy shawl like a ministering angel.

The king sat on the floor of the room; his sobs audible beneath the tear-soaked shawl covering his head. Nathan coughed lightly, drawing the king's attention.

David raised his eyes and got to his feet out of respect for Nathan. "Peace be upon you, my lord prophet," David declared. "What brings you to me now?"

"Peace be upon Your Majesty. I see how inopportune a time it is for any Israelite. This is the hour of repentance and reunion. However, I must speak to the king about a very important subject," Nathan apologized. "Yom Kippur is the time to right wrongs. I heard of an awful incident, one the king must urgently address.

"*There were two men in a certain city, one rich and the other poor. The rich man had a great number of sheep and cattle, but the poor man had nothing except one small ewe lamb that he had bought. He raised it,* and it grew up with him and his children. It shared his food and drank from his cup; it slept in his arms and was like a daughter to him. Now a traveler came to the rich man, who refrained from taking one of his own sheep or cattle to prepare for the traveler who had come to him. Instead, he took the poor man's lamb and prepared it for his guest."

The prophet finished, looking into David's face, waiting for the king's judgment.

David's wrath rose; the rich man's audacity offended him. In anger, he decreed: *"As surely as the Lord lives, the man who did this deserves to die! Because he has done this thing and has shown no pity, he must pay for the lamb four times over."*

Nathan looked straight at the king, looking into his eyes, as if trying to penetrate deep into his soul. Pointing an accusatory finger at him, he declared: *"You are that man! This is what the Lord, the God of Israel, says: 'I anointed you king over Israel, and I delivered you from the hand of Saul. I gave your master's house to you and your master's wives into your arms. I gave you the house of Israel and Judah, and if that were not enough, I would have given you even more. Why then have you despised the command of the Lord by doing evil in His sight? You put Uriah the Hittite to the sword and took his wife as your own, for you have slain him with the sword of the Ammonites. Now, therefore, the sword will never depart from your house, because you have despised Me and have taken the wife of Uriah the Hittite to be your own.' This is what the Lord says: 'I will raise up adversity against you from your own house. Before your very eyes, I will take your wives and give them to another, and he will lie with them in broad daylight. You have acted in secret, but I will do this thing in broad daylight before all Israel.'"*

David's face turned as pale as his prayer shawl. The harsh words penetrated like a blade stabbing his heart, shedding his blood within him. A shiver gripped his body, his legs failed him, and David dropped to the ground. "Oh, oh, woe is me! I have violated God's Word! I have sinned against my Lord, the God of Israel, and I have transgressed His precepts. I killed Uriah, so the sword will never be removed from my home. I took Bathsheba, dishonoring God in the people's eyes."

Nathan the Prophet looked at the humiliated king on the ground, weeping over his sin. Nathan's heart, connected to David's heart, went out to him; he sobbed with the man on the floor. "It is revealed and known to God that your sin was only against Him, and by the law of man, you are exempt. Uriah the Hittite deserved death. Bathsheba was a free woman when you took her. Still, God despises the way you did it. A person of your rank and position must be beyond reproach; the act you have done seems, in human terms, to be a vile act. Indeed, if another man had done so, no one would have said a word. But for you, it was forbidden! You represent the Creator of the Universe; you serve and worship him! Your act allows those who oppose the God of Israel and His Kingdom to take the high ground!

"However, your immediate and unequivocal confession does you credit. If you had sinned with a married woman, you would be subject to the death penalty, and you would never be permitted to marry her. Similarly, if your killing of Uriah had been forbidden, you would be condemned. God, however, knows all secrets. He recognizes the truth of your intentions and motivations. *The Lord has taken away your sin. You will not die. Nevertheless, because by this deed you have shown utter contempt for the word of the Lord, the son born to you will surely die.*"

Nathan left the king sobbing on the ground before his Maker at Yom Kippur's end.

David paced the halls of the palace, as Bathsheba's cries and sighs in childbirth echoed down them. His lips voiced a silent prayer for the welfare of mother and baby. It seemed like an eternity, as Bathsheba's screams and groans tore at his heart. Many hours had passed since her nurse had entered his room and informed him that the time had come. He feared and dreaded what was to come; he knew the sentence on the baby's head, hoping for it to be abolished. He had never told Bathsheba what Nathan had said; it would be unbearable for her. Her cries intensified as the baby made his way out. A pregnant woman has the superhuman ability to endure the pain only because of the anticipation. The strength of the soul overcomes the pains of the body, knowing a newborn is on the way.

"Soon enough. Soon he'll be out. Push hard. Soon you will have a child, hold on," the midwives said, encouraging the spirit of the woman in labor. "One more push, just one, Bathsheba, and he's out."

Her final scream pierced the heavens, followed by a sigh of relief. The sound of a baby's cry could be heard.

"Congratulations, dear Bathsheba, you have a son," the midwife said as she placed the newborn baby on his young mother's body.

Bathsheba produced a pained smile. "I have a child," her lips whispered softly, embracing the son on her lap with tired arms.

The door opened: "Congratulations, Your Majesty," the midwife said to David, "You have a son."

"Thank you," David said, his lips numb. "How's Bathsheba?" he asked worriedly.

"She's fine," the midwife replied with a slight smile, looking at the worried king. A thought crossed her mind: All men are the same, no matter what their job; but at moments like this, they all look the same, like scared little children.

The midwife encouraged him: "Don't worry, Your Majesty, she and the baby are fine. In a few hours, she will begin to regain her strength; the difficulty is already behind us. Bathsheba is young and strong; she will recover quickly. Soon you will be able to visit her, Your Majesty."

David thought: She will need that strength and resilience, with what lies ahead. He blurted out softly, "Thank you very much."

"Dear Father, I have sinned, I have transgressed Your precepts, I have defamed Your name. But how did the child sin? Why should he be punished for my crime? What wrong has he done?" David lay on the floor of his room, not eating or drinking for six days. A few hours after Bathsheba gave birth to their son, the news had come that something was wrong with the child.

"I don't know what's wrong, Your Majesty," said the midwife, "but the baby is not breathing properly. He is struggling to breathe. I've never seen a situation like this." The midwife tried to encourage him: "Don't worry, Your Majesty, I'm sure everything will be fine. In the end, God willing, he will make it through."

The midwife left and David collapsed on the ground crying. "Please, Father, have compassion on the child; remove my sin from him. Let not the child die for my iniquity. I have called upon you, O Lord. God, I cry. Cleanse the infant of my sin and spare his life."

The sound of crying could be heard through the door. Six days of fasting, yelling and crying, echoing throughout the palace, cutting into the hearts of all who heard it, motivating them to pray for the newborn prince.

Zadok and Jehoshaphat stood by the door, exchanging glances as they asked each other: Who should break the bitter news to the king?

"I dare not tell him," Zadok told Jehoshaphat, as if reading his mind. "I was told that it's been a long time. For six days, he hasn't stopped crying," he said worriedly.

"Not only does he cry all the time," Jehoshaphat added, "he hasn't eaten a morsel or drunk anything since the news came to him that the boy was sick. Every time we brought him food, he wouldn't get up from the ground; the servants who brought the new meal found the last one untouched. I hope the bitter news doesn't break his spirit completely. I'm afraid he'll hurt himself when he learns about it."

Zadok shrugged. "There is no choice; we must tell him. The child must be buried; it cannot be postponed." Jehoshaphat nodded, and the two entered the king's room.

Lonely rays of sunlight penetrated through the thick curtain covering the window. After a week of being sealed, the chamber's air was stifling. Zadok and Jehoshaphat looked at their king crying on the ground. "Your Majesty," said Zadok. David looked up dimly, bathed in tears, staring through him. The ministers exchanged glances, trying to find the words. "Your Majesty," Zadok repeated.

"Is the child dead?" asked David, surprising them with his pointed question.

"Unfortunately, yes," Zadok spoke in a rush, trying to get it all out as soon as possible. "Your son passed away an hour ago. The healers and midwives did all they could to save him, to no avail. It is God's decree. We share the king's sorrow."

The two anxiously awaited the king's reaction. David got up from the floor, went to the corner of the room, and washed his face from the basin. "My brothers and comrades, give me a few minutes. I will bathe, change, and return to you."

Zadok and Jehoshaphat looked at each other in astonishment while David was in the bathroom. He emerged several minutes later to say: "Please, come with me; I should go to the house of the Lord to thank Him for His acts." When his ministers seemed shocked, he explained: "One has to thank God for the bad just as one thanks for the good! Whatever God does to us, we must thank Him," he concluded, turning to leave the palace, toward the tent where the Ark of the Covenant rested.

Once he had finished there, he returned to the palace and said to his servant: "Please bring me bread to eat." The servant rushed to fulfill his master's wishes. The king sat and ate his fill.

Zadok could contain himself no longer: "Please, Your Majesty, explain to me the meaning of your actions. For the living child, you fasted and wept; now that he has died, you rise and eat?!"

David looked at Zadok, a slight smile on his lips: "My lord priest! *While the child was alive, I fasted and wept, for I said, 'Who knows? The Lord may be gracious to me and let him live.' But now that he is dead, why should I fast? Can I bring him back again? I will go to him, but he will not return to me.* As long as my boy was alive, there was hope to annul the bad decree; now, the sentence has been carried out. Why fast now? One day, in the World of Truth, I will meet my son, whom I did not get to know. For now, we must go on living."

A year later, the mood in the palace had been utterly reversed; a week had passed since David and Bathsheba welcomed their second son. A festive atmosphere enveloped those gathered in the hall. Early in the morning, the people gathered for the baby's entry into Abraham's covenant.

David was wrapped in phylacteries and a prayer shawl, at the circumcision chair.

"*Blessed is he who comes in the name of the Lord,*" the crowd shouted joyfully and relievedly as the baby was brought to his father. Nathan presented the newborn, his face beaming. David responded with profound emotion:

I rejoice in Your promise
Like one who finds great spoil.
The sacrifices of God are a broken spirit;
A broken and a contrite heart,
O God, You will not despise.

In Your good pleasure, cause Zion to prosper;
Build up the walls of Jerusalem.
Then You will delight in righteous sacrifices,
In whole burnt offerings;
Then bulls will be offered on Your altar.
His voice echoed through the great hall:
Blessed is the one You choose
And bring near to dwell in Your courts!
The crowd responded:
We are filled with the goodness of Your house,
The holiness of Your temple.
David closed his eyes to intone a prayer:
If I forget you, O Jerusalem,
May my right hand cease to function.
May my tongue cling to the roof of my mouth
If I do not remember you,
If I do not exalt Jerusalem
As my greatest joy!

The silent crowd connected with the king's longing for the building of the Temple in the Holy City of Jerusalem.

David read the creed of millions of Israelites throughout the generations, willing to give their souls and the souls of their children to their Creator, to accept His Kingship over them, to bear witness to the belief that He alone created everything, and to designate His name over the entire universe.

Hear O Israel, the Lord our God, the Lord is one.

The audience repeated the king's call with reverence.

David exclaimed, testifying to the belief in the eternity of the Creator.

The Lord reigns!
The Lord has reigned!
The Lord will reign forever and ever!

The audience echoed the king's recognition of the everlasting King of Kings.

The king repeated his call, and the crowd followed.

David prayed for the health of the baby.

O Lord, save us, we pray.
O Lord, save us, we pray.

The crowd prayed after the king.

David offered a supplication for human success:

We beseech You, O Lord, cause us to prosper!
We beseech You, O Lord, cause us to prosper!

The audience echoed David's prayer.

David handed the baby over to Nathan as he sat on the circumcision chair. Nathan put the infant on the throne next to it, announcing three times: "This is the seat of the Messenger of the Covenant, of blessed memory."

A hush fell over the crowd in anticipation of fulfilling the command. Nathan the Prophet prepared the baby for his entry into the covenant.

David closed his eyes with the knife in his hand, in the city of Jerusalem, Mount Moriah, in the same place where Abraham held the knife to slaughter his son by God's command. David sat ready to circumcise his son. His knees symbolized the altar to which Isaac had been bound. David, like Abraham, was willing to fulfill his Creator's command, whatever it might be.

A memory ran through his mind. Absalom, his clever third son, had once asked him: "The Creator is perfect, so why not create man with no foreskin?"

David had replied to his son: "The perfection of man is in fulfilling the Will of his Creator. A person who lives on earth and does not fulfill the Creator's Will is not a complete person at all. When one circumcises his son properly, he proves that he believes in the Creator of all. It is not easy to take a blade to the body of a newborn." David went on to explain: "The circumcised baby receives its perfection precisely by the person who circumcises, fulfilling the Creator's command. The act of circumcision proves the connection to perfection between the act of the Creator and the act of man, the integrity of the connection between us and God."

"Blessed are You, Lord our God, King of the World, Who sanctified us with His precepts and commanded us to bring him into the Covenant of Abraham our Patriarch," David recited, continuing: "Blessed are You, Lord our God, King of the World, Who sanctified us with His precepts and commanded us concerning circumcision."

The audience answered "Amen" loudly.

David leaned over the child, and fulfilled the covenant himself.

A light cry arose from the infant's mouth, opening their hearts to prayer.

David raised his voice and recited: "Blessed are You, Lord our God, King of the World, Who has kept us and sustained us and brought us to this time," thanking his Maker for allowing him this opportunity.

"Amen," responded the guests. "Just as he entered the covenant, so may he enter into the Torah and the precepts, the marriage canopy, and good deeds."

Nathan raised a glass and recited blessings over the wine and some fragrant myrtles. The prophet closed his eyes and recited: "Blessed are You, Lord our God, King of the World, who sanctified the beloved one from the womb, set His statute in his flesh, and sealed his descendants with the sign of the holy Covenant. Therefore, as a reward for this, the Living God, our Lot, our Rock, has ordained that the beloved of our flesh be saved from the abyss, for the sake of the Covenant which He has set in our flesh. Blessed are You, Lord, who makes the Covenant."

Nathan took a sip, then said: "Our God and the God of our ancestors, preserve this child for his father and mother, and his name in Israel shall be called..." He leaned over to David.

"Solomon," David told Nathan.

The prophet said to David, "The Lord commanded me to tell you that he would also be called Jedidiah."

David amended: "Solomon Jedidiah."

Nathan continued: "Solomon Jedidiah, son of King David and Queen Bathsheba! May the father rejoice in his offspring, and may his mother be glad at the fruit of her womb, as it is said: *May your father and mother rejoice, and she who bore you be glad.* And it is said: *I passed by and saw you weltering in your blood, and I said to you: 'You shall live through your blood;' and I said to you: 'You shall live through your blood.'* And it is said: *He has remembered His covenant forever, the word which He has commanded to a thousand generations; the covenant which he made with Abraham and His oath to Isaac; He established it for Jacob as a statute, for Israel as an everlasting covenant.*

"Give thanks to the Lord for He is good, for His kindness is everlasting. Give thanks to the Lord for He is good, for His kindness is everlasting. May this infant Prince Solomon Jedidiah, son of King David and Queen Bathsheba, become great. Just as he entered the covenant, so may he enter into the Torah and the precepts, the marriage canopy, and good deeds. May this verse be fulfilled in him: *May God make you like Ephraim and like Manasseh.* Amen, so may it be His Will."

David prayed and the audience was silent, listening to the melody of the king's rhythm, drawn into the lyrics of the ode:

> *A song of ascents.*
> *Blessed are all who fear the Lord,*
> *Who walk in His ways!*
> *For when you eat the fruit of your labor,*
> *Blessings and prosperity will be yours.*
> *Your wife will be like a fruitful vine*
> *Flourishing within your house,*
> *Your sons like olive shoots*
> *Sitting around your table.*
> *In this way indeed shall blessing come*
> *To the man who fears the Lord.*
> *May the Lord bless you from Zion,*
> *That you may see the prosperity of Jerusalem*
> *All the days of your life,*
> *That you may see*
> *Your children's children.*
> *Peace be upon Israel!*

CHAPTER FIFTY

Amnon and Tamar

"What troubles you, brother?!" Amnon's cousin Jonadab asked him. "You don't look good. You've seemed ill for a few days now. Are you all right?"

Amnon, King David's eldest son, lay down; he had been bedridden for two weeks. His manservant had called Jonadab to try to figure out what was wrong with him.

"It's nothing." Trying to deflect the question, he murmured softly: "I'll be fine."

"Don't tell me it's nothing," Jonadab urged. "I know you too well for you to put me off so easily. You've been gone from the study hall for a fortnight. At first I thought your father had given you a mission, but then your man told me you've been lying about all this time. I came to see what happened to you."

Jonadab was Amnon's longtime best friend. Their family bond paled in comparison to their close relationship as study partners. For years they'd sat together in the royal study hall, bringing them closer every day.

Amnon tried to evade: "No, don't worry. I'm probably just under the weather."

"Under the weather? Are you joking?" smirked Jonadab. "You've never missed a day due to illness, and suddenly you're under the weather for two whole weeks?"

Amnon looked away, watching the greenish curtain waft with the breeze blowing into the room. "You wouldn't understand…" he said desperately.

Jonadab snarled: "Oh, I wouldn't? What is going on with you? Tell me."

His mind struggling to find a remedy for his condition, Amnon thought to himself: Jonadab is a very clever young man, with extraordinary wisdom and deep perception. He is quick-witted, and his counsel is usually sound and practical. If he doesn't know how to help me, no one else can." Amnon began to reveal his heartsickness to his best friend: "You know my sister Tamar?"

"Of course."

"Whenever I think of her, my heart shudders. I love her completely, and I want her. I know that if I ask my father to marry her, he'll never allow it. That's why I look like this. My whole body is aching and tender from the intensity of my love and desire for her, but I know my cause is hopeless. There is no cure for what ails me," Amnon finished, a tear welling up in the corner of his eye.

Jonadab put a hand on his forehead, straining his mind to solve the thorny problem. "Tell me, Tamar's mother, Maacah, is a war bride, right?"

"Yes," Amnon sighed.

Jonadab's feverish mind began to work vigorously, disentangling the legal knot: "So a war bride is a foreign woman captured in war by an Israelite. The Torah allows the Israelite to have intercourse with her, on the condition that he brings her home, converts her properly, and makes her his wife in every respect. That is what Uncle David did with Maacah, who is the daughter of King Talmai of Geshur. The war he waged on her homeland lasted a while, and your father was in the field for several months. He came home and had to wait a month before marrying Maacah. Six months after your father returned home, Tamar was born. Am I right so far?"

Amnon nodded, trying to understand what his friend was getting at.

"It follows," Jonadab resumed his analysis, "that Uncle David is not legally Tamar's father, because she must have been conceived on the battlefield, before Maacah converted. A proselyte is like a newborn baby, with no previous lineage."

Amnon looked at Jonadab, hope glimmering in his eye. "Yes..." he said eagerly.

"It follows from all this that according to the laws of the Torah, you and Tamar are not siblings. You have different mothers, and while David is your father, she has no father at all, legally speaking." He smiled. "All you must do is ask him for her hand."

The light ignited in Amnon's eyes faded. "He'll never agree," he said sadly.

"Why? Why do you think so?" asked Jonadab in wonder.

Amnon explained: "You know my father, he is a righteous and pious man. You are right that by the letter of the law, Tamar is not my father's daughter, so we are not siblings. However, he has always raised her as his own. She dresses like the other princesses, and lives among them. My father wouldn't let me marry her, because it looks like incest. Were he to explain the legal logic, it would make Tamar some sort of foundling, upsetting her, her mother, my father, and her brother Absalom. On top of that, it's been less than two years since the story of Bathsheba. My father will not want to start making excuses again for the royal family's apparently forbidden unions." Amnon seemed to despair of life.

"Listen to me carefully, my friend," said Jonadab. "Your father loves you completely, you are his firstborn. If Uncle David sees the situation you are in due to your love for Tamar and how it makes you ill, he will present any explanation, excuse, or explanation necessary. Your father is a wise and righteous scholar. He knows that by law, she is permitted to you, and therefore he will not refuse you if he understands that preventing her from you brings you to such a state. Lovesickness can sometimes be lethal. You look like you won't survive if you don't marry Tamar," Jonadab said worriedly to his friend. "Listen to me what you'll do: Your father knows you're sick, but he doesn't know the reason. When your father comes to visit you, ask him that your sister Tamar come to you and prepare food for you here, so you can eat what she makes in your presence."

Jonadab mused: The king will see his son's distress in his love for Tamar and will agree to give her to him as a wife. Tamar, too, when she sees Amnon's love for her, will agree to marry him. After all, she's not legally David's daughter. When she agrees, it will be easy to persuade Maacah and Absalom as well.

"And what will come of it?" asked Amnon.

"When your father sees that you love her so much, he will let you marry her. Your father knows human nature, and when you tell him that you must eat from Tamar's food, he will understand everything." Jonadab concluded: "You must listen to me."

"My beloved son, what is it? Are you in pain? Did the healer visit you today?" David asked his firstborn, who appeared to be on his deathbed, anxiously.

Amnon answered weakly: "I don't know what happened to me, father. I'm weak all over my body. For several days, I haven't eaten anything. My whole body hurts and aches, and the healers don't know what I have. Please help me, Father!"

David's face took on a grim countenance; sorrow filled his heart. "My son, you must eat! I don't know what ails you, but if you don't eat anything, your body will be even weaker, and you won't be able to overcome the illness that afflicts you. You must force yourself to eat. Is there anything your soul desires?" he asked lovingly.

Amnon looked at his father, hoping for the success of his scheme, and answered feebly: "Could my sister come and make her delicious pancakes? Maybe the wonderful aroma of her baking will arouse my appetite, and I'll enjoy some."

David turned to the sentry at the door: "Run and bring my daughter Tamar here. Her brother Amnon is sick, and he longs for her pancakes." The guard hurried off.

"Your sister Tamar is so kindhearted, she will surely prepare lunch for you. You know, Tamar is very modest. She never leaves the house. But for her brother, she will. Eat what she prepares for you and rest. Now I have to go; they're waiting for me in court. Tomorrow morning I will come to you again, and I want to hear that you ate to your heart's content," David told Amnon, worried about his young son.

"Well, Father, I'll do my best," Amnon said in a low voice.

Tamar stood in Amnon's doorway. Her gentleness and nobility were evident from her hesitant steps as she entered her brother's sitting room. "Father said you asked me to prepare food," she said in a weak, shy voice. Tamar's eyes were downcast, abashed. "Father said you were sick and wanted me to make you pancakes."

"Yes, sister, please," Amnon said, eyeing her hungrily. He thought:

She is so stunning, her flowing clothing cannot hide her beauty. She wears a royal striped gown with a tunic over it, trying in vain to hide her wondrous figure. The hood on her head covers her hair, but her striking face shines like the full moon. I love her so much.

Amnon watched as she came in and went into the small kitchen, where a fire was crackling, ready to cook. Every movement became etched in his mind, intensifying his drive.

"Brother, here you go. The pancakes should give you strength," she said, placing the pancakes on the heavy wooden table next to her brother's couch.

"Thank you, sister," he said in a broken voice, "but I've spent so much time languishing here on my sickbed, it dulls my appetite. In the bedroom, it is much more pleasant. The maid just freshened up in there."

Tamar took the pancakes to the bedroom on the orders of her brother, who hastily got up from the couch.

"Get everyone else out of here," he whispered to the guards standing outside. They hurried to fulfill the crown prince's words.

Amnon entered the room after his sister, quietly locking the door behind him. "Come, sister, please serve me your pancakes," he said, sitting down in a chair next to the wide bed in his inner chamber.

Tamar walked over to her brother with the tray of pancakes in her hands, her eyes looking at the ground, too shy to direct them at her brother Amnon.

The tray fell out of Tamar's hand as she felt her brother's strong grip on her arm. Deathlike dread descended upon the pious young woman, as her body was touched by a man.

"Come to me," Amnon said, holding his sister.

Terror, trepidation and trembling filled Tamar. She pleaded shakily: *"No, my brother! Do not humiliate me, for such a thing should never be done in Israel. Do not do this disgraceful thing! Where could I ever take my shame? And you would be like one of the wretches in Israel! Please speak to the king, for he will not withhold me from you."* Tamar wept, but to no avail.

"Get out of here!" Amnon shouted at Tamar, who was sitting sobbing on the floor. "I told you: leave my house immediately. I don't want to see your face in my home!" Amnon yelled, grabbing Tamar's arm wildly and hurling her out of his bedroom.

"Please, brother," she begged through her tears, "Do not compound your misdeed. You wronged me sorely, but to cast me into the street is far more wicked." She cried, humiliated to the core. "You have taken my maidenhood; at least marry me so you and I may be spared greater disgrace."

Amnon looked at Tamar with loathing. His vile and violent hunger satiated, all that was left within him was a void that could not be filled. The desire and love soured into contempt and hatred: "I don't want to hear or see you in my house anymore!" Amnon shouted. The power of the disgust he felt for himself blinded him. The desire to distance himself from any connection to the despicable act he had committed deafened his ears to Tamar's pleas. "If you don't get out of here immediately, I'll call the guards to force you out!" he screamed.

Tamar continued to weep.

"Guard!" screamed Amnon from the door of his bedroom.

The guard opened the door in a panic.

"Throw her out and lock the door behind her," he said, pointing to the humiliated Tamar, whose striped gown was torn.

The guard, who went to fulfill his master's will, grabbed the arm of the woman lying on the ground, dragged and pushed her out of his master's house, and locked the door behind her.

The world seemed grim and gloomy...

The road seemed endless...

The narrow streets seemed threatening to the sobbing, wandering young woman. She had ashes on her head, and her striped gown was torn and dusty, unable to hide her shame. Her tears ran down her cheeks, smearing the grime on her face. Despised and humiliated, she followed her feet … wherever they led her. Cries of devastation and grief rose from her mouth as she stumbled along. The people who crossed her path turned away abruptly, allowing the woman dressed like a princess to continue on her way. She groped like a blind woman past every building, trapped in the darkness of her situation, unaware of the passersby. Her ears heard nothing but her own soulful screams. Guilt suffused her though she was the victim; why had she allowed herself to be alone with Amnon in his home? A stone in the road tripped her, and she rose to her feet awkwardly, unaware and unaffected by the blood streaming from her grazed knees. She raised her hands to tap her head in sorrow and disbelief over her fate.

A door appeared before her somehow: a refuge from the cruel, uncaring world; a portal to safety and security. She pounded on the door, as if trying to break it...

Eternity passed, but the door would not open...

She tapped, she knocked, she pounded, until her blood smeared the door, a parody of the paschal lamb. "Please open the door," her lips murmured as tears fell.

Another eternity passed...

The door was opened by Absalom, and Tamar fell on the threshold, weeping.

Absalom looked in horror at his older sister, disheveled ... disgraced ... disfigured. With tears in his eyes, he helped his sister into his home. A maidservant was summoned in panic to assist the poor princess. The maid embraced the girl, gently leading her to the interior of the house, washing and dressing her, bandaging her wounds, and changing her bedding.

Time passed, and Absalom waited...

But not patiently. His anger and fury at the unknown perpetrator filled his heart.

He felt sorrow, sadness, and sympathy for his sister, so pious and so grievously humiliated.

The desire for revenge overwhelmed him.

The pain on his older sister's face was etched in his mind.

He thought angrily, dwelling on the crime committed against his sister: I'm going to kill the bastard who did this to her! His blood will run on the ground, just as my sister's did! To commit such an act is tantamount to murder. I am the blood redeemer, and I will avenge her!

"She'll be fine," said the maidservant who entered the room; her face showing how she shared the siblings' pain. "The wounds on the body are just superficial wounds, some scratches that will pass quickly. In a few days, the scars will disappear," she murmured, knowing that her consolation was no consolation.

"The scars on the body will disappear," said Absalom painfully, "but what about the scars on her soul?"

"She wants you to come in," said the maid, "I'll go make her something to eat in the meantime." The maid headed toward the kitchen, while Absalom went to see his sister.

Tamar sat in the corner of the room, curled up in herself, recoiling in her sorrow, reclusive with her pain. Her head slumped on her knees, gripped by her arms.

"My sister," said Absalom gently.

Tamar lifted her head, and the light in her eyes seemed to have gone out. The joy and mirth that used to fill her face had vanished, replaced by grief and sorrow.

"Who did this to you?" he asked in a soft, sorrowful tone.

Tamar paused in shock: "My brother ... my brother did this to me."

"Your brother Amnon?" he said contemptuously, the hidden rage erupting.

Tamar nodded.

"How? Why? What have you to do with him?" he asked in confusion. His anger at the man who had done this to his sister grew endlessly, knowing that his brother was the bastard.

"He was sick. Father told me to go cook for him. I made him food and when I came to give it to him, he grabbed me and..." Tamar burst into gasping tears, the power of memory bringing back the terrible nightmare again and again. "Where shall I take my shame? Maybe I made him do this to me?" she stammered, guilt and self-flagellation filling the chambers of her heart.

Absalom approached his sister, and in a comforting voice, he supported her: "No, sister, not at all. You have nothing to be ashamed of, you are not to blame for anything, and you should not feel an iota of guilt. Amnon is the bastard who is to blame for everything, and he will pay for it. Don't worry sister, you will stay with me for now. Rest assured, I'll take revenge on this villain, but don't tell anyone else what happened. Try to forget what he did to you. I know it's impossible, but what was, was. The past cannot be changed, my dear sister, but you must not live trapped in this memory. You should try to distract yourself from this with other things. I know that it seems impossible now, but you must remain silent and not publicize it. People won't understand; you have to maintain your dignity."

Tamar nodded and wiped away her tears, "Thank you, dear brother."

"Take care of yourself, my dear sister," said Absalom: "Now I will call the maid to bring you food and drink. You must recover your strength."

"Mother, you promised me food! I'm hungry!" the boy cried, his loud tears merging with his helpless mother's silent ones.

"I know, my dear soul. I know you're hungry; so am I, but I have nothing to give you to eat," she said, hugging her skinny little son in her feeble arms.

"But what can we eat? I'm starving," he beseeched her, with his sunken eyes tearing up.

All his mother could do was pull her child into her lap and hug him as tightly as their pangs of hunger allowed. "My son, what can I say? For three years, our land has been stricken by drought. Not a drop of rain has fallen! The market stalls are empty, because there's nothing to buy. Nothing grows, and people grab whatever they can find. Stealing food from each other, battling and bickering over anything to fill their bellies. What can I do, my child? I'm weak! From whom could I possibly pinch or snatch something? Even when there is a morsel for sale, the bullies and the brutes shove me out of the way. I am at my wit's end, my love!" she said desperately.

"Mother," said the boy, searching for a solution to their dire circumstances: "Let's go to the king! Surely the palace has food! The king is just ... he will feed us!"

Her reply lay somewhere between laughing and crying: "My sweet child, who would let us in to visit the king? Does the king's guard admit vagrants to the throne room?"

The boy looked at his mother pleadingly. In a choked voice, he invoked the late head of the household, who'd perished of hunger weeks earlier: "Father, of blessed memory, was one of the king's warriors. He told me bedtime stories about his adventures," he recalled wistfully. "About how heroic and righteous the king is, about his wars, his battles, and his victories. Father told me how much the king loved the people. I know Father wouldn't lie to me. Father loved the king and admired his virtue. Surely the king will not turn us away! Mother, take me to the palace, please." He stood and tugged at his mother's torn sleeve. "Come, we must seek out King David."

Jehoshaphat entered King David's chamber, his face sagging and drooping. Anguish twisted his face: "Your Majesty, a widow and her son seek an audience."

Every day people came to petition the king for a morsel of bread or a drop of water. Hunger was no stranger in the palace either; the royal household was on a strict diet, sufficing only to stave off hunger and thirst enough to function, nothing more.

"Bring them in, please," the king said in a pained voice.

The fractured family entered the throne room. The widow was pulled along by her son, forced to face the king in her rags. The king looked at the two with compassion, their eyes sunken, their faces blackened by hunger. Their clothing was in tatters but seemed to swallow their shrinking bodies. Their outstretched palms were bony, their skin dry and cracked. The widow's eyes seemed to be dead, extinguished.

The boy had never met the king before, but he knew from his father's stories that he needed to bow. His eyes shone as he reminisced. "My king," the boy began to speak, without asking permission: "My father, of blessed memory, was one of your soldiers. Do you remember him? Tobijah, son of Gabriel the Hebronite, do you remember him?"

"Of course," said David, a paternal smile on his face: "You cannot forget a heroic, wise, and righteous man like your father."

"Father tells me—" The boy paused to rephrase. "Sorry, he used to tell me all the time about the wars and battles you fought in together, about your strength and might," he said with the enthusiasm typical of his age. "My father, of blessed memory, praised the king for his character and virtue. My father loved you very much. He always took care of Mother and me, but now…" Tears welled up in the boy's eyes: "Now Father is dead. He perished weeks ago, leaving no one to help Mother and me." The boy began to cry: "My king, I am hungry; my mother is hungry. We have nothing to eat or drink. It's been over a week since I've had anything decent. Please my king, help us, for we are starving," the boy burst into tears, along with his mother.

The king wiped away his own tears and motioned to Jehoshaphat to bring the boy and his mother food.

"Sit down, my son. Please sit down, ma'am," said the king. "They will bring you food soon. What's your name, boy?"

"David, son of Tobijah, son of Gabriel the Hebronite," answered the boy proudly, "Father named me after the king."

David smiled. "Listen, son, while they bring the food, I'll tell you a little story about your father. You probably haven't heard the tale, because even your father didn't know about it: how your father Tobijah saved the whole camp in wartime."

The boy's eyes went wide, as his ears perked up to hear of his father's heroism.

"We were besieging one of the cities of Aram," the king began to recount. "It was late. Most of the fighters were sleeping, as I walked around the camp. It was freezing, with hailstones falling from the sky and gale-force winds threatening to uproot every last tent the soldiers slept under. We were conducting a siege, but the Arameans didn't know how low our own supplies were running. With provisions dwindling, our troops were hungry and weak, and I considered retreating to Israelite territory — I was quite discouraged. I walked around the grounds trying to settle on a course of action. The camp was silent, until I heard a low moan in the distance, a sincere prayer for salvation. I followed the sound, until I found your father Tobijah. He was wrapped in his prayer shawl, beseeching God in the cold and wet conditions. I listened to his words. Tobijah's supplication was unforgettable: 'Please, Heavenly Father, Merciful Father, just as You helped Abraham against Chedorlaomer and his allies in the Battle of Siddim, just as You subdued them before him, so may You help us prevail now!' I knew it was not mere happenstance that led me to your father's side; I searched my heart, wondering why God had brought me to hear those words. Then it hit me, like a thunderbolt. When Abraham threw straw and dirt at his enemies in the Battle of Siddim, they turned into swords and spears that overwhelmed the enemy.

Now the hailstones, striking the ground so powerfully, could be used instead of straw and dirt. I didn't wait a moment! I ran and woke up all the fighters. Our company of climbers used their ropes and hooks and quickly scaled the city walls. All the sentries there had gone indoors to avoid the hail, sure that we would not attack in such fierce weather. Our climbers came down the other side and threw open the city gates. The troops, including your righteous father, entered the city and captured it. The battle was brisk and brilliant. Do you understand who your father was? I couldn't tell him about the miracle he had wrought. Fortunately, now I have the chance to tell his son."

David looked at the boy, whose eyes expressed endless admiration for his father.

The servants entered bringing food for the widow and her son, but they didn't notice. The tale of Tobiah had roused their hearts, filled their bellies, and satisfied their souls.

"Your meal is served; please, enjoy it while it is fresh," said the king, pointing to the table set for the mother and son. "Lord Jehoshaphat, please call the high priest."

CHAPTER FIFTY-ONE

Famine

"For Saul and for the house of blood, he who put the Gibeonites to death," said High Priest Abiathar, interpreting the words of the Urim and Thummim on his chest.

The king and his ministers were shocked. When David had asked Abiathar to find out the reason for the three-year famine, no one had expected such a reply. Over the course of the drought, the king and his court had sought to improve the people's behavior, but to no avail. Regulations and edicts had been promulgated to eliminate idolatry, promiscuity, and violence, with officers of the law and justices of the peace appointed to stop transgressors and prosecute offenders, but nothing had worked.

Abiathar elaborated sadly: "King Saul was not eulogized properly but hastily buried, like a commoner. Moreover, there was never a reckoning for the injustice committed against the Gibeonites, who were left defenseless after the massacre of Nob."

Prince Amnon slammed his palm on the table. "It makes no sense! This cannot be! Did the wicked Saul, who pursued my royal father relentlessly, merit mourning and elegy?! And who cares that some sojourners died?! Is that why we've been starving for three years?! The Gibeonites lied their way into Israel, so Israel must suffer?!"

"Silence!" his father ordered. "You know nothing of Saul, King of Israel. He was a great and righteous man. You cannot imagine it, so bite your tongue!" King David was furious at himself, at Amnon, and at the injustice. "As for the Gibeonites, do not denigrate the sojourners. Three dozen times, the Torah tells us to love and respect them, because that was our status in Egypt. The Gibeonites accepted upon themselves the yoke of the Lord's commandments, and to harm them is utterly beyond the pale. Yes, they approached Joshua, son of Nun, under false pretenses, pretending to be from a far-off land, but he and the leaders of Israel swore an oath to protect them, an oath which still binds us. Of course, there is divine wrath at our failure! I understand why there is a famine now. It was my duty to rectify that injustice, and since I did not, we are all paying dearly." Everyone present looked down at the stunning rebuke from God. "We must repair this breach immediately. Jehoshaphat, bring the Gibeonite leaders to me urgently. We owe them an immense apology, and we must appease them so they forgive us. Only then will the famine come to an end."

"Peace be upon you, King David of Israel," said the head of the Gibeonite delegation as he entered the throne room and bowed. David looked at the man, whose old worn clothing did not hide his boldness before the king: his face hard as steel, his eyes stiff and sharp, his body cast as lead. "Your Majesty summoned us."

"Yes, I asked you to come to me, because I know that we, the People of Israel, owe you an apology. As King of Israel, I apologize for what we did to your people." David saw the shadow of a smile pass over the man's face.

"Apology?!" the man asked with feigned naïveté. "Apology for what?"

The king felt the cynicism with which the Gibeonite spoke, repulsed with disgust at his words. "For mistreating you," he said in a soft voice.

"For 'mistreating' us?!" The Gibeonite sounded harsh and bitter. "King Saul of Israel wreaked utter destruction upon us, and you say we were 'mistreated?' Our blood and our land were forsaken. Our lives were cast to the dogs! But you say we were 'mistreated?!' Apology rejected! What more could you want from us?" The Gibeonite turned his back on the king, as if about to leave the room.

"Halt, you may not leave!" David ordered. He beseeched the Gibeonite leader, who turned back: "We want to atone for our actions. I know why you reject our apology; our actions were unacceptable, but I hope not unforgivable. Know that I have issued a decree that no Israelite may harm any Gibeonite. You and your people will receive the respect due to you as sojourners in Israel. Violence, assault, and thievery against you will never be tolerated again. We seek to ease your mind, to reconcile with you for our past misdeeds. I can guarantee that in the future, you will face no abuse, but how may we compensate you for the past?" David looked at his fierce interlocutor and asked: "What will convince you to grant your pardon and bless us? Name your price, so that you may no longer begrudge Israel for your people's suffering!"

The Gibeonite smirked. "Our price? Neither gold nor silver, neither ransom nor blood money." The man's voice grew louder: "We have no issue with the People of Israel, but with the House of Saul. We demand revenge! We seek vengeance upon the son of Kish for our blood! Do you want to appease us? Then avenge us! We will accept nothing else but the blood of the man who tried to destroy our people."

The words echoed in David's head: *revenge ... vengeance ... avenge us.* He struggled to clear his thoughts, looking at the man who stood before him, trying to mollify him. "But what good will revenge do for you? Ask for anything else, and I will give you: wealth, honor, prestige. Whatever you ask, I will not withhold it from you."

"We seek nothing but revenge! We must avenge the blood of our children and kin! *As for the man who consumed us and plotted against us to exterminate us from existing within any border of Israel, let seven of his male descendants be delivered to us so that we may hang them before the Lord at Gibeah of Saul, the chosen of the Lord.* Hand them over, and you will be forgiven; if not, you will continue to starve!" The man looked at the king, his harsh gaze permitting no other alternative.

"Please, ask for anything else," David pleaded.

"No!" said the Gibeonite leader boldly. "Only vengeance on the House of Saul!"

David realized he had no choice. The death toll from the famine only rose and mounted daily. He thought: These Gibeonites have not a whiff of pity in them; they are not true Israelites. "Your request is granted," the king whispered somberly.

It was two days after Passover, the season of freedom, the time of redemption, amid the rebirth and renewal of spring; but the famine still reigned.

At midday, the sun was blazing and the air aflame. The men stood by the pavilion of the Ark of Testimony. The decree had been signed; the deed must be done. The heat wave added to the feeling of distress for all those summoned to the pavilion.

There were eight of them, the sons and grandsons of Saul. Of the eight, only one would survive to witness the sunset. Two were the sons of Rizpah, daughter of Aiah, Saul's concubine. Five were the sons of Merab, daughter of Saul, wife of Adriel the Meholathite. The eighth was Mephibosheth, son of Jonathan, son of Saul.

King David stood before the men of the House of Saul, pain and sorrow filling his heart, his eyes tearful. "My brothers and comrades, my beloved," he said weakly to the men. "You know what we are doing in this place, you know the decree. You eight are the descendants of King Saul of Israel. Unfortunately," David choked back the tears, "seven of you will die. This is a harsh act which tears our hearts asunder and cleaves our souls, but it is our duty. All of you will pass in front of the Ark of Testimony: whomever the Holy Ark draws in will become a sin-offering for the House of Saul and all Israel. I'm sorry..." David began to cry, his tears swelling, his voice choked: "The Good Lord will atone for all the house of Israel." David sat down on the ground, mourning for the seven descendants of Saul who would die. He held his face in his hands: "Please God, have compassion on Mephibosheth, son of my beloved Jonathan, to whom I swore that I would deal kindly with his seed," he whispered in prayer.

The condemned began to march toward the Ark of the Covenant, accepting the decree. A slight tremor ran through their bodies on their slow death march.

A woman began crying. It was Michal, daughter of Saul, who'd raised Merab's sons as her own. On this bitter day, she knew, most of them would die — if not all.

Rizpah sat in silence.

Her sons approached the Holy Ark, one by one, to be drawn in between its staves.

One...
Two...
Three of the sons of Merab approached for the Holy Ark to absorb them.
Three...
Four...
Five...
The disabled Mephibosheth rolled toward the Holy Ark in his chair.
He approached...
And passed by unimpeded...
A slight sigh was heard from David...
The last two sons of Merab approached, knowing that the Holy Ark would draw them in. As it did...
Six...
Seven.
Abiathar reflected that it was reminiscent of the Yom Kippur service, like the blood of the sin offerings sprinkled between the staves of the Holy Ark, one upward motion and seven downward motions. The high priest would mark his progress...
One...
One and one...
One and two...
One and three...
One and four...
One and five...
One and six...
One and seven...
Seven descendants of Saul as a sin-offering for the Israelites.

He recited the prayer he would recite on Yom Kippur within the Holy of Holies: "God, may it be Your Will, that these may be like the sin-offerings of Yom Kippur. If it is a hot year, let it be rainy. Let the scepter not depart from the House of Judah. Let Your children not rely on each other for support. Let the prayers of travelers to stop the rains go unanswered."

The Gibeonites eagerly awaited outside the tent to receive their booty, to have their vengeance on the House of Saul.

"The time has come; we will finally repay the House of Saul. It is a holiday for us, the revels of revenge!" The Gibeonite leader stood on a small platform prepared for the big celebration. Behind his back were seven tall pillars ready to hang the sons of Saul. The crowd, thirsty for bloody vengeance, stood by, cheering as they saw the descendants of Saul being led to the pillars. Excitement gripped the crowd as the ropes were wrapped around the necks of the descendants of Saul. The drumbeat became deafening, its rhythm speeding up, rousing the blood in the hearts of those seeking revenge. The Gibeonite leader raised his hands, ready to give the signal.

The crowd eagerly watched the raised hands, in anticipation of the exciting moment. A tense silence ensued once the drums fell silent. The Gibeonites looked to their leader, who had subdued the People of Israel. His eyes were filled with joy at the sublime moment. Suddenly the leader lowered his hands, giving the signal.

The seven prisoners were hoisted up...

The nooses tightened...

The descendants of Saul flopped about...

Swinging...

Trying to take one last gasp...

Breathing their last...

It was as if a volcano had erupted among the spectators, the lava of their vengeance spewing forth in an inarticulate scream of joy. The Gibeonites yelled and reveled, and the heat of their enthusiasm froze the blood of the Israelites who stood at a distance, witnessing the atrocity. The sound of music and melody, song and dance, congealed and reverberated among the reveling crowd, with food and drink distributed to the attendees, who frolicked amidst the gore of their retribution. For many hours, they romped amidst the slaughter, with their celebration, the dance of retaliatory violence, continuing day and night.

"Please, let us bury our dead," David asked the Gibeonite leader. "You have what you wanted, so now allow us to bury them." David looked at the audacious man standing before him, with a monstrous, bloodthirsty leer still smeared on his face.

"They're ours," he replied boldly. "Your sin will be atoned only when the rains come. Until the first drop falls, they are ours; when the skies open, take their corpses."

David pleaded, trying to mollify him, promising anything he could think of, but the Gibeonite was impassive. "When it rains, you can retrieve them," he declared.

David addressed the delegation that had come to bring back Saul's children. "These people are not true Israelites. They show no pity! From this day onwards, no Gibeonite will ever be allowed in the assembly of the Lord. Such cruelty has no place in Israel!"

Heat...
Scorching...
Haze...
The blazing sun beating down on every head...
Animals and birds of prey foraging for food surrounded the seven hanging pillars.
Days...
Weeks...
Months...

Rizpah, daughter of Aiah, concubine of King Saul of Israel, stood fiercely against the forces of nature, against the wild beasts and birds which were seeking to scavenge the flesh of the seven executed young men. Her only shelter was a piece of sackcloth stretched across the rocks to protect her head from the blazing sun and chill of night.

"*He is the Rock, His work is perfect; all His ways are just. A God of faithfulness without injustice, righteous and upright is He,*" her lips murmured at all times, as she saw her two sons and the five sons of Merab hanging from the tree.

The seventeenth of the month of Marheshvan arrived, the day of the Flood of Noah. Rizpah stood in prayer before her Creator: "God, for about six months, I have been on guard over your sons, preserving human sanctity and dignity. Passersby marvel at the punishment imposed on the seven sons of the king of Israel, for the harm their father did to sojourners in Israel. People marvel at this nation that honors those who join it, who cleave to You. Now, Heavenly Father, the time of winter has come, the time of rain. For more than three years, not a drop of rain has fallen onto the land. The drought is severe, and your people are thirsty and hungry. Please, Dear Father, until now, I have not prayed to You, for it was not the rainy seasons, and untimely rains are a curse, not a blessing. Now, my Father, show Your people that You have forgiven their iniquity, that You have accepted these seven public sacrifices." Rizpah's eyes were on the sky, her arms raised like two sun-bleached sticks to the heavens.

Small bits of clouds begin to appear, carried on the wings of the hastily blowing wind. Small drops of rain fell, looking like tears in her eyes, tears that hadn't fallen from her eyes since the day her two sons and the five sons of Merab were hung.

"Thank you, Father, thank you for accepting the sacrifices with good will, to open the gates of heaven and bestow a good bounty on your people."

"Hurry up, go take down the bodies of the seven hung men. Exhume the bodies of King Saul of Israel and his sons, which were buried in Jabesh Gilead. Prepare a burial place for the eleven righteous men in the land of Benjamin, near the tomb of Kish, father of King Saul," the king commanded his men.

David looked out the window, seeing the raindrops slowly falling to the ground, moistening the thirsty rocky soil. He listened to the slight murmur tapping on his window. "Spread the news throughout the country, to come to mourn in the territory of Benjamin. Those who cannot make the journey must observe seven days of mourning and eulogy for Saul and his seed in their towns."

The messengers left urgently. The eighteenth of the month of Marheshvan was a day of eulogy and mourning at Kish's tomb. David mourned, eulogized, and cried over the death of Saul, his sons and his grandsons. He spent seven days weeping and lamenting the death of the righteous.

There were seven days of torrential rain; the heavens sobbed with the king over King Saul of Israel and his descendants.

The people gathered one by one. The heavy downpour saturated the cracked earth, filling the dry cisterns, and revived the plants of the field.

CHAPTER FIFTY-TWO

Rizpah

Rizpah was led to King David, the limbs of her skeletal body like a sun-bleached tree, her face slender and blackened by hunger and the scorching heat of the long summer. She was in her mid-forties, bent, dragging her feet like a crone whose spine no longer held her up. She leaned on a maidservant who accompanied her.

"Rizpah daughter of Aiah, concubine of King Saul of Israel," David turned to the enfeebled woman standing before him. "I heard about what you did, about your courage and bravery. Woman of valor, your actions are commendable!"

Rizpah lowered her gaze, ashamed to look up at the king: "I did what I had to do, Your Majesty," she replied weakly, discomfited by the praise lavished on her.

"Not every person could do what you did," David observed pleasantly. "Each person deals with what that soul has the power to accomplish; no one faces a trial beyond their capacity to withstand."

Rizpah remained still, silent, shut off.

He looked at her. "Rizpah, daughter of Aiah, you know that the royal scepter can only be handed from one monarch to another." Her face seemed empty, devoid of the will to live. "No commoner may marry the former wife of a king, or his concubine."

Rizpah nodded. She was condemned to die bereaved, a childless widow. She was aware that her relationship with Abner had been contrary to the law of the Torah.

"Rizpah, concubine of King Saul," David said in a soft, gentle voice: "I am going to ask you a difficult question; you need not answer now. Think about it, then reply."

Rizpah raised her eyes in his direction, gazing past him. "Yes, Your Majesty."

"Rizpah, daughter of Aiah, concubine of King Saul, will you marry me, Israel's king?"

Rizpah was so stunned; her legs could not withstand the weight of her blasted limbs. Her knees trembled. Her maid steadied her. Her eyes widened in shock. She knew her appearance, skin blackened by the sun stretched over a skeleton. "Deceive me not, Your Majesty," she pleaded in a whisper. "I am an apparition from the netherworld, a refugee from the grave. Please don't mock me." Her eyes brimmed with disgrace and shame.

King David rose from his throne and approached her. "Neither deceit nor mockery, my lady," he said compassionately, stopping some distance from the trembling skeleton. "Rizpah, daughter of Aiah, I would never joke about this. You are a true woman of valor! A great and holy soul! Your fortitude and bravery testify to the sublime source from which your regal spirit was hewn. You said you look like death, but your actions prove that great life flows through your veins. Your state does not define you. Look within, Rizpah, look into your heart," the king whispered, as if sharing a secret: "Deep within your soul, look at the place where its light resides, a spot that sometimes seems dark and blackened, covered by layers of sorrow and grief. Remove the sorrow from there, and let it be released from you. Cleanse your heart; let your tears wash the sadness and grief from your midst," David whispered, as if trying to heal the shattered, desolate soul. "Open the gate that traps your tears inside you. Let your spirit escape the dark abyss where melancholy rules. Open your heart to the joys of inner life. Give yourself the right to cry, to be you, to be Rizpah, daughter of Aiah."

The woman collapsed to the ground, as the maid lost her grip. The maidservant rushed to help her mistress up, but David waved her away. "Weep, Rizpah, daughter of Aiah; weep for King Saul. Weep for your two sons hanging from the tree, for Abner, son of Ner. Weep for all the sorrow and grief you have suffered in your life. Cry the sadness out of you. Cry the poison out, pure soul..."

With a gasp, a tear began to form in the corner of Rizpah's eye, to

David's relief.

A few moments passed, an internal battle to maintain her fortification.

Rizpah lifted her head, wiping away the rebellious tear:

"I'll think about it, Your Majesty," she declared, as she struggled to stand, aided by the maidservant's arm. "I'll think about it," she repeated.

Rizpah staggered out of the throne room, supported by her maidservant.

Two days later, David summoned Rizpah again. Her face looked the same, but her body seemed steadier. The maidservant walked alongside, providing the grieving woman only minor support.

"Rizpah, have you thought about what I said?" the king asked hopefully. He scrutinized her drooping face, trying to find a trace of vitality in her burnt-out eyes.

"Yes, Your Majesty, I considered your proposal," she replied weakly, "but I still find it mistaken. I searched within myself for the light Your Majesty spoke of but found only darkness. I searched within myself for the joy of life but found fear of death. I asked my eyes to shed tears but found a stone lying on my heart. Begging Your Majesty's pardon, I must decline. My king misjudges me," she whispered — sharply, decisively.

The king rose from his throne to pace the chamber, looking heavenward as if asking for help. He strove to discover the inner workings of the human mind, mired in melancholy. "Rizpah, you say that you found dark instead of light, fear of death instead of joy of life?" He paused; several minutes passed in silence. Rizpah shifted uncomfortably, searching for her maidservant's supporting hand. "I know you were looking, Rizpah, but consider this. There are several kinds of searching. Perhaps you lose a penny and spend a few moments looking for it: if you find it, fine; if not, oh well. But imagine if you mine the earth, looking for gold and jewels; it may take years of backbreaking labor. You may happen upon a rich layer, but if not, you will find nothing more than rocks and dirt. What about if you had a jewel and dropped it, but you didn't know where? You would keep searching until you gave up. But there is one more type of searching, which never ends. Imagine that a young prince was entrusted to your safekeeping in a certain place. If that boy disappeared, would you ever stop looking? No, because the price to pay for such a failure would be your life!" The king looked at Rizpah lovingly: "Pure soul, you searched for light and joy, but only as if it were a penny. You sat on your own for a few minutes, and when you couldn't find your light, you decided it was nowhere to be found. Am I right?"

Rizpah nodded reluctantly, like a child caught red-handed.

"Listen carefully to my words, soul so beloved to God. Pay heed to my directive." The king's voice sounded gentle but firm, pleading but commanding. "This search is not pro forma. You must not do it as if to discharge an obligation, to say, 'I searched but did not find.' This is not to please anyone, not even me. This is your journey, the journey of your life. You are a great, fierce woman, as I told you at our previous meeting. You have done a tremendous act of devotion." The king was silent for a few moments: "Everything you have done is null and void compared to the path which lies before you, the journey to find yourself. You must invest time and effort in this search! Put your all in trying to find Rizpah! If you do not find yourself, your life will be in vain, your deeds for nothing, your experience worthless. Every person must undertake such a search for self. This quest is neither privilege nor indulgence; man's search for meaning is the holiest of missions, without which even the greatest and noblest acts are of no account. Return to your home, dear soul; go back to your search, give it time. Put all the enormous mental powers within you into it. Speak your truth, pour out your heart, and let your spirit break through the iron walls. Don't let go, don't despair! Seek, search, sift through the ashes of your soul, until you begin to discover your light and vitality." His voice dropped to a whisper: "Find within yourself your love for the soul of Rizpah." He gazed into the opaque depths of Rizpah's eyes, searching for a spark of life. "Go home, holy soul, come back to me in about a week. Please, do what I ask. Sincerely seek yourself."

The silent Rizpah bowed her head: "I will do as Your Majesty requests," she whispered, as if left with no choice.

Rizpah sat in her room, examining, exploring, trying to discover the light, to obey the king's orders. Searching herself for Rizpah, probing, analyzing, plunging in.

"Rizpah, where are you? The king said you dwell inside me. The king promised that if I searched for you, I would find you. Who are you, Rizpah? Tell me! Talk to me!" she begged, trying to find an opening, a crack in the fortified wall. She strove to embrace emotions, to shed a tear, to pierce the armor around her personality, and to shatter the cocoon around her which was preventing her from starting over after her trauma. "Cry, Aiah's daughter, for the crushed soul of Rizpah, the haze of despair and depression, the snare of sorrow which allows no hope of escape. I want to live..." she whispered to herself, disbelieving her mantra: "I have to live! I must live!"

It took many hours before the torrential tears came; the dam burst, shattered into shards, as her eyes released the flood which had been trapped in the depths of her soul. It was purifying, flushing out the poison that had accumulated inside her body, allowing her to expel the sorrow and melancholy. The deluge released the psychic forces which had been drowned in a deep trench of despondency and depression.

Rizpah fell to her knees, head shrouded, dress wet from the torrent of her tears.

Crying for Rizpah...
Sobbing for Saul...
Weeping for her sons...
Mourning for Abner...
Lamenting her widowhood...
Bemoaning the People of Israel...
Crying for everything...

Inside, she felt the fetters of her spirit being released one by one. Each tear carried away a thread of the burial shroud around her soul. As the sadness that was weighing her down to the center of the earth melted away, she felt lighter. Every sigh and moan, she knew, untangled the knots binding her spirit, taking a brick away from the burial chamber entombing her soul.

Her cries increased, the released sorrow and heartbreak breaching the walls...

For a while, the only sound was the wails washing over her, excising the decay and detritus out of her soul.

Then Rizpah grew silent. The sorrow that had swamped her life was gone, leaving her desolate and empty. Withdrawing into her melancholy had allowed her to barricade herself, in a place that was safe, secure, and stable, though miserable.

But now her psyche was a wasteland...

The dark disappeared, but no light shone...

The mourning faded, but relief did not dawn...

The sadness dissipated, but joy did not come...

Rizpah sat still, feeling how her heart had become an empty space, a dark starless night, the depths of the ocean ... lifeless.

Rizpah looked into herself but saw nothing. The void enveloped all of her, and she groped blindly — an animal with no feeling, a stone dormant from time immemorial.

Rizpah was still ... silent...

Empty...

Desolate...

Like the absolute vacuum of space...

Three days had passed since the darkness, sadness, and melancholy were purged.

In place of all the bad, only a void was left...

Rizpah believed, understood, and knew that the king's words were correct. The bad place could be filled with good...

If darkness comes out, there should be light...

Light that could fill Rizpah...

Rizpah continued on the path laid out for her by the king.

Looking...

Searching...

More!

Longing to find the place the king told her about...

Silence...

Observation...

Convergence...

Weeping silently...

The will of the human spirit...

Then there was an eruption, like an undersea volcano. The earth cracked, and lava streamed forth, shaking the ground violently. From deep within Rizpah, a cry erupted. The yearning, the desire to find herself, sheathed in a shell, covered in a cocoon. The scream erupted: "Daughter of Aiah, *aieh* (where) are you? What are you? The king said that you exist, that you are alive, but I find no trace. The king said you are great and holy, where are you hiding? Rizpah…! Reveal yourself to me…" She wilted, weeping, whimpering… for her spirit, for her soul, for her inner self.

Suddenly she saw a distant figure, a lively and laughing woman, filled with joie de vivere. "Do I know her?"

The woman giggled and moved closer, walking as lightly as if she were dancing.

"Who is this woman?"

Her vitality and vivacity were undeniable, spreading a fragrant aroma that never seemed to dissipate.

"What does she have to be so happy about?"

Rizpah saw the woman throughout her life, her ups and downs, her joys and woes. The woman smiled and continued on her way.

"What makes her happy?"

The woman looked forward, leaving the past behind her. She extended her hands to the future. She enjoyed every moment, every situation. She dealt with life's crises with a smile, shaking her head at difficulties, letting them pass over her, continuing to live with a smile.

Rizpah saw how every challenge she overcame made the woman greater; every difficulty strengthened her vitality; every leap over a crisis made her happier. Every adversity became an advantage; all opposition became an opportunity. Rizpah marveled at the woman who turned darkness into light, grief into joy.

The woman approached Rizpah, standing in front of her.

"Who are you?" asked Rizpah.

The woman's smile was dazzling. "You know who I am. But do you know what you are?"

Rizpah was surprised by the answer, but more so by the question. "What am I?!" she repeated the woman's question. "You mean: who am I?"

"No, I mean what are you?" The woman looked deep into Rizpah's eyes. "Who you are, I know better than you! But what are you? What have you done to yourself? I want to know! You are me, your innermost spirit and truest self, your soul," the woman replied compassionately. "Why are you doing this to us? Why would you imprison us in the darkness of oblivion? Why are you killing us? You subdue the light that flows from within, a light that can illuminate the entire world by its glow. Why do you think you're to blame for everything you're going through? Why do you torment yourself with things that do not befit you? Why do you want sadness and sorrow, indulging in anguish and angst, sinking into the depths of despair and despondency? What does all the melancholy that fills your heart give you? Why don't you give it an outlet? Why carry everything inside you? To poison us?"

"Why are you blaming me?" Rizpah protested. "What should I do when life has been so cruel to me? When the burdens are unbearable? I didn't choose that! It is the Will of Providence! Don't blame me! Didn't I purge the grief, sorrow, and melancholy?"

The woman smiled, locking her gaze on Rizpah, penetrating her soul: "You know that's not true. Life is cruel to those who see cruelty. Life is harsh to those who view it harshly, who see it as unbearable. Only you chose to feel this way! True, there is Providence. Heaven dictates what a person faces; but the manner in which things and cases are received, man chooses. See the good, and all will be good; see the bad, and all will be bad. A person has the right and the duty to choose how to live life, but the choice is expressed through accepting events. To paint in black, you mix all colors together; to reverse the process, you must know how to separate the hues."

"You're talking nonsense!" cried Rizpah, trying to entrench herself in place, rejecting the accusations leveled at her, stepping back.

"No, Rizpah. You know I'm not talking nonsense," the woman said lightly, moving toward Rizpah and clutching her bony hand. "Darkness is not a reality in itself; darkness is the absence of light. Let the light shine within you..."

Rizpah felt the warmth of the woman's hands penetrate her, spreading throughout her battered and bruised body, breathing life into her.

"Look at the abundant grace bestowed upon you… Look at the goodness that fills your life… Don't look at the bad at all… You have life… You have vitality… Let yourself forget the bitterness of the past… Wipe that acrid taste from your mouth… Don't think about what's been taken from you… Be grateful and glad with what you had and what you have… Embrace the memories of good without getting lost in them… Be glad for your time with Saul, who is still linked to you, even if he is no longer in your world… Be glad about your sons, about the time you got to be with them. You'll meet them again in the future. Think of the bounty bestowed upon you, to have those boys for the years you did. Some women have never felt the joy and love of hugging their children. Many would be willing to swap with you, if only to experience that moment of happiness, of hearing a child say: 'Mother, I love you.' To see that smile, to observe that child sleeping in bed, to quietly adjust that blanket to ward off the chill of night."

Rizpah stared at the woman, tears running down her cheeks.

The woman gazed at Rizpah with compassion: "You have learned to cry, Rizpah, an important lesson, second to none; but do not cry for what has been taken from you, cry for what has been given to you as a free gift. Don't cry out of self-pity, don't cry over pain and suffering. Do not be like the ungrateful borrower who is indignant when the lender returns, as if you were the true owner. Cry out of gratitude and gladness! Open your heart with tears of joy for the gift you've received, for the moments of happiness you've experienced, for the life granted to you at every moment."

Rizpah felt a new torrent burst from her eyes, warm tears sweeter than honey, a cry of happiness and joy bursting from her throat, uniting with the Giver of All Good, savoring the moments of joy and love. She felt the influx of light fill her entire being, the blood flowing through her veins like a life-changing, swiftly flowing stream. Her life passed before her eyes, moments of joy and happiness, love and affection, rejoicing and celebration. Each tear seemed to carry within it a treasure trove of beautiful vitality and vigor, merging and uniting with the woman.

Rizpah wept with joy and gratitude for the good…

A cry of love… A long cry of resurrection…

Rizpah rose to her feet, and the feeling of exhaustion that filled her body disappeared. A feeling of joy took its place, accompanied by a sensation of lightness and vitality. Rizpah looked on, as if she were in a dream. She sensed joy in her heart, discovering animation and jubilation within her.

"Thank you... Thank you..." She whispered with a happy smile to herself.

Rizpah rose, bathed, dressed in her finest, and then anointed and adorned herself.

To her maidservant, she said with a smile: "My dear, run and tell King David that the soul of Rizpah, daughter of Aiah, wishes to meet him."

King David, sitting next to his writing desk, was overwhelmed by the resurrection of the dead he was privileged to witness.

Watching Rizpah walk toward him, her legs carrying her like on a cloud, feather-light, approaching the king. The king looked at Rizpah, observing how the dead face was now filled with new vitality and vigor, a smile on her face — something not seen for thirty years, since King Saul's death; the smile of a living person.

"Your Majesty King David, I thank you very much," Rizpah said with a sheepish smile, her eyes fixed on the ground. "I did what you told me; I searched and found the soul of Rizpah." She looked up, meeting the king's gaze. "Yes, I, Rizpah, daughter of Aiah, very much desire to marry Your Majesty, King David of Israel."

CHAPTER FIFTY-THREE

Vengeance

A summer morning greeted Absalom as he came to see his father. The rising sun warmed the world waking to a new day with its rays. It was the festive season, between Passover and the reaping festival of Shavuot; every day of the seven weeks was eagerly counted. The warm weather of spring was having its effect on the people; warm winter clothing had been stowed away, and was being replaced by light and breezy attire.

"Good morning, dear father," Absalom bowed to his father and rose to kiss him.

"Good morning, my dear son," said David. "What brings you to me at this early hour? Aren't you supposed to be in the study hall?"

"Yes, Father, usually at this hour, I am in the study hall, but tomorrow the shearing of my sheep will begin at Baal Hazor. I am holding a feast for all my shepherds and workers; I have to show my workers gratitude and generosity. From you, I learned that we have to be very respectful to our employees, so I'm giving them a big and beautiful banquet. I also told them that this year, the king and his sons would probably join us, and the workers were very happy. Therefore, I have come to ask you, Father, to join us, along with all the princes," Absalom said.

"Why trouble yourself, son? If I come with you, my entire entourage will come with me, and that's too much trouble for you," David tried to dissuade him.

"No, Father, it's no hassle at all. It is always a joy to host you, and everything is ready. Father, I would really like you to join the celebration," Absalom pleaded.

"Please, son," David requested, "Do not ask me for too much. I am an old man, already in my sixties. I've had enough fetes and feasts, and the journey is too much for me. I want to sit in my hall and study the holy Torah. Please go without me. Take your brothers with you, rejoice together, and make your people happy."

"Well, Father," Absalom said in disappointment, "if you cannot make it, please make sure to send Amnon as your representative. I know he's your right-hand man, but for a day or two, you can spare him! As a consolation prize, let the crown prince preside."

David thought: He wants Amnon to come! I thought that what happened between Amnon and Tamar two years ago would cloud the relationship between Absalom and Amnon. Poor Tamar, who has been living with Absalom at home for two years; she is dejected, refusing the suitors that arrive at her doorstep daily. That unfortunate incident has left Tamar as a widow in her brother's house. I should have thought about it beforehand, forbidding seclusion between a man and a woman, even if she is single. The Torah forbids seclusion between a man and a married woman, but not an unmarried woman. Unfortunately, hindsight cannot fix what has already happened. I banned such seclusion, fencing the serious breach in the wall of modesty within Israel. If such a case can happen with a virtuous and modest woman, what about those who are not? But what has been done cannot be undone. People say that there is no change in the relationship between Amnon and Absalom. The bond between them needs to be tightened; brothers need to socialize together a lot. A bottle of wine brings hearts together. Let them rejoice together; nothing could be better."

Absalom coughed lightly to get the attention of his brooding father.

"Excuse me, son, I was lost in thought and forgot you. I told you I'm an old man!" David said with a grin. "Of course, why not? Tell Amnon I approve. He can go with you and your brothers; I'll manage on my own. Go and rejoice, and may God bless you with all the blessings written in the Torah."

"Cheers, dear brother Absalom," Amnon cried at the banquet, lifting his wine glass.

"May you have a good life and peace, my brother Amnon," answered Absalom, raising his own water glass. Absalom was a handsome man, sturdy and strong. His long hair was ruffled by the light breeze blowing across the field where the shearing was being celebrated. All the adult princes had come to Absalom's banquet to share his joy. Their cups were filled with wine, but Absalom was known to have taken a lifelong Nazarite vow. He never cut his hair, drank wine, or approached the dead. He was known as a holy, righteous man, abstaining from worldly lusts and pursuits. Once a year he trimmed his long golden locks; he gave their weight in gold as a donation for the Temple's construction. Absalom looked at his intoxicated brother, overwhelmed by the hatred he had to hide. He told a servant: "Make sure my dear brother Amnon's wineglass is always full, understand?"

The servant ran to pour wine for his master's brother. Amnon drained his glass immediately, gesturing to the servant for another. "Cheers!" said Amnon drunkenly, swaying like the grass of the field in the blowing wind.

Absalom moved away from the table a bit, motioning to two of his guards. He whispered to them: "*Watch Amnon until his heart is merry with wine, and when I order you to strike Amnon down, you are to kill him. Do not be afraid. Have I not commanded you? Be courageous and valiant!*"

"But my lord..." one of the guards began.

"No buts! Did you hear what I told you? I am not allowed to kill him; I cannot approach the dead. Believe me, I would gladly kill this villain. You know what he did to the princess! Such a depraved man does not deserve to live. Shechem son of Hamor, did a similar deed to Dinah, daughter of Jacob, so Simeon and Levi, her brothers, killed all the men of the city, because they held Shechem, son of Hamor, to account. If Amnon had the slightest shred of decency, he would have taken my sister as a wife afterwards, as the Torah says. But this villain scorns the words of the Torah and thinks that because he is the firstborn, he can do whatever he wants. I tell you, go and kill him! You must not fear anything; you are fulfilling the command of the king's son. Were I a commoner, you would be liable for killing a man under my order, but since I have royal authority, it is as if you act under coercion. In any case, you will be slaying a man who is condemned to die, so just do as I have commanded you."

The two guards approached Amnon, holding wine jugs. Amnon held out his empty glass to the guard: "Come on, laggard, don't I deserve some wine?" he said to the guard, disdain evident on his flushed face.

"Please, my lord," the guard says, pouring wine from his jug into Amnon's glass with one hand raised up, as he drew his sword with the other. The guard behind Amnon also drew his sword: "Please, my lord, receive what you deserve!"

Two swords lodged in Amnon's body, one in his stomach and one in his back. Amnon fell to the ground, his glass full of wine flying out of his hand, staining the clothes of the princes sitting stunned around the table.

"Right, my lord, did you get what's coming to you?" the assassin said, half-grinning.

The door to David's study opened in a panic. David and the men with him looked up from their texts. At the entrance stood one of Amnon's young servants. Sweat poured from his face and soaked his clothing. His face was a mask of horror.

David jumped up as if bitten by a snake. "What happened?" he asked in alarm.

"Absalom killed all the princes," he said, weeping hysterically, smacking his face. "No one survived!"

"Ohhh!" David's hands went to the collar of his garment, tearing the fabric, exposing his chest. "Ohhh!" he sobbed over the loss of his children.

Everyone present tore their clothes as well, in stunned mourning at the great loss.

Jonadab, son of Shammah, David's nephew, leaped at the boy and grabbed his arms. "Whom did you see killed?!" he asked the boy firmly, bringing him back to reality.

The boy, as if trying to understand the question, tearfully replied: "When they killed my lord Amnon, I fled for my life. Absalom must have killed them all!"

"I understood, thank you," Jonadab responded, walking over to the king, who was crying, lying on the ground. He declared: "*My lord must not think they have killed all the sons of the king, for only Amnon is dead. In fact, Absalom has planned this since the day Amnon violated his sister, Tamar. So now, Your Majesty, do not take to heart the report that all the sons of the king are dead. Only Amnon is dead."*

The bereaved king looked at Jonadab, mutely hoping that his other sons were safe.

The sentry in the tower observed a mass of people arriving on mules from the direction of Baal Hazor. He sent a messenger to inform the king.

Jonadab said to David: "Behold, the princes have returned, just as your servant said."

The king's sons entered the study where the king sat on the ground, mourning his firstborn. With torn garments and tearful faces, they recounted the slaughter at the shearing, from its beginning to its bitter end.

Meanwhile, Absalom sought asylum with King Talmai, son of Amihud of Geshur, father of his mother Maacah.

CHAPTER FIFTY-FOUR
The Lady of Tekoa

"Your Majesty, a widow from the town of Tekoa has come to the palace, weeping and pleading for an audience," said Jehoshaphat.

The king sat on his throne. The light had gone out of his eyes when Absalom assassinated Amnon. His joie de vivre and jolliness had shriveled up, leaving his face as desolate and desiccated as a desert.

Three years had passed since Absalom murdered Amnon. David's heart had been inundated by the drive for vengeance, to execute the killer of his firstborn. Grief refused to leave the king's heart, seeping in time and time again, making him miserable. The knowledge that his firstborn had been murdered, and that his killer had escaped justice, left him no rest. At the same time, his love for Absalom made him desperate to find a way to pardon his crime or commute his death sentence.

"Bring the woman in, please," David said with a sigh, his soul tired of royal difficulties. Petitioners came to his palace day and night, pouring out their hearts, detailing their troubles. The king absorbed all their grief and distress, until his spirit felt like an overflowing sponge, a jug of wine overfilled. Every crisis, every illness, every calamity penetrated the king's soul and threatened to tear him apart. He dedicated hour upon hour to hearing their complaints and pleas, as they begged for help. It left his bruised and battered heart further beaten by the misfortunes of his people.

A woman staggered into the room, her legs struggling to bear her skinny body. She was in mourning attire, with dust and ash dirtying her head and clothing. Life seemed to have passed her by. Her tear-streaked face seemed to announce that sorrow and grief were about to drag her to the netherworld. With heavy steps, she approached the throne, to fall on her face and weep in her grief. "Save me, O King," she sobbed repeatedly.

The king sympathized with her anguish and agony. He absorbed her tears, her sorrow filling him. "What brings you here?" he asked the wretched, kneeling woman.

"Indeed, I am a widow, for my husband is dead. And your maidservant had two sons who were fighting in the field with no one to separate them, and one struck the other and killed him. Now the whole clan has risen up against your maidservant and said, 'Hand over the one who struck down his brother, that we may put him to death for the life of the brother whom he killed. Then we will cut off the heir as well!' So they would extinguish my one remaining ember by not preserving my husband's name or posterity on the earth." The woman bemoaned the bitterness of her fate, from the death of her husband and her older son to the desire of her family to kill her younger son, either to redeem the firstborn's blood or to inherit her late husband's estate. "I am hiding my son, but my family wants him to be handed over. I tried to reason with them. Yes, the blood redeemer may demand the life of a manslayer, but that is not the case here! My younger son was attacked by his older and stronger brother, and he had no choice but to kill him. It was self-defense! Moreover, there were no witnesses, nor anyone to issue a warning. However, they still seek to execute my younger son, so they can pay me off and inherit my husband's estate."

The king looked at the woman with sympathy: "Go home, and I will send men to investigate the case. You need not surrender your son to the blood redeemer. If they demand him, send word to me, and I will support you. However, if it turns out that your son is a murderer, and fratricide was committed, then he must face justice. He must be tried and sentenced, without partiality or bias. I am sorry for your predicament, and my heart goes out to you, but justice must be done. My kingdom cannot be a place where bloodshed is ignored, or the land will be overrun by killers. As a king, I must not pardon a murderer or give a murderer a light punishment. Such offenses must be harshly punished, for the good of the entire nation," the king ruled.

The woman kept crying as she said: "Your Majesty is right that murder cannot be ignored. If such a crime goes unpunished, what will keep violent people from slaughtering their countrymen? Still, there is no concern that the average man will kill his brother, the child of his father and mother. It is improper to punish good, decent people for such an aberration, since slaying kin is not the way of the world. On the contrary, it is the way of kinsmen to avenge their brother's blood. At the same time, the Torah does not order one to do so; it merely provides a dispensation if a blood redeemer kills a manslayer in the heat of passion. It is not an active obligation; if a potential blood redeemer stays his hand, he has neither violated a negative command nor nullified a positive command. It is akin to divorce; the Torah prescribes the proper method for doing so, writing a bill of divorce and so on, but there is no active obligation to go down that path. In my case, the blood redeemers do not act in the heat of passion, but to fill their pockets with my husband's money. As I said to the king, my son acted in self-defense. The clansmen do not want to redeem my older son's blood, rather they wish to pursue their own fortune; they seek a pretext to execute my younger son and inherit my husband's estate. Should the law of the Torah be that a blood redeemer who slays one who has committed fratricide is liable to death himself? Then you will have an endless cycle of violence, a countrywide flood of bloodshed."

The king gazed at the woman thoughtfully: *She is a wise woman, presenting her case cleverly and convincingly. I cannot help but see the similarity to my situation. Absalom saw himself as a blood redeemer for Tamar. Amnon's violation of her was akin to murder, as the Torah says: "This case is just like one in which a man attacks his neighbor and murders him." There was no warning of Absalom either. I would be the redeemer of Amnon's blood, but I am not obliged to avenge his blood.*

"And now, Your Majesty," the woman interrupted his thought, "after presenting my case, my king can decree that the blood redeemers withdraw, and then my son can come out of hiding and return to my house."

David considered this, accepting the wise woman's words. "You're right. *As surely as the Lord lives, not a hair of your son's head will fall to the ground.* By royal decree, anyone who harms your son will be punished. I will send my couriers to notify the blood redeemers of my ruling."

"I thank Your Majesty," the woman said, a slight smile forming on her face. "Does my king give me leave to speak freely?"

"Speak," said the king, looking forward to hearing what else the woman had to say.

"Your Majesty's subjects are not wicked, as in the tale I told. God forbid! Did the king not wonder how the family could plan to kill my younger son? After all, there were no witnesses and no warning when he struck his brother and killed him. Your Majesty needn't retract this just verdict, but the truth is that my sons are not at stake, but Your Majesty's." She took in the king's astonishment. "For the unspeakable act committed against his sister, Princess Tamar, Prince Absalom killed Crown Prince Amnon. Although there were witnesses to the act, there was no warning. Therefore, in a court of law, he could not be found liable. By royal edict, he could still be punished to prevent the setting of a precedent, but as I already argued, fratricide is an aberration that goes against human nature. As for the blood redeemers, the king can decree that not a hair of Absalom's head fall to the ground. In fact, Absalom did not kill anyone; it was his guards. He who commits a crime on the orders of another is liable for his own action. If you say that they were coerced by Absalom, well and good, but that is a matter for the Heavenly Court, not human judges. If he deserves death, God will do what is good in His eyes and execute him; if not, then why should Your Majesty kill him?! Now, if the king sees fit for Absalom to live, should the prince do so among foreigners in an unclean land? Let the king's son return home from his hiding place, just as Your Majesty decreed regarding my child!"

The king gazed at the woman with a mixture of anger and hopeful joy — anger for the subterfuge; hopeful joy at the thought that he might be able to welcome home his wayward son. In response, the woman said: "Let Your Majesty not be furious with his maidservant for spinning a tale out of whole cloth. The people know how the king's is pained by this situation. I said to myself that I must go to the king and present a parable, so that Your Majesty might solve his problem by solving mine. I told a tall tale so my king would remain impartial and judge well. *And now your servant says: May the word of my lord the king bring me rest, for my lord the king is able to discern good and evil, just like the angel of God. May the Lord your God be with you."*

The king's face turned thoughtful: Even though she is a wise and clever woman, someone gave her the details, a man who is wise and knowledgeable in Torah law — and the workings of my heart. She spoke well, and the parable was brilliant. My son Absalom need not die, nor languish in exile. But who sent her?

The king stared into her eyes: "I must ask you something; do not hold back!"

The woman looked at the king, a slight tremor of fear running through her body, in awe of the crown. "Please speak, Your Majesty."

"Do I detect Joab's hand in this affair?" asked the king.

She was amazed by the king's discernment. *"As surely as you live, my lord the king, no one can turn to the right or to the left from anything that my lord the king says. Yes, your servant Joab is the one who gave me orders; he told your maidservant exactly what to say. Joab, your servant, has done this to bring about this change of affairs, but my lord has wisdom like the wisdom of the angel of God, to know everything that happens in the land."* Her face expressed admiration for his wisdom.

"Thank you, my daughter, for your words and your brilliant analogy. May the Lord bless you!" King David said to the woman, dismissing her. His eyes had reignited.

"Did you call me, Your Majesty?" said Joab, bowing deeply to his sovereign.

"Yes, indeed, my friend Joab," said the king with a smile. "It was clever of you to recruit that lady of Tekoa to plead your case. You may have the honor of carrying out my verdict. Go to Absalom and bring the boy back home. After all, whoever begins to fulfill a good deed ought to see it through to completion. However, he is to go back to his house; I do not grant him a royal audience."

Joab bowed down to the king, happy that he had succeeded in influencing David, bringing a smile back to the king's face. Now he could return the prince to his father. "Long live Your Majesty, King

David forever. *Today, your servant knows that he has found favor with you, my lord the king, because the king has granted his request."*

Joab went to Geshur to bring Absalom back to his home in Jerusalem.

"Give your father a little more time, and then he will grant you an audience," Joab advised Absalom. "For now, the king is not ready for you to come before him. I will appeal to him to relent. I am sure that it will not be long before your father summons you to stand before him as you used to do."

Joab went on his way, while Absalom remained in his home.

CHAPTER FIFTY-FIVE

Absalom

"Fire! Fire! Get water, the field is on fire!" Screams and shouts filled the darkness of the night. Joab's manservants, maidservants, and soldiers battled the blaze amid the barley. The column of smoke rose skyward, making the dark night even darker. The improvised firefighting brigade was soon unrecognizable in the smog of sweat, soot, and smoke, running to and fro to stop the conflagration from spreading. Joab looked over his vast field in flames, an inferno blazing in the gloom of the dark night.

"Lord Joab!" One of the army chief's loyal fighters came to his master gasping, announcing: "We caught three boys red-handed, trying to flee. This was arson!"

"Arson? Who would want to burn down a barley field? Bring them to me," Joab said wearily. He'd seen enough war for a lifetime; yet here he stood, his white beard blackened by the soot, his forehead stained, seeing his crop literally go up in smoke.

The three boys were led to Joab, their faces frightened, their bodies trembling at the army chief's fury. He skewered them with his gaze. "Why did you set my field on fire? Who sent you to do this?" he demanded angrily.

One lad screwed up his courage to say with a quaver: "Prince Absalom bid us."

"Why?" Joab asked, puzzled.

"I don't know, my lord. Our prince ordered us, so we did it," he replied innocently.

Absalom's door flew open angrily, the sentry posted there shoved out of the way by the enraged Joab, who made his way toward Absalom, who sat there smiling.

"Peace be upon you, Joab," Absalom smirked. "What brings you to me?" he teased.

"What brings me to you?! You know very well what brings me to you!" Joab's pent-up rage seemed about to erupt at Absalom, who dared to betray him. "Why did you do that? What possessed you? Did you think I wouldn't find out you were behind it?"

"On the contrary, I knew you'd figure it out; I counted on that," Absalom countered boldly. "You didn't want to come when I summoned you, so I had no choice. You cannot avoid me. It's been two years since you brought me back from Geshur, two years that I've languished in Jerusalem. I am so close to my royal father, but I have yet to see him. Whenever I seek your help to get me an audience, you ignore me." His casual tone became caustic. "Why did you bring me here? Why bring me to the capital, if I am still in perpetual exile? My four children have died during these two years, probably due to my father's displeasure with me. My three sons and my daughter Tamar are gone. Since I've come back to the city, I have known only misery. Better for me to stay in Geshur than to be so close to my father and still banished from his presence. My father hates me! I have lost four children, but he didn't see fit to come and comfort me. You told me that my father told me to return to Jerusalem, that you persuaded him to pardon me. He has not forgiven me; he still resents me and wishes me ill. I summon you, but you ignore and evade me. So now you've come?" he said with a venomous smile. "Tell my father that if he still views me as guilty, he ought to put me to death; but if my sin is forgiven, let him grant me an audience and welcome me back to the palace! I'm sorry, I tried to ask nicely, but you didn't get it! Now you do."

Joab looked at Absalom's face, twisted in sorrow and anguish. He saw a son in mourning, distanced from his father. "I'll talk to your father," Joab said and departed.

King David sat on his throne. Above his head, the royal crown of King Hanun of Ammon shone. He wore garments of sky-blue, with gold and silver threads.

Absalom stood in the brightly lit entrance. His cloak was golden, to match his tresses, which reached his shoulders.

The son looked at his father...
The father looked at his son...
David struggled with mixed feelings. He still harbored resentment over the murder of Amnon, but his heart ached for the son who had been so far away for so long.

Absalom bowed to the ground, in tears: "My royal father, I am so sorry. I beg your pardon for my actions," he said in a low voice.

David rose, walked over to his beloved son and extended his hand to help him up. Tears welled up in his eyes as he hugged his son, whispering: "I love you, Absalom."

"Brother, what are you doing here?" Absalom asked the man standing before him.

The man looked at the prince standing before him at the city gate, where petitioners gathered to seek the king's justice. For about a year, the man had been hearing about Prince Absalom's presence at the city gate, greeting all the litigants. The prince's face radiated light, his smile and expression captivating the man's heart. His majestic beauty and the glory of his face were incomparable. The humility he projected was a contrast to his high status as the king's son. Behind him was the prince's chariot, drawn by six noble horses, with fifty guards alongside. The man wanted to bow to the king's son, but Absalom grabbed his elbow and embraced him.

"You don't have to kneel before me," he said gently. "We are just men of Israel, you and I. Where are you from, my friend? Why have you come?" he asked pleasantly.

The man looked at the prince embracing him lovingly: "I am from the Tribe of Dan, and I come here to seek the king's justice."

"Really? Tell me more?"

The petitioner looked at the prince. "I am a simple man of no great means. The Lord has blessed me with eight children. I borrowed money from my neighbor to support my family. With the loan, I bought three cows, whose milk I sell to support my household. My loan is overdue, but I cannot pay it back right now. I have to marry off my children, so I don't have the money right now to pay him back. My neighbor is a very rich man; he has money and property, but no children. I asked him to forgo my debt, but he refused, demanding that I return the money I borrowed from him. He doesn't need that money — he has more than enough — yet he pressures me. I have come to ask the king to order him to forgo my debt, or at least postpone the repayment by a few years," he concluded, confident that he was in the right.

"Isn't he ashamed?!" yelled Absalom, "Asking you to repay the loan?! Why does he need the money? You're right! He's rich! You are poor! He ought to forgo your debt and offer you more. Oh, I'm sorry, brother, but the king will not see it that way; he'll order you to pay up, in full. You will find no relief in the king's court; he will not order your debt absolved." He began to tear up. "I pity you, my dear brother! If only I could judge Israel! Brother, go to the king's court and then come back to tell me about it."

Over the course of many hours, petitioners entered the court, after having discussed their case with Prince Absalom, who showed respect and consideration.

Eventually, the man from Dan came out, dejected and deflated.

As he approached Absalom, the prince asked him: "How did you fare?"

"Exactly as my lord predicted. King David said my neighbor has the law on his side, and I must repay the loan. He gave me just a month to do it." His gaze was downcast. "Doesn't he understand what being poor is like? Doesn't he care for the people?"

Absalom's gaze was sympathetic. "A man who sits in an ivory tower cannot understand the sorrow of the common man. The pain of the oppressed does not mean much to the hedonists in the throne room. I'm so sorry, my brother; I feel your pain." He gestured to one of his guards. "Go with him, my dear brother, he will give you some money from my purse, so the king's cruel verdict won't be your undoing."

The man obeyed and returned with his hands full of gold coins, by Absalom's order.

"Thank you very much, my lord," he said to Absalom, trying again to bow to the prince, who stopped him once again.

"I only wish I could give you much more," Absalom said as he embraced and kissed the man. "If I become king, I can give you much more."

"Thank you so much, Prince Absalom! God willing, you will be king soon. The people need a ruler like you, who understands the grief of the common man. We don't need a king who sits in his palace and doesn't acknowledge our sorrow. You are the real king; everyone already knows this and wants it to be true."

Absalom kissed and hugged the man and said goodbye to him, as a friend separated from his old friend.

"Dear Father, I have been in Jerusalem, the Holy City, for about four years; it has been two years since we reconciled. Still, I have not yet offered a thanksgiving offering to God. I must go to Hebron and offer sheep to express my gratitude to God. I made a vow while I was in Geshur that if you would take me back and accept my penitence, I would make an offering of thanksgiving to the Lord."

David looked at his son, thinking: For two years my son has served me faithfully, going out and coming in before me as a slave before his master. His humility and modesty are evident from his actions. He has truly repented! His desire to make a thanksgiving offering in Hebron is praiseworthy; he can certainly find sheep there.

David felt a wave of love for his son and sympathy for Absalom's misfortune. To lose four children in such a short time, leaving him childless, was unspeakable. "Go, my son, in peace, make your sacrifice and then return to me."

"My dear father," Absalom lowered his eyes. "Can you write me a letter asking people to accompany me? I don't want to go alone to Hebron. Can you instruct in your letter that two people of my choosing accompany me? It is not befitting your royal honor for the prince to travel on his own." His request seemed sincere.

"Of course, my son," David said, picking up his quill.

In the emptiness of the night, barking echoed through the city. An autumn wind blew, carrying the fallen leaves, raising them to heaven in a ghostly dance. A man walked down the street, holding his cloak against his body, hiding from the chill of the wind. A cat ran out from around the corner, startling the passerby.

A wide door stood in front of him, its brown color looking more like black in the darkness of the city. The moon hid behind dark clouds, emerging intermittently as the breeze blew them past.

Knocking on the door disturbed the quiet on the street. Through the door, a commotion could be heard. It opened to reveal a large party, eating and drinking with great joy. They fell silent at the new arrival, moving aside to let him pass. "The king's counselor Ahithophel the Gilonite," they whispered as he made his way in.

"Follow me, my lord! Our master is waiting for you," a man gestured to Ahithophel.

Ahithophel made his way toward the inner room confidently. His boldness, along with his erect but slightly careless gait, made clear that he knew his own importance and greatness. He did not seek approval from others based on external appearance. His face was still chiseled and youthful, by virtue of his coal-black beard. He was known for his vigor and excellent advice. Though no observer would have guessed it, he had married off children and grandchildren already — including his eldest granddaughter, Bathsheba, mother of Solomon. Seven years later, he still resented how David's relationship with Bathsheba had begun, without consulting him.

Wise and clever, holding a grudge in his heart, Ahithophel stood before Absalom.

"Who are all these people?" he asked Absalom without preamble.

Absalom smiled, delighted at the bond between him and the king's counselor. "I asked my father to give me a letter asking two people to accompany me. I must have presented that letter a hundred times, so we now have two hundred bound to me."

"Two hundred more, two hundred less, what of it?" declared Ahithophel dismissively. "The entire nation is with you. We have spies scattered throughout Israel, waiting for your signal to start the revolution. Act quickly, blow the shofar, and declare yourself king. Your father is still unaware of the impending rebellion. Gather your loyalists, go up to Jerusalem, and destroy your father's house," Ahithophel hissed, eager for the coup.

"When dawn breaks, we will raise the banner," Absalom replied. "We will blow the shofar, declare our revolution and ascend to Jerusalem."

As the night came to a close, the east began to brighten. The morning was still overcast, as fierce autumn winds blew across the city, carrying the sound of trumpets echoing throughout the town, then the region, and then the country.

"Long live King Absalom of Hebron!" the cry arose, and the land trembled.

"Your Majesty," came a cry of panic as the door to David's chamber was thrown open. "Prince Absalom has declared a revolt in Hebron. All over the country, rebels are flocking to him. He has launched a coup, and the people have been seduced to join him." The lad, sent by Hushai the Archite, the king's companion, trembled in fear of Absalom. "Hushai urged me to tell you that this rebellion is very serious. Absalom has stolen the hearts of all Israel, and he is on his way to Jerusalem."

David closed his eyes, a tremor running through him as he recalled Nathan's prophecy, the rebuke after the Bathsheba incident. For years, he had known its time would come, the terrifying vision echoing in his ears: *"This is what the Lord says: 'I will raise up adversity against you from your own house. Before your very eyes, I will take your wives and give them to another, and he will lie with them in broad daylight. You have acted in secret, but I will do this thing in broad daylight before all Israel.'"*

Like waves crashing on the rocks, thoughts pounded his mind: My son rebels against me, Absalom wants to seize the throne. Is this not the prophecy being fulfilled? My dear son leads a revolution against me, not a slave, not a foreigner! My son wants the crown, but he won't destroy my house! He wouldn't kill me! He might slaughter his brothers, so they cannot challenge him — or my wives, their mothers, for the same reason! My concubines should be safe, as they pose no threat to him. I must flee quickly, give him the chance to come to his senses. When his blood stops boiling with a lust for power, his mind may rule his heart once more!

David hastily rose, digesting the bitter news, devising a plan to save his kingdom from his wayward son. "Run like the wind," he ordered the lad, rousing himself like a lioness racing to rescue her cubs from an approaching enemy. "Assemble ten of my guards to gather my eight wives and all my children. Individually, they are to sneak out of the city, to my residence outside the walls, in a matter of minutes. My concubines shall stay to protect the house; Absalom will not harm them. Then the guards must spread the news to all soldiers and servants who remain loyal to me; they too, should make their way to my residence, with whatever they can carry on foot. No chariots, no horses, no uniforms — they must get out of the city undetected."

Within the hour, David stood at the entrance to his residence outside the city walls. His loyal soldiers, servants, and household members passed before him. Great and faithful families were horrified as they marched toward an unknown future. His face was impassive as he watched the exiles, banished by his rebellious son and his lethal plot; but David blamed his own sin for this catastrophe.

Ittai the Gittite and the six hundred warriors he leads appeared from the bend of the road, bowing to their king. "Why are you coming with me?" the king asked him. "After all, you are a foreigner among us, already an exile from your homeland. Reside with the new king; he will not hurt you. And if you cannot abide him, go back home. That would certainly be better than accompanying me in my wandering and displacement!"

Ittai, a warrior loyal and devoted to David, who had taken it upon himself to fight for the king of Israel and be his servant, looked in shame at the deposed monarch. He swore: "*As surely as the Lord lives, and as my lord the king lives, wherever my lord the king may be, whether it means life or death, there will your servant be.*" His face was determined: "I am with Your Majesty, until the day I die; do not bid me to leave."

"Ittai, my friend and comrade, take your place among my ranks," said David, showing Ittai and his men where to go.

David and his men headed toward the Judean Desert, where he'd hidden from Saul decades earlier. Once again, the windblown wilderness welcomed him into its bosom, this time seeking refuge from his wayward son rather than his mad father-in-law. This time there were tender women with him, as well as pampered children, accustomed to luxury and comfort, crying as they wandered in his wake.

The Kidron Valley lazily greeted the newcomers, the murmur of its stream audible from far off. A gentle breeze rustled the leaves on the enormous sycamore trees along its banks, a song to accompany the sedated current. The refugee caravan considered how to cross, when they suddenly heard an approaching squad and tensed up: were the newcomers friends or foes?

Ittai the Gittite quickly backtracked to see who was making the noise, then hurried back to David's side: "Your Majesty, do not worry. These are not hostile people, but holy men: Zadok and Abiathar, the priests with the Levites. They bear the Holy Ark."

The people halted while the newcomers joined them. They were relieved to see the bearers of the Ark of the Covenant, who brought it to the edge of the stream.

The king approached the priests and greeted them: "Zadok, why have you come here and removed the Ark of the Lord from its place?" the king wondered.

"Your Majesty is God's choice to be King of Israel, and so the Holy Ark must be here."

David demurred: *"Return the ark of God to the city. If I find favor in the eyes of the Lord, He will bring me back and let me see both it and His dwelling place again. But if He should say, 'I do not delight in you,' then here I am; let Him do to me whatever seems good to Him."* His people were dispirited by this decision. Having the Holy Ark in their midst had seemed a good omen; now it would leave as suddenly as it came.

Zadok expressed his displeasure at the idea of leaving the king and returning to Abasalom's Jerusalem, which he had just fled. "If Absalom hears that we have come to you, he may kill us all. I beg of Your Majesty, do not send us back to Jerusalem," Zadok pleaded for his life and for those accompanying him.

The king was lost in thought: All those people in Nob, the city of priests, perished because of me. I cannot permit another bloodbath among the seed of Aaron.

The people gazed at their sovereign, awaiting his word. "My friend Zadok, ask the Urim and Thummim whether to return to Jerusalem," David commanded.

Zadok did so, and the reply was clear. "Return to the city safely."

"Go back to Jerusalem with the Holy Ark," the king commanded. "Your son Ahimaaz and Abiathar's son Jonathan are with you. I will stay in the wilderness until you send word through them what my son Absalom is planning."

David and his people climbed. Their faces were hooded and their eyes wet as sorrow filled their hearts. David even removed his shoes, mourning and sobbing over his expulsion from the Holy City. The mountaintop afforded them a final look at the capital. It was lush and green in autumn, with the horizon being painted in various shades of green and brown now that summer was gone, the sun peeking through thick clouds filling the sky.

David turned his face toward the Holy City, focusing on the pavilion he had made for the Ark of the Lord. He prostrated himself toward the site of the Divine Presence.

The reverie was broken by someone shouting: "Your Majesty! Your Majesty!" It was Hushai the Archite, climbing the mountain after David and his people, dirt on his head and his robe torn. Slowly, he made his way to the king, leaning heavily on his staff. His white beard was stained with earth, his hands were scratched and bruised. His azure eyes were reddened from the tears he had shed. He was wizened but wise, feeble but intelligent. At his age, walking on level ground was hard, let alone scaling a hilltop. He trudged, dog-tired but dogged. A paragon of purity and righteousness, the king's companion and friend, he could not abandon his comrade.

"Dear Hushai," David called out, running to help the elderly man. "Why did you follow me? You ought to have stayed in town!"

"Your Majesty is my master and my soulmate; how could I abandon you?" The old man tried to catch his breath after the challenging climb.

The king embraced Hushai: "My dear, unfortunately, you will not be able to come with me. We need to keep up a grueling pace, and it will be beyond your ability. I know you want to stay with me, but it would endanger me and my people. Return to Jerusalem, my soulmate; God willing, I will see you there!"

"But Your Majesty..." Hushai tried to argue

"No, Hushai, don't try to convince me. It's too difficult and dangerous. If you love me, please do what I tell you. Go back to the city, present yourself to Absalom; tell him that just as you were with me, you will be with him. Everyone appreciates your clever and kind advice. Absalom is no fool, so he will doubtless accept your offer." A plan began to form in his mind. "Ahithophel the Gilonite is his co-conspirator. You must subvert the counsel of Ahithophel. You are the only one who can do it. Return to Jerusalem and work against Ahithophel. You are not alone; I sent Zadok and Abiathar there too. Whatever you hear and discover, you can pass on to them, and their sons will convey the information to me. Do this for me, as one who loves me." David dropped his voice to a whisper: "But before you go, let us speak privately."

The wise eyes looked at David lovingly. "Of course, Your Majesty. What is it?"

"I am suffering, my people are suffering, but I am deeply troubled by the reputation of my Lord. How does it look to the world for me to flee like this? Is it not a desecration of the name of Heaven? Perhaps if I make myself appear as a heretic or an idol worshipper, for appearance's sake, observers will find the fault in me and not in God. Otherwise, they may say that the Holy One acts unjustly, perish the thought!" There were tears in his eyes, distressed by the very idea of apostasy, even if it's a pretense.

Hushai regarded him kindly. "No, Your Majesty must not do this. On the contrary, this situation validates the Torah's words. The passage of the war bride precedes that of the wayward and rebellious son; one leads to the other. Maacah was a war bride, and now her son Absalom is a rebellious son. The Word of God is true!"

David embraced Hushai, grateful for the comfort he gave him. Hushai, regretfully and unwillingly withdrew, to make his way slowly back to the capital.

As evening approached, the wind grew stronger, carrying dirt and sand. The children's stomachs were grumbling with hunger, but there was nothing for them. In their panicked flight, in fear of Absalom, they'd left without food or supplies, relying on God's mercy.

A man arrived at the camp with two laden donkeys. He bowed to the king. "Peace be upon Your Majesty," he said aloud.

"Ziba?" asked David, "What are you doing here? Why do you bring laden donkeys?"

"Your Majesty King David," the servant began. "I heard of the king's exile, so I took it upon myself to bring gifts, food, and provisions for the king and his people. Thus my king will be refreshed and be able to ride rather than walk."

"But what of Mephibosheth?" asked David.

"Unfortunately, my lord, Mephibosheth is sitting in his home in Jerusalem. He hasn't left the city," he reported with downcast eyes. "Apparently, he thinks that this is his chance. He expects Absalom to kill Your Majesty, and for the court to then sentence him to death. Then the crown will return to the house of Saul — specifically, to him."

David fumed: "After all I did for him! I welcomed him to my table, and he turns around and tries to seize my throne?!" Mephibosheth's perfidy enraged him. "Ziba, Mephibosheth is an ingrate. With all I have bestowed upon him, he plots against me! Henceforth, you shall eat his crops and produce," he decreed in his wrath.

"As Your Majesty wishes," Ziba said, bowing and prostrating himself, a hidden smile forming on his face. He thought happily: I have succeeded!

"*Get out, get out, you worthless man of bloodshed!*" the shout echoed. A stone hit David's shoulder as he and his people followed the path at the foot of the mountain.

It was late at night. The people were drained and exhausted by the circumstances in which they'd been swept up. The young children had fallen asleep on top of the donkeys carrying them but were awakened by the shouts. On the incline stood the chief justice of the court, Shimei, son of Gera, Saul's uncle, screaming.

"Debaucher! Bastard! Butcher! Brute! Abomination! You deserve what has befallen you!" Shimei complained bitterly, throwing stones at the caravan, cursing and slandering King David. "*The Lord has paid you back for all the blood of the house of Saul, in whose place you have reigned, and the Lord has delivered the kingdom into the hand of your son Absalom. See, you have come to ruin because you are a man of bloodshed!*" Shimei, bold-faced, was gripped by deep resentment of David and his kingdom. It was a surprise coming from an elderly man, a great sage of Israel.

David lowered his head and continued walking, trying to protect his body from the shower of stones falling on him. The women hunched over their children, trying to protect them, turning their backs on the condemnation of the disturbed old man.

Abishai drew his sword and approached King David. His face red with fury, his eyes spitting fire, he demanded: "Why would this dead dog curse Your Majesty?"

David lifted his head, tears in his eyes: "What am I to do with you, sons of Zeruiah? If he curses me, perhaps it is by God's command! Who could tell him to be silent?"

"Cursing the King of Israel is high treason! The penalty is death!" Abishai countered. Their men followed the argument between the king and his deputy army chief.

"Listen to me, Abishai," said David, observing his people. "Look, my son, my own flesh and blood, is trying to kill me. That is truly extraordinary, for a son to try to kill his father. On the other hand, it is natural for this Benjamite to hate me; he is Saul's kinsman. Let him curse, as the Lord told him. Every person has a role decreed by God; people do not act of their own accord. The Lord told him to curse me, so he cursed me. True, God lets guilty people sin and innocent people save, so Shimei must be liable for something in Heaven's eyes. Regardless, we must leave it to God's reckoning; He may see my distress, my tears, and my humiliation, and show me pity."

David and his men walked slowly through the valley as Shimei, son of Gera, cursed, cast stones, and flung dirt at the humiliated convoy.

"Long live the king! Long live King Absalom!" Hushai declared as he bowed. What was once David's throne room looked strange and foreign occupied by a usurper.

"Hushai the Archite?" asked Absalom, puzzled. "Do you not bear the title of king's companion? You have abandoned your friend!"

Hushai smiled at Absalom: "Your Majesty, I am the king's companion, whoever that may be, as chosen by God, and the people of all Israel. That is whom I accompany and abet. Moreover, do I not stand before the son and heir of King David? As I served Your Majesty's father loyally, I will serve my King Absalom."

Absalom approached Hushai, embraced and kissed him: "I am

overjoyed that you also stand with me, my dear. You shall be my aide, just as you were my father's."

As the days passed, Absalom found himself desperate for good advice. His father's throne room, so familiar to him, was now where he received dire reports daily. The civil war raged on, with many thousands of dead all over the country, tens of thousands wounded. Robbery and looting, as well as abuse and cruelty abounded in Israel.

He thought: How will I ever establish my reign and calm my kingdom? The resistance is fiercer than I thought. David's loyalists fight boldly and confidently, refusing to accept the revolution. I must demonstrate my legitimacy and confirm my victory over my father. We must stop the fighting by getting his supporters to surrender unconditionally. We need to make the entire nation accept my authority."

"Guards, summon the king's counselor, Ahithophel the Gilonite!" he ordered.

Minutes later, Ahithophel stood before him: "Yes, Your Majesty," he said happily.

"I need advice, my dear friend," said Absalom. "I must stop the fighting and establish my dominion over the entire nation. What is your counsel, Counselor?"

"Your Majesty, in order for the people to accept your authority, you must first prove to them that you will not retract it," Ahithophel said, as if he had carefully considered the matter and had been waiting for just such a question. "The people fear that you will regret your actions and restore your father to his throne; if so, he will take revenge on all those who joined the rebellion against him. Still, he will spare you, his beloved son, just as he has forgiven you for killing Amnon. Therefore, you must prove to the people that you despise your father. My advice is that you take his ten concubines for yourself, publicly demonstrating your contempt for him. It must be before all Israel, in broad daylight. Then your kingdom and your kingship will be secure."

"Are you serious?" asked Absalom. "Do you think the people will accept that?"

Ahithophel chuckled as he gestured: "Oh, they'll be shocked at first, but it will show you're serious. All of Israel will be awestruck, and the resistance will fall apart. Tell your men to pitch a tent on the roof of the palace, and then summon your father's concubines."

Absalom thought: Everyone knows that his advice is sound and his word is true. An audacious and depraved act, but the right course to seize the scepter of rule.

Absalom looked at Ahithophel: "As you say, I will now do." He headed to the roof.

Some hours later, Absalom summoned Ahithophel again. "I did what you advised me," he said, feeling the vileness of what he had done, a far more terrible act than what had been done to his sister Tamar. "What is our next step?" He felt as if he were atop a boulder that was triggering a landslide, helpless to stop it.

"Now," Ahitophel declared, "it is time to slay Your Majesty's father. I would choose twelve thousand warriors to pursue David this very night. I would attack him in the dark, when he is weary and discouraged; I would sow fear in his camp, prompting his men to flee. Then I would strike him down, and the whole nation will be yours for the taking. One man's life is all that is keeping you from bringing peace to the land."

Absalom chuckled. "How pragmatic your counsel is, Ahithophel. You are a man of action! What say you?" he asked the elders who had joined his rebellion.

One of them stroked his beard uneasily: "It seems to me that it is worth hearing another opinion on this subject; if this plan fails, we will pay dearly."

Absalom looked at the old man, his doubts penetrating his heart, leaving a void within him. "Call Hushai the Archite," he told the guard. "Tell him I need his advice."

Hushai entered the king's chamber; the elders regarding him with suspicion. Known as a close friend of King David, his very presence made them uncomfortable. Hushai bowed deeply to Absalom: "Your Majesty summoned me?" he asked in awe.

"Yes indeed, my dear Hushai. I need advice on how to act now in order to establish my rule. Ahithophel advised me to send twelve thousand warriors tonight to chase David, to try to capture him and kill him. What do you think of this plan?"

Hushai laughed out loud, indicating contempt and disdain for this scheme: "To chase David now?! You know his father and his men; they are bold and bitter, like a bear whose cub has been killed! Your father is a man of war and will not let the people rest. If you try to hurt him now, you will fail in battle. His men will fight fiercely now. You know them: Joab, Abishai, Ittai. Sending a small force is a bad idea. Do you think twelve thousand will suffice? True, they number less than two thousand fighting men, but they would rout such a force easily; and if you are defeated in your first battle, even the best of your warriors will abandon you. My advice is that you gather soldiers from Dan to Beersheba, as numerous as the grains of sand on the seashore. Then we can overwhelm him, falling upon him at once. He would have nowhere to hide, neither he nor his men. That is what I advise Your Majesty to do."

One of the old men who had questioned Ahithophel's plan was enthused: "Now we're on the right track. A small army against King David and his men? That's suicide! Hushai's strategy is better than Ahithophel's."

Absalom summoned Amasa, whom he'd appointed as army chief. "Assemble all the fighting men throughout Israel; in a few days, we'll attack David en masse."

Meanwhile, Ahithophel went home, wrote a will and hanged himself. He knew that Absalom was doomed and feared being held accountable for supporting the coup.

At twilight, the horizon was painted in reddish grays, a few rays of sun bursting through the thick curtain. In the streets of the city, shouts and screams could be heard, along with the clang of swords. Crime and strife bedeviled the town, which Absalom's men occupied. They searched for nests of resistance to the new king.

An old man stumbled down the street, leaning on his staff. On his head was a hood that covered a bit of his face, a shield from the chill of the approaching night. The soldiers walked past him with barely a glance. An anonymous grandfather posed no military threat. Still, an officer ordered him to halt. "Where are you going, old man?!"

The old man looked at the officer, eyes penetrating his soul, drilling into his heart: "From light to darkness, from darkness to light.

From here to there, from there to here." With probing eyes, he uttered words without context: "Once for white, now for black. The black of now is the white of later. From good to bad, from bad to good. From lie to truth, from truth to lie." The old man gave a short laugh: "Wisdom is stupidity, stupidity is wisdom. Are you wise or stupid?" he asked, and continued on his way, leaving the officer confused, wondering about the old man.

"Just a crazy old man," the officer told his men, disbelieving his own words.

Near the pavilion of the Holy Ark, the old man looked sideways. Finding no hostile observers, he ducked inside a house. It was mostly dark, broken only by the faint light of two candles in the center of the room. At the table, Zadok and Abiathar sat; they rose to honor Hushai the Archite. The aged face glowed. "Quickly, there is no time! You must urgently send your sons to King David to tell him to flee, to cross the Jordan quickly. He must get away! Tell him about my plan, as well as Ahithophel's."

Minutes later, a serving girl emerged from the house, making her way directly to the outskirts of the city. She was holding a basket of clothing, hurrying to Ein Rogel, the spring where the laundresses did their work.

"Jonathan, Ahimaaz," she whispered into the bushes. The two young priests peered out, recognizing the maidservant's voice. "Your fathers have a message for you to pass on to King David," she whispered to the lads, detailing the parts of the mission.

"Thank you," the two said, disappearing into the foliage again.

Before they could sneak out, they noticed that one of Absalom's boys was lurking in the area. He seemed to be looking for some hideaway in the area.

"Quickly," Jonathan whispered, "We must go! In a matter of minutes, that lad will find us and inform Absalom. We have to sneak out the back. My father's friend lives nearby; if we can make it there fast enough, he will provide shelter and refuge."

The next minutes were full of running, evading, and hiding, with pursuit on their heels.

When they got there, only the lady of the house, the wife of

Abiathar's friend, was present. Wise and clever, she was faithful to God and David. "Quickly, get into the cistern!" she whispered to the fugitives, pointing to the pit in her yard. Jonathan and Ahimaaz jumped in. She spread a sheet over the mouth, then placed wheat on top.

Mere moments later, Jonathan and Ahimaaz heard the lady speaking to Absalom's men. "Who, my lord? Jonathan and Ahimaaz? Yes, they were here. I gave them something to drink, and then they headed back to Jerusalem, I think."

"My lord, they're not here," came the voice of a soldier.

"Well, let us return; maybe they're back in town."

Soon after the conversation had ended, the lady of the house moved the wheat, rolled back the sheet, and sent the young men on their way to King David.

Jonathan and Ahimaaz arrived at David's camp, telling him about Ahithophel's plan, Hushai's scheme, and everything he needed to know.

The king and his men crossed the Jordan before daybreak. The citizens of Mahanaim received them with great honor, presenting gifts and food to the exiled king.

Across the Jordan, David's ranks swelled with the loyalists and the faithful.

One day, as the sun was about to burst forth and banish the dark, casting off the shadows of night, he surveyed them. About ten thousand troops prepared for the campaign, coming together as an organized army. They were divided into three brigades, headed by Joab, Abishai, and Ittai respectively. Each brigade had officers of thousands and hundreds, delegating authority, preparing for battle against the impassioned and disorderly mob that Absalom had assembled.

King David, refreshed and reinforced, stood at the gate of the city of Mahanaim, with his small, loyal army before him. The king was dressed for battle, ready to fight to restore his kingdom and liberate his capital.

The three brigadiers came to speak to him. Their faces were fierce and determined, dedicated to the cause of the Davidic restoration. They had one quibble.

"Your Majesty," Joab eyed David in his battle gear, "must not go to war with us. Our enemy has one goal: killing my king. They are not interested in us. If we flee or lose, the enemy will leave us in peace. But if Your Majesty is on the battlefield, they will be relentless, until my king is slain. Moreover, if Your Majesty leads us, they will know that this is the totality of our manpower; but if Your Majesty remains in the camp, we may lead them to believe that we are only the vanguard, striking fear in their hearts. The most important thing is that someone must remain behind to pray. Who better than our king? Therefore let Your Majesty stay while we go into battle, so we can concentrate on our combat and not be preoccupied with our king's welfare."

Hearing the legitimate arguments, David thought: Joab is an extremely talented army chief; he makes excellent points. My presence on the battlefield would be a distraction. I ought to stay here. He told his men: "Do what you deem is right."

David stood on a large rock at the entrance to the city and addressed his army. "My brothers, my comrades, the bravest and truest! Today, you go out to battle your enemies — but they are your brethren too! The cause of this coup is mine; I sinned before our Creator, and this is His punishment. Consider the People of Israel; you engage in combat with revolutionaries who defy the kingdom established by the Lord. I acknowledge it is very difficult in the heat of battle to think of the enemy as a beloved brother. Be careful: do not pursue those who flee, do not punish those who surrender, do not put to death those who are wounded. These are our kinsmen, incited and ignorant. Spare the children of Abraham, Isaac, and Jacob, your family. Go in peace and return in peace!" The king looked at Joab, Abishai, and Ittai: "Please, take it easy with the lad Absalom."

The large meadows on the Jordan's east bank were yellowish-brown. Absalom's men were like sand on the seashore, stretching across the amber fields. The Forest of Ephraim was to their back, while before them were cultivated fields. Sheep and cattle, mostly owned by Ephraimites on the west bank, were enjoying the lush eastern territory of Gad, Reuben, and half of Manasseh. Animals were then slaughtered without their owners' knowledge, to feed Absalom's army. The usurper walked among his troops, hugging and kissing them, encouraging them ahead of the planned assault on David's camp. At noon, the sun stood high in the grayish sky, warming the warriors, who were enjoying a post-meal nap during the midday heat.

Suddenly, the screams and shouts of combat and consternation filled Absalom's encampment. David's forces had attacked suddenly and boldly. Absalom's army tried to recover from the shock of the small-scale raid, only to find itself under assault from the north and the south. Any thought of counterattack was abandoned as alarm turned to panic. In disarray and dismay, they began to flee, fearing David and his men. The forest to their rear seemed to offer refuge, but its treacherous terrain soon claimed more casualties than any blade. Twenty thousand warriors fell in the field and glade, and Absalom's fighters fled every which way, though David's men did not give chase.

Helplessly, Absalom screamed at his men to turn around and fight. Their cowardice enraged him. His sword flashed as he attacked his own fleeing fighters. "Weaklings! Feckless traitors!" he shrieked to all around him, seeing his imminent downfall.

He thought: I must escape! All I can do is save myself.

He leaped onto his mule, fleeing into the twists and turns of the dense forest, thinking: I need a place to hide for a few days until the rage subsides. My father will have compassion for me ultimately. I must evade and dodge until cooler heads prevail.

On the battlefield, bodies were scattered by the thousand, their blood turning the ground into a marsh. The wounded were screaming, begging for mercy, as David's men rushed to help their brethren. Joab meandered through the killing fields, searching, wondering: Where is the usurper? Where is the attempted patricide, who threw the pardon for his brother's murder back at his father's face? Where is the ungrateful arsonist who targeted the estate of the man who rescued him from exile?

"Have you seen Absalom?" Joab asked anyone who crossed his path. "Did anyone notice where Absalom fled to? Have you stumbled over his worthless corpse?"

Finally, he ran into Cushi, a dark-skinned sojourner who had enlisted in David's army. He was a conscientious soldier known for his speed. "Lord Commander Joab, I saw Absalom," he reported.

"Where is he?" Joab demanded urgently, desperate to find his enemy.

"I saw him in the depths of the forest, caught by his hair in an oak tree! I gather he tried to ride his mule under an overhanging branch, but he was caught by those golden tresses of his." He laughed: "He is swinging like a windchime, making an awful sound."

"Why didn't you kill him? The usurper, the rebel, the high traitor was in your hand, and you didn't slay him?! I would have given you money and power had you done so? Why did you leave him like that?" shouted Joab at the fighter.

Shock gripped Cushi: "Kill him?! King David ordered us not to do that. We heard the royal command. To execute a rebel in defiance would be an act of treason! Would I transgress the king's explicit order for treasure or honor?! Had the king ordered him killed, he would have been dead long ago. But His Majesty told my lord, along with Lord Abishai and Lord Ittai, not to spill Absalom's blood. I heard it with my own ears. How could I stand in front of the king and lie to him, to say that I didn't do it? My lord wouldn't have helped me in such a shameful situation either, I have no doubt."

"Don't you worry about that!" Joab sputtered. "To execute a traitor is to fulfill the command of our king and his King! Show me where he is, and I'll do it myself."

Cushi led Joab and ten of his warriors to the oak tree.

Absalom was suspended between heaven and earth. The hair he took such pride in had become a hindrance to him. His beautiful eyes were filled with horror at the situation he found himself in. His body was exhausted from his attempts to free himself from the snagging branch.

"My friend Joab, help me," he called out in a choked voice, as he saw the army chief approach.

"Lowly traitor," Joab hissed from between clenched teeth, "you stole your father's heart, the heart of the court, and the heart of Israel. Therefore, your death will be threefold as well." Joab took out three sharp and pointy pikes, and advanced toward Absalom, whose face was a mask, frozen by the fear of death.

"Die, you traitor!" said Joab, sticking the pikes in Absalom's heart. "Strike down the traitor!" he commanded his boys. The ten fighters drew their swords and struck the prince who had seized his father's ten concubines. "Throw his corpse into the pit and place a heap of stones over it!" commanded Joab, "He is not worthy of being buried in the tomb he prepared for himself. Absalom's Monument, which he had the audacity to build for himself while he was still alive, will remain empty of this coward's carcass."

Joab took out his shofar and sounded a great staccato blast. Absalom's coup was at an end. There was no need for anyone else to die, now that the usurper was underground.

CHAPTER FIFTY-SIX

The News

Ahimaaz, son of Zadok, excitedly told Joab. "Let me run and tell the king that his enemies are dead, and the revolution is over."

Joab sighed. "*You are not the man to take good news today. You may do it another day, but you must not do so today, because the king's son is dead.* Our king will not rejoice at the news, so I will send another man to inform the king." Joab looked around, and his gaze fell on Cushi, whom he called over. "Go to the king and tell him what you saw: the victory, the hanging of Absalom on the tree, and his death."

Cushi bowed down to Joab and ran off to carry out his order.

"Please, Lord Commander Joab, let me bring the news of victory to the king," Ahimaaz begged Joab. "Let me run! I can overtake Cushi."

"Why, son, would you want to bear this news? The good news is our victory, but the bad news is his son's death. Why would you want to bring bad news to the king?"

"Even so, I would run now, my lord," Ahimaaz pleaded.

"Then run," Joab conceded.

Ahimaaz moved as nimbly as a gazelle as he set off, focusing on his destination. His feet floated over the ground; he leaped over stones and rocks. In a matter of minutes, he pulled ahead of Cushi, racing back to Mahanaim to spread the news.

"Your Majesty!" cried the sentry, "there is a lone runner approaching."

David, eager to know what had happened, was waiting at the city gate, his face contemplative, his brow furrowed in sorrow. The sentry's shout interrupted his troubled thoughts. He whispered: "If he is alone, he must be bringing news."

"Your Majesty, another man is running after him," the sentry observed.

"He must be bringing news too!" replied the king, rising from his seat.

"Your Majesty! By his run, it seems to me it's Ahimaaz, son of Zadok."

"A good man, who must bring good news." A slight smile formed on his lips.

Ahimaaz came to the gate, and King David came out toward him. Ahimaaz bowed to the king: "Peace be upon Your Majesty," said Ahimaaz, "*Blessed be the Lord your God! He has delivered up the men who raised their hands against my lord the king.*"

"How fares the lad Absalom?" David asked Ahimaaz, his heart uneasy.

"I cannot say," Ahimaaz demurred, seeing the king's concern for his rebellious son. "Perhaps Cushi can speak regarding the prince's status, when he arrives."

Minutes later, Cushi arrived, gasping before the king. "*May my lord the king hear the good news: Today the Lord has avenged you of all who rose up against you!*"

"How fares the lad, Absalom?" asked the king, hoping for a good answer.

"*May what has become of the young man happen to the enemies of my lord the king and to all who rise up against you to harm you,*" Cushi gladly exclaimed to the king, as if bearing welcome news of the death of his enemy.

"*O my son Absalom! My son, my son Absalom! If only I had died instead of you,*" King David slowly buried his face in his hands, walking on the roof, mourning the death of his son. "*O Absalom, my son, my son!*" His heartbreaking cry shattered the silence of the night, echoing throughout the city. The people returning from the war, filled with joy at the victory, became mourners when they heard that the king was grieving for his son. The warriors, who had laid their lives on the line and won the day, snuck into the city silently, as if defeated in battle.

"Silence! Are you not ashamed?" The call surprised David, who wept bitterly for his dead son. Joab, hearing the king's cry, had gone up to the roof and stood before David. *"Today, you have disgraced all your servants who have saved your life and the lives of your sons and daughters, of your wives, and of your concubines. You love those who hate you and hate those who love you! For you have made it clear today that the commanders and soldiers mean nothing to you. I know today that if Absalom were alive and all of us were dead, it would have pleased you!"*

Joab's diatribe shocked the king. The army chief went on, his voice angry and defiant. "Are you weeping over a rebel who wanted to kill you and all your people?! Men have given their lives out of loyalty to you, and you are now rebelling against them. 'My son, my son Absalom,'" he said sarcastically, mimicking the king's voice. "Your evil son would be willing to slaughter you and all those who accompany you, if only given the chance. If he'd had his way, dogs would now be feasting on your flesh and the bodies of all those who love you; yet you whine as if you have lost some great love." Joab's rage was growing. "Now go! Get down there! Speak to the hearts of your servants. I swear to you, if you don't go out, no one will spend the night at your side. They will abandon you, to the last man. I tell you, if you do not come to your senses, the evil that comes to you now will be worse and more bitter than all the evils you have known from your youth until now!"

The king looked up and, seeing the truth in Joab's words, wiped away his tears. "You are right," he said in a whisper, "I will go down to the gate of the city, and I will greet my people upon their triumphant return."

CHAPTER FIFTY-SEVEN

The Return

Jerusalem was abuzz with nervous anticipation of King David's return.

One youth said to an old man: "Believe me, I know him, he won't let it go by quietly, he'll kill us all."

"What are you talking about? You just think you know him! He will forgive us and act as if nothing happened. Just seek his pardon and he'll grant it," the elder objected.

"You're crazy! We rebelled against him! We put another on his throne! Apologize and everything will go back to normal?! It seems you don't understand the gravity of what we have done. Don't you know what high treason means?" the youth yelled.

The man stroked his white beard: "Yes, I know what it means, but do you realize what will happen if we don't restore him, if we are left without a king over the people again? You're still young, you don't know what happened before David. You did not live under the iron fist of the accursed Philistines. You were born only after David became king and liberated the entire nation from the hands of our enemies. You don't have memories like me: the oppression, murder, looting, and humiliation we suffered before you were a twinkle in your father's eye. David fought his wars when you were a baby in the cradle; Fortunately, you did not have to live as a slave to a foreign people. You think you do, but you don't know King David. When I was your age, I served under him," the old man said nostalgically. "I was privileged to see his heroism and daring in the face of the enemy. He saved this nation! I saw him carry one of my wounded comrades, like a father cradling his child. With his soldier's blood on his face, David bandaged and comforted that boy." The elder's eyes filled with tears: "I remember how the king cried with the bereaved families, orphans, and widows. I saw with my own eyes the pain that filled the king's heart over the sorrow and suffering of his people. You young folk don't know who King David is! Oh, what foolishness it was to follow your folly, to hand David's scepter to a scoundrel like Absalom." The old man buried his head in his hands and burst into tears.

The youth looked at him with mixed feelings, finally asking: "What should we do?"

The old man stopped sobbing. "As I told you, we must restore King David, seek his pardon, and swear allegiance to him. I tell you, he will accept our return; he'll forgive us. Who like him knows and appreciates the magnitude of the virtue of repentance!"

"I hope you're right," replied the young man, sounding unsure.

All over Israel, such conversations took place. The revolt, which ended by Absalom's death, left the people confused, with no king, no leader, no shepherd, and no guide.

They were worried about David's return, lest he take revenge...

They felt terror and fear, lest the nation be left without a ruler...

They were overwhelmed by anxiety about what was to come...

A hush fell over the marketplace as the people gathered around a platform to hear the two priests David had sent, Zadok and Abiathar. "Dear members of the tribe of Judah!" cried the former. The cool autumn breeze at dusk heralded the coming of the rainy season, as the crowd's hearts fluttered like leaves. Their faces were filled with worry, concern, and anxiety about the future. Zadok went on: "Judahites, you are kinsmen of King David, you love and treasure him! Why should you be the last to bring the king home? All of Israel's tribes have sent emissaries seeking a royal pardon, begging our sire to take back his throne. If all of them seek to restore King David, why not you, his cousins and compatriots? If you fear retribution, the king has sworn that he will not seek vengeance, that he pardons all who followed his son. If you feel shame, there is no better remedy than restoring the Davidic monarchy."

"What of Amasa, son of Jether, who was Absalom's army chief?" someone asked.

"If Amasa is present, let him step forward. The king has a message for him!"

The crowd parted to let Amasa come forward and climb up to the platform. He looked down, head bent, shoulders slumped. He moved slowly, dreading his fate.

"Amasa, son of Jether!" Zadok addressed him. "His Majesty King David has sworn an oath to appoint you as Lord Commander of the Army of Israel, in Joab's stead. Since Joab violated the king's command to spare Absalom's life, His Majesty has chosen you, his kinsman, for this prestigious post." Amasa shrugged and looked at the priests. His gaze showed that he was suspicious of what they were saying.

Zadok went on: "His Majesty knows that this revolt was decreed by the Lord; he does not seek to blame or avenge this act. Israel needs a king to lead it, and His Majesty is ready to welcome everyone back to him, as if nothing had happened. It is your duty to convince your tribesmen to restore King David and welcome him back."

The trumpets sounded on the banks of the Jordan. The entire tribe of Judah, headed by Amasa, son of Jether, had arrived to greet the king returning from exile and accompany him to his capital, Jerusalem. King David was dressed in royal garb, and positioned on a regal palanquin. A soft wind danced through the treetops, bending the branches as if bowing before their king. The murmur of the river merged with the singing of the crowds gathered to herald their king's return. The sun's rays shone through the high clouds, lighting up the caravan as it approached the river's edge.

"Long live King David!" the people shouted.

Shimei, son of Gera, suddenly appeared, disembarking from a boat on the Jordan River. He bowed and prostrated before the king. "Long live King David! King David forever!" he exclaimed. A thousand members of the tribe of Benjamin accompanied Shimei, along with Ziba and the sons and servants of Mephibosheth.

"I have brought ferries to transport Your Majesty and his men," Shimei said, bowing to the ground. "Let Your Majesty disregard what his servant did, the disrespect he showed the King of Israel. It was not only I, the king's servant, who sinned against Your Majesty. Please accept my repentance and request for forgiveness, and I will return to serve Your Majesty. I have come, as the highest rank of all the House of Joseph, to seek the king's pardon! Please forgive me, Your Majesty!"

From among the king's men, Abishai, son of Zeruiah, came out, his sword flashing in his hand, his face red in fury: "Today you will lose your head, Shimei, for cursing the Lord's anointed when he fled Jerusalem!" Abishai began to advance toward him.

"Stop!" cried David. "What am I to do with you, sons of Zeruiah, who always trouble me? Need we kill a man in Israel today?! Today I am King of Israel again. It is a day of rejoicing, not revenge! The day when Israel restores its king! I swear to you, Shimei, son of Gera, he who repents and seeks forgiveness will not die."

Abishai withdrew and sheathed his sword, glaring at Shimei.

Barzilai the Gileadite, a wealthy and venerable man from Mahanaim, who had provided for the exiled king and his men, accompanied David on his return.

"Please, my beloved Barzilai, accompany me to my capital, Jerusalem. There I can repay you for the wonderful kindness you have shown me and my people," David asked Barzilai. "My gratitude to you knows no bounds, and I must repay you well. How can I do that if you remain here?"

"Your Majesty knows that his servant is an elderly man. How can I leave my home and my homeland? What might my king give to a man of my age? I cannot taste food anymore, I cannot listen to music, I cannot even see Your Majesty's beautiful face. Why should I be a burden to Your Majesty? I appreciate the gesture, but there is no point to it. I want nothing more than to live peacefully in my home, die in the city of my ancestors, and be buried alongside them. If the king wishes to reciprocate, take my son, Chimham, and accord him the favors Your Majesty wishes to grant me."

"My beloved friend Barzilai, I will do as you say! Your son will be like mine, and he will eat at my table," said the king, kissing and hugging his friend as they parted.

The king's chair was put onto the ferry, to bring him across the Jordan River. The Judahites as well as five hundred Benjamites accompanied David on his return journey.

However, this aroused consternation among the other tribes. "*Why did our brothers, the men of Judah, take you away secretly and bring the king and his household across the Jordan, together with all of David's men?*" They felt left out … insulted.

The men of Judah were unsympathetic. They made their case aggressively: "*We did this because the king is our relative. Why does this anger you? Have we ever eaten at the king's expense or received anything for ourselves?*"

"*We have ten shares in the king, so we have more claim to David than you. Why then do you despise us? Were we not the first to speak of restoring our king?*" The other tribes wouldn't relent either, screaming in anger and disappointment. "You're the last tribe to accept our sire. Were it not for his letter, your revolt would still be going on. Now, like bootlickers, you grab at him, as if you want him more than we."

The quarreling and shouting echoed back and forth. The argument was so loud that neither side could hear the other. They hurled vitriol and insults at each other, an unending roar which even King David himself could not quell.

Suddenly, a shofar blow interrupted the yelling. A Benjamite named Sheba, son of Bichri, held it aloft. The people fell silent, waiting for him to speak. His shout echoed throughout the entire crowd, seeping in like poison in a wounded body: "*We have no share in David, no inheritance in Jesse's son. Every man to his tent, O Israel!*"

Sheba, son of Bichri, waved his hand, as if signaling to the people of the ten tribes to follow him, as if deposing the king and disposing of his kingship.

The other tribes of Israel spun on their heels, turning their backs on King David and his tribesmen.

They followed their new leader, Sheba, son of Bichri.

CHAPTER FIFTY-EIGHT
Sheba Son of Bichri

Silence prevailed in the city, an ominous quiet. The streets were deserted, the bustling city hushed. The whistling wind was the only sound, sending a chill through every soul in the city.

In the semi-dark of the chamber, only footsteps could be heard, the monotonous sound of a man pacing back and forth. King David was restless. Absalom's coup had ended, but now a new revolt had erupted, courtesy of Sheba, who was trying to rekindle the fires of rebellion and revolution, to reignite disputes and debates among the people, who had not yet calmed down from the recent turmoil. Absalom's inferno had claimed tens of thousands of Israelite victims, and flames were still licking at the edge of the camp, threatening to envelop it.

The king sat alone in his room, memories flooding his mind. The last meeting with his son, whom he would never see again, had taken place in this room.

Sorrow filled the king's heart. A few hours earlier, his ten concubines had arrived before him. They had been crying, pain etched on their faces. Humiliation, disgrace, shame, suffering and sorrow suffused their hearts. After Absalom's depraved acts, they were widows in their husband's lifetime, shut up in the palace. It tore at the souls of the unfortunate women. The sound of their cries echoed in the king's ears, filling his heart with sorrow for his precious concubines, who had been torn from him by his son.

Footsteps approached his door, followed by light knocks. He was ripped from his reverie, pulled from the depths of sorrow in which he had been immersed. "Amasa, come."

"Your Majesty summoned me?" asked Amasa, the newly appointed army chief.

"Yes, I need you to gather the Judahites; bring them here in three days. Do not tarry; we cannot let Sheba's rebellion go unanswered. We must not let him gain power. He must not be given time to poison the people with his toxic words. You know what they say: when there is just one crack in the dam, it can be mended; when it widens, the torrent becomes unstoppable. Do not delay; this is your first mission."

"Yes, Your Majesty, I will do as you say at once!" Amasa bowed to King David and left in a hurry to carry out the first order given to him as commander-in-chief.

After three days, Amasa had not returned. David paced anxiously, dwelling on the rumors of Sheba's growing strength. He thought: The poison that seeps into the chambers of the human heart can cause terrible destruction.

David summoned his deputy army chief. "Abishai! I sent Amasa to gather the Judahites. I ordered him to come back to me within three days, but he's late!"

Abishai nodded, the thought crossing his mind: It serves you right for replacing my brother Joab with the incompetent Amasa, who's a snot-nosed child by comparison.

David observed: "Sheba's revolt may harm us more than Absalom's coup. Take all my men and pursue him, or his power will only grow. Waste no time, go now!"

Abishai hurried to carry out the royal order, gathering the king's guard and sentries. In the meantime, Joab gathered the king's warriors, and the brothers led the army.

For hours, they marched through hills and valleys, alongside fields and orchards that were longing for the rain to come. Joab and Abishai led the skilled warriors north, where they heard Sheba was mustering his forces, in the Abel-Bethmaacah area. Loyalists flocked to them, providing intelligence and information.

At twilight, the sun was setting in the west, enveloped in distant clouds. Over the hill at Gibeon, they found Amasa and a handful of warriors gathered from the tribe of Judah making their way to King David in Jerusalem. The forces met at the summit.

Joab saw Amasa advancing toward him; anger filling his heart at the laggard who'd replaced him. "Peace be upon you, Brother Amasa,"

Joab said as he extended his arm, as if he wanted to hug and kiss his cousin.

"Peace be upon you, Lord Joab," Amasa replied, still awed by his predecessor.

Joab kissed Amasa, tugging his beard affectionately. Then Amasa grunted and moaned, his smile fading, stunned to find that the short dagger from Joab's waist was buried in his chest. He fell to his knees, breathing his last.

"Traitor!" snarled Joab through his teeth.

The people with Amasa fell silent, shocked and astonished by the brutal scene.

"We continue to follow the king's orders," Joab said coolly to his men. He and Abishai resumed the chase for Sheba as if nothing had happened.

Amasa's men were still silent, unable to recover their composure. One of Joab's followers walked over to his corpse and declared: "*Whoever favors Joab, and whoever is for David, let him follow Joab!*" He moved the corpse to the side of the road and covered it with a cloak. "To fight King David's enemies, follow Joab!"

This time, Amasa's men got the message and hurried to join the sons of Zeruiah.

They were soon joined by thousands, then tens of thousands. From every tribe and region of Israel, people came to realize that David was the rightful King of Israel, while Sheba was an unfit, untrue upstart, motivated by lust for power and honor.

Bethmaacah was a large city near Israel's northern border, fortified by two walls. Its populace valued peace and quiet, and its streets were filled with children at play shouting. The merchants loudly and proudly traded their goods in the colorful market.

In its center, a man stood on a platform, raising his voice to address the crowd, which was somewhat indifferent to the speaker. "My dear brethren, my precious countrymen, I ask you: How long? How long will we be ruled by those who think only of their personal prestige and position? How long must we submit to those who have but one goal, accumulating wealth and power? How long, my brothers, will the son of Jesse subjugate us? He seeks only to benefit himself and his dynasty. Why does he deserve the crown? Why does his house deserve greatness? He is corrupt! My dear countrymen, we must depose him. Israel needs a new king! We the people need a ruler who does not pursue honor and power, one of us, a man who thinks only of the good of the nation." Sheba went on, gesturing, his gaze humbly lowered. "We must put a man on the throne who deserves it more than Jesse's son."

An old woman called out: "Who did you have in mind? Who meets the requirements you're looking for? Do you think of yourself?" she pressed caustically.

"Ahh... Ma'am, I haven't thought about it. But if no one else steps forward, I'd be willing. I seek no office or title or honor, but I'll accept the crown," Sheba stated bashfully, which his questioner responded to with a light, hoarse laugh.

Sheba went back to laying out his political, security, and economic ideas.

Suddenly, the sound of shouting — not from children at play, but from men at war — broke up the crowd. The sentries warned the townspeople that a hostile force had arrived. Soon, there were thumps on the outer wall, and battering rams shook the stones.

Commotion and cacophony erupted, people running wildly, shoving with their arms and pushing with their bodies. Mothers screamed as they ran to scoop up their children, to find shelter or at least shield them. The city's defenders ran to collect weapons of war from their homes, to face the assault.

With a sickening clatter, the outer wall collapsed.

The sentries on the inner wall were surprised at the old woman who came slowly up the stairs. Despite their protestations, she shooed them away and stood on the battlements. She cleared her throat and called out: "Lord Commander Joab, son of Zeruiah! Captain of the Guard Jashobeam, son of Hachmoni!"

Her voice echoed over the army that had gathered outside the city. She made a striking figure; her garb was that of a crone, but her voice was that of a maiden — firm and majestic, youthful and uplifting. David's fighters looked up at her, and she seemed to tower over them, as she authoritatively summoned the veteran army chief from the top of the wall. They saw the old woman standing tall and confident above their heads, raising her voice toward the veteran army minister. "Hear me, hear me, let Lord Commander Joab approach so his maidservant may speak to him!"

Though the words were deferential, she seemed to be in command. Her face was creased, but her stature unbowed. Joab stepped out from among his troops.

"Are you Joab?" she asked, without any special etiquette.

Her majestic voice amazed Joab. "I am," he said, feeling like a small child standing before the teacher, caught red-handed, knowing a reprimand was coming and getting ready for it.

"Hear the words of your maidservant," she said, though her tone was authoritative.

"I am listening," he said in a whisper.

The woman pronounced, in a voice which froze people in their tracks on both sides of the wall, like the Voice at Sinai: "You well know what the Torah says about warfare. *'When you approach a city to fight against it, you are to make an offer of peace.'* The Creator, Blessed be He, tells us to seek peace even when we engage foreigners. Now you approach a peaceful and faithful town in Israel, and you raise a siege ramp against it without warning. Would you gobble up the Lord's inheritance?"

Joab stood in silence, accepting the reprimand from the honorable woman. "God forbid that I do so!" he said apologetically, covering his face. Joab explained: "I come here because a rogue by the name of Sheba, son of Bichri, from the hill country of Ephraim, has committed high treason. Deliver him to me, and I will leave your town in peace."

"So it is him you seek? You have struck terror in the heart of our town just for him? Wait a bit, and you will have his head in your hands," the woman promised, then climbed down the stairs.

A few minutes later, she returned with a round bundle. "Here is his head," she told Joab. "Present it to His Majesty King David. It is a gift for him from our city, which remains faithful to him."

The woman threw Sheba's head down with obvious disgust, then returned to the people of her town.

Joab sounded the shofar, dismissing his army. Each man could now return to his home and his job. Joab returned to Jerusalem, to the undisputed King of Israel.

CHAPTER FIFTY-NINE
Census and Censure

A few days later, life was beginning to return to normal in the Holy City. The people were now at rest; the peace which had reigned before Absalom and Sheba was restored. Law and order had been reinstated, and David's subjects came from all over the country to welcome him back to his throne, seeking his pardon for the coup.

"Your Majesty, a petitioner seeks an audience," said Jehoshaphat, "Mephibosheth, son of Jonathan, son of Saul."

David shifted uncomfortably on his throne. He had expected Mephibosheth to be the first to accompany him. Hadn't David showered Mephibosheth with kindness? Yet it was Ziba, his servant, who had shown up, revealing that his master exulted at David's exile, hoping to restore the dynasty of Saul. The ingratitude shocked and disturbed David. "Yes, bring him before me!"

Mephibosheth's chair was brought in by two bearers and set down. Jonathan's son immediately threw himself to the ground, sobbing. "Welcome back, Your Majesty!"

David looked at the man lying on the ground, his clothes dirty, his hair unkempt, his body filthy and sweaty. "Why didn't you come with me, Mephibosheth?"

"Your Majesty," cried the poor man, "my servant tricked me. I asked him to saddle my donkey so that I could go into exile with the king, but he did not do as I said. He left me alone in my home and went to you. There was nothing I could do. I am unable to travel on my own, as Your Majesty knows. All I wanted was to be by your side, but I was trapped. I wanted to repay your generosity to me and my father's house. I am and have always been Your Majesty's faithful servant. What I would have given to accompany you! Your Majesty is like an angel of the Lord, and after my king had given me my life, what more could I ask? Your Majesty will do as he sees fit." Mephibosheth wept, sincerity and sorrow in his sighs and sniffles.

"Restore him to his chair!" David ordered the bearers. He felt grief and compassion at the humiliation and crying of his friend's disabled son. "Mephibosheth, I rewarded Ziba for what he claimed, and the king's word cannot be revoked. Still, I will modify the decree as follows: Ziba will work your fields. When the produce comes in, you will split it as landlord and sharecropper. The fields belong to you and your family; Ziba has no portion in the land, but the crops you will share."

Mephibosheth looked at David with open love: "I would not object if Ziba took it all. My greatest joy is the privilege of witnessing my king safely restored to his throne."

Mephibosheth's observation was correct: the Davidic restoration was complete. The revolts were quelled, and peace reigned. Jerusalem was filled with joy and prosperity. The markets were full to the point of bursting, with fruits, grain, and vegetables in every color of the rainbow. Species and perfumes filled the air. Children played in the streets again, their laughter breathing life into the vibrant city's residents and visitors.

"Joab, our capital and our country are at peace. Life returns to normal. My subjects are pleased with me, and our borders are safe, even along Philistia." David recalled the last war, shivering slightly as he remembered the last battle with the Philistines. He had nearly lost his life to Ishbibenob, Goliath's brother. Just before certain death, Abishai had appeared like an angel, saving him. The four great heroes of Gath had been Goliath, Ishbibenob, Saph, and Ishmadon, all sons of Orpah, Ruth's sister. That made them cousins to David; but now they had all fallen into the hands of David and his men — who had made him swear never to set foot on the battlefield again.

"Yes, Your Majesty," Joab agreed, pulling David out of his reverie.

"The time has come for a census. Count my subjects, the numbers of our soldiers across Judah and Israel."

"Why?" asked Joab, puzzled.

"For no particular reason," David answered firmly, "I want to know how many Israelites there are, from Dan to Beersheba. Bring me their numbers."

"But Your Majesty, why do that? However many they are, may the Lord increase them, and may my king see it." Joab knew that counting the people was forbidden.

"Joab! Do what I told you immediately!" commanded David, and his voice made clear that nothing could dissuade him. "You may go," he told the army chief, returning to his study

For more than nine months, Joab dragged out the census. He hoped that David would come to his senses and call it off; but the king, as if moved by a higher power, remained impervious to logic and reason. He had to know the number of his subjects.

Joab returned to the palace, his gaze lowered, and sorrow filling his heart: "I have done as Your Majesty ordered," he said weakly.

"And..." David prompted, eager to get the information.

"Israel numbers eight hundred thousand sword-wielding warriors; Judah, five hundred thousand," Joab said softly, as if trying to hide what he had done.

"Thank you," the king whispered, his head in his hands. "Thank you, that's all."

Joab bowed and left the king's presence.

The king began to weep: "*I have sinned greatly in what I have done. Now, O Lord, I beg You to take away the iniquity of Your servant, for I have acted very foolishly.*"

Gad the Visionary entered the king's chamber, a venerable elder. His snowy beard was a gleaming white, his eyebrows almost transparent. His body was rail-thin, and the robe he wore was as azure as the sky. Beneath the turban on his head, his steely green eyes shone.

"Peace be upon you, Lord Visionary," said David, rising to greet the man out of his respect for the visionary through whom God communicated. He sensed that Gad had not come to bring good news.

"Peace be upon you," the visionary replied softly. He knew that the revelation he was charged to deliver would be difficult for the king to accept.

David cleared his throat: "What brings my lord today?" He knew it would be bitter.

"Your Majesty, I experienced a vision at night, a message for my king," said Gad, postponing the moment he would have to elaborate. "It pertains to the census conducted among Israel and Judah. What made Your Majesty do that?"

"I don't know," said the king, "I don't know what made me act so foolishly." David lowered his eyes apologetically for his rashness. "What does the Lord say?" he asked, knowing that he had sinned, ready to accept his punishment.

"Three paths lie ahead," said the visionary with great sorrow. "Your Majesty must choose one. *Do you choose to endure three years of famine in your land, three months of fleeing the pursuit of your enemies, or three days of plague upon your land? Now then, think it over and decide how I should reply to Him who sent me.*"

The king sat down at his table, head in his hands, tears streaming down, pondering: The first choice is seven years of famine, but three years of famine almost consumed the nation. Tens of thousands died while starving people almost lost their humanity in their quest to feed their households. Seven years of that would be unbearable! The second choice is three months in the hands of the enemy. Who knows how much death, abuse, robbery, and looting that would entail? Our foes look forward to the moment they can attack us. The third choice is three days of a terrible plague that consumes the masses of Israel. If I choose hunger, people will say I did so because I am rich and trust that I will have the food to support my household. If I choose war, they will say that I trust my soldiers to protect my family. I must choose the last option because in the plague, all are equal; may God have mercy on our souls." David looked up at Gad: "*I am deeply distressed. Please, let us fall into the hand of the Lord, for His mercies are great; but do not let me fall into the hands of men,*" he whispered.

For three days, emissaries from all over the country came to the king's palace to describe the tragedy. David sat on the floor of his room wearing sackcloth, with ashes on his head. For three days he fasted, beseeching God to annul the decree, to soften the severe blow, to moderate the terrible verdict.

David heard a blood-curdling cry and ran to his window,

overlooking the city. A young woman cradled the body of her son, looking accusingly at the palace.

A black cloud hovered over the city, akin to the plague of darkness in Egypt; it stifled the rays of the morning sun, which struggled to emerge through to banish the gloom of death. The malevolent cloud appeared like a formidable Angel of Destruction, baring its sword, seeking to eradicate Jerusalem. The cloud was centered above the threshing floor of Araunah the Jebusite, as if preparing to wipe out the Holy City in one fell swoop. The cloud had the appearance of the Angel of Death, readying to consume everything.

David looked up, feeling his blood freeze within him, a block of ice chilling him to the bone, fingers of frost gripping his heart. A scream erupted from his soul, as if from the depths of the earth, emanating and rising from somewhere in the depths of his spirit. His hands grasped the sackcloth over his chest, baring his breast: "Oh…" A primal yell burst from him, splitting the sky, ascending to bang on the Gates of Mercy. "Oh… Behold, I have sinned, and I have transgressed," he cried to Heaven, "but these sheep, what have they done?!" David wept, grieving the victims of the plague. "Direct Your hand at me and at my father's house!!" he shouted, begging for his people Israel, trying to annul the decree against it.

It seemed like an eternity that he waited there, but it was just a few minutes before Gad the Visionary arrived. David was still frozen, his body shivering as his wide-open eyes expressed the horror he had witnessed. Gad entered without David's notice, as the king struggled to his feet. Gad placed a soft hand on the king's shoulder. David shook off the horror: "Your Majesty," he whispered, "Come to your senses, my king! You must act. The Lord orders Your Majesty to bring an elevation offering."

"An offering? Where?" wondered the king. "Where is the place of the altar?"

"Under that, at Araunah's barn," Gad whispered, pointing at the black cloud.

The word "that" sent an icy shiver through the king's body.

A few hours later, a caravan of people made its way up the hill. King David, dressed in sky-blue royal clothes, contrasting with the black cloud on high, led it. Zadok the Priest was on his right, dressed in the high priest's vestments, the Urim and Thummim on his chest. To his left was Gad the Visionary, dressed in white. They were followed by the justices of the Supreme Court, the priests, the Levites, the tribal chiefs, and the masses of the Nation of Israel. The Levites were singing and chanting, their musical instruments providing melodious accompaniment, their quavering voices contrasting with the dramatic spectacle before them. The cloud of back death hovered over the threshing floor, as Araunah the Jebusite and his four sons hid inside. It suddenly appeared as they were filtering through. They were bewildered by the sound of the choir and the crowd.

Araunah, the former King of Jebus, had converted after the conquest of the city by King David and his people. His white beard peeked out of the doorway, followed by his eyes, wide open with renewed fear and astonishment. The menacing cloud of death was still there, and beneath it, the royal caravan. Araunah came out, in fear and awe, bowing to the King of Israel who had spared his life, the king who had welcomed him under the wings of the Divine Presence some thirty years earlier.

Araunah looked at David with reverence, thinking: He too has aged a lot; the king is no longer the same young man I first met. The many years and hardships had left their mark on him. "Peace be upon Your Majesty, King of Israel," Araunah's voice shook. "Why does Your Majesty come to his servant?" he said fearfully, fearing that his actions might have caused the cloud of death to appear.

The king looked at Araunah musing: He has aged a lot since our last meeting; the horror of the black cloud of death also seems to be taking its toll on him.

"Peace be upon you, Araunah. It's been a long time since we last met," David said. "I come here for a very important reason, my friend. I want to buy this threshing floor so I may build an altar to God. This will end the plague and disperse the black cloud."

"Buy it?!" asked Araunah, puzzled. "Why should the king buy the threshing floor from me? Please, Your Majesty, accept it as my gift, along with animals and wood for the offering. I would gladly give the king all that is mine. No purchase necessary; just remove this black cloud from my land!" Since his conversion, Araunah had felt he owed his life to David. Any other conqueror would have eradicated the defeated monarch and his heirs. King David, on the other hand, had let him join the Chosen People, though Araunah had previously blasphemed and cursed the king and his God. Now the king came to banish the cloud of death overhead, and David wanted to pay him to save him and his family? "God bless Your Majesty, take whatever is needed!"

"No, my friend and comrade. I appreciate your gesture, but I must pay you the full price for this piece of land. I will not offer my Lord a gift from another. It is inappropriate to give the King of Kings what we have received free of charge. The altar must not stand in a place which is one man's private property, even if he would make it a gift. I will buy the site, the animals, and the wood for six hundred golden shekels."

Araunah was astounded: "Six hundred, Your Majesty?! That is a dozen times what it's worth, perhaps fifty golden shekels at most!"

"I know, my friend, but this must be a permanent sale, never to be redeemed or resold. On this site, the Temple of the Lord will stand, a place for the Divine Presence to dwell among the People of Israel for generations to come. I will collect fifty shekels from each of the tribes of Israel, so that no tribe can claim ownership over the other. Every one of our people will have a stake in the House of God — every individual, every tribe, and the Nation of Israel as a whole." David gestured to Jehoshaphat, who signaled to two carters. Their load was a hoard of gold coins. "Here is the payment for the threshing floor, animals, and wood, my good friend. And now, let's get to work."

David raised his hand, motioning for tribal princes to appear before him. "Everyone must take a rock to build the altar," he commanded. Within a few minutes, Araunah's threshing floor had been transformed into an altar for elevation and sin offerings.

King David took one goat, rested his hands on its head and recited a confession: "Master of the Universe, Creator of All, Eternal Ruler, You treat Your people with grace and all Your creation with great mercy. Your Holy Torah says that if a ruler errs and sins, he must offer a goat to atone. I, Your servant, acknowledge that I committed a great sin, an unacceptable act. God of Mercy, please spare Your nation, the

People of Israel, and forgive my offense. May my offering be accepted with goodwill." King David slaughtered his sin-offering. Zadok caught the blood in a designated vessel, sprinkled some of it on the horns of the altar and poured the rest of the blood at the foundation of the altar. The fat of the sin-offering was then burnt on the altar.

Zadok laid his hands on a bull, followed by all the princes of Israel. He repeated the process with its blood and fat.

"God, please show Your people Your strong hand, the power of Your mercy, and Your love for Your people Israel," David prayed, but the black cloud still hovered overhead.

"Please, our Father, act in Your great and awesome name," David continued.

Out of the gloom of the black cloud appeared two pillars of fire, which consumed the darkness, illuminating all the surroundings of the threshing floor. One pillar of fire landed on the altar, consuming the fat. The second pillar burnt up the carcasses of the bull and the goat alongside the altar.

The king and the people, who had been standing to watch the scene, fell on their faces at the awesome sight. A moment later, as the king and the people began to raise their heads, the pillar disappeared, its place taken by a small column of smoke. The black sky became clear, and the warm sun's rays shone benevolently on the whole congregation, bringing smiles to drooping faces.

"It's over," Gad the Visionary whispered to the king. "The plague has stopped; the sacrifices have been accepted with goodwill."

The Levites began singing and playing, as the people began to laugh and dance.

"This is the House of the Lord God, and this is the place of the altar," King David said. "Zadok the Priest, bring elevation offerings and thanksgiving offerings to God for all the good He has done for our people Israel!"

The singing of praise rose to a crescendo; the music poured directly from their souls, raising them ever higher, binding their spirits to their Creator. The sun's warmth enflamed their hearts to a roaring fire, as they watched the priests burn the thanksgiving offerings on the altar.

King David, on the other hand, wrapped his cloak more tightly around him. His body was still shivering, despite the heat of the bright day. The cold inside him would not lessen its icy grip, no matter what he did.

CHAPTER SIXTY
Abishag of Shunem

"We must find a solution! King David keeps trembling with cold. All the blankets piled on him fail to warm his body." Zadok's face expressed concern. "Since the time of the plague, he has not been able to overcome this chill."

Beniah, son of Jehoiada, the new chief justice of the Supreme Court, was also troubled. "Blankets will not help his situation. Something happened to the king's blood during the plague; what he saw was so chilling — literally — that we cannot grasp how it changed him. The king told me that the Angel of Destruction towered over the site, using the hem of his cloak to wipe the blood of seventy thousand Israelites off his sword. Since then, his soul has been frozen; he shakes and shivers."

"But we have to do something about it! It is impossible for him to be in such a situation. The king is no longer young; he will soon be seventy. More than age, there is the trauma of everything he has undergone, which weighs upon him. I cannot bear to see our king suffer like this," Zadok whispered, lest they be overheard.

The two loyalists were at David's door, their faces sharing his pain and sorrow.

"I have a solution," Benaiah whispered, "but I am unsure the king will accept it."

"What's your proposal? We will convince him," urged Zadok.

"Blankets and clothing don't produce heat, they just trap it, keeping it from dispersing."

"That's right."

"If his body cannot produce the necessary heat, he needs another body. I have consulted the greatest healers, and they confirm it."

Zadok was confused: "So what's the problem? Our king doesn't lack for wives!"

"It's not that simple. Firstly, the king's wives and concubines are not much younger than he, so their body heat is insignificant. Secondly, you know that the king has chosen to spend the last years of his life celibate, sanctifying himself before death."

"Yes, I once heard from him that he asked God to let him know when he would die, but God refused." Zadok smiled. "The king told me he dared to ask God to tell him at least which day would be his last, so God told him it would be the Sabbath. King David asked if he could die the day after, to avoid desecrating the Sabbath, but such a delay would take away from his heir. The king asked that his death come earlier, but that was also denied. God told him He loves the king's study more than any sacrifices and offerings by his son Solomon. It's funny, the king talks about conversing with the Creator as if it's a normal, everyday thing, as if everyone is as close to the Lord. Since then, the king sits from the beginning of the Sabbath until nightfall the next day, immersed in Torah. The king says he'll at least die studying." Zadok laughed: "As if during the rest of the week, the king doesn't study. Every spare moment, he devotes to studying, so at the end of every Sabbath, King David holds a thanksgiving meal for having another week of life, a week of study." Zadok stifled himself, recalling where he was. "For our purposes, let him marry a young woman."

"Don't you understand? King David has eighteen wives, and that is the limit of the Torah. As Nathan the Prophet teaches, a commoner may marry as many women as he can support, but the king is limited to eighteen," Benaiah explained.

Zadok shifted uncomfortably. "Let him divorce one and take another in her place."

Benaiah quipped: "He would never do that. You know the king; he is all heart. He saw each of his wives as if she were the love of his life, and he loves them all just as much today. The king would never divorce any of them. Haven't you seen how it hurts when people come to his court for a divorce? He begs them to try to reconcile, to build bridges, to straighten things out. If he sees that the issue is financial, he gives the husband a job with a good salary as long as he promises not to divorce his wife. He tries with all his might to dissuade the couple from parting. He explains what matrimony requires, talking to each individually. He tells the husband that he must treat his wife as a queen, provide her with all her needs, and appreciate her. He explains that it is forbidden for a husband to rebuke his wife, much less raise his voice at her. He must elevate, compliment, and raise her up. He tells the wife to honor her husband as a king in his castle — never to degrade him, not even in her heart; not to criticize his actions; not to critique him." Benaiah sighed. "How many precious hours he invests in his efforts to prevent divorce. How many tears he sheds when he sees a couple with children seeking a divorce. The king sits day and night with the couple, explaining the damage they cause to their children because of their reluctance to understand each other. He explains the disservice to their offspring, who are like orphans as soon as their parents separate. God Himself grieves then! 'Even the altar sheds a tear,' the king says. But you think he'll divorce one of his wives? Even if he were willing to divorce one of his wives, he wouldn't take a new wife, because if he married a woman, he would have to be intimate with her. There's no way he'd agree!"

Benaiah stroked his beard, considering the enigma. After a few minutes of silence, he said with a slight smile: "I think I have an idea…"

King David lay on his bed, his body shaking under the blankets covering him from head to toe. His eyes were closed, as he listened to his second-born, Chileab, son of Abigail. The young man was reviewing his studies and discussing complex issues, bringing a smile to his father's face.

"My teacher Mephibosheth said that the Torah is to be studied for its own sake, which is a commandment from God. The study of the holy Torah transcends everything. I told him that in my opinion, although Torah study has enormous value, if it is done heartlessly, it is like a dead body without a soul. Case in point: Doeg and Ahithophel were Torah scholars but wicked. He asked me what I thought the purpose of Torah study is, and I told him that it is the pursuit of virtue, to perfect one's ethics, to turn one into a superior creature, to embody humility, to make one truly human."

David grinned. "What did he say?"

"He told me I was right," Chileab replied happily.

The king seemed thoughtful: "Both of you make good points, but you miss the real purpose. These are all means to bring forth the Light. Studying Torah, correcting virtue, transforming a person into a pure and transcendent creature — it all forms a vessel to house the Light of God. There are great Torah scholars, as you said, who are wicked. There are people of virtue who may suddenly violate the Word of God. Neither achieves their true purpose." David's face lit up as he sat up. "The complete, true purpose is for man to connect, or should I say to merge, with the Creator — to contain within him the Light of the King of Kings and radiate it outward to all around. Moses was privileged to be such a vessel, to contain the Light of God within him and spread it outward; the skin of his face glowed for this reason, which the people could not process. The revelation of God through such a man overwhelmed them, so Moses wore a veil to make it bearable. Like Moses, one must be a great lantern, holding the glow inside and shining it on each person to the greatest degree possible. It is man whose mission it is to reveal the reality of God to the world."

The door opened quietly, and Benaiah entered. Seeing the father and son engaged in Torah study, smiling, and their eyes shining, he didn't want to disturb them.

"Tell me about Father," a young voice addressed him. Benaiah suddenly realized that another prince was in the room, twelve-year-old Solomon. His eyes were pleading. "Lord Benaiah, surely you can share something with me about Father."

Benaiah met the child's gaze, then looked at the reclining king, memories flooding his mind. "It's been a while, more than forty years since I met your father. At the time, he was not the king, but his son-in-law, a fugitive. For forty years, his life has been intertwined with my life, years of upheaval and conflict." Benaiah looked thoughtful. "So you want to hear a story? Over four decades ago, when I first served with your father, I was still a teenager. We would hide in forests, caves, and deserts from King Saul and his men. Several hundred of us hid in the Cave of Adullam. It was reaping time, very hot. We concealed ourselves from King Saul on one hand, and from the Philistines on the other. We stood at the entrance: your father, Asahel, and Abishai. We observed a Philistine garrison hiding in the tall wheat fields. Your father debated whether we should burn the wheat fields to expose them. We didn't know what to do, since it would mean destroying someone else's crop. Now, the Supreme Court was in Bethlehem, but there was no way to reach it. The sun beat down on our heads; sweat dripped down our faces. Your father spoke innocently about the fresh, cool water in his hometown's cisterns. We entered the cave at nightfall, and I sat by the small fire with Abishai and Asahel. We wanted to make your father happy; you can't imagine how much we loved and admired your father. I was a young man, fleeing the king's tax collectors. I was lost, broken, and bereft; I had no idea what to do. I was confused in my mind, not understanding Providence, and resenting being in exile. When I met your father, he explained, encouraged, strengthened, and supported me. He taught me faith and confidence, he put me on my feet." Benaiah spoke longingly of a time gone by, a difficult time, but full of memories. "My whole desire was to make him happy. I had an idea, and I told it to Abishai and Asahel; they both agreed with me. In the dark of night, the three of us descended toward the Philistine outpost, hidden in the fields of Bethlehem. We entered the field quietly, attacking the sleeping Philistines, until we reached the gate of Bethlehem. We eliminated the whole garrison — not so many, a few dozen. We entered the city and consulted the Supreme Court. Then we eliminated the guards stationed by the cistern, drew water, and returned to the cave. We were overjoyed to bring him joy. We came to him in the morning light, our hearts racing; it was as if we were walking on clouds. Your father was engrossed in prayer when we arrived, so we waited for him to finish. We went over to him, gave him the water, and explained where it was from. We were sure he would be happy, but he turned as pale as a ghost. 'Did you risk your lives to ask a legal question?! To bring me water?! It is forbidden to do such a thing under any circumstances! So Samuel the Ramathite told me: Whoever endangers his life for words of Torah, his statements are worthless. We will not accept the ruling you received! As for the water you drew, it will be a holy sacrifice,' your father declared, spilling it out. 'Drinking this water would be like drinking your blood.' The shock that befell your father, when he heard that we had taken such a risk for him, did not escape my memory. He couldn't accept that someone would do that. He always saw himself as the least of his people."

Benaiah put his hand on Solomon's shoulder: "Virtue, my son, virtue must be appreciated. You must work very hard to acquire virtue."

Solomon looked at Benaiah, the veteran warrior: "Thank you very much, Benaiah. I love hearing these stories so much, especially about Father."

Benaiah smiled. "I think your brother is done." Chileab rose from his chair beside his father's bed. "Excuse me, I must speak with your father now, Your Highness."

"Peace be upon you, my dear friend," the king greeted Benaiah. "Did you come to visit an old man?" he said with a smile.

"How does Your Majesty feel?" asked Benaiah worriedly.

"What shall I tell you, my dear? I'm cold! Clothes don't warm my body. I'm afraid it's because I cut off the hem of King Saul's cloak, peace be upon him. Now, as punishment, I'm always cold." The king shivered under the thick blankets.

"Your Majesty, I think I have a solution for this. You have to agree to what I'm telling you," Benaiah said, concerned that the proposal would not be accepted. "Clothes cannot warm our king's body. We need to bring a young woman to warm the king." King David tried to resist, but Benaiah continued: "Excuse me, Your Majesty, let my king permit me to finish. The king cannot function in this way; the king must see to his subjects. We will bring the king a young woman, who will lie next to Your Majesty under the covers. Her body temperature will warm the king and heal him." The king tried to say something, but Benaiah pressed on. "I know Your Majesty cannot marry her; the king already has eighteen wives and can't take anymore. And I am aware that divorce is anathema to the king. I also know that it was the king who decreed that it is forbidden for a man to be secluded with a woman, even unmarried. I have already spoken with the justices of the Supreme Court on this issue, and they conclude that since the prohibition of seclusion is based on the concern that the man and woman may became intimate, Your Majesty's age removes that concern. Should my king say that he is not too old and could rise to the occasion, we may have another person in the room, so it would not be seclusion at all. In order to prevent unnecessary talk and malicious thoughts on the part of the people, we will look for a clever woman to be the king's aide. This will provide a pretext for her presence. Moreover, in order to avoid unnecessary talk, we will select a plain one, so nobody thinks that the king lusts for her." Benaiah concluded his remarks, awaiting the king's response.

King David looked thoughtful: "You've thought of everything," he said with a smile. "You have come prepared to answer my every objection."

Benaiah smiled, "Your Majesty has taught me well how to prepare to offer advice."

"I agree, but there's one thing you haven't thought about! You know that even though I'm old, I still must worship God. I must correct what I have done wrong in my life. You know what people are still talking about. People think I took Bathsheba because I desired her beauty, that I took a man's wife."

Benaiah burst out: "That's not true, everyone knows that Bathsheba is..."

"Hush, my dear friend, you know as well as I do, that when I give a lesson, I often am asked by some wag or wit: 'Your Majesty, what is the punishment for adultery?' I know what they are alluding to. I usually answer: 'An adulterer dies by strangulation, but he has a portion in the afterlife. However, whoever embarrasses his fellow in public has no portion in the World to Come.' They smile as if they were talking about someone else and not about me. It is revealed and known to the Creator that I am so drained by these experiences, that you could shred my body and not a drop of blood would fall on the ground. I, too, constantly ask myself whether there wasn't some element of lust in my taking her. Even though deep down I know this is not true, doubt gnaws. Therefore, my dear friend, do as you suggest. Find a young woman, a clever one; but make sure that she is the most beautiful. Not just a pretty face, but the most exceptionally attractive maiden, the kind that any man would desire. I will be with her, she will lie with me, and I will not transgress at all. At least in this way, I will prove to myself, to some extent, that taking Bathsheba was not a lustful act."

Two weeks passed, and Benaiah brought Abishag of Shunem before King David, a very clever, young woman of rare beauty, of such exquisiteness that all who saw her fell silent. The maiden served the king and warmed his cold body.

CHAPTER SIXTY-ONE
Coronation of Solomon

The door to Bathsheba's room opened hastily. At the entrance stood her young handmaid. Panic appeared on her face. "Your Majesty," she cried, her distress shocking Bathsheba out of her chair.

"Has something happened??? Bathsheba asked fearfully.

"Your Majesty, Nathan the Prophet has come to the house to speak with my queen," she replied. The young woman, who had never met Nathan, was frightened when she opened the door of the house and saw a man who looked like a white angel standing in the doorway. The excitement of seeing the prophet left her trembling.

"I'm coming," Bathsheba said, following her handmaid, arranging her headscarf.

"Peace be upon you, Lord Nathan the Prophet," Bathsheba said, bowing to the venerable man. "What brings my lord to my house? Has something happened?"

"Yes, Your Majesty," Nathan replied. "Have you not heard that Adonijah, the fourth-born son of our king, has seized the crown? Adonijah took Joab, Abiathar, chariots, cavalry, and fifty men running before him. He called all the king's sons and the tribesmen of Judah, and they are holding a kind of coronation ceremony."

Bathsheba's mouth opened in astonishment: "But King David told me..."

"I know what the king promised Your Majesty. That's why I'm here. I also know that it is God's will that your son Solomon reign. Our king is unaware of what Adonijah is doing; you know he has been bedridden for quite some time. Therefore, go immediately to the king and tell him what's going on. After you enter his bedchamber, I will come and confirm your words. Quick, there's no time to waste!"

Bathsheba left hastily, hurrying to the royal bed chamber.

"Your Majesty," Abishag whispered to David, who was lying on his bed. The king opened his eyes slightly, detaching himself from his holy thoughts, not quite seeing the young woman. "Queen Bathsheba is here; she wishes to speak with Your Majesty." The king heard the tone Abishag used to refer to Bathsheba, the envy and grievance of being excluded from the privilege of royal matrimony.

David ignored it. "Please bring her in."

Bathsheba approached the bed, bowing before the king. The king gestured with his hand, motioning for her to approach. He saw the tears welling up from the corners of her eyes: "What troubles you, my wife?" he asked softly, "Why are you crying?"

Bathsheba wiped away her tears: "Your Majesty, you swore that Solomon our son would reign after you and sit upon your throne. Now Adonijah rules, and you don't know?"

David sat up, astonished: "How do you know Adonijah has made himself king?"

"Your Majesty, hear what your son, the one born to Haggith, has done! He took Abiathar and Joab, and all the princes except Solomon. He gathered many sheep and cattle and Judahites for a coronation ceremony by the Stone of Zoheleth, which is by Ein Rogel." Bathsheba pleaded and prodded. "And now, Your Majesty, the eyes of all Israel are on you, to announce who will sit on the king's throne after him. If Your Majesty fails to act now, the people will assume, once the king has been gathered to the World to Come, that this coronation was what you wanted. My son Solomon and I will lose out. Either they will kill us outright, or they will denounce him as a bastard and me as an adulteress." Bathsheba sobbed inconsolably, wiping away tears again and again.

Abishag of Shunem approached the king's bed: "Your Majesty," she whispered in his ear, "Nathan the Prophet has arrived; he seeks an audience as well."

"Bathsheba, my wife, don't cry!" said David softly. "Everything will be fine. Wait a few minutes outside, as Nathan wishes to speak with me. I'll summon you soon."

Bathsheba left and Nathan entered, approaching and bowing to the king.

"Come near, my friend and comrade," he said weakly to Nathan. "What say you?"

"Your Majesty, I've come to ask a question," Nathan said. The king nodded. "Did Your Majesty command that Adonijah be crowned king and sit on the king's throne?"

"Why do you ask?" asked David innocently, as if unaware.

"Your Majesty, Adonijah took Joab, Abiathar, the officers of the army, and the ministers of the government. He also took many sheep and cattle, and together with all the princes, they are holding a feast. All the people are shouting loudly: 'Long live King Adonijah!' I, Zadok, Benaiah, and Solomon did not receive an invitation." Nathan the Prophet looked insulted: "If it was Your Majesty's will to do so without informing Your Majesty's servant, so be it; but I wish I had been informed," Nathan said, knowing that Adonijah had acted without King David's consent or knowledge.

"Wait a few minutes outside, my friend, and I'll call you," the king requested.

Nathan the Prophet left the king's presence.

"Abishag!" cried the king, sitting up a bit in the bed. "Call Bathsheba, tell her to come."

Bathsheba and Abishag approached David, astonished to see that he had gotten to his feet without assistance — erect and alert, like a hero girding himself for battle.

The queen thought: My husband! My king! That's the man I married, not the invalid I saw on his deathbed minutes ago.

Abishag panicked, grabbing at him: "Your Majesty, be careful not to fall!" She felt the taut and tense muscles of his body.

"Don't worry!" he smiled, breaking free of her grasp.

"Bathsheba!" His firm, authoritative voice ripped Bathsheba from her reverie, cutting her off from her reminiscing. *"As surely as the Lord lives, who has redeemed my life from all distress, I will carry out this very day exactly what I swore to you by the Lord, the God of Israel: 'Surely your son Solomon will reign after me, and he will sit on my throne in my place.'"*

Bathsheba fell on her face, bowing in thanks to the king, tears of joy streaming down her face. She exclaimed: "*Long live my lord King David forever!*"

"Abishag!" King David said commandingly, sending a shiver down the young woman's spine. He was neither old nor broken, she realized, with a sense of shame, of a missed opportunity. She recalled how she had teased him, saying he refused to marry her not out of piety but a lack of passion or potency. Now he appeared like a young lion, ready to fight. "Abishag!" he roared.

"Yes, my lord the king," she said in renewed awe.

He glanced at her, grinning at the storm he sensed raging within her. "Run, call Nathan the Prophet, Zadok the Priest, and Chief Justice Benaiah, son of Jehoida. Tell them to come to me urgently!"

The young woman stood frozen and disbelieving. "Make haste, my dear, hurry up!" ordered the king, as if he were a father chiding his reluctant daughter.

Abishag shook off her thoughts and went to do the king's bidding.

The chamber which had been darkened recently by heavy curtains was now thrown open to the sun's rays. King David stood by the open window, enjoying the warm breeze. David felt the blood flow through his veins again, warming his cool body, infusing him with restored vitality. He pondered: Just as my third-born Absalom revolted, now my fourth-born Adonijah shows his rebellious streak. My son from Haggith plots to seize the throne while I live, yet without my knowledge?! Where did I go wrong with him and his big brother? What made them act this way? Have I failed to educate my sons? I gave them everything; they lacked nothing; they were pampered from the day they were born. Why would they do this? They were royal princes, denied nothing, given everything they asked for.

David recalled an argument with Bathsheba: Apparently, she was right not to pamper Solomon. She was a stern parent, restricting his pleasures and indulgences. She disciplined him for acting up. Setting clear and severe boundaries in every aspect of life — perhaps that is the best course? Bathsheba insisted that Solomon didn't grow up as a spoiled child, punishing him herself for serious misdeeds. She seems to have been right with her maxims: "A man without limits is not a man but a savage." "You cannot be a prince over men until you are a prince among men." What did I say? "A child should receive love." But she said: "He is showered with affection, but the real love is to give him an education. He should not be allowed to do whatever he wants. Not setting boundaries is love of self, not love of the child. Do you think it's easy for me to rebuke and punish him? It hurts me more than it hurts him, but there's no choice. If I don't, he will grow up feeling that there are no rules, that he may do whatever his heart desires." She seems to have been proven right, not I.

David shook himself from his reverie, trying to plan his next steps.

Zadok and Benaiah entered together, along with Nathan, who'd been waiting outside the door. The sunny room surprised the three newcomers, who had recently witnessed its ambience of gloom. "Your Majesty," cried Benaiah happily and ran toward David by the window. "Is everything all right? Does my king feel well?"

David looked at the three, his gaze alive and alert: "My health is good, but what of the health of my kingdom? My friends, you know the dire situation better than I do. Adonijah has seized the royal scepter, with Abiathar and Joab as his accomplices. Let me make this clear: Solomon will succeed me, no one else." David inhaled deeply. "And his coronation will be today! God's people will see a new man on the throne this day, and you three will place him there. *Take my servants with you. Set my son Solomon on my own mule and take him down to Gihon. There Zadok the Priest and Nathan the Prophet are to anoint him king over Israel. You are to blow the ram's horn and declare, 'Long live King Solomon!'* Benaiah, you will take the shofar and the anointing oil, the same prepared by Moses almost five centuries ago. Finally, take Solomon to my throne room and seat him there, for I have appointed him over Judah and Israel!"

Benaiah studied David's face with admiration. The elderly invalid had vanished, and the firm and fierce monarch had returned. He exulted: "*Amen! May the Lord, the God of my lord the king, so declare it. Just as the Lord was with my lord the king, so may He be with Solomon and make his throne even greater than that of my lord King David.*"

A crowd left the palace, headed by Chief Justice Benaiah, son of

Jehoiada, leading the royal mule, on which sat Solomon, son of David. Next to him, Zadok the Priest wore the vestments of the high priest, while Nathan the Prophet was in snow-white garb. The king's guard came next, in full uniform, followed by the king's ministers and servants, the musicians and poets of his court. It was afternoon, and the gurgling spring greeted the visitors, along with birdsong and rustling leaves. The pines emitted a sweet smell, as a small fawn leaped, fleeing the crowd coming down the hill. The fountain flowing into the stream gave the royal caravan a sense of freshness.

"My dear brethren!" declared Nathan, his back to the spring and his face to the people. "This is a joyous day for Israel. David, King of Israel, anointed by Samuel the Seer, prophet of God, is passing the royal scepter to his son Solomon." Nathan stopped, hearing the applause of the growing crowd. He quieted them down again by raising his hands. "Loyal servants of the king! We have a privilege. Since ancient times, the People of Israel have never had a true monarchy, a dynasty passing from father to son. Today, we are witnessing it!" The applause rose to a crescendo, overwhelming the sounds of nature. "Solomon, son of David, come here!" called Nathan.

Twelve-year-old Solomon was slender, wearing a sky-blue robe embroidered with gold and silver threads. His eyes which were as azure as the sky, expressing intelligence and wisdom, were slightly lowered. A large golden dome was already on his head.

Solomon advanced toward the prophet, his steps measured and considered, the march of a man who knows himself but is not overly proud.

He stood before the prophet at the edge of the spring.

"King Solomon, son of David, kneel before your Creator!" said the prophet.

Solomon fulfilled the command and knelt.

"Zadok the Priest, rise and anoint Solomon of David with the oil as King of Israel!" the prophet commanded, taking the dome from Solomon's head.

Zadok complied, pouring some of the oil on his fingers as he approached Solomon. Above Solomon's eyes, Zadok placed his fingertips and dragged them over the head, bringing them to the nape of the neck. He poured the rest of the oil over Solomon's head, blessing him: "*May the Lord bless you and keep you. May the Lord cause His face to shine upon you and be gracious to you. May the Lord lift up His countenance toward you and give you peace.*"

The crowd applauded thunderously. Benaiah's shofar was blown, shaking the skies all the way to the Heavenly Throne. "Long live King Solomon!" cried Benaiah, and the people echoed his call.

"As this spring bursts through the rock, spraying as if out of nowhere and reviving the world, so will your wisdom! Your influence and your kingdom will swell like the flowing stream," Nathan blessed him.

The music and dance, cheering and trumpets, grew louder, until the earth quaked and the sky shook. Solomon was carried on the shoulders of the warriors leading the new king to his palace, to sit on his throne.

"What's ... what's that noise? What's the commotion about?" Adonijah asked Joab. He stammered, his face red from wine and rich food.

"I don't know, Your Majesty," Joab replied. "I don't like the sound of the shofar I hear at all! It is not a typical ram's horn, but the shofar of Benaiah, son of Jehoiada. Why would he be blowing it? Look, Jonathan, son of Abiathar, is coming." Joab recognized his characteristic run. "A good man, who must bring good news," Joab smiled.

Jonathan arrived puffing and panting, standing in front of Adonijah.

"Jonathan, my good friend," Adonijah grinned. "Come, you are a good man, and good men bring good news!"

Jonathan looked at Adonijah and Joab, his face frightened and confused. He stammered, "But…" then blurted out his report: "*Our lord King David has made Solomon king. And with Solomon, the king has sent Zadok the priest, Nathan the prophet, and Benaiah, son of Jehoiada, along with the guards and heralds, and they have set him on the king's mule. Zadok the Priest and Nathan the Prophet have anointed him king at Gihon, and they have gone up from there with rejoicing that rings out in the city. That is the noise you hear. Moreover, Solomon has taken his seat on the royal throne. The king's servants have also gone to congratulate our lord King David, saying, 'May your God make the name of Solomon more famous than your own name, and may He make his throne greater than your throne.'*

The faces of Adonijah and Joab turned pale; fear gripping their hearts. "What did King David say?" asked Adonijah fearfully.

"And the king has bowed in worship on his bed, saying, 'Blessed be the Lord, the God of Israel! Today He has provided one to sit on my throne, and my eyes have seen it," Jonathan whispered, struggling to get the words out.

The crowd, eavesdropping on the conversation, began to whisper among themselves, and it was not long before they took to their heels out of fear of Solomon, leaving Adonijah and Joab alone.

Solomon sat on the throne, with King David's servants and ministers passing before the freshly anointed ruler. Benaiah stood next to the chair, his face smiling.

One of the servants came up and whispered something in Benaiah's ears, and his face grew serious.

Benaiah approached the king: "Your Majesty," he whispered, "Adonijah, son of Haggith, fears for his life. He has taken hold of the Altar before the Ark of the Covenant, grasping its horns, claiming sanctuary. He will not leave without an oath that he will not be harmed if he lets go."

Solomon looked at Benaiah: "If he is ready to acknowledge me as my royal father's one true heir, then he has nothing to fear. Not a hair of his will fall to the ground." Solomon's face hardened: "But if I find any evil in him, he will be put to death!"

Adonijah came to Solomon, his face pale, bowing before the true heir of David: "Long live King Solomon," he said in a whisper.

"Go home!" Solomon commanded his brother.

CHAPTER SIXTY-TWO
Last Will and Testament

It was late at night, the starry sky overhead, the palace quiet. David sat at his table, engrossed in study. The Holy Torah illuminated his face with joy. His white beard gleamed in the candlelight. Gentle Solomon gazed at him in wonder and admiration.

"*In the beginning, God created the heavens and the earth,*" David read longingly, as if studying the verse for the first time in his life. "God's first creation was the very reality of time. In the beginning, the concept of time was created; time is not a reality in and of itself. There is no time without God's Will; apart from the Divine Will, there is nothing in the universe. Creation is making something out of nothing. When God wanted to create the world, the creation of the world began. Then God brought it all into being: this world and the World to Come; spiritual and physical dimensions; and all the classes of angels, from cherubim to seraphim. Everything is made by the Creator, from the top of the upper spheres to the bottom of the lower spheres. Behold, my son, and be wise! There is nothing else besides Him, nothing acts except by His Will."

David became immersed in reflection: I must convey to my son his duty in his world, his way of leading himself and the people of Israel.

"My beloved son!" His voice became purposeful: "*I am about to go the way of all the earth. So be strong and prove yourself a man.*"

"Father, don't talk like that..." Solomon didn't want to dwell on his father's impending demise.

David deflected Solomon, his voice commanding and firm: "You must be strong, my son, even though you are young. You must treat your people wisely and considerately. It is not easy to lead any people, let alone the People of Israel. You must make sure that the people follow the path of God if you want to be a loyal king to God and His people. If you make sure that the people keep the commandments and live in faith, the people will have the abundance they deserve. *Keep the charge of the Lord your God to walk in His ways and to keep His statutes, commandments, ordinances, and decrees, as is written in the Law of Moses, so that you may prosper in all you do and wherever you turn, and so that the Lord may fulfill His promise to me: 'If your descendants take heed to walk faithfully before Me with all their heart and soul, you will never fail to have a man on the throne of Israel.'"*

"But Father..."

"Listen, my dear son, there is no escaping from this moment. Death comes as the end of every man, and my end draws near. As God is my witness, I tried to worship Him with all my heart. I tried to lead His people on the right path. I taught faith and belief; I invested my time in bringing the nation closer to its Creator. I have clarified the ways of repentance and God's leadership. I hope I succeeded to some extent."

"Father, do you really think the end is near? That you will soon leave me alone?" Tears welled up in Solomon's eyes.

David took his son's hand: "I'm about to leave this world, but I am not really leaving You. I will always be with You. As long as you give me a place in your heart, I will be there. I am moving from this reality to a higher reality. We must quit this world as a person who quits his job and goes to another job." David stroked Solomon's hand: "My son, I leave to you what I have taught you: Torah, morality, faith, and the closeness of God. In the Book of Psalms that I have composed, there you can find me at any moment you want; there you can find yourself; and most importantly, there you can find God's closeness." David grew serious. "My son, there are a few things you must do when you sit on the throne after my death, difficult but necessary tasks. I ask neither in vengeance nor anger. Joab murdered Abner and Amasa in cold blood, and he must not die a natural death. If that happens, he will have no atonement for his misdeeds. Act wisely, to make sure he does not die in his bed. Reward the sons of Barzilai the Gileadite for the kindness their father showed me. As for your master, Shimei son of Gera, who bitterly cursed me while I fled from your brother Absalom, there is a great cloud over him for his sin. I swore I wouldn't spill his blood, but you must use your wisdom to make sure he, too, doesn't die a natural death, which would prevent him from having atonement for his transgression."

David looked at his beloved son's face: "Now, let's keep learning. It's a shame to waste even one moment..."

CHAPTER SIXTY-THREE
Afterword

The holiday of Shavuot fell on the Holy Sabbath. Four hundred and seventy-six years to the day after the Torah was given to Israel on Mount Sinai, a healing sun shone in the afternoon, caressing Creation with its rays. Only the chirping birds disturbed the silence of the day. A light breeze blew between the leaves of fruit trees, releasing their intoxicating smell. The melody of study could be heard in the center of the orchard, a gentle love song. David sat there, in the courtyard of his palace.

On the table in front of him sat a small Torah scroll, always lovingly bound to the king's right arm when he was not studying it. The Torah commanded: "*It is to remain with him, and he is to read from it all the days of his life, so that he may learn to fear the Lord his God by carefully observing all the words of this instruction and these statutes.*" David leaned over the scroll, looking at the shiny black letters. His face was smiling, his eyes were shining, as his lips moved in pleasure, thirstily drinking the words of the Torah.

"*I am the Lord your God, who took you out of the land of Egypt, from the house of slaves,*" he whispered. David thought: Four hundred and seventy-six years ago, it was on the Sabbath, on Shavuot. "*Who took you out of the land of Egypt,*" from the realm of debauchery. The Torah speaks to me in the second person. It is my duty to see myself as one coming out of Egypt, to defy the slave masters who try to deny me freedom. All I have to do is to want to be released, to be free. There is nothing that obliges me to be a slave — not the time, not the place. But I'm a slave anyway! Is God not my master, as the Torah dictates? Did we go from slavery to slavery? From slavery in Egypt to slavery to God? What is a slave? What makes a man a slave instead of a freeman?

David mused, his eyes closing, his fingers kneading his eyebrows unconsciously: A slave is one who has a master over him. In Egypt, we were slaves to Pharaoh, who in his wickedness enslaved us, forcing us to serve him out of hatred. The very fact that we were slaves to him was his purpose, cruelty for the sake of cruelty."

David opened his eyes, and a twinkle of love ignited in them. He reflected: Even today we are slaves, but we serve the King of the World. Our service is based on love, as our Master wants the best for His servants, as parents want for their children. Yes, He tries and tests and charges us, even chastens us, but it all stems from the love of our Heavenly Father for us. We remain ignorant of this, and this is why we see our Lord's service as oppressive or coercive. It is like a little boy who wants to jump into the stormy sea, thinking what fun it would be to play in the ocean waves, but his father forcibly stops him; like a mother who powerfully distances her son from a dangerous spot, out of her love for him.

The sun showered love on David's head. "Oh... *Create a pure heart for me, God, renew the right spirit within me,*" the king whispered. "Give me a pure heart to be a genuine servant of the Lord of Truth."

Every Sabbath, he would study, pray, and commune. Ever since he learned that he would pass away on the Sabbath, he had not rested for a moment from the work of his Creator. His lips whispered, humming, fervid, speaking at all times: "*How I love your teaching, all day long, it is my conversation...*" his lips murmured.

A loud hiss could be heard from among the fruit trees. The chirping of startled birds distracted the king from his musings. David got up to see what was causing the noise.

His lips hummed...

He walked, descending the three stone steps...

"*How I love your teaching...*"

The second step was broken...

The sound of whispering stopped...

David fell, his neck breaking...

The voice of prayer fell silent.

His last words echoed: "*I love your teaching…*"

David returned his soul to his Creator with love...

Printed in Dunstable, United Kingdom